Semana Santa

David Hewson is a columnist for the *Sunday Times*, and the author of three novels. *Semana Santa*, his first, was highly acclaimed and was selected for the W. H. Smith Fresh Talent promotion.

DAVID HEWSON

SEMANA SANTA

HarperCollins*Publishers*

HarperCollins*Publishers*
77–85 Fulham Palace Road,
Hammersmith, London w6 8jb

This paperback edition 1998
1 3 5 7 9 8 6 4 2

First published in Great Britain by
HarperCollins*Publishers* 1996

Copyright © David Hewson 1996

The Author asserts the moral right to
be identified as the author of this work

ISBN 0 00 651062 0

This novel is entirely a work of fiction.
The names, characters and incidents portrayed in it
are the work of the author's imagination. Any resemblance to
actual persons, living or dead, events or localities is
entirely coincidental.

Typeset in Minion by
Rowland Phototypesetting Ltd,
Bury St Edmunds, Suffolk

Printed and bound in Great Britain by
Caledonian International Book Manufacturing Ltd, Glasgow

Semana Santa

1

La Soledad.

The words echoed around the old woman's head as she woke slowly, fitfully, from fast-fading dreams. Outside, through the arch and pillars of the keyhole door, the noise of the city rumbled like the low growl of an unseen animal. The scent of oleander mingled with the fumes of diesel and cigarettes. From her wicker chair, its points and cracks now biting into her bones, she could see across the garden to the courtyard. A handful of orange and lemon trees dotted with wrinkled fruit, dusty in the afternoon sunlight, waxy red seed husks on a lone pomegranate, the sudden drift of cat's urine on the unseasonably hot late-afternoon air.

Caterina Lucena watched the ghosts reassemble and populate another place: bright, gay, noisy. The sound of laughter rang from gleaming wall to gleaming wall, the tiles sparkled new in the sun. She could see the figures drifting from group to group, as they had done more than sixty years ago when, as a young girl, she had watched, filled with awe and admiration, from this very room. All of the great people of the day had visited in their time. Even, once, Lorca himself. She had seen them sip fino and manzanilla beneath the orange blossom, heard them talk about things she could not comprehend. She had watched their faces change over the space of two seasons, shift from bright, optimistic good humour to, first, a muted concern, as faint as gossamer, then to visible anxiety, and finally to fear, simple, naked, brutal.

And all the time the trees blossomed and bore fruit. It stood on the branch unpicked, gathering dust from the carriages and cars she could hear beyond the wall.

One day, she came down from her small, sunny room, woken by something she did not recognise. The ground was littered with rotten fruit. It was as if a sudden earthquake had shaken them from the tree. They lay on the dry brown earth misshapen and decaying. Flesh and pulp peeped out from beneath the torn orange and yellow skins. There was something obscene, something frightening about the sight.

A lifetime on, she floated above herself as she was then, watched the young girl in her white and pink cotton dress, loose and cool in the sun, standing outside the courtyard's gold-and-blue-tiled door, looking down at this bitter harvest in shock and foreboding.

She waited, waited. It would come. It always came.

From beyond the courtyard wall an explosion erupted, a noise so huge, so violent that it seemed to rip apart the world. The air, the sky shook with the sound. She screamed and time took leave of its senses, the seconds turned to hours, as if to extend the pain they promised.

The trees became electric. Their branches snapped, as if to attention, as if a fibrous thread of muscle, tight as steel, ran through the sap and suddenly tautened in fury or fear. They clenched like fists then released themselves and the air filled with leaves and twigs and the sweet, sickly aroma of rotten fruit. The blast of the cannon came to her, bringing with it a new odour, the sharp smell of cordite and burning.

Overhead, the sound of wings, the frantic cry of birds, flapping, flapping, flapping.

A shape forms before her line of vision, floating down from the sky, tears of blood against pure white, close enough to touch. It falls with the speed of a single, descending feather, slowly, almost gracefully. She can see the red, deep and real, on its feathers, she can see the bloody gore around its neck where the blast removed the head. At the back of her skull, she can feel herself screaming. But there is no noise, there is no pain, there is no sensation at all. The world has become nothing but this single occurrence: a headless dove descends in front of her with an unearthly slowness.

She watches its neck twitch frantically from side to side. She sees the blood pump and spill from its still-beating heart. The drops fly slowly through the air, perfect red pearls, half frozen in their motion. They spatter her dress, her skin. She can see the red on her arms, sense it sticky on her neck. As she screams, she can feel the light red rain on her tongue, and she cannot stop herself *tasting* it, fresh and warm and salty, licking the roof of her mouth in an automatic reaction whose very thought starts to overturn her stomach long before the physical sensation becomes real.

Time pauses. There is a moment when the dove is frozen in front of her as if to say: *this* is the point. And then the seconds become real again. It falls to the ground with a sudden, brutal flop, and as she begins to retch she knows that this event, though only the precursor to other, worse happenings, is one which will mark her for the rest of her life. In another time, a young girl vomits dryly in the court-yard of her ancestral home, the small, shattered corpse of a dove at her feet. Outside, the sound of arms, the smell of blood.

La Soledad.

Doña Caterina watches her ghost recede, slip slowly away

in the afternoon sun. There is a sudden anger in her: *why now? Why do the dead not lie buried?* Tears prick the corners of her eyes. She feels ashamed of the sour, dry taste of stale manzanilla in the throat. A little lunch, a drink from the plastic container the part-time maid buys around the corner, sweaty, sleep-filled afternoons. But at least the dreams had stayed away, for years, almost to the point where she could forget them.

A sound draws her attention. For all her frailty, her eyes, her ears, remain as sharp as ever. In the corner of the courtyard there is a movement. She watches as a figure darts behind a tangle of purple bougainvillaea and scrambles for the far wall. It is half hidden by the trees. All she can see is red, red everywhere, no face, no *identity*.

A deep red, the colour of doves' blood.

She feels the anger rise still further in her, strains her hands against the arms of the wicker chair and lifts herself upright. Her bones ache. She grips the old cane she must now use always and her incapacity fuels her fury.

'Shit, shit, shit,' she screams through the open door. The sound echoes around the tiled courtyard. Her voice comes back to her like the cawing of a crow. The tears prickle her eyes afresh.

'You thieving little shits! You prey on an old woman instead of working for a living. You come here. I give you what for. I shove my stick up your ass, you little shits!'

There is a rustle of leaves from the corner of the courtyard, a grunt of exertion. The red figure lifts itself over the wall.

She feels relief, and shame for realising it. These are her days: to wake, to eat, to sleep, then to count the pesetas to make sure she can do the same tomorrow. And now to shout at young thugs who come to rob her.

She sits back in her chair and looks around the room.

The most valuable items have gone already, shipped to the auction room in Calle Mayor. The paintings, the porcelain, the Chinese rugs. All the fabric of her memories of childhood is now dispersed. In her mind's eye, that active, protean part of her imagination which she now, by preference, chooses to inhabit, she can see the apartments of the *nouveaux riches* in the new quarter where they live, squashed into little boxes, cheek by jowl, like the poor, but with TV sets and loud radios. Her life, her ancestry, enclosed by their thin, plaster walls, lending faint authenticity to their shallow, mundane existences.

Now, nothing is missing. She is certain almost immediately. Everything that remains is a firm, tangible cornerstone in her life. To lose one vase, one shard of reality from the past, would be something she would notice immediately.

Doña Caterina blinks and realises that, for a short span of time, her mind had disappeared. No thought, not even the old and welcome prick of anger, that sudden stab of feeling that kept her alive. Old age was beginning to fossilise her, slowly, day by day. The process had begun decades ago, with the gentle fall of a headless dove. Now it was accelerating towards its inevitable end. It meant nothing to her.

She sniffs the air and begins to know. It is the smell, the old smell.

Once more, painfully, she pushes herself out of the wicker chair. She wears an old, faded print dress which now hangs baggy on her bones. Blue roses, once the colour of the sea, are pale etches against a black background pattern of leaves. Her hair, grey with gingery brown streaks, is tied back in a severe bun. Her face, lined and walnut brown, still wears an aristocratic aspect: a stare that could wither the unwary, the bent nose that has run through her family at least since

11

the Reconquest, cheekbones that flare beneath the eyes, almost to points. She looks like a fragile old eagle searching for prey as she struggles to the downstairs door, leaning on her cane.

Doña Caterina turns the handle and walks into the hall. It is smarter than her own room. The entrance is large and airy. Sunlight pours through the dusty glass panes which surmount an ancient double door studded with brass. The floor is swept, the tiles gleam as brightly as hundred-year-old ceramic can. On one wall of the rectangular hall hangs a huge, floor-length mirror, its surface scarred by flaking mercury. She can see herself in it across the room: an ethereal, faded creature who seems to melt into the background of the mansion.

This is how the great families end, she thinks, in decay, in shabbiness, in the pale glory of their past. The fools in the war had it wrong. There was no great turning point, no single, apocalyptic moment. Everything simply . . . *fades* until nothing remains except a dispersed collection of random ephemera, unconnected save for a history no living person could discern.

She sniffs the air again and a cold feeling runs down her spine. She begins to realise what had woken her, and it was not the thug in the garden.

She shuffles towards the other ground-floor rooms. They are unoccupied but, in these days, who knows? The further she walks from the staircase, the more the smell recedes. Still, she takes the chain of keys from her pocket, rattles them in the ageing locks, and looks inside, postponing the inevitable. Nothing but furniture covered in shrouds, like misshapen ghosts waiting for something to rouse them. All three are the same: still, dusty, lifeless.

After she closes the door on the last, Doña Caterina sits down in a small upright chair next to the mirror. There is

12

a more comfortable seat on the other side of the room, but she does not want to see her reflection in the glass. Even the sight of her own face might frighten her.

'The Angel Brothers,' she says to herself, and shakes her head. They had paid well this last year, and they had, in a sense, not deceived her. They were in residence only rarely. They had reputations, they said. This was true. They showed her the articles in the newspapers: the exhibitions in London and New York, the profiles in the glossy foreign magazines. But they had *reputations* too, and this also became apparent. The banging of doors at midnight. Strange visitors in strange clothes. An otherness that, on occasions, frightened her, gave her a chill that was too familiar.

One day, in the hall, she had seen them both come downstairs, holding hands and giggling like children, dressed in some outlandish suits of leather that made them look foolish. She was not ignorant; she knew of such things.

'You are from Barcelona,' she said and stared them in the eye with that eagle gaze that no one, not even the Angel Brothers with their bloodstreams awash with substances, could ignore.

Pedro, the quiet one, the one with fair hair (was this dyed? she wondered), nodded.

'You are brothers? You are *genuine* brothers?'

'Sí, Doña Caterina,' he said (and she realised that, for some reason, the second seemed incapable of speech). 'We are more than brothers. We are *twins*.'

She stared at them both. There was no resemblance whatsoever. She could not believe it.

Pedro looked hurt. 'This is true. We would not lie to you. Look.'

He shook his brother, whose eyes seemed dark, unfocused and unfathomable. 'We will show the good woman.'

They both unzipped their leather jackets and started to

pull out the tails of white, frilly cotton shirts from their trousers. Doña Caterina could smell a fragrance from their bodies, heavy, strong and feminine.

'See here.'

Pedro pointed to a pale scar on his waist. His fingers were smeared with paint: red, blue, yellow. His nails were long and dirty. The mark on his body was about four inches long and two high, with further, smaller weals around the edges, like vicious tears in a self-inflicted wound. It was on his left side. The other brother simply held up his shirt to reveal a pale, slim waist. A near identical scar sat there on the right.

'See,' said Pedro. 'I am the right twin. Juan is the left. We were joined thus almost until the age of two. We are not merely brothers, we are twins. We are not merely twins, we are heavenly twins.'

He giggled, as if through drink, though there was an energy to him which could not have come from alcohol.

'This is the secret, the secret of our art. For our first two years we were a being with two minds. Now we are two beings, two minds, yet when we *create*' – he used the word as if it were holy – 'we create as one. Two minds, a single purpose.'

She looked at him, the distaste sour in her mouth. 'You please keep quiet at nights,' she said. 'And you do nothing to bring this house into disrepute. What is permissible in Barcelona may not be permissible here. Not under my roof, at least.'

'We will bring you nothing but honour, *Madame*.' He used the French glibly: he had done this before. 'One day there will be a plaque upon your door.'

She had left them there, stumbling out of the portico, to return God knows when. And, true to his word, the noise had abated. This last month she had hardly heard them at all. The money was welcome. No, the money was *essential*.

As she stands up she realises this is almost what she fears most. She is too old to take in new people. This was why she had never tried to fill the other rooms. The task of finding new 'guests', vetting them, watching them, making sure they paid on time, this was all now beyond her. The Angel Brothers, whatever happened behind their locked doors, paid regularly and no longer disturbed her. They were her security until the end came. There was nothing left to sell, except the house itself, and that, she knew, would kill her as certainly as any disease or young thug from the street.

Doña Caterina sighs, walks past the huge mirror without looking into it, and makes for the stairs. Once she had slid down the banister into the arms of her father. *Once.* Now she grips it with wrinkled, tortured hands, shuffles one foot onto the step, follows it with the other, carries on this way, one step at a time. There are twenty-seven steps – she had counted them when she was four years old – and each one takes her the best part of a minute. At the top of the stairs she sits down. Tears now streak her cheeks. Her breath comes in gasps. The door to the apartment is half open and the smell is unbearable: a fetid, miasmic odour that chills her to the bone.

La Soledad.

The phone, *their* phone, she knows, is on a small table a footfall beyond the open door. Nothing in the world, not God himself, could persuade Doña Caterina to cross that threshold. She sits for a period of time she could not calculate, the memories, the terrors racing through her mind with a cruel clarity that brings bile to her throat.

When the world stops spinning she wipes her face on her sleeve, stands up, takes hold of the banister and sets off down once more, step by step. The sunlight is fading through the glass over the door. Outside there is the sound of birds greeting the twilight. It takes her another twenty minutes to reach the phone in her room.

At the emergency call switchboard in the big police headquarters behind the Plaza de la Paz, a red light flashes. Miguel Domingo, an overweight civilian who thinks he really has better things to do with his time than sit taking weird phone calls, watches it flicker in front of him. He finishes a can of San Miguel, takes a bite of fat ham swathed in bread, chews, swallows, belches, then reaches for the key. With as much bored aggression as he can muster, he flicks the switch and bellows, '*Digame.*'

But it is a minute before Doña Caterina can stop sobbing and begin to talk.

2

At six in the morning the big trunk road is quiet. Within the hour the heavy lorries arriving from Cadiz, Seville and Cordoba by the new motorways will begin to choke the dual carriageway, pumping clouds of black diesel into the palm trees that line the highway, getting into fights with the locals trying to drive to work from the suburbs. Now it is close to peace.

Maria Gutierrez keeps up a steady fifty kilometres an hour in her plain rented Seat Ibiza, her eyes, half dead, aching, watching the road. The little red car hangs in the inside lane for as long as possible. She does not hurry, she lets the traffic push her along, drifting with it, trying not to think about where it leads. It is ten years, a decade, since she has been to the city, and to return is to intrude upon her own, unwanted past. Her hair flies out from her head, uncombed and tangled, loose in the dusty wind that blows in through the half-open window. It is a pale brown, streaked with blonde, too young, too wild for her, a relic of yesterday. Her bright, clear blue eyes, piercing, a little staring, dart from road to street and back again, looking for directions, registering sights that stir old memories, rustle the past which lies buried somewhere in her head. They are deep, intelligent, old eyes, set in a pale, alert face that is more striking than attractive. Maria Gutierrez is thirty-three: she has the eyes of someone a decade older and the hairstyle of a twenty-year-old.

Seven hours earlier, in the dead of night, she left her tower block apartment in Salamanca, in the new city: bright, clean, antiseptic. The tower blocks are the precise number of feet distant from their neighbours specified by the city authorities. There is correctness, exactitude here, and some kind of cold, dull comfort in the place's mute, grey stone form. Rubbish collections do not occur at three in the morning. Singing, all-night parties, and loud family rows are all discouraged. No one knows each other: they get up in the morning, go to work, come home, go to bed. This is the north, this is the new city: remote and filled with an unspoken sense of loss. But safe, too. In the north, emotions know their place. Below the surface, below stairs, where they cannot touch you.

In the south it is different.

Maria Gutierrez drove for six hours in complete darkness, along motorways she did not know, liking the blackness, liking the anonymity, the security it promised. Then, as the sun rose bright and yellow and fearless along the ridge of mountains to the east, she came to the city.

The trunk road skirts the old quarter along the line of the outer walls first built by the Arabs in the ninth century, shortly after it was captured. Three hundred years later the Christians returned, triumphant. From behind the same walls they launched the campaign that two centuries later was to complete the Christian Reconquest of Spain. Another civil war, five hundred years on, destroyed half of the honeyed stone. The town planners of the sixties finished most of the job, pushing them aside to make way for a traffic artery of asphalt.

The signs of the old boundaries remain: an arched gate here, a fragment of wall there. A boy, someone entranced by her hair, her eyes, had shown them to her once, when she was at the university, when her emotions used to play

18

tricks, before she learned how to master them, to keep them tight inside. She passes them now and, in that little internal mirror that leaps out from nowhere, unbidden, unwanted, she can see his face. She wonders where he is: if he is alive. Somewhere in her head stirs a dim memory of their final argument, the moment when his intensity, his closeness became too much. When she chose the safety of being alone over the dangers of being two. The recollection rolls over in its sleep and, for a moment, she lets her mind go still in case it wakes, holds her breath until all inside is silence once more.

The car passes the old turn-off to Cadiz, moves inside the line of the old city walls, follows the ring road to the right, and then begins to travel towards the river, a sluggish brown mass some two hundred yards across. On its way from the mountains in Cazorla to the Atlantic, the Guadal-quivir makes an odd detour around the low rock on which the city was first built. It flows around both sides, forming a small, natural island, easily defended, though too small to contain the kind of population the city soon came to attract. Past the tangle of ancient brickwork and timber that marked the medieval wharves – once Columbus docked here – past the pleasure boats waiting for the day's visitors. Behind the burnished handrail on a small steamer someone polishes the deck, a cigarette dangling ash over the glittering wood.

She is running directly by the water's edge now. Only a narrow footpath, set at a lower level, separates her from the water. On it a small group of teenagers is practising for the fiesta: trumpet, horns, drums mangle one of the old melodies. It floats briefly through the half-open window as she passes by, then, mercifully, drifts away, across the water, towards the open green spaces of the Alfabia park on the opposite bank. Doves flap in the air, as if disturbed by the cacophony.

Four bridges lead into the old city, each named after the

four quarters they serve: Carmona, Veracruz, Santana. And El Viejo. The old one. The barrio. She remembers the name – she cannot help it, the mirror is there and this time it will not go away – thinks of small rooms in small apartments, small beds, the sound of an iron frame creaking under the weight of two bodies. She need pass only two of the bridges, before turning into El Viejo, but, instead, circles the city once, taking another twenty minutes, hovering at the edges, looking for some excuse to turn back, following the pavements, watching, thinking about the day ahead. There is no excuse. Today will be a quiet day. The big celebrations, the climaxes, are days away, at the weekend. The week, Semana Santa, is only just begun. The temporary crowd barriers seem all in one piece: no overnight revellers have thrown them in the river. No one has set fire to the wooden seat galleries installed for the parades. Not a single slumped form occupies a riverside bench.

The bridge to El Viejo comes up on her right, golden and old, with three graceful arches across the Guadalquivir. She signals, looks in the mirror, then turns onto the narrow single-track road. The light is on green, the car speeds through with a rush of wind noise from the walls. She drives beneath the Almohad Gate, a vast, triumphal arch weathered by the centuries and more recent pollution, and turns into the Plaza de la Paz, turns left again, into the barrio. She remembers the street, finds the little underground parking lot, leaves the car, then walks back to ground level. The apartment is where she expected it. She opens the door, walks upstairs, throws her bag on the floor, throws open the window to air the stuffy room, then lies on the bed, staring at the ceiling.

The sounds and smells of the city float through from outside. A decade on, they are the same.

3

'Maybe she is a lesbian. Must be. That's it. A lesbian. Possibly. Definitely.'

Sergeant Felipe 'Bear' Torrillo was listening intently and going red in the face. This was unusual only for the time of day. Six feet tall, 250 pounds, with a face like a giant cherub, Torrillo shook with mute anger. He was listening to Quemada, the squad loudmouth, and wishing he could tear himself away.

'See, Torrillo. You don't understand these things. Lesbians, they all feel deep down they're guilty about it. So they badmouth us all the time but really, deep down, they want to hang around getting to know what dick feels like. You take my word for it. You look over there' – Quemada stabbed a finger at the slight figure in the waiting room across the office and made sure she knew he was pointing at her – 'you're looking at one real-life lesbian. You go down the market and buy a cucumber, see if I'm wrong. They like hanging round cops, you bet they do, they like it 'cos they know we're real men, not the little faggots they normally hang around with. You know why they do that? They just hope one day we might fucking *cure* them.'

The electric light gleamed on the smaller, older man's bald patch, reflected on the thin, bright line of his smile, the thin, bright fabric of his office suit. A year separated the two men but it looked more like a decade. Torrillo stood and quivered in a loose cotton suit that hung around

21

his bulk in creased folds, chestnut hair long and gathered back around his face into a short ponytail, some relic of a long-past spell on the drugs squad. Quemada looked like a bank manager on an inadequate salary, almost a foot shorter and way overweight with a greased swatch of hair plastered in a circlet around the perimeter of his bald head. He wheezed as he spoke and beads of sweat stuck out on his forehead. Quemada shuffled a mess of paper on a desk that looked as if someone had upturned a waste basket on it.

'You tell your little lesbian: she wants curing, maybe I could see my way to being the doctor.'

Three of the other cops behind him laughed dryly, read the look on Torrillo's face, then went quiet.

'You are one dumb shit, Quemada,' the big man said stony-faced. 'One dumb shit.'

Torrillo hunted around for something else to say, lost the battle, repeated himself again, then watched the door open and Rodríguez walk into the room. The Captain sniffed the air: cigarettes, sweat, cheap *chorizo* and stale farts. He glanced at the figure in the waiting room, looked at Torrillo, whose face was now scarlet, and pointed to his office. The two men walked down the corridor, Torrillo opened the glass door for them both, then they went in and sat down.

In his leather chair, dressed in a dark-blue barathea single-breasted suit, Rodríguez looked across the square to the cathedral, the queer mix of Christian gothic and Moslem mosque that brought the tourists swarming through in long crocodile lines every day of the week. This was the view, *his* view. He had owned it for more than a decade. The way he stared out at it, silent, pensive, when the cases got tough, the way he came back with some insight when the rest of them were struggling, these were things that had moved somehow into station folklore. They called him 'the old man' years before he deserved it, but he accepted it nonetheless. From the chaos and corruption that had been the police force under Franco he had fashioned something that performed, worked, achieved something. And if they didn't always understand how he did it, then that was all part of the myth, the magic. Sometimes you didn't *need* to understand everything.

The Torre del Oro, the three-hundred-foot clock tower that once served as a minaret, cast a long, narrow shadow across the square. It was 8.30 in the morning and in the Alarcon, the little bar the policemen used, Rodríguez could see a good proportion of the morning shift eating piles of *churros* out of greasy sheets of paper, gulping down cups of coffee and chocolate, glasses of coñac in front of them. Torrillo watched the Captain settling in, felt, with an unwanted pang of unease, the concern that had been bugging him more and more recently. The old man, the detective they had all looked up to for longer than anyone cared to remember, was *looking* old. There was a time when everyone hung on his word. When you knew that however bent anyone else was around the department Rodríguez walked between the lines, followed the book, settled things that no one else could even begin to see. But it had been a long time since anything was settled. Now he looked old and comfortable and satisfied. He must have been pushing past fifty-eight, retirement was winking at him from the horizon and he was starting to wink back: a little *casita* down by the coast. Some time for the family he used to talk about so much. Torrillo could see him in retirement now, the animated, tanned face slowly turning dull mahogany under the sun, the dark, lively eyes losing their shine. It was happening already. They all knew it. When things got tough, when a case was stalled, there was a time, when they were deep and miserable in their cups at the Alarcon, that someone would say 'the old man will fix it'. The time was passing. The generation was on the change, and with it the way of the world.

Torrillo took it all in, took in how much the old man was winding down, wondered why anyone should blame him, then asked, 'Jesus, why us?'

Rodríguez looked at his sergeant and smiled. 'Why not us? She wants to learn. Who better to learn with? It's a compliment.'

'*They* don't seem to think so.' Torrillo jerked a thumb at the outer office.

'*They* are – what was the phrase I heard through the door? – dumb shits.'

Torrillo laughed. 'Me too. Sometimes.'

'Sometimes.'

Rodríguez's eyes gleamed with good humour and, though it might not last, alertness. Torrillo reminded himself that no one in the building – *no one* – looked like that, especially at this time in the morning, during Semana Santa.

'You bring her in. Then get some coffee. We'll run through the schedule like normal. Then get some work done.'

Torrillo lunged to his feet. Big patches stained his armpits already. 'Sure. There's something going on out there this morning, something new. Don't know what. They came in with something for you just before you arrived.'

Rodríguez nodded then glanced at the report on his desk. He was still looking at it when the door opened and Maria Gutierrez entered.

Torrillo followed her, closed the door, then coughed. 'I'll get some coffee.'

'And some water for me, please,' she said in a quiet voice. The accent was light but definite: northern, middle class, firm.

Rodríguez looked at her. The memo he had received about the attachment – which he had scarcely read – prepared him for somebody else. Maria Gutierrez was short and slight, little more than five feet. She wore a pale-blue cheesecloth shirt and faded baggy jeans that looked as if they came from a cheap street stall. Her hair seemed to shoot outwards in a wayward tangle from her head then get sunk by gravity somewhere along the way: Rodríguez could not decide whether this was a deliberate style or simply a lack of care. Set against her delicate, striking face, it had a kind of disordered elegance, but this was not a woman who sought to make herself attractive. She wore no make-up on fair, untanned skin that seemed more north European than Spanish. Bright, intelligent blue eyes stared back at him, returning the appraisal. Rodríguez wished he had read the memo properly. He could not guess her age: it could have been anywhere between twenty and thirty. Age was never one of his strong points.

Torrillo returned to the room, placed three black coffees in clear glasses on the desk, then handed her some water in a plastic cup.

'Thank you,' she said. 'And thank you for taking the time to let me see you work.'

Torrillo smiled and blushed at the same time.

'Señora Gutierrez,' said Rodríguez. 'You are a student at Salamanca?'

'No, Captain. I am a professor at Salamanca.'

'Ah.'

'A professor of humanities. I thought this information would have been passed on to you.'

'Humanities?' said Torrillo, bewildered. 'This is a police force. What sort of place is this to look for humanities?'

'I am a professor of humanities by qualification. My role is currently in the public policy department.'

25

She made the point pleasantly, patiently.

'We're working on a number of projects that examine the way police forces go about their work. It's part of a project being paid for by the Government which eventually may produce recommendations for formal training and investigation programmes. These are new times for universities, Captain. We have to pay our way, so we take on these contracts. That's not my decision. We have carried out studies in Madrid, Barcelona, and Malaga; we are working on others here and also in Burgos and Santander. Eventually, there will be a report ... There is a methodology for the project which you can have if you wish. Basically, our brief is to observe, to follow through on a single case, and report afterwards on its handling.'

'A metho*what*?' Torrillo's brow furled in puzzlement.

'A methodology. A procedure, if you prefer.'

'Procedure, that I prefer. That's a police word.'

'Captain?'

Rodríguez's attention had returned to the report. He withdrew his attention reluctantly.

'Captain, don't you want me to outline how I want to work?'

'Please be brief. I have a letter here from Madrid telling us you must be accommodated and given a free rein as far as is practical. So you are welcome to join us on attachment but, as I am sure you understand, our primary role is to do the jobs we are paid to do. I will help you as far as I can, provided – and it is important this is understood – provided that it does not interfere with our work.'

The blue eyes flashed wide and Rodríguez, as he understood he was meant to, recognised the ice behind them.

'Of course. It is not for me to get in the way. I merely wish to follow your work, to observe, make notes. And when I have completed the attachment ask some questions of you and your sergeant. A debriefing if you like. And I will send you a copy of the final report.'

Rodríguez waved his hand over the desk, waved at the volumes lining the walls of the office. 'Reports, reports, reports. A policeman's life is made of paper.'

She sat, expressionless.

'No. I am sorry. Of course I would like to receive your report. For now, I must concentrate on a different one.'

He picked up the sheet of paper immediately in front of him. 'The idea, if I understand it correctly, is that you follow a single investigation from beginning to end – whatever that may be.'

She nodded.

'The end may be somewhat inconclusive, of course. We have a good detection rate here, but no one is perfect.'

'I understand that. The easiest thing is to assign me to follow your team on a case that attracts a significant manpower resource and then I'll cut it off once the investigation is either concluded or you begin to wind it down.'

'I see,' said Rodríguez and looked again at the paper on his desk. 'Are you squeamish, Professor?'

The blue eyes didn't blink.

'Well. We shall find out. You have heard of the Angel Brothers?'

'The artists? Yes. Of course. Who hasn't?'

Torrillo shook his head. 'Me.'

'Well. You will get to know them. They were found dead last night. Killed, probably. Most inconvenient at the start of Semana Santa, I must say. I had hoped to engage your attention with an explanation of our excellent systems for traffic control and crowd management, Professor, but it seems this is not to be. The house is in Carmona. I will be placing Lieutenant Menéndez on the assignment. He will meet you in the parking lot.'

27

She did not move. 'Last night, Captain?'

'As I said.'

'And it is now nearly 9 am the following day? Does it take this long for a senior policeman to arrive at such events?'

'They were found last night by a very old lady. She is very frail and, understandably, somewhat confused. When she phoned the emergency switchboard she simply complained about a very bad smell. Nothing more.'

'And?'

'The operator put her in touch with a plumber, which is not easy at that time of night. When the plumber arrived, *he* called us and explained the true situation. I think it is fair to say there was a problem with our – how would you put it? – methodology. Please. Lieutenant Menéndez is waiting.'

Torrillo stood up, walked to the coat stand and put on his jacket. She followed him out of the door, scribbling frantically into a small pocket notebook as she walked.

Torrillo stopped at the despatch desk to sign out. Quemada sat at the adjoining table grinning stupidly for everyone to see. He looked her up and down, sang little clucking noises, shrugged his shoulders, made a downturned grin as if to say: maybe, on a bad day.

Maria Gutierrez stopped scribbling, leaned over and stared Quemada straight in the face, so close she could smell the tobacco on his breath. Torrillo caught the sudden charge of atmosphere in the office and turned to watch.

Quemada bent over the table, flexed his arm. A flabby wad of muscle formed between elbow and shoulder.

'You like biceps, lady?' Quemada grinned.

'Not when they're between the ears.'

Torrillo burst out laughing, a big loud rumble of a sound that caught around the office. Quemada sat silent, red-faced amid the noise. Maria Gutierrez straightened up, tucked her notebook into a small grey leather valise and walked out of the door to a ripple of light applause.

Torrillo looked at Quemada, whose chin was still almost on the desk, and felt a twinge of sympathy.

'She may be a lesbian, friend,' he said. 'But if she is, she's *our* lesbian.'

Then he followed her, down two flights of stone stairs into the parking lot. Outside, Torrillo walked over to a big Ford saloon and opened the door for her. The man in the front didn't even turn round.

'This is Lieutenant Menéndez,' Torrillo grunted, half embarrassed.

'Good morning, Lieutenant,' she said to the dark-suited back in front of her. There was no reply.

Two minutes later they were speeding out of the front entrance of the police station, in silence. The heat had come early this year: it hung heavy and humid in the air.

In the square, gangs of workmen were starting to complete the temporary grandstands along the route of the main procession planned for the following Sunday. They climbed and hung on the huge skeletal frames like insects inspecting the bones of a long-dead beast.

Torrillo turned right at the Torre del Oro, waited for the traffic light to turn green going into Campillos, then drove past the huge circular wall of the bullring, a mellow gold in the morning sun.

'Semana Santa. Phooey.'

He made ready to spit out of the half-open window, then remembered there was company in the back.

Menéndez scanned the streets, then turned round to look at her. A thin, cold face, no more than thirty, angular, with a light, black moustache. The Lieutenant was dressed in a neat dark-blue suit with an immaculate white shirt and dark-red silk tie. He looked like a stockbroker.

'Tradition is not a strong point in the police force, Professor,' he said, in a flat, monotone classless voice. 'We tend to live day by day.'

'Tradition,' Torrillo barked out of the open window. She watched his little ponytail, gathered together with a plain elastic band, jittering as he spoke. 'Holy Week – holy *shit!* You know what they do? They spend the first three days of the week on their knees, and the next four on their backs. Drinking or f— . . . well, you get my point. We get maybe a hundred thousand visitors here for Holy Week and they're all the same. Three days spent crying' – his voice turns falsetto and for a moment he takes his hands off the wheel and presses them together – ' "please, sweet Jesus, *please* save us, we have been very, very bad this last year." Then it's straight into the park to the feria, all night long in the *casitas*, and watch all that free fino loosen their pants. You're a cop during Semana Santa you're either directing traffic or lost drunks or just dealing with people in trouble 'cos they can't decide whether to fight or fuck. Excuse my language, lady, you're not writing this down too, are you?'

Torrillo looked in the mirror and saw her smiling amiably.

'Good. I wouldn't want you to write that down. Might give the good people who pay our wages the wrong idea.'

The car negotiated a tight, narrow corner, against white stone walls, past pedestrians stumbling along tiny pavements. Then the street opened out into a wider thoroughfare. The houses looked bigger, with massive wooden doors, most half-open to reveal shady courtyards, lit by splashes of colour: geranium red, jacaranda purple.

'Carmona. There. You see the parish church? Best Virgin in town, they say. Now where I come from there are *no*

30

virgins in town. Carmona, they still got a few hereabouts. And most definitely we do not say the f-word here,' said Torrillo. 'You do that people faint away dead in the streets, they're so delicate.'

Torrillo watched as a horse and carriage, full of passengers who looked more than a little drunk, slowly turned into a side street. He pointed with an index finger that looked like it came off a meat counter to a large, old, four-square mansion along the street. A white Citroën ambulance estate car was parked outside, with two police vans. Torrillo drove through iron gates that needed a coat of paint, then parked in a gravel drive underneath a tangled mimosa tree. Like a taxi driver, he hurried to get out of the car first, swivelled round, then opened the back door.

'You can call me Bear if you like. Everyone else does, except the Lieutenant.'

Maria Gutierrez swung her legs out of the back seat of the Ford and stood up. The top of her head came somewhere close to Torrillo's chest.

'Bear.'

'I think it's affectionate. Most of the time anyway.'

When they turned to the house, Menéndez was already deep in conversation with one of the officers from the scene of crime squad. His face, tanned and angular, now hidden behind dark glasses, was quite unreadable.

4

'I gather the Captain asked you, Professor, but I guess I have to ask again. Are you squeamish?'

They were standing in the hallway. It reminded her of a European arthouse film of the 1970s: faded grandeur, dust, a pervasive sense of decay. Menéndez's face bore the signs of slight impatience.

'I will follow you and leave if I must.'

'Good.'

They walked up the stairs, past men in white overalls dusting with fine brushes, drawing ink circles around marks that seemed barely discernible. The smell got worse as they approached the top. She took out a handkerchief, shook a little cologne on it, then briefly clutched it to her nose. It helped a little.

Menéndez and Torrillo walked into the apartment without exchanging a word. She followed in their joint shadow.

It was an astonishing sight. The door opened to an immense room, open and sunlit through huge panel windows at the front. In the centre was a hulking, dark shape surrounded by forensic officers. Over it hovered a noisy swirl of dark, buzzing flies. From time to time a white hand would attempt to swat some away: it was a hopeless task. Some deep, primeval instinct told her not to face the thing in the centre, not yet.

She looked around the perimeter, she looked at what appeared to have no interest for the police officers: earthly possessions of the late Angel Brothers. A marble fireplace dominated the long, left wall of the room, with a large gilt mirror over it. On the marble shelf stood an ormolu clock almost three feet high: the hands were set at midnight. The opposite wall was covered in a hotchpotch collection of modern art: a mural which she dimly thought might be by Gilbert and George, a Warhol silk-screen, several pieces which were probably by the brothers themselves. Close to the door was something more personal: a single plasticised board on which newspaper and magazine cuttings were stuck with pins. She looked at them: a picture from an English magazine of the brothers at a London party. A review of an exhibition in New York. Amateur snapshots of the brothers in the company of various members of the international glitterati.

Between her and the far windows was a jumble of disordered furniture. Could they have lived like this? No. The furniture had been pushed back from the centre of the room to make way for whatever now occupied it. In another situation, she could have laughed at the incongruity of the styles. Four dining table chairs looked like English Chippendale. The table, however, was a vinyl representation of a semi-naked woman kneeling on all fours, carrying the perspex top on her back. She wore knee-length leather boots, the vagina was open and grotesquely exaggerated, and the breasts almost swept to the floor. Her eyes were closed, her mouth open: an expression, it occurred to her, male artists of a certain age seemed to associate with ecstasy.

From the centre of the room came Menéndez's voice: low, firm and questioning. She could put this off no longer. Maria Gutierrez walked towards the small crowd and heard the murmur of men's voices blend into the buzzing of a thousand flies. Torrillo noticed her creep gently behind him and, automatically, stepped back to let her have a better view. She blinked and was amazed that she did not throw up on the spot.

The Angel Brothers lay directly beneath a small, modern chandelier which dipped low from the ceiling. Their corpses were posed side by side, as if by an undertaker, on a dark-red velvet coverlet spread over an oversize double bed. Each was wearing costume which she guessed as being Spanish court style, from something like the mid-seventeenth century. One twin wore green, one wore red. Velvet and brocade jackets, velvet trousers, gathered at the knee, white knee socks, dull black leather shoes. The body on the right held a small ornamental sword across its chest: it looked like a cheap theatrical prop. The other brother had one hand on a small jewel chest – again of uncertain origin. Menéndez reached forward and opened the lid. Inside was a collection of paste jewels. Menéndez's hand was encased in a throwaway plastic glove of the sort used by counter girls at the supermarket delicatessens.

Both brothers had been dressed in white, frilled shirts, of the type still worn by horsemen and followers of the bullring. The arm holding the sword covered most of the corpse's chest. Its sibling's was open to view, however, and she could see, in the centre, a huge wound, marked by a dried black stain. Around it were what appeared to be darts, English darts of the kind found in some pubs. Short ribbons, red, yellow and blue, had been tied to them, and the points were stuck hard into the flesh. At least six darts pierced the body from close to the neck to the navel, a small black stain on the shirt beneath each. Elsewhere on the chest, other stains denoted wounds that had no obvious cause.

Menéndez moved to the other side of the deathbed, then lifted the rigid arm holding the sword. Beneath it, the same pattern could be seen: a large central wound, a pattern of darts with ribbons, a small number of other bloodstains.

34

He returned to the other side, and touched the shirt. It was not buttoned. He lifted it and for a second she thought she would be sick. The flies had not come from outside. There were maggots moving within the body, yellow and white, made alive by its putrefaction.

A little unsteadily, she turned and walked out of the room, walked downstairs, out of the front door, then sat on the front step of the mansion. Even there, the air seemed tainted by the smell from inside the house. She wondered if it would ever leave her.

With her vision swimming, Maria Gutierrez walked to the police Ford, opened the back door, then passed out on the seat.

Menéndez never saw her go. He was walking around the bier transfixed, examining the bodies, lifting pieces of clothing, prodding the wan, waxy flesh with a pencil, then dictating short notes into a small tape recorder. For safety's sake, Torrillo scribbled down the asides in a small notepad. Menéndez had never asked him for this. It simply seemed to make sense.

The rest of the crew stood back and waited. No one spoke. They watched the detectives at work, a few bored, most intrigued.

Outside, the city came to life. Birds sang in the mimosa trees lining the avenue beyond the courtyard wall. A procession went by, first in silence, with a welcome whiff of incense floating in through the window, followed by the noise and happy chatter of the crowd. The charter jets turned finals three thousand feet overhead and landed thousands more visitors to the pageant through the wholly inadequate portals of Murillo, the city airport. The morning hustlers tried half-heartedly to drum up some business among the tourists and the locals, but found the combination of the heat and a short-lived religious fever too much for most. A policeman was knifed, not seriously, when he intervened in a bar brawl which began as a civilised argument over football. In the Plaza de la Paz, seven members of a religious sect erected a stall which detailed the imminent end of the world: next Sunday. 'Before or after the bullfight?' asked a concerned spectator, watching them assemble their banners. And they thought he was joking. A lorry illegally overladen with smoked garlic overturned on the ring road and caused a traffic jam that tailed back to the Cadiz motorway. In the heat and anger, one man had a heart attack, several fights ensued, and a baby girl was born prematurely to a teenage mother, delivered by the female bus conductor.

And Maria Gutierrez slept and slept, through a nightmare in which headless doves tumbled out of the piercing blue sky, falling to the ground like red rain, over and over and over again.

She woke with a jolt, the shocking scarlet images still imprinted somewhere on the cerebral retina that lived inside her head. There was a moment when she had forgotten where she was, then she recovered, sat upright, straightened her jeans, ran a few fingers through her hair, checked in the driver's mirror, and got out of the car. A man with a doctor's bag was walking through the big entrance.

'Late as usual,' she thought, then checked herself. She was there to observe the cops, not become one of them. Least of all, to start thinking like one.

Menéndez and Torrillo were walking down the staircase when she came back into the mansion. The Lieutenant looked preternaturally alert, absorbed in a way that precluded interruption. The work – the killings – had energised **him** and there was something dark, something almost sinister, about the energy it had released. His face seemed to glow, his deep brown eyes snatched at everything around him. They caught her. He waved gently, almost effeminately, with one hand, towards a door at the side of the room, then walked over, Torrillo in tow.

'You're feeling better?'

She nodded.

'Good. It's a shocking sight. Most people would have collapsed on the spot. You did very well. And now . . .'

She waited.

'Now we must talk briefly to the lady who owns the house. I think she has little new to tell us but it will be an interesting interview, in any case.'

Menéndez motioned to the door. They walked in. A local policewoman in a blue uniform that was too tight for her bulky frame stood next to the old woman who sat bolt upright in an old, fading armchair, gripping its wings tightly. She looked ancient, too old to be alive. Her face looked like a Greek mask, resolute, impassive, filled with tragedy. As they walked towards her, she lifted her eyes to them, deep, incisive eyes, measured Menéndez to be the superior, made a gesture for him to sit down, and said, 'You know who I am. I want no scandal. The family name is still good enough for that in this city, I think.'

5

In fact, Menéndez was able to tell Caterina Lucena more about the brothers than she could tell him. He had asked for the criminal files and cuttings from the newspaper library to be brought to the house, skimmed through them briefly. They revealed almost everything that had already been in the public prints, sanitised for *Hola!*, suitably juiced up for *Esquire* and *Playboy*.

Pedro and Juan Angel had been born thirty-four years before in one of the poorest ghettos of Barcelona. They were Siamese twins of a kind, joined at birth at the waist, but only marginally, though this was unknown to the doctors at the time. The connection was simply through the flesh: they shared no internal organs. But in the Spain of the time they were medical freaks, and no one knew how to diagnose the case.

Their father was a deckhand working on long-distance freighters. A year after their birth, he sailed on a ship to Kowloon and was never seen again. Most people felt he could no longer face the medical bills being charged by the Hospital of the Virgin. Shortly before their second birthday, the Angel Brothers were separated by a simple operation paid for by public subscription, and thereafter they fell out of the newspapers, disappeared from the public consciousness.

This was partly an act of social convenience. The newspapers had first painted a picture of a poor honest ghetto family bravely facing up to an unusual predicament. Barcelona is a large city but a small place. Such fictions have limited lives. Their mother worked as a dockside prostitute, most hours of the day, and the city soon knew of it. The operation duly salved the public conscience and let people become concerned about other matters. It changed nothing for the family. The mother continued to work as a prostitute, leaving the children to be brought up most of the time by an aunt who had six children, all boys, of her own. She resented the task, and in particular resented the fact that they were male. She had prayed to the Virgin Mary for daughters, ever since her first son, but the prayers had not been answered. Pedro and Juan were slight, quiet, effeminate children, however, so, for the aunt, the answer seemed obvious. For the first eight years of their life, both were treated as if they were girls. They wore dresses, big, fancy, flouncy ones on Sundays, they went to dance classes, they took part in the parades. They used girls' names – Anna, Belen. On occasion, when they were in their Sunday best, with a little rouge on their cheeks, someone would smile and say: '*Guapas.*' No one connected them with the Siamese twins any longer. That story had been confined to the past.

When they were eight the brothers exposed themselves during Communion classes and were duly expelled from both the church and the school which the church ran. The general view was that their predicament was of their own making and their future their own responsibility. Both took this to heart and spent the best part of the next decade and a half living on the street, hustling as juvenile prostitutes, selling both hard and soft drugs, and becoming involved in the familiar round of juvenile crime: stealing handbags and cameras from tourists, joy-riding cars, minor hijacks of goods around the docks. They spent four periods in reform school, and later jail, before they were twenty-two, always together, since they refused to be separated. It was during their final prison spell that they took up art classes.

On their release, the brothers declared themselves to be artists and produced a series of works that spawned increasing fame and controversy, first in Barcelona, then internationally. They sold a set of bull's testes encased in Perspex for $32,000 through Sotheby's in New York, then outraged Catholic opinion by inflating a hundred-and-fifty-foot replica of a condom outside the cathedral of the Sagrada Familia in their home city. Later works included a stillborn lamb shrink-wrapped in plastic which fetched £25,000 in London. (Torrillo, on hearing this, said, 'I must tell my cousin Carlo, he's a sheep farmer in Antequera. I think he could have let them have one just like it for, I don't know, maybe even half that price.') An item simply entitled *Still Life*, which consisted of a cardboard box full of Kleenex tissues into which the brothers had masturbated, remained unsold when it appeared in Los Angeles with a reserve price of $50,000.

By the time they were thirty, four years before their deaths, the Angel Brothers were established on the international modern art circuit. They had appeared as walk-on celebrities in three Almodóvar movies and designed an ad campaign for Benetton. The magazines estimated they were both dollar millionaires, with four homes around Spain, one on the French Riviera, and a small apartment on the Lower East Side in New York.

The police files also showed that they had not altogether given up the past. Both had been fined for possession of heroin during the mid-eighties – Menéndez was struck by how the brothers always seemed to become involved in events together, never alone – and both had been warned over an incident in Barcelona in which a twelve-year-old boy complained of sexual abuse and various perversions but dropped the accusations when, it appears, he was paid off. They admitted to habitual drug abuse and, two years before their deaths, revealed that they were HIV positive, though there were no signs of the onset of full-blown AIDS.

Menéndez left out the more salacious parts of the story. She was an old woman. She probably still had high Catholic values. When he had finished, she was glaring at him.

'They paid and they were hardly ever here,' she said, angry that she had to say that she needed the money. 'They were not ... not *my* people. But they paid.'

Menéndez thought about the geography of the house. 'You heard nothing, you saw nothing.'

'I did not say that.' The old woman spoke firmly. 'You did not ask me before.'

'Please ...'

She took a sip of water from a glass on an ancient side table. 'When I awoke yesterday afternoon I heard something in the courtyard. Someone, one of these young thugs, had been in the garden. He climbed over the wall.'

'Why did he not walk out of the front gates?'

'Because they are locked, and they are high. You must have seen this.'

'Did you lock them yourself?'

She stared at him contemptuously. 'Do I look as if I am capable of that? The maid does it. The part-time maid. She comes when the Angels ask her to. When they do not, she still helps me. It is an understanding.'

'What did this person look like?'

'Red. He was wearing red. It was a long way off. Behind the trees. I only glanced, but ...'

'Yes?'

'My eyes are not so good.'

She drained the glass and turned to the policewoman. 'There is a bottle of fino in the case over there. I would like some.'

41

The officer returned with the bottle: a cheap supermarket brand Menéndez did not recognise.

'I think he may have been wearing a costume.'

'What sort of costume?'

'A . . . robe. Perhaps. I know I could not see a face and . . .'

She broke off and for a moment Menéndez thought she was about to cry.

'I think we have asked enough questions. I am grateful for your help.'

She nodded, clutching a grey handkerchief to her face.

'These trees. You mean the ones by the vine?' He pointed to the left of the courtyard.

'No, no. There. At the back.'

'Ah. Now I understand.'

'He was a thug. A thug from the street.'

'Yes. Perhaps.'

Torrillo was squinting at the back of the garden. Menéndez closed his notebook.

'Doña Caterina. I must ask. You are owed money for their tenancy, I assume?'

She looked at him with suspicion.

'We have found cash in the brothers' room. I will ensure that a full six months' tenancy is paid from it – this is, I think, the city minimum these days.'

She nodded, clutching the damp handkerchief. 'It is the smell. The *smell*.'

'I know,' said Menéndez. 'I know.'

6

Torrillo lurched the Ford back towards El Viejo. It was mid-afternoon and the streets were half empty. He held a huge cheese sandwich in his left hand, out in the breeze of the open window, and took chunks out of it whenever the traffic permitted.

'What will you do next?' She sat in the back of the car feeling distant from their thoughts.

'The initial medical report will be waiting for us when we get back to the station. The cause of death is fairly obvious, I think. There are minor wounds to the chest on both parties – you saw the darts, but there are other wounds too, though no sign of the weapon that caused them. None of these were serious enough to kill. My guess is that there was one large thrust to the heart – perhaps with a sword, I don't know – which killed each man. The pattern seems to be identical.' Menéndez paused. 'Everything about the Angel Brothers seems to be identical.'

'So?'

'So we follow our procedure. We determine the cause of death. We find out what we can about the last hours of the deceased – this may not be easy, since I think they have been dead for at least a week and I still do not understand why two rich men, with homes all over the world, should rent an apartment like that and use it so seldom. And we talk to the people who knew them. We have a diary, a contacts book, from the apartment. But . . .'

He stopped and seemed reluctant to go on.

'But . . . ?'

'But . . . You're interested in our methodology? It's simple. Most murders are simple affairs. Domestic. Lovers' quarrels. They are not . . . *complex*.'

She was scribbling into her notebook again.

'What we have here, Professor, is what appears to be a ritual murder of two well-known and highly eccentric men who seem to have no reason to be where they are. And the pose . . . their bodies, that was a pose, you agree?'

'Yes.'

'I think the Angel Brothers had some curious tastes in dress but it did not extend, I suspect, to, what – doublet and hose? Almost. Had they been to a fancy-dress party or something? I don't know. It was somehow . . . formal.'

He looked in the driver's mirror and could see she was smiling.

'Policemen don't follow art, Lieutenant.'

'You call that art?' mumbled Torrillo through a mouth half full of bread. 'My cousin Carlo could . . .'

'Sure, sure, sure.' Menéndez signalled him to silence. 'I think the Professor has something to tell us.'

'We have time for a small diversion?'

'How long?' said Menéndez.

'Five minutes. To get there. How long after that depends on you.'

She shuffled herself upright in the back of the car and looked out of the window.

'You know the old fish market, in Veracruz?'

'Closed down five years ago,' said Torrillo. 'They're talking about making it a tourist attraction once the smell finally goes.'

'Take me there.'

The car turned off the main road, navigated a series of

44

narrow back streets, past complaining pedestrians, hanging washing out of windows. An old crumbling building, barred with planks, a regional poster outside, loomed ahead of them.

'Left, maybe three hundred yards, then left again. It's a dead end. There should be a sign for the hospice.'

Torrillo chuckled grimly. 'The hospice? Sure. I know it. My uncle was there. Walked in like a lamb, three months later out in a box.'

They turned into a blind alley and parked the car on a yellow line. Torrillo pointed to an old iron gate in the stone wall. 'You want me to come? I hate these places. Spooky.'

'Finish the sandwich and follow us,' said Menéndez and got out of the car, the woman close behind him.

They walked through the door and found themselves in a cool cobbled courtyard, crossed it to the single door in the apex of the opposite side and walked through to a desk. Behind an open diary and an old-fashioned inkwell sat an elderly nun dressed in white and grey. She finished reading the notice in her hands and then looked up at them. Her manner was neutral.

'The chapel, sister,' said Maria. 'It is open?'

The nun rattled some keys at her waist and pointed to a battered wooden donations box. Menéndez threw in a thousand-peseta note and whispered, 'I hope this is worth it.'

They walked to the end of a long corridor decorated with blue and white tiles depicting scenes from the Bible. An old man, incredibly thin, with a face that spoke only of despair, watched them from a wheelchair. The nun opened the door and ushered them in.

Torrillo caught up in a couple of steps. Maria took in, with a little surprise, his sudden turn of speed. 'It's cold in here,' he said. 'These places always make me feel cold.'

It was dark too and their eyes took time to adjust to the lack of light. At the end, on the altar, gold candelabra glistened. Above, a small spotlight shone on a painting of the Ascension, the colours radiant even in the gloom. Along each wall of the chapel were more paintings, dimly lit: scenes from a hospital, Abraham about to sacrifice his son, two canvases of the Virgin and Child.

'Follow me.'

They walked with her down the centre of the room, towards the altar.

'Now turn round.'

They did and Torrillo's mouth dropped open like a trapdoor. 'Jesus . . .'

Above the entrance was a canvas six feet across and three feet high. Two small lights played on it from either end of the frame. The picture looked like a photograph, rendered in oils, of the scene they had just left: two men, in red and green formal dress, lay dead on a bier. Their skin was putréfying, maggots crawled from their eye sockets. In the right-hand corner of the frame a spectral hand – the hand of God – appeared with a set of scales, weighing the worth, the soul and the heart of each, and finding them wanting. In the lower left-hand corner, the fires of hell burned.

'Artists in life, artists in death,' she said, with more than a hint of smugness. 'Perhaps the Angel Brothers would have approved.'

7

Captain Rodríguez came straight from the press conference, the camera flashes still hurting his eyes. There was a blackboard in the corner of the office. Menéndez stood in front of it, chalk in hand. The two detectives newly assigned to the case, Velasco and a still-blushing Quemada, had joined Torrillo and Maria Gutierrez. It was nearly 9 pm. Outside the sun was dying, painting the city burnished gold. A new shift had come on duty as they assembled, with a mixed murmur of greetings, jokes and the odd catcall. Rodríguez did not look like a man about to go home.

'Questions,' he said, then began to write on the board.

1. Who did the brothers know in the city? Who have they seen recently?
2. Why were they here?
3. Who had a motive to kill them?
4. What is the significance of the way they were killed? The darts?
5. Why were their bodies laid out after the fashion of an old painting?

'Any more?'

'Sure,' said Torrillo. 'How many people are we looking for here? These Angel guys couldn't have been a pushover. They wouldn't just lie there letting you stick darts in them. Were they tied? What?'

Rodríguez pushed forward a piece of paper on his desk. 'Drugged. It says here in the medical report. Common hospital anaesthetic.'

'So we're looking for someone with access to drugs? A doctor or something?'

'Maybe,' said Menéndez. 'But you have to remember the Angels were junkies. A good proportion of the dope they used probably originated in the health service in the first place. If it was their pusher who killed them he'd be able to get hold of anaesthetic as easily as heroin. Could mix them together so they'd inject themselves with it. But it's a point.'

6. How, exactly, did it happen?

'Any more?'

'Boyfriends,' said Quemada. 'These queers, it's always the same. They fight like alley cats. Normal situation – man beats up on his wife, few bruises, that's all. No problem. Queers, you get knives, the whole fucking lot. Boyfriends. Mark my words.'

Rodríguez looked underwhelmed, ringed item three on the blackboard and the detective shrugged his shoulders.

'Any more?'

'Why did he come back?' The two new detectives turned to gaze stonily at Maria. 'Don't you want to know?' she said. 'They were dead for a week. Why did he have to come back to the house?'

'Lost something. Forgot something. Most likely,' said Quemada.

'Yeah. Most likely,' Velasco agreed. She looked at the new man and tried to figure out his place in the station hierarchy. And hierarchy there was, even so early on, that was clear. A pecking order, rigidly enforced without a word being spoken, and Rodríguez was at the top, not just out

48

of rank but also through some simple, unspoken sense of status. Velasco looked in his mid-thirties, with dark sallow skin the colour of a tobacco stain, a gaunt, unhappy face shadowed by stubble. He wore a crumpled polyester suit that shone in the light of the office, its fabric a swirl of different, mirrored colours. Velasco thinks it looks smart, she said to herself. He thinks wrong.

'Most likely?' she asked. Quemada's fat little suit quivered as if it didn't expect an answer. 'Then why did he leave the door open? Why didn't he just go in, get what he wanted, then close it like he did before? It's as if . . .'

'Captain?' Quemada's eyes pleaded with Rodríguez. 'I understand we got to have the lady here but do we really have to listen to her?'

Rodríguez stiffened, with a slight pomposity the men had all come to recognise, looked at her and said, 'We need all the ideas we can get. And I didn't see any of you getting the line about the painting. Go on, Professor.'

She could hear Quemada grunting as she spoke.

'It's as if he almost *wanted* the bodies to be found. Not just any time, but then.'

'Why would he want to do that?' asked Rodríguez.

'I don't know.'

'No,' said the Captain, and made a note on his pad. 'But it's a good question.'

7. Why did he come back and leave the door open when he left?

'Any more?'

Torrillo tapped the table with his pen.

'Sergeant?'

The big man grunted. 'You know this Caterina Lucena, right?'

'I know *of* her. Most of us who grew up in the city do. Very old, very distinguished family. Last of the line. The rest of her family got wiped out in the Civil War.'

'Yeah, well.' Torrillo poked a finger in his ear and twirled it around. 'I got to say, Captain, it just sort of struck me she might not be telling the whole truth there.'

'Why?'

'She is one old lady who is on the ball, right? I mean, maybe she's *old* but I don't think her brain is on the way out like she wanted us to think.'

Rodríguez said nothing.

'Well, that's the way it struck me, Captain. Like, take that line about not seeing anything in the garden but some guy dressed in red, no face or something. Her eyesight looks pretty good to me. She knew when the Lieutenant was pointing to the right place and the wrong place. How come she didn't see any more? Is she just old and batty or maybe scared she knows who did it and he might come back?'

Rodríguez turned to the board and wrote.

8. Did Caterina Lucena lie?

'Guess that's the nub of it,' said Torrillo.

Rodríguez drew a line underneath the last question, then turned to them.

'Go through the diary and the address book we found at the flat. Talk to Barcelona and Madrid – that's where the brothers lived most of the time. Track down contacts, appointments. Find out who they used to spend their time with when they were here. When they arrived. What they did.'

Velasco brushed some invisible crumbs off his suit and stood up. Quemada picked up their papers and they left by the glass-fronted door, followed by Menéndez.

Rodríguez looked at Torrillo and said, 'You're off duty, Sergeant. It's been a long day and it's likely to be another long one tomorrow. Get some sleep.'

'Get some food first,' the big man grumbled.

'Professor?'

She was barely awake. The day seemed to have drained her entirely. Her notepad lay on her lap, untouched for a good half-hour.

'Captain?'

'It's late and I don't think it advisable that you should walk home at this hour. The streets are busy this week. Sometimes things get a little lively. I will drive you.'

'I can take a taxi.'

'If you can find one. Please. I insist.'

They walked down two flights of stairs to the police car park. Rodríguez opened the passenger door for her and held it as she climbed in. He walked round, got into the driver's seat and buckled his seat belt.

'You are staying in the barrio?'

'A friend has loaned me his apartment. He is a psychologist. Recently he moved to New York.'

'You are staying alone?'

She tried to read his expression in the street lights and failed. 'Yes.'

'Would you please tell me how you knew about the painting, the one in the hospice?'

'I lived here when I was a student, briefly. Doing postgraduate work. Some people spent their student days in bars and discos. I preferred the galleries. It really is quite a well-known painting, in artistic circles. The artist was from Seville, Valdés Leal.'

'I have heard the name.'

'Not Murillo, but part of the same era. The Golden Age. If you were from Seville, you would know him well, I assure

51

you. He did some minor religious work but he is best known for his . . . horror pictures? Yes. I think you can call them that. There is another, still in Seville, which is particularly gruesome. Murillo used to say that he could not look at it without holding his nose.'

'And what is their purpose?'

'A very specific one. Valdés Leal was highly religious. The purpose of the painting is to point out that in the midst of the glories of life there is death, that life on earth is transient and ends in decay and corruption, and that we are judged at the end of it, where salvation or damnation awaits us.'

'Do you think the Angel Brothers would be familiar with his work, with this particular picture?'

'Absolutely.' She was adamant. 'It is designed to shock, it contains elements that offend, even nauseate, it is apocalyptic. When the brothers encase the corpse of a rotting lamb in Perspex and ask the wealthy to pay tens of thousands of dollars to own it, aren't they making the same point? I can't begin to imagine they would be unaware of him. Can you?'

'No. As you explained it to me, no, I cannot.'

She pointed to a turning on the right. 'It is the third house along. Where the optician is. I have an apartment on the first floor, above the shop.'

The car drew to a halt on cobbled stones.

'May I ask you a question, Captain?'

'I will answer if I can.'

'Caterina Lucena. Who is she? People seem intrigued by her.'

He sighed and looked out of the window. 'It's not a pleasant story, particularly after a day like this.'

'I would like to hear it all the same. You have a way of whetting one's curiosity. It would be unfair to leave me in the dark.'

'And you don't have sufficient food for nightmares already?'

'Sufficient is sufficient. More cannot make it worse.'

'Perhaps not.'

She waited. Rodríguez now looked old and tired under the light of the street lamps. The contrast with the men he led was more marked than ever. He might have been a university lecturer, one of the polite, distinguished old men she had grown to like, grown to admire at college, men who talked and talked and talked into the night, spinning tales, spinning history.

'The Lucenas are an old family, very old. They date back to the Reconquest. There is a story to that. The dynasty was founded by a soldier – I forget his name – who was given lands in the south for defending a particular fortress when it was besieged by the Moors.'

'This was unusual?'

'The way he did it was. The Moors laid siege for six months without success until they managed to capture his daughter who had been travelling elsewhere in the country. They took her to the fortress walls and called to him, saying that unless he surrendered they would cut her throat. Without hesitating, he reached for his belt, threw down his dagger and said: "Use this."'

'What happened?'

'The Moors capitulated and left the girl unharmed. Thereafter, the Lucenas seemed destined to be, not just brave, but braver than the rest. Read the military histories, the name is there always, from the Armada to the Peninsular War. When Caterina Lucena looks down that aristocratic nose at you, she is looking from the same grand high viewpoint of centuries. Could you not feel that *pride?*'

'I could. And I couldn't understand it.'

'Doomed pride, of course. Since she is a spinster and

53

none of the family survived the Civil War except her.'

'None?'

'None. People here do not talk about the war. Even my father, who lived through it, rarely spoke to me about it. Only a few stories come out, and one of those is about the Lucenas. Something strange, something dark happened to the people here. Left and right divided, became blood enemies. The Lucenas were on the left, the aristocratic left, and for a time they were in the ascendancy. Then the right started to win, through mobs, through street gangs, through violence. One day, when the news came through that Lorca had been murdered by the Falange in Granada, a group of Falangists – at least a group who *claimed* to be Falangists – drove to the Lucena mansion. Where you were today. It seems that they had been *inspired* by what was happening in Granada. The Lucenas had their own guard outside. There was a battle, but the guard was outnumbered. The gang broke in, took away everyone inside. Caterina's mother and father, other relatives, brothers, sisters, I forget how many. They were kept for some time in a makeshift prison used by the Falange, on the outskirts of the city. La Soledad. Then, just as happened to Lorca, one day they were taken outside, told to dig a ditch, and then to stand in it.'

She waited, knowing what was to come.

'They turned a machine gun on the entire family, twelve, maybe fifteen people. The ditch was their grave.'

Rodríguez gazed out into the night, his eyes unfocused.

'And Caterina?'

'She was the youngest of the family. Thirteen, fourteen. When her father realised what was happening, he pushed her to the ground and told her to lie there. The bodies, as they fell, protected her. This is what we understand – this is a story which has been through some retelling, you see, and, as far as I am aware, Caterina herself has never spoken

54

of it. The anecdotal version is that she lay underneath the
dead and dying bodies for the best part of a day, some say
with a minor wound, some say not. In the early evening,
when other prisoners arrived to fill in the ditch, she clawed
her way out from under the bodies and ran away. How, no
one knows. Some say that some of the prisoners helped her
and were shot for doing so. But this is conjecture.'

A small group walked past the car in silence, dressed
from head to foot in pure white. They spoke in hushed
whispers, soft voices ringing faintly against the stone walls.

'How do you live with such a thing?' Maria said.

'How? Perhaps it is easier for her. She is Caterina Lucena.
Remember the father in the Reconquest, remember the
dagger thrown down from the ramparts. It is her destiny
to overcome adversity, *any* adversity, or so, I presume, she
feels.'

'This is a terrible city,' she said, without thinking. 'I felt
that when I was here before. As a student. There is something dark, something unnatural about it. It threatens, even
when it is gay.'

'No,' Rodríguez replied, and there was a new firmness to
his voice. 'This is a *real* city. As your painting by Valdés
Leal is a real painting. As the Angel Brothers, dead on their
bier, are real. It threatens only because it does not seek to
hide that which we would rather not see. It uses the nearness
of death to help us appreciate the brightness of life.'

She looked at him in the dark, trying to see the expression
in the eyes that now glittered blackly in the reflection from
the windscreen.

'And that is what you like. That is what fires you.' It was
a statement, not a question.

He reached past her and opened the passenger door. The
evening air entered the vehicle, cool and gently perfumed
with orange blossom.

'I must go back to the station. Please excuse my rudeness.'
She picked up her case and put it on her lap.

'When should I return?'

'When you wish. We will have a case meeting at 10 am. You are, of course, welcome.'

'I will be there at ten.'

'Observing?'

She shrugged her shoulders. 'What else?'

Rodríguez scrutinised her in the dark and she was very conscious of the fact. His was an interesting face: fine-featured, pleasant, welcoming. But behind it, when you could almost hear him thinking, there was something else, some keen, aggressive intelligence that he held in check until it was needed. She did not envy anyone who became the focus of the Captain's professional attention, even at this closing stage of his career.

'I have no objection if you do more than observe,' he said finally. 'None at all. Menéndez is an intelligent man, better trained than most. Ambitious too. But he thinks along straight lines. They all do. They deserve to be jolted out of it.'

'That's not my job.'

'No,' he said, and his eyes were positively glittering now. 'No, it isn't. But I think you should say what you feel must be said.'

She paused for a moment then said, 'You're testing him, aren't you?'

Rodríguez laughed. It was a pleasant, deep sound. 'You are a professor, aren't you? I prefer to think I am cutting our little lieutenant free for a while. He has worked under my shadow for a good time, now he must work on his own a little. I shall stand back and see where that leads. I am not a fool. He sees himself as captain; of course he does. But I think I have a few years left in me yet. And who knows? Perhaps this curious little case will show us what our friend Menéndez is made of.'

'I see,' she said and climbed out of the car.

'Captain?'

He smiled innocently up at her from the driving seat.

'I do not wish to be part of any office intrigue. I must make that clear.'

'Nothing, my good Professor, could be further from my mind. Our primary objective is to solve this case as quickly and efficiently as possible. But I want to find out if Menéndez is fit to follow me. And find out I shall.'

Then he pulled the door shut, and the little engine gunned, with a cloud of fumes. The red car drove off into the thick, velvet night.

Maria Gutierrez turned the key in the lock of her apartment. The sound of metal on metal echoed down the long, polished hallway. Her loneliness pulsed inside her, and behind it, shapeless and only dimly recognised, the faint, ragged edges of fear.

8

'Come on, Bear. You speak a little English. You went on the course last year.'

The more the man in the seat in front of them gabbled, the more Quemada begged. Semana Santa was beginning to hot up. The office held two prostitutes under caution, one pickpocket, a couple of tourists who complained of being robbed. And Quemada's man, who was a mystery.

'This guy is driving me crazy, Bear. He's quacking more than a duck with its ass on fire and I don't get a word of it. Just deal with him until the tourist cops come along, will you?'

Torrillo wiped the back of his hand against his sweating forehead and cursed the weather. It was hot enough for mid-summer and he had another reason to sweat – he didn't like to admit to Quemada just how little English had hung around once the induction course had ended, and how much of that had got jumbled up with the tourist street talk you just picked up as a matter of course over the years. He leaned over to the man in the chair, stared dolefully at him long enough to win a moment of silence, then said, in slow, loud, deliberate English, 'Shut the fuck up!'

The man paused, looked hurt, then said in a loud American voice, 'This is the limit. This is the *fucking* limit. You get me the American consul and you get me him now. I've had a bellyful of this goddamn city and when you find out who you're dealing with you're sure gonna be sorry you . . .'

Torrillo looked at him again, then said, more loudly, '*Shut the fuck up!*'

'*Aw, Jesus,*' the man screamed. 'That the only English you know? I'm here trying to report some fucking vicious lunatic trying to maim me and I get some baboon with a fucking ponytail . . .'

The American lurched to his feet, face going red. He wore a red nylon football jacket and red training trousers. A good six feet tall, athletic build, dark hair, about thirty years old, Torrillo judged. He looked as if he could handle himself, and he was starting to get mad.

'*Shut the* . . .'

'*I been here two hours now and I want the American consul.*'

He was thumping the table with both fists. It bounced up and down when he hit it.

'I want him now. I want a ticket home. I had a goddamn bellyful of this place. I been bitten by mosquitoes, I been robbed blind by your fucking barmen, I got hustled at seven in the morning – *seven* in the morning – by some broad with a moustache my old man could have done justice to. Jesus, you guys go for it at that time of day, huh? I can't train 'cos it's hot enough for a fucking Turkish bath out there, in spite of everything your oh-so-nice tourist people in New York say – mild spring climate, Mr Famiani, *mild climate, my ass* – and finally, and this is just the icing on the cake, you understand, just the pee-ess de la refucking-sistance, when I just eaten some meal I wouldn't serve to a fucking pig, when I'm just going to go home to my hotel and try to get some sleep, if and assuming you fucking people can shut your goddamn noise long enough to let me close my eyes, some goddamn fucking *lunatic* comes at me out of nowhere, yammering like he's some character

59

out of a Looney Tune number, and has the infinite goddamn nerve to throw *this* at me . . .'

The American reached into his pocket, quick as a flash, pulled something out, held it in front of him, neat and tight, between finger and thumb.

Torrillo glanced at it, glanced at the redness of the man, thought for a second, looked him in the eyes, then, without even drawing back his arm, punched him straight in the face. It was like being hit by a brick wall. The American's nose crumpled, then his body arched backwards, flying across Quemada's desk taking a sheaf of papers with it. The metal object in his hand flew in the air, then fell, scuttering and scraping noisily across the dusty, plasticised floor. The man came to rest in a heap, head fetched up against an iron swivel chair, blood starting to pump from his nose. There were tears in his eyes and this time he really was screaming, screaming like crazy, and Torrillo just couldn't make out a word.

Torrillo walked over, past the heap on the floor, bent down, reached under a desk space, retrieved something, and held it up in his hand: a brand-new, bright, shiny dart, the silver shaft stained with dark brown from the point to halfway along the shank, a yellow ribbon tied to the base of the plastic feathers.

Torrillo put it safely on a desk, a good six feet away from the man in the red jacket and the red trousers, then walked over to him. He reached into the desk drawer, pulled out a pair of handcuffs, roughly turned the man around, cuffed one hand, cuffed the other. Then he pulled him up, sat him down on one of the metal office chairs, hard on his backside, hands behind his back. Blood and snot ran down from his nose, over his gaping mouth, then dripped off his chin.

Torrillo said, in a slow, quiet voice, 'Shut the fuck up.'

The American started to sob, gently, blowing bright pink snot bubbles out of his mouth and nose.

Quemada looked at the shaking heap on the chair, looked at Torrillo, shook his head and let out a long, low whistle.

'Jesus, Bear. When you deal with someone, they surely know they been dealt with.'

9

Forty-five minutes later, Menéndez, Torrillo and Maria
Gutierrez were sitting in the interview room. A police doctor
was dabbing at the face of the man they now knew to be
Freddy Famiani, age thirty-two, a professional athlete from
Laguna Beach, California. The doctor had applied a large
plaster to a dart wound in Famiani's upper arm.

Menéndez's English was passable, Maria's fluent. Between
them they had managed to piece together enough of the
story to realise the mistake, take off the cuffs, call a medic,
calm Famiani down a little, persuade him that he really had
no need to call a lawyer or the American consul, and no
permanent damage was done.

'Doesn't look so bad. I just gave him a little slap,' said
Torrillo when the doctor finished wiping Famiani's face. 'I
hit him real hard he'd still be sleeping.'

Maria did not translate the words.

'The Sergeant believed you were about to assault him,'
said Maria. 'There has been an attack by someone answering
your description, using the darts you pulled out of your
pocket.'

'An attack?'

'A serious attack,' said Menéndez.

'Serious? Like someone, someone got killed or
something?'

Menéndez said nothing.

'Shit.' Famiani ran his sleeve across his face. 'Anyone'd

think this was New York the way you guys go on at each other. You got some water?'

Torrillo opened the door, walked to the water fountain and returned with a plastic cup.

'Got to keep up my liquid intake,' said Famiani. 'Important. Like these.'

He reached into his jacket pocket and pulled out a bottle of pills. Menéndez watched him shake two into his hand and then wash them down.

'Nothing illegal, Mr Policeman,' Famiani said. He sniffed away some blood. 'Vitamins. Salt. Good natural stuff. I like to win fair and square when I run. Maybe that's why I don't win so often.'

Menéndez took out a pen and started to write.

'Your name is Frederick Famiani. You are from Laguna Beach, California. You arrived here last Wednesday, by train from Malaga. When did you arrive in Spain?'

'A month ago. Saw some old buddies down on the coast. They run a tennis school near Mijas. Teach the golden wrinklies how to serve overhand. Jesus, some way to make a living. Then came here. Do some sightseeing, some more training. Goddamn tourist people in New York said the weather would be, and I quote, "mild". Some kinda mild.'

'Why are you training?'

'You don't follow sports or something? Next month, the Berlin Marathon. One *big* event, fifteen thousand runners, and one fucking *huge* purse. All around the wall, in and out the Brandenburg Gate. Came fifteenth last year, reason is I was a little under the weather and, to be perfectly frank, this was my first European race and I just wasn't used to running through all that dog poop. Enough of it on the streets to make you barf, man. Even worse here. You run a marathon here you call it the slippery brown Nike special and I'll just *slide* all the way from start to finish. This year's

63

different, see. This year the dogshit don't faze me. And I'm fitter too. Leastwise I was until you guys started taking slugs at me. You get sued much here? No? That surprises me. Do *not* move to America. You'd never get professional indemnity insurance. I could make a lot of money out of this back home. Jesus. More than a whole year of marathons.'

'Do you know anyone in the city?'

'No one except you charming people though some of the places I go training there's all sorts of ladies keep wanting to say hello. They just naturally friendly or they have some kind of, uh, ulterior motive?'

He smiled at Maria. 'Say, you're sort of pretty. You a cop too? Naw. Not possible. Pardon my mouth. My trainer says if I could keep it shut more often I'd win more races: cut down on wind drag and conserve my energy. Know what I mean?'

Famiani looked into the cold blue eyes and found silence sometimes came naturally.

'And tell me again, please, this time slowly and in detail, how you came to acquire this.' Menéndez held up the dart, now encased in a plastic exhibit bag.

'Er. Not quite right, my friend. *It* acquired *me*. OK?'

Famiani gulped down some more water. Torrillo thought this could take for ever.

'See, I like to run early in the morning and late at night. You don't bump into people so much and it's cool. Good discipline for a runner, you know. Get out of bed early, hit the road. Eat some supper, wait for it to digest a little, do the same. So I'm staying in some semi-converted flophouse over, like' – he pointed out of the window, beyond the Torre del Oro – 'like, over *there*, which is not exactly of Holiday Inn standard and comes complete with piped groin music from the neighbouring bedsprings, you know what I mean, and it seems to me the best place to train is this

64

park. You know the big one with the pigeons and stuff?'

'The Alfabia?'

'Yeah. There's this big blue and white sign on tiles at the entrance? Little arch? Sort of a canal with little bridges on it?'

Menéndez nodded.

'So I get up around five, eat some breakfast, if that's what you can call it, and I go there, like I done the last three mornings. Then last night, I got to thinking maybe I take a run late in the evening, too. Before I go to bed. And that's where it happened.'

'What happened?'

'The guy stuck me with the dart.'

Famiani rolled up his sleeve.

'Here. You can't see it now 'cos of the Band-Aid but the fucker threw that thing right at me from, like, no further away than you are now. Just walked right out from behind one of them little bridges then threw it at me. You know what? I think the fucker was gonna throw another one, too? The lights aren't too great there but I saw him. He was like reaching for something else. I could see him. Like another dart. I dunno. Maybe it was something bigger than that? It was hard to tell.'

Famiani shook his head. 'You know something else? I think that crazy fucker was surprised. I think he actually expected me to, like, start something, there and then. He had this kind of aggressive pose. You know? You get to read it when you go around the streets a lot like I do. It's the OK-punk-let's-start-something look. Someone tried something just like it in Marina del Rey once just because I nearly bumped into his shopping cart or something. Not with the dart, you understand, just kind of . . .'

He threw up his fists.

'This all comes of a bad diet, you know. Yin and Yang

seriously out of kilter, my man. Too much red meat and shellfish, bad for your inner balance and that sort of stuff. You should talk to my trainer Benny, he knows about these things. Fish, chicken, steamed vegetables, keep you regular, keep you harmonious. You guys should try it. What I've seen, most the time you people live on lard. Your choice but *distinctly* unharmonious.'

Menéndez kept scribbling and spoke without looking up from the page. 'But instead you ran?'

'*Ran?* Some fucker throws one of those things at me you bet I ran. I was out of there faster than shit off of a hot shovel. Shame there weren't no prizes around 'cos I would have won 'em, you bet your ass.'

'Did he try to follow you?'

'Didn't stand a chance.'

'And you can describe him.'

'Nope.'

All three looked at him and waited. Maria said, 'I am sorry, Mr Famiani. Perhaps you did not understand the question.'

'Sure, I understood it. You said: can I describe him? And I said, no, I can't. You people listening to me or did I miss something out? I didn't even see the guy. Just . . . *it!*'

'Maybe I should slap the little shit around some more,' Torrillo said in Spanish.

'*Hey, hey, hey!* I think I got a little whiff of that one,' Famiani spluttered. 'I'm not trying to be funny with you, really. Scout's honour and all that stuff. Just that it's true. All I saw was that funny kind of costume thing you guys wear when you're waving your incense around and stuff.'

'Costume?'

'Yeah. You know. Like the Ku Klux Klan. Bad taste if you ask me, making your church stuff look like the kind

of things those bastards wear. Your country, you understand, your choice. But seems bad taste to me.'

Menéndez tore off a piece of paper, drew a figure on it
with the pencil.

'You mean like this?'

'Yeah. Didn't I say that? This long fucking cloak that goes
all the way to the ground, with the flappy arms. And the
big pointy hat, slitty eyeholes. I didn't see *nothing* behind
that. Nothing. Not even the eyes.'

'His hand.'

'Sure, his hand. Must have seen that. He pulled out that
fucking dart with it. Then after he stuck me I saw him
fumbling around inside of that cloak like he was looking
around to pull out something else. I dunno what. A Uzi?
You have them here? Spooky watching him fumbling
around like that, man. You seen that bit in *Alien*? Where,
like, the guy has got this *thing* in his stomach and it starts
to writhe around inside him, kind of pushing up his T-shirt
on the way out? *Gross*. It was sorta like that. Writhing. You
bet I ran the fuck out of there. And like I said, wasn't no
way he was going to follow, not if he was Jesse Owens. Not
with that outfit round his ankles. My old man could have
beaten him out of there.'

'Can you describe his hand?'

'White. Fingers on it. How else you gonna describe a
hand for chrissake? What next? You gonna give me *hand*
pictures to look at, see if I can find one I recognise?'

'And there was nothing on his dress? No jewellery?'

'Dress? Jewellery? This some kind of queer thing? Jesus,
this place is fucked up. No. There was nothing on his *dress*.'

Famiani sniffed again, then stretched his long legs.

'Nothing more I can tell you. Can I go now? I wanna
catch an afternoon train to Madrid. Benny's meeting
me there. No offence but this place gives me the serious

heebie-jeebies. Guys in *frocks* throwing fucking darts at you . . .'

Menéndez scribbled down contact addresses in Madrid, Berlin and California.

'You need to go back to the park with one of the detectives to identify the exact place where the attack took place. I will assign someone to you. After that we will happily drive you to your hotel and then to the station if you wish.'

'Kind of you, but I guess it's the least you can do in the circumstances.'

'If you think of anything else, here is my number.' Menéndez handed over a small, white business card, with the city coat of arms on the top.

'Sure. Nothing more to tell, you know. This was all over in a few seconds. Thank God. And I'm not the kind of guy goes around looking closely at things when I'm running in any case. Running requires *focus*.'

'Thank you,' said Menéndez, stony-faced.

'Tell the big guy he doesn't need to see me out. I been helped enough for one day.'

Famiani stood up, wiped his nose on his sleeve, grabbed one ankle up then yanked it up behind him to stretch the muscle, released it, then did the same with the other leg, gave a little grin.

'Don't feel too bad, all things considering.'

He walked to the door, took hold of the handle, then turned back to them.

'The dress. It was red, kind of. I said that, didn't I? Sure I did. Deep red. Like scarlet. Weird. The Klan kinda like 'em white which makes sense, I guess. Red's a new one on me and to be perfectly frank with you people, you're welcome to it.'

10

Quemada and Velasco played footsie with the legs of their desk and looked unhappy. The incident with Famiani had taken them well over the end of their shift, which should have seen them off duty at nine, and they did not like kicking their heels in the main office while Torrillo and the woman had all the fun elsewhere. They watched glumly as the American came out of the interview room, booked in with one of the day team for a visit to the park, then left with some passing crack about how nice it would be to get the hell out of town. Torrillo beckoned for them to follow down the hall into Rodríguez's office. They came, sizing up the woman from behind as they did so. Same faded, floppy jeans, different cheesecloth top. Hair still looked like it needed some care and attention. But all things taken into consideration, it seemed best to suppress the wisecracks.

Menéndez opened the drab green door and led the way in. Bright sunlight came through the windows in big, thick chunks that shone as dusty shafts of light across the room. The blackboard was unchanged from the previous evening, but the Captain's desk now looked awash with paper, much of it torn-off pages from notepads, covered in scribbled writing. The Lieutenant sat down in the leather chair, suggested they did the same, sent Torrillo for some coffee, waited for him to return, then said, 'The Captain asked me to take this meeting for him. He's busy. Well?'

Velasco took a deep breath, unconsciously polished both

knees of his suit with his sweating palms, and wondered why his partner always left it to him to do the explanations. This chalk and cheese partnership seemed to work fine most of the time. It had for the best part of three years. Yet still, in spite of the jokes, in spite of the odd bout of frantic, spontaneous drunkenness together after work, he still felt there were ways, many ways in which he didn't know Quemada. Velasco stifled his little bundle of inner resentment and said, 'You aren't going to like this.'

Then he took a long gulp of overstewed coffee and began.

'The way we see it this place in the old girl's mansion it must have been something like, I don't know, a kind of rumpus room for the boys.'

Menéndez was writing again and didn't look up. 'Explain.'

'Well, you see, we spoke last night to loads and loads of the people they knew in Madrid and Barcelona and the duty captain even gave us permission to make a long-distance phone call to New York and talk to some people there.'

'And they knew about the apartment here?' asked Menéndez.

'Well, kind of,' said Velasco. 'See, these guys, it's not like they have a family around them we can talk to. All they have is *acquaintances*. Far as we can make out, they had their homes in Madrid and the rest of it and they lived there when they were doing business. You know, seeing agents, people who used to buy their junk, going to parties with the kind of people you see in the magazines, being *seen*. But it was like they didn't have a *life* there.'

'Yeah.' Quemada pulled out a notebook. 'See we spoke to their agent, some foreign guy called Mendelsohn in Madrid, and when we asked him who the brothers' friends were he just said, none. They didn't have none. So I says, well, who did they see, like who did they spend their time with? And he says, whoever invited them to their parties. It was like their life was just about parties, just about drumming up business. Nothing else. Now seems to me that these boys are not the sort to have no acquaintances at all. So I ask him: where they go to have fun, least the kind of thing they called fun? And he says he's not sure but he thinks they used to come here, 'cos sometimes they'd be away for a few weeks, when they got sick of all the partying with the nobs, you see, and when they'd come back, he said, they were *glowing*. And the guys in Madrid and Barcelona turned over their houses there and they're clean, 'part from some dirty books and a few grams of pot. Whereas . . .'

'Whereas it looks like that little old lady's house was knee-deep in spunk and spit most of the time the boys were in it.' Velasco smiled. That was one line he wasn't going to let his partner steal. 'They found enough syringes in the drawers to run a medium-sized infirmary. No dope though, that's funny. Other stuff too. Kind of kinky stuff: handcuffs, rubber suits, things you could get beat up with. There's a bare bed in one bedroom. Some traces of blood, not the brothers'; it's being tested now. Not enough to make it look like someone got serious hurt, you understand. Fun and games.'

'We made some calls too,' said Quemada. 'Around the network. The rent boys knew them, some pretty well apparently.'

'Any names?'

'Not at the moment. We plan to talk to some people tonight. The important guys in this business don't work days and God knows where they go when they go off duty.'

'Good.'

Menéndez picked up a sheet of paper from the pile on his desk.

'You went through their diaries?'

'Yeah. They were too smart to put down anything there. Maybe they kept some private diaries somewhere but we haven't found anything.'

'Did they go to the bullring?'

'Yeah,' said Velasco. 'Quite a lot. Madrid, Barcelona. A couple of times here. That was one of the circles they moved in too, you know. The agent said that. Bullfighters' parties; they liked getting their pictures taken with these guys.'

'Turns queers on. The suits and all that stuff,' said Quemada.

Menéndez rubbed his eyes with the backs of his hands. He looked as if he had not slept. 'You boys are nearly two hours over your shift already. Can you spare me another half-hour?'

They nodded. They didn't like Menéndez, particularly didn't like the way he kept chasing the Captain's job. But they liked to hear him think.

'Good. Take a break, we'll resume in fifteen minutes when I've assembled my notes. Try to put some direction on this thing.'

They broke up. The two detectives finished their paperwork. Torrillo took Maria round to the Alarcon where, in the middle of a gaggle of noisy cops, he ate two huge slices of toast, soaked in bright-red pork dripping, washed down with a coffee and a *copa* of brandy. She sipped a mineral water and, after thirty seconds, gave up trying to wave away the clouds of cigarette smoke that spilled over them from every side.

'You writing this down in your report?'

'What?'

' "And after an hour they then go to the bar around the corner to stuff their faces with lousy food." '

72

She laughed and Torrillo thought that was something that didn't happen often.

'No.'

'So what will you write?'

She thought. 'I don't know yet. I have some notes but . . .'

Two traffic cops pushed their way to the bar and barked out orders.

'Jesus,' bellowed Torrillo. 'Can't you see there's a lady in here?'

One of the traffic cops turned to look at him from behind opaque sunglasses. 'Sure I can, Bear. Just can't figure out why, that's all.'

From behind the sunglasses, someone observed her.

'Hey!' said the traffic cop. 'I know who she is. Quemada told me. She's the ice queen. Stands out a mile. You worked out how to teach these guys to do their jobs yet, lady?'

Maria could feel the blood rushing to her cheeks. The opaque sunglasses continued to stare at her, stifling the words in her throat.

Torrillo bellowed, 'Goddamn bike riders think they're something out of the movies . . . get out of my way.'

Then he barged past the motorcycle cop to the corner of the tiny bar, neatly stacked a pile of dirty plates and glasses to make way for their own, then slowly turned a half-circle that pushed open enough space for Maria to stand with a degree of comfort. She placed her glass of water on the grubby plasticised table and, for a moment, wished she had never given up cigarettes.

'Ignore these people, Professor. Big mouths go with the job usually. It don't mean anything.'

'No,' she said, and wondered whether she should feel amused or angry. 'No.'

'You were saying . . .' The big man wanted to get the conversation back on track as fast as he could.

73

'The thing is, Bear . . . I'm meant to be writing about existing methodologies, pardon me, existing *procedures*.'

'Yeah?'

'And I'm still trying to work out what they are.'

He squinted, screwing up the big round face. 'You mean like: where's the handbook?'

'If you like.'

Torrillo wondered whether he could trust the woman. Was this just some kind of plot from upstairs to come in and shackle them with more rules and regulations and paperwork? Trouble was, she just didn't *look* like someone from upstairs.

'There are kind of handbooks for most things. But you can't write a handbook for the kind of things we got on now.'

'I appreciate that.'

'And also you got the Captain.'

She waited, silently, for him to say more.

'The Captain's different. He's got kind of a feeling for these things that means most times you don't need a handbook. Sure we cover the points, but it's what you get out of the points, that's what matters.'

He gulped down more coffee and she found herself wondering why he looked like this. Why the ponytail, why the canvas suit that would have looked more in place on the road manager of some rock band?

'It's a question of intuition, inspiration. Comes from up here' – he tapped his head – 'not some handbook. Tell you a story. When I was a kid, I used to go up and stay with some relatives near Santiago. You know around there? It's *green*. All the time. It just rains all the time and it makes things green, not this burned-out kind of scrub we got here. I used to be into birds those days. Down here you see stuff like eagles, buzzards, hoopoes, the fancy stuff, and you take

74

it for granted. Up there, they used to have these blackbirds everywhere and they fascinated me 'cos we just didn't see that many and they're clever birds. You can watch them, and think about them, and try to guess what they're doing. Point is, I used to watch those blackbirds hopping over the grass, looking out for worms, and I could *never* work it out. You see them, they have their head cocked a little to one side, those eyes going out from the side of their heads, and when they pounce, they pounce somewhere else. Somewhere you know they weren't looking. I watched that for hours on end and never could figure it. Till one day it hit me and I realised how stupid I was. I kept expecting them to look for the worms. They weren't. When they cock their heads, they're *listening* for them. Listening for the rustle in the grass, whatever it is a blackbird can hear down there. The Captain, he's like that. You think he's looking for something somewhere, really he's listening, listening really hard, some place else altogether. So we go out there, we find the stuff for him, we come back, and we wait. While he listens. Not the kind of stuff you get in a handbook.'

She drained her glass and looked at the cheap plastic watch on her wrist. 'I think the point about handbooks, Bear, is that they're there to support the intuition. They're there to give you something to work with when the inspiration is somehow missing. When you listen and hear nothing but the wind.'

'Well, there you have me, Professor. See, I've worked with the Captain a long time now. We all have. You know for a lot of us he's like some kind of a legend. The man who always got there. I can't recall a situation where the intuition *did* fail. In the end.'

'In the end.'

She looked at him, curious, calculating the degree of trust.

'He's not a young man, Bear. He looks tired sometimes.'

He grinned. He didn't mind. He half expected it.

'Yeah. You know, pardon me for saying, but at times you sound like that creep Menéndez. He's after the Captain's job. I guess you already worked that out.'

'He's ambitious. What's wrong with that?'

'Nothing. It's just that it's not nice to show it so much. And you might at least wait for the guy to retire. He ain't got long to go.'

'Bear,' she said, 'will you do me one favour?'

'If I can.'

'Please call me Maria. Ask the Captain to call me Maria too. And Lieutenant Menéndez. If he can bring himself to.'

'Thank you, Maria.'

'*De nada*,' she said and smiled. Twice in one day. That's good going, thought Torrillo. Sometimes the ice queen melts a little.

Rodríguez was behind his desk, behind the paper mountain, but the blackboard had been wiped clean. He waited for everyone to arrive, thanked Quemada and Velasco for extending their hours – 'We get overtime for this, Captain?' asked Velasco hopefully, then shut up when there was no reply – then stood up with the chalk in his hand. Menéndez crouched over a notebook, a ballpoint darting over the page.

'I see three obvious routes of inquiry. Velasco, Quemada. You stick with the one you've already started.'

'Sure, Captain,' said Velasco.

'That one we doing or all three?' asked Quemada.

'All three,' said Rodríguez.

'You mean, chasing the rent boys, squeezing what we can get out of them?'

'Yes.'

'Fine.' Quemada yawned. 'Just so's I got it clear. It's been

76

a long night and I'd appreciate these things spelled out for my dim-witted brain.'

And even this little act of insubordination rankled for Torrillo, who glared at Quemada from across the room, watched him stare at his shoes, smart a little, then say, 'I get the second line of inquiry. It's the guy in the red suit, right? There many of them about?'

'Jesus,' said Torrillo. 'It's Semana Santa. Got to be ten thousand of them out there.'

'Ten thousand people wearing penitents' outfits, maybe even more,' said Velasco. 'Not thousands wearing red ones. You got, maybe, sixty brotherhoods of penitents in all, most of 'em wear white, a few black, a few brown. Not many red. Not that I can recall.'

Rodríguez picked up a sheet of paper from the desk. 'Three. The Brotherhood of the True Cross, Proven.'

'That's not like the True Cross, Unproven, or the False Cross, or something else? These religious guys really kill me,' said Quemada.

'You're plain ignorant,' said Velasco. 'I got relatives involved in all this stuff and it's tradition. They work all year round doing things you never heard of, raising money for charity, some of it police charities too. You shouldn't badmouth it.'

'Yeah, well, one of them isn't raising money for the cops, he's raising *work* for us.' Quemada was bent forward with his thumbs holding open his eyelids.

'The Brotherhood of the True Cross, Proven,' Rodríguez continued. 'The Brotherhood of the Everlasting Flame.'

'You can forget that one,' said Velasco. 'I had a cousin was big in that one. The costume's red, sure, but more sort of orangey red. No way someone is going to describe that one as scarlet. Besides, I don't think there's much life in it any more. My cousin packed it in years ago. He wears black now, don't you know. And while I'm at it, you can forget the first one too. Probably. My memory serves me right, they merged with the Everlasting Flame a couple of years back. Happens a lot these days. Religion isn't what it was. Young kids prefer to ride motorbikes and score dope down the park, some of 'em anyway. May not be in the directory yet, but they're the same. They wear the same dress.'

Rodríguez scribbled on the paper in front of him. 'Good. They're out, unless I decide otherwise. That leaves the Brotherhood of the Blood of Christ.'

Quemada's eyes lit up. 'Say, I heard of that one! I heard of that!'

Velasco gasped and rolled his eyes. 'Christ, everybody's heard of that one.'

'Yeah,' said Torrillo. 'Everyone.'

'I haven't,' said Maria.

'You're doing time and motion, lady, you're not part of the investigation,' Quemada said immediately.

Maria wondered why the words felt so hurtful. They were, in a sense, accurate. She looked across to the Captain for some sign, some recognition of where she stood in the pecking order. He seemed oblivious to Quemada's remark.

Rodríguez went on. 'The Brotherhood of the Blood of Christ is relatively recent. It dates back to the Civil War. It has maybe two thousand members in the city. There's a small office, a secretary to the brotherhood. Menéndez will talk to him later.'

'Say,' Quemada sat upright. 'I know where I heard of that one. That's the one the cops join, the ones who get the God urge, right? That's the one you join if you're a cop.'

'Jesus, sweet fucking Jesus,' Velasco moaned and put a hand to his head. ' "The God urge?" And they wonder why this fucking society is going down the tubes.'

'They don't make the membership records public,' said Rodríguez. 'We could threaten with court action to get them if they turn difficult. But I think it's true to say that membership of the brotherhood is fairly tightly controlled. Police. City officials. Politicians, some local, some national.'

'What kind of politics?' asked Maria. 'A little to the right of Christian democracy?'

Rodríguez nodded. 'I said it dated back to the Civil War. Maybe even directly to the Falange. It's mellowed over the years, of course. It's also shrunk a lot in size. No influence any more. Does you no good with a socialist administration.'

'So you a member of this thing, Velasco? You snorting incense in your spare time?' Quemada looked at his partner with genuine bemusement.

'No I am not,' the officer replied, vehemently. 'And even if I was, that's a hell of a thing to ask, even of your partner. Besides, there's no saying we're looking for someone there. We're looking for some crazy who likes wearing the uniform, that's all. For God's sake, you can probably hire these things from some fancy-dress place, just like you can get witch costumes for your kids come Halloween. Maybe he just borrowed it for the occasion.'

Menéndez looked up from the page and said, 'Probably not. I've already checked with the six main costume supply companies in the city. None of them supplies penitents' costumes for rent – they think it would be in bad taste.'

'Then maybe he made it. His mother ran it up for him.'

'Maybe,' said Menéndez. 'But even if he did, we should assume some association. Direct, or indirect, through a relative or acquaintance, perhaps. Why else would he pick red? White would be more anonymous.'

'Not much more,' said Torrillo. 'We still got a couple of thousand of them walking around out there. We can't

79

stop every one, and even if we did, what would we ask them?'

'Yeah,' said Velasco, full of gloom. 'Next year I'm going to take a holiday for Semana Santa, you know. This could lose me my religion it goes on like this. And the third thing we're supposed to know? These two maybe I could have worked out but you lose me on the third thing.'

'The darts.' Rodríguez opened the drawer of his desk and took out an evidence bag. The sharp silver objects looked dull and harmless behind the semi-opaque plastic. He held it by the cream card tag tied around the top.

'With the brothers, he threw the darts into their bodies before he killed them. We know that from the pattern of the bruising. They did *not* pierce the skin after death. With Famiani too – which we must assume was another murder attempt – he threw the darts *before* he tried to use some other kind of weapon.'

'The brothers would have let this guy stick darts in them anyway, probably,' said Quemada. 'They took them in the arms and chest. There were marks on their backsides that looked as if they'd had them there too before. They'd have *let* him do that as some kind of weird turn-on. Seriously.'

'And then he gave them dope that knocked them out and then he killed them,' said Velasco.

His partner nodded. 'Which he had to do because he couldn't take them both on at the same time. Yeah. Makes sense. I can see it.'

Maria asked, 'What would have happened to Famiani if he had stayed to fight? What do the brothers tell us about that?'

'After they were hit with the darts, they were wounded, deep, in the shoulders and the side of the abdomen, using some sort of long, pointed instrument,' said Rodríguez. 'These weren't fatal wounds. They were deliberate, planned,

80

they were not designed to kill. But they would have been painful, if the brothers were still conscious.'

'It was like he was goading them?' asked Torrillo, his face a picture of innocent bemusement.

'Yes. And then . . .'

Maria smiled – three times in one day, Torrillo thought – then put her hand in the air, like a schoolgirl with an answer.

'Professor?'

'And then he killed them with a single thrust to the heart with a long blade?'

She could feel their eyes turn to examine her. A flash of momentary annoyance ran across Rodríguez's face then disappeared.

'Correct.'

'That's it. The bulls. It is a simulation of the bullring. And almost accurate. The red of the costume represents the capes of the *banderilleros* when he begins the killing. He then – and this is a sign of some practicality on his part – he then reverses the natural order. The darts, with their ribbons, he throws next, to goad the victim further. *Then* he becomes a picador and uses some kind of lance. Finally he is transformed into the matador. He finishes the fight, he makes the sacrifice, with a single thrust to the heart with the sword.'

Velasco looked puzzled. 'I met people who copied things before, and they always try to be precise about these things. They're a little manic. That's why they copy. They wouldn't dream of doing things anything other than exactly right. If he's trying to copy real life, why doesn't he do it exactly?'

Maria leaped in with the answer. 'Because, as I said, he is practical. He is not trying to copy real life, he is trying to adapt the form of a real-life ritual to a new situation, that of murdering a human being, who is not as stupid as a bull. The sight of the darts would not alert the brothers. They would probably see it as part of the game. When the lance, or whatever weapon was used, would appear, the pain, the seriousness of the wounds, would betoken something else. Similarly, with Famiani, many men would have responded to having a dart thrown at them with violence and aggression.'

'I'd have beaten the living daylights out of the little fuck,' said Quemada.

'No, you wouldn't. You'd have died. When you tried, you would have met with the lance. And when you were incapacitated by the lance, you would have met the sword.'

'So we're looking for a sexual pervert who's a member of the Brotherhood of the Blood of Christ and has something to do with bullfighting?' asked Torrillo.

'We are looking at connections across these three areas,' said Rodríguez.

'I got a good bullfighting contact, from way back,' Torrillo said to Menéndez. 'We could speak to him after we talk to the brotherhood people.'

'Good.'

'And the other questions?'

The way they looked at her, Maria began to feel she had intervened once too often. There was something unspoken in the room. Something that could not be said in front of her.

'The motive?' she said. 'Caterina Lucena? The choice of the painting as some kind of motif for the killing? The randomness of this – Famiani surely was random, so how do you know the brothers weren't also?'

'Priorities, Professor. There is no point chasing what we don't know until we have run down what we do. The meeting is at an end.'

Velasco stumbled to his feet and groaned. 'And I'm supposed to fucking sleep after that?'

'No problem,' said Quemada. 'Think of Jesus. That could send *anybody* to sleep. We're on duty at six.'

They started to file slowly out of the room.

'Professor?'

She halted at the door.

'May I have a word in private?'

The rest of them exchanged glances, then left. She returned and sat in front of the chaotic, jumbled desk. Rodríguez rubbed his eyes.

'Excuse me. I spent most of the night reading.'

She nodded. 'You need to rest too, some time.'

'I will. Some time. Do you mind my asking, is this useful for your report?'

'Yes.' She knew of no other answer to give.

'It is not a conventional case. It tells you little of routine practice here.'

'Do you have many conventional cases?'

'Oh, yes. Most of our work can fit into a standard set of procedures. Even the murders. You might find it more instructive to postpone your attachment until this case is finished.'

Rodríguez tried to read behind her cold, blue eyes, but it was impossible.

'Is that what you want? For me to leave?'

'I think you should consider the option. To come back when our workload might be more useful for your report.'

'You didn't answer my question.'

'No. I did not. It should be your decision.'

'If you feel I am hindering your investigation . . .'

He waved her into silence. 'Not at all. Not at all. If I thought that we would not be having this conversation. Look.'

83

He reached behind him and opened a file. It bore her name.

'This is the confidentiality document you signed when you came here, yes?'

Maria looked at the page, filled with jargon and caveats, and her signature at the bottom.

'Yes.'

'You did not read it, of course, I cannot understand how anyone could read this sort of language. Or what kind of person could write it. But you know what it means?'

'I think so.'

'It means that all operational information you hear and see here – *everything* – is confidential. It must not be disclosed to any third party without the written permission of a senior administrative officer in the National Police.'

'Yes. I've agreed to that.'

'I understand that but it is as well that you remember you have signed this.'

'Will you answer my question?'

Rodríguez looked at her across the desk and, for a moment, she could see the hidden flash of intelligence, of ruthlessness, in his face, could imagine how they had come to hold him in such esteem. Then it disappeared behind a civil servant's smile.

'Yes. I hope you will stay, for the duration of this case. This is not a normal investigation. There are aspects to it, perhaps sexual aspects, which may benefit from the opinion of an intelligent outside party. You are clearly intelligent, though I would be grateful in future if you would let me present my findings uninterrupted.'

Maria could feel him hesitate. 'I have the feeling, Captain, you are about to say "but".'

'But . . . you must appreciate what we may be facing.'

'I think I do.'

'What?'

'Someone who has killed two people and attempted to maim a third.'

'That is only part of it, probably.'

'Then what?'

'There is a pattern, one that is familiar even to detectives like our friends Quemada and Velasco, though they were unwilling to talk about it while you were here. The Angel Brothers were clearly no random killing. They must have been familiar with their killer to have allowed him into their apartment and let him become so intimate with them. The attack on our friend Famiani, on the other hand, appears to be purely opportunistic.'

'And the pattern?'

'It may be one of two things. Our man may have killed the Angel Brothers and then simply discovered that he *liked* it. Or he may be working to an actual cycle. Remember, *he* alerted us to the bodies by returning to the Lucena house, breaking in again and leaving the door open. He *wanted* the bodies to be found.'

'Either way, you expect him to try to kill again.'

'Most certainly. My guess is that there is some cycle in this, some cycle linked to Semana Santa itself. The city goes a little crazy at this time of year. That has only just begun. The pitch will increase daily until Sunday, with the final parade, then the bulls. It is customary for our arrests, across all categories, to increase exponentially with each day of the fiesta. Perhaps the passions rise, whatever. All killings of this nature come to an end – either because the perpetrator is caught or because the cycle itself ends. There are very few instances of continuous multiple murder, over a period of years. The psychology of the killers means that something happens to end it. Maybe they purge themselves of the desire. They get married. They find God.'

'I understand what you are saying.'

'Do you? We are facing here someone who is certainly intelligent – intelligent enough to model the death of two modern artists on a canvas hundreds of years old, intelligent enough to see the parallel between the two, as you saw it. This person, or persons, may be dangerous in more than a mere physical sense. I have seen tough, dim, insensitive policemen destroyed by the simple evil other human beings may inject into this world. What you said about this city last night, that gives me concern. You must not think of it this way or it may harm you.'

'I was tired. I was depressed. I don't know why.'

He looked at the file again. 'You know I read this for the first time last night?'

'Yes?'

'You were married.'

'Yes.'

'No more?'

'My husband died. A sickness. He was ill, suddenly. Two years ago. He was thirty-two.'

'And that is when you switched from teaching to research?'

'Yes. I wanted to change something about my life. It seemed wrong to carry on as if nothing had happened.'

'And still his death depresses you?'

'Sometimes.'

'I see.'

'Is this relevant?'

'Your peace of mind is certainly relevant to me.'

'So I may continue?'

'Yes. I would be glad of it. You will make a visit shortly with Menéndez and Torrillo. I am doubling the manpower on the case from midday. At two thirty, we will have another press conference appealing for information. It will be a delicate affair. To stir sufficient concern to generate a response without scaring people so much we have a panic. But perhaps during Semana Santa we will be wasting our time in any case. Who watches TV, Professor? Who reads the papers?'

'I would prefer it, Captain, if you called me Maria.'

'So the Sergeant said. Very well.'

'Thank you.'

'And if this becomes too much for you, Maria, you will not be too proud to tell me. I may need your help, we have so few women on the force, and it would enable me to do my job better if I did not have to worry about you.'

She almost laughed. 'I shall ensure my mental state does not interfere with your professional competence, Captain.'

The invitation was not returned.

'I would appreciate that. Now. Will you please ask Sergeant Torrillo to step back into the room?'

Bear was leaning on the water fountain, threatening to topple it over. He looked into her face, saw colour in her cheeks, something close to amusement.

'*Fourth* time today, Maria,' he said. 'This could become a habit.'

11

Out on the street the atmosphere had changed. Through the half-open window of the car, now struggling to get through the crowds, Maria could almost touch the difference. It was electric. A choir of young boys, dressed in white, carrying crosses and hymn books, crossed the square slowly, like a military formation, a balding priest at the head. On the pavement, crowds watched, snapping cameras, shuffling their feet, reading programmes, trying to decide what to do next. A hopeful gypsy woman sang an impromptu melody on the corner next to the pharmacy, then thrust an arm through the car window looking for change. Torrillo barked something, and the hand disappeared as fast as it had come. Bodies brushed, sometimes fell, against the car as it struggled to get free of the crowd. The bell of the great tower chimed overhead, scattering crowds of pigeons into the sky, now a deep eggshell blue, with the faintest trace of high cirrus in front of an indolent fading half-moon. Morning smells – coffee, fat frying, the sweet perfume of *churros* and sugar – mingled with the aromas of Semana Santa. Incense and horse dung, diesel and cheap wine. A group of dancers in traditional dress, black headdresses outlined against the sky, clattered past in a cloud of crude, mephitic perfume, laughing in young, unspoiled girlish voices, heels clicking on the cobblestones, with heavily made-up faces and bright, carmine lips, humming tunes to the occasional click of a castanet. Behind them followed a man and woman on horseback, immaculately dressed, he in the grey suit and round hat of a Jerez *caballero*, she in white jodhpurs and blood-red hunting jacket, black leather boots past her knees. They both rode with one hand on their reins: in the other they carried a small glass of sherry. Far off, in the distant corner of the square, close to the side entrance of the cathedral, Maria could see the focal point of the crowd, gold and gaudy under the sun, a huge carved wooden platform, supported on the shoulders of a group of men who wept and sweated in the heat. In the centre, behind glass, she could just make out the figure of a Virgin, cross in hand. It looked like an old-fashioned wax doll. In the train of the Virgin came a group of penitents, slow, silent, and anonymous.

They were dressed in white.

And then the car broke free of the mass, shook off their sluggish momentum, turned sharply into the wider avenue of El Cano. Torrillo sped into third gear and left the crowds behind. They disappeared, like bees focused on a single honey pot. The streets were almost deserted, many of the shops were closed. Down one narrow alleyway, at its very end, she saw the signs of another procession, heard the blare of a trumpet and the rattle of a drum. Then it faded, disappeared into the warren of paths and streets, medieval and earlier, that made up San Isidro, the oldest quarter of the city, the oldest part of El Viejo. The barrio of the barrio, where the locals lived almost on top of each other, screamed out of windows, seemed never to sleep, grew up with the map of the tangled skein of turnings and little squares around them already imprinted inside their heads. She had stumbled into it once, as a student, walked for hours trying to find a way out of the maze, never once feeling threatened but always alone, a stranger, out of place in a tiny, enclosed world which was somehow separate even from the city itself.

Torrillo braked, then parked the Ford by the side of the cobbled road, next to a pharmacy, running the vehicle so close in to the wall that they had no choice but to get out of the driver's side doors.

'We'll have to walk from here,' said the Sergeant. 'It's not far.'

He ducked under a dark narrow arch which smelled of cats' piss and they followed, Menéndez bringing up the rear. The alley opened out enough to let two donkeys pass almost in comfort. The walls were whitewashed, lit by flashes of geranium red. The smells of the barrio, washing, flowers, urine, drains and food, everywhere food, filled the air. A child screamed, a mother scolded, a television set babbled from behind a half-open door, from an upstairs window came the unmistakable sounds of a couple making love, the frantic creaking of bedsprings, the moans of passion.

They walked into a small, pretty square, pretty enough to attract the tourists, if they felt brave enough to wander off the heritage tracks the council had patiently set out for them in the safer parts of the city. In the centre, a Renaissance fountain ran with water, a statue of a colt, rearing on its hind legs in the middle of a scallop shell.

Torrillo pointed to the sign on the wall. 'Plaza del Potro. It's here somewhere.'

The Sergeant asked in the shop, a hotchpotch collection of bread, biscuits, cheese and meat, housed in someone's front room, then came out and headed for the building on the opposite corner. There was a closed door, painted light cream, and a phone with a series of buttons beside it. Torrillo punched one, spoke and, when the buzz came, pushed his way inside.

The office was on the first floor, a simple, elegant room, well furnished, with teak desks and cupboards, leather furniture and the smell of polish. Miguel Castaneda, the general secretary of the Brotherhood of the Blood of Christ, sat in the most expensive-looking chair of all, pushed back from behind a vast desk. He looked at least seventy, short, squat, leathery-faced, and peered at them unpleasantly from behind rectangular gold-rimmed glasses, shifting in his chair with a slow, reptilian deliberation.

'No. The answer must be no, Lieutenant. Our membership lists are a matter between the brotherhood and God. We do not hand them out for public consumption.'

Menéndez looked around the room. The walls were covered with old black-and-white photographs. Franco's face, white, imperious, sometimes a little befuddled, peered out of many. Once, the general was in full uniform, at the head of ranks of penitents, another time in a business suit, watching a parade pass, looking bored.

'We are not talking about public consumption, Don Miguel. The records will remain confidential within the police force, that I assure you.'

Castaneda made an unpleasant noise, clearing his throat. 'The police force, the police force. Twenty, thirty, forty years ago, you could have made such a promise. Not now. You are pawns, Lieutenant. You are servants of this poisoned state.'

'We are policemen, sir, investigating two murders and an attempted murder, all acts committed by someone we believe to be either a member of your brotherhood or someone closely connected with it. You have a public duty to assist us.'

'Duty?' Castaneda glared at them and let the word hang in the air. '*Duty?* You do not know the meaning of the word. None of you do any more.'

'We have a duty to safeguard the citizens of this city,' said Menéndez. 'To do this we must, we *must* examine your membership records. As far as I know, every one of your

91

members is innocent. Do you not realise that, until I can place them outside the remit of our inquiries, every one of them must be regarded as a suspect?'

'That is a ridiculous statement, Lieutenant, as you must know unless you are a fool, which I presume is not the case. The purpose of the brotherhood is charity, tradition, worship. And duty. Yes. True duty. You are wasting your time. Wasting *my* time.'

'We could go to the courts to force this. It would take time, however, and it would be easier, it would be quieter, if you were to offer your cooperation.'

'You could try. Do you have any idea of the kind of men who belong to this brotherhood? They are not street urchins. They are not the thieves of the gutter you normally deal with. I could pick up the phone here and now and speak to one of your superiors. I could talk to any number of high court judges.'

'I don't doubt it. Nor that they will know their responsibility in this matter too. This is an official police investigation and you *must* help us.'

'Lieutenant, you do not understand. It is *inconceivable* that any of our brothers could even contemplate being involved in the kind of crimes you are investigating. These brothers, these sodomites?'

Castaneda said the words with obvious distaste. 'You are a policeman. You know where to look for the kind of scum that moves in these circles. And it is *not* here.'

'And yet we have firm evidence that these crimes were committed by someone wearing the dress of the brotherhood.'

'Impostors. Charlatans.'

'But why the brotherhood? Why choose it?'

Castaneda shrugged his shoulders. 'It is of no concern to me.'

Maria spoke. 'Perhaps there is a compromise. If we were to give you certain details, you could check them against the records yourself and tell us if there were any matches.'

Castaneda looked at Menéndez. 'The woman is with the police?'

'She is a civilian who is helping us on the case.'

The old man shook his head. 'Incredible.'

'We're looking for someone with a close connection to bullfighting,' said Torrillo. 'How about it?'

'I doubt there is a man in the brotherhood who does not follow the bulls.'

'And you have people in the business? Administrators, judges, matadors, too?' asked Menéndez.

'Of course. We return to the original question. To answer this, I would have to give you our entire membership list, and that is not possible.'

'What about him?' Torrillo nodded towards a small poster in the corner. It advertised the corrida which marked the end of Semana Santa the year before. At the top of the list of contestants, in big, bold sans serif letters bigger than anything else on the page, were the words 'El Guapo'. By the side of it was a picture of a young man, with blond hair that looked dyed, grinning to show perfect teeth. More of a pop star than a matador, thought Torrillo. They didn't look like that when, briefly, he had followed the bulls. 'I can't see any other posters for the ring here. What about Mateo? Are you a fan, sir, or what?'

The old man wriggled, visibly. 'He's a very popular matador. Some purists might not approve of his style, that is not for me to judge.'

'Is he a member of the brotherhood?' asked Menéndez.

The old man sighed. 'This becomes tedious. The membership is closed. I say nothing on this subject and my silence means nothing. He may be. He may not be. My silence does not say either.'

'Is he here, in the city, now?'

'I believe, I have read in the newspapers, that he will be the most experienced matador in the ring this week. He comes from the city. This is no secret so, yes, I expect he is here already.'

Torrillo walked over and looked more closely at the poster. He rubbed the paper, cheap and thick and glossy, between his fingers and stared at the photograph until he could see the dots that formed it.

'Don Castaneda. He is a very' – the words came slowly – '*pretty* boy. If we were to examine the list of parties attended by our murdered Angels, do you think it possible they might have met?'

Castaneda laughed, and it sounded like rocks rumbling around in a well. 'If you're suggesting what I *think* you're suggesting you are somewhat far off the mark, Sergeant. El Guapo is a *swordsman* outside the ring as much as he is in it. It goes with the job, as they say. But don't take my word. Discover this for yourself. Do what you will. This interview is at an end.'

'I will have to take this further,' said Menéndez.

'Do what you wish. I have work to do.'

He showed them to the door of the first-floor office and they walked down the narrow wooden stairs. When they got to the bottom Torrillo grimaced, kicked at the floor, and swore.

'What is it with these old farts? He's got nothing to hide. Why can't he just *cooperate*?'

'He will,' said Menéndez. 'He just wants to make us work for it, that's all.'

She looked around, saw the 'Servicios' sign and said, 'Excuse me. I have to go.'

Menéndez nodded and said, 'We'll wait outside.'

She followed the sign and found a door marked with a silhouette of a woman with a fan, went inside, hung her bag up on the hook, pulled down her jeans and sat down. From the gap above the door she could smell strong, dark tobacco. It curled inside the tiny washroom, hung in a grey cloud close to the ceiling, then drifted slowly out of the half-open window. When she had finished, she stood up, zipped her jeans, then washed her hands in the small, clean ceramic sink, using the tiny tablet of pink soap that sat damp and semi-liquid in the recess. She dried her hands on a worn green towel, wiped them on her jeans out of habit, picked up the bag, threw back the bolt on the door, turned the handle and pushed.

Nothing happened. Nothing. The door moved an inch, then bounced back. Something was blocking the way, something that gave, just slightly, when she tried to get out. The smell of cigarette smoke grew more acrid. She felt something run over her skin, along her spine, puzzled over it, wondered to herself: why?

She pushed again. The door gave a little further, maybe three inches. She could see sunlight staining the polished tile floor and something else, the corner of something, before the door gently, but firmly, pushed back on her.

Maria tried to work out what was happening, wondered if she ought to shout for Torrillo and Menéndez. But they were outside, beyond earshot. She looked at the window. It was too small to get through, and in any case, she didn't know where it led. There was nothing else to do. She yanked down the handle again, put all of her slight weight against the door and pushed. It moved reluctantly again, two, three, four inches. Then as she tried harder, it moved free. She was off balance, tipping forward, feeling the gravity greet her momentum and draw her towards the tiles, gleaming in the sun. She stumbled, banged her knees, rolled over to cushion the blow and found herself cowering on her back, knees drawn up to her stomach, hands around her shins, underneath the shadow of a scarlet giant, clad, head to foot, in blood-red cloth, eyes mere slits, but staring at her, down at her from a point that seemed close to the ceiling.

He was vast, anonymous, deadly.

The giant started to pull its hands out of its pockets and Maria found herself screaming without knowing when she had started, screaming at the top of her voice as she rolled over the polished floor, struggling to get away from the figure that loomed over her, rolling and rolling, her hands flailing. Her bag opened and scattered its contents on the floor. She saw the hands come slowly out of the folds of the cloth, saw them draw back slowly, fingers unclenching, slowly, deadly slowly, saw white skin, tufts of hair, felt she saw the pores, wide and open and fat and greasy under the sun. And saw the fingers open to reveal empty palms as the room became dark.

Torrillo was the first through the door. She was lying on the linoleum screaming, the man had his back to the toilet doors, hands high up in the air, fingers waving. Torrillo stood between them. She backed up towards the door, gasping, her cheeks wet.

'Police,' Torrillo barked at the man.

'You OK?' Menéndez said to her, eyes hooded.

'He scared me.'

She looked confused.

The man pulled off his hood. He looked about thirty, with a tidy, short-clipped moustache and beard, florid skin, pale-brown unfocused eyes. He continued to wave his hands in the air and swayed gently against the door.

'I'm all right,' said Maria.

She picked herself off the floor, brushed off the dust from

her jeans, straightened her shirt, casually picked up the contents of her bag, packed them back in. 'He scared me. That's all. I couldn't get out. Then when I did, he was there. It happened so quickly.'

'I didn't know there was anyone in there,' the man said. 'The men's was locked or something, no key, so I was just waiting for the lady to come out. I guess I got a bit drowsy.'

The voice was slurred and common. What looked like wine stains spotted the front of the cloak. 'I didn't mean to frighten anybody. We just drank so much out there on the parade that I had to like . . . go to the toilet some time. I didn't mean to frighten her.'

Torrillo grunted then frisked him up and down. From a pocket in the robe he took out some coins, a set of car keys, a few thousand pesetas, a packet of cigarettes, a cheap disposable lighter, an ID card. Torrillo looked at the picture on the card then looked at the man. He matched. Torrillo wrote down the name in his notebook.

The man grasped his groin. 'I really got to go, please. You get to drink an awful lot at these things.'

Menéndez nodded towards the door.

'Thanks, sir.'

He carried the hood in one hand and started to lift up the cloak before he even reached the door. Maria saw white, hairy legs, short blue socks, open-toed sandals, then a pair of cream Y-fronts. The man stumbled into the toilet, half closed the door, and they heard a groan of relief followed by the sound of a stream of liquid hitting water.

She looked at Menéndez and said, downcast, 'Oops. Mild panic attack. Sorry.'

'Two thousand or so of those people out there,' said Menéndez. 'You can't get spooked every time you see one of them.'

'No,' she said, and Torrillo noticed there were still tears

in her eyes. The two men walked in front to leave her in peace. She followed along the alley, watched Torrillo duck under the arch again, climbed silently into the back of the car.

'I'm fine now,' she said.

'Good,' Menéndez nodded. 'There'll probably be cameras at the press conference. It's worth bearing in mind.'

Inside the building, on the ground floor, the man in the red robe waited until they were out of earshot, then waited another five minutes, went to the front door and flipped the inside latch. Then he went back to the washroom, looked at himself in the mirror and smiled. Calm. No fear. No tics. No doubts.

He tried to remember what he had learned last time out, tried to fix the memories in his head, since he knew that when it all started to happen it happened fast. Then he straightened the point of the hood, put it back over his head, and let himself out of the women's toilet. He pulled out the set of keys Torrillo had looked at, picked the right one, unlocked the mortise on the men's toilet door, went in and retrieved the kit he had stashed behind the cistern. It was wrapped in oilcloth and about three feet long. He unrolled it, took out a pair of plastic surgical gloves and rolled them carefully on to his hands. Then he walked up the stairs towards the office where Miguel Castaneda now sat bolt upright, talking fast and furiously on the phone.

He pushed open the door and the phone went straight back onto the receiver. The old man looked like a little old bull, walnut brown and full of fury.

'Who the hell are you?' he barked in a voice made high by anger. 'Just walking in like this. You knock before you walk in here.'

The man reached into the folds of the oilcloth roll, pulled

out the first dart, felt the metal, cool and hard and comforting through the plastic gloves, pulled back his arm, felt the muscles flexing. The little missile flashed through the air, first black, then silver, as it crossed the shadow cast by the venetian blind.

Castaneda opened his mouth to shout and the dart hit him straight in the left eye, shattered the lens of his glasses, punctured the cornea then stabbed into the back of the socket, and sent him reeling backwards out of the leather chair. The noise. There was too much noise.

'Shit,' said the figure in red.

He dropped the set of tools on the floor, picked up the sword, and went to the other side of the office. The old man writhed, pulled the dart out of his head. Blood and mucus oozed out of the frayed socket. Castaneda was now rocking frantically from side to side, gurgling, trying to scream.

The hooded man plunged the sword into the old man's throat, ran it through the windpipe, almost severing the spinal cord. A fountain of blood shot up the blade. The point bit into the carpet and then the soft wooden planks below, pinioning Castaneda to the floor. The old man lay there, becoming still, making low guttural noises.

Just to make sure, he leaned on the blade with all his weight, fixing it firm in the wooden floor. Then he went back to the oilcloth roll, picked out some more implements, returned and looked at his handiwork. It wasn't perfect but then, even in the ring, you couldn't get it right all the time, even in the ring there were unforeseen circumstances. The hooded man wiped his hands on his cloak, grabbed two more darts, pulled out an improvised spike made out of a garden fencing tool and set out to bring what artistry he could to the situation.

Twenty minutes later, after he had rifled the filing

cabinets, he went downstairs, and walked to the toilet to clean up. He took off the cloak and hat, pulled out the sports trousers and pale-blue shirt he had hidden in a plastic refuse sack behind the cistern, washed off the blood from his hands and arms, carefully removed the make-up, the theatrical beard and moustache, then checked in the mirror. He put the costume in the plastic sack, rolled that up in the oilskin, put the items he had taken from the filing cabinet in a wrinkled Continente supermarket bag, looked around to make sure he had left nothing, then walked out of the cubicle.

On his way out, on his way to the door, he saw something on the floor, bent over, examined it, picked it up and put it in his jacket pocket.

'Dumb fucking cops,' he said.

Then he walked out into the bright afternoon sun, walked slowly around the barrio, looking at the trash collection containers. When he found one that was almost full to the brim, he looked around to check he was alone, then pushed the oilskin underneath the top layer of trash. He stood back. It was well hidden by bags of rotting food, empty wine bottles, plastic oil containers. He walked for ten minutes to another part of the barrio, sat down in a small café and ordered the *menú del día*: *sopa de picadillo, chuleta de cerdo con patatas, flan*, and half a carafe of chilled red wine. Six hundred pesetas. While he was waiting, he used the phone to call the rubbish department, asking for a priority collection at the container he had just used on the grounds that it was now full and starting to smell. The council official put it on the afternoon round.

When he finished the meal, he walked to another part of the barrio, let himself through a small door, walked upstairs to a neat, white-walled, two-room apartment, showered, dressed in a clean robe, poured himself a sparkling mineral water, sat down on the cheap Habitat canvas sofa, turned on the TV and started to zap the channels.

The press conference was live on Channel 8. The media now had a name for him: El Matador.

He grinned. He liked it. The cops were on the screen, the big one silent, the old one, the Captain, talking, talking about precautions and vigilance and the need for information. They gave a freephone number and promised confidentiality. He could see, from the calm expressions on their faces, that they knew nothing about Castañeda.

The camera angle shifted to the side and, for the first time, he could see that she was standing behind them, watching, attentive, fair hair loosely combed and tied back with a ribbon, clean pale skin. She looked different from the kind of women he'd known, the little bags on the street. Then her face moved, started looking for the camera. She turned, right, then left, then right again, looked into the camera, looked through, looked into him, searching, quizzical. For a moment, the world stopped moving, the buzz subsided. He was quiet inside. Alone with her. It felt good.

He reached over for his jacket, reached inside the pocket and pulled out the address book. It had a shiny, plasticised cover with a pattern of flowers and was no more than a few millimetres thick. Most of the pages were blank. The few entries in the book were written in hard, black ink, in a fine, feminine hand. They were old. They were all in the north of the country. He flicked to the front. On the owner's page there was her name, an address in Salamanca, a work phone number, a home phone number, a fax number, an e-mail number. On the same page, scribbled in recent pencil in the same hand, was an address in the city, not far from where he was now, with a local phone number. There was no other name attached to the address.

He closed the book, fingered the cover, felt its texture,

looked at the woman on the screen, her hands clasped demurely in front of her. He thought of how many times those fingers must have used the book, wondered how many of the entries in the pages belonged to her lovers, wondered what they might have done together in the long, dark nights, looked at her closely on the screen, tried to *imagine* what she would be like, how her skin was to touch, how it would feel to push hard into her and feel the flesh give gently, moistly, like a rose, opening.

When he was hard enough, slowly, in front of the TV, he started to masturbate, one hand on his penis, the left on the address book. The programme broke for the ads – *don't forget your summer Casera, buy a Renault Clio now, drink Osborne brandy and meet beautiful women.* He felt it approaching now, felt the pressure beginning to build. He rubbed the base of his penis with the little book, gently, feeling the cold, shiny cover against his skin. Then, when it was getting closer, he opened up the middle pages, held them open beneath the pink, livid head. It was all over, with a small, involuntary spurt that made him arch a little upwards. He reached for a tissue from the box on the table in front of him, and wiped the semen carefully off the page. The ink looked fuzzy on an address somewhere in Madrid.

He examined his fingers, saw bloodstains alongside the cuticle, tut-tutted, and went back into the bathroom to look for a nailbrush.

12

'El Matador. *El Matador?* Jesus. That's wonderful. That is *all* we need. Semana Santa. Tourists. Crazies. Drunks. As if that isn't bad enough, we got the press ramping it all up with El Matador. Who thinks of these things?'

Torrillo was talking to himself out of the window as the car sped through the suburbs. Menéndez was in the front passenger seat, on the carphone, making notes, speaking occasionally. Maria sat in the back and watched the world go by. This was part of the city the tourists never saw. Grim high-rise apartments rose among junk yards and refuse sites. Tanned figures in grubby clothes walked slowly, aimlessly around the pavements. A few checked through the refuse, picking for something worth acquiring. They passed an olive pressing plant, the air filled with an overpowering, acrid smell. By the side of the road, twenty feet high, were piles of olive husks, dry and brown under the sun. More small factories, a tyre plant, car scrapyards, a roadside stall selling fruit, oranges, big green melons, avocados and tomatoes. They left the high rises behind, then the factories began to peter out. Small allotments, with low, leafy vegetable crops, spread out across the red earth, the odd shack dotted between the fields. Men and women worked on the land, dressed in black, stooped underneath frayed straw hats, hacking at the earth with their hands.

Menéndez's phone call went on and on. Torrillo let his anger burn out of him. Maria sat in the back wondering: will this story let me sleep tonight, Bear? And out of nowhere, as sharp as a sickle, came the thought, sudden and cold and cruel.

The green mask and the red velvet walls

She thought of the time, two years ago, when Luis had returned from the hospital and told her of the tests. They had sat around the little kitchen table, the table where, only the week before, they had made the decision, finally, to have children, to become, in his words *(no, not hers, not hers)* 'whole', and felt its presence there. Unknown, unseen, life-threatening. This thing that came from somewhere – *where?* – outside him entered his body, poisoned his being. This thing that they did not know, could not put a correct name to, this thing that was *eating* him.

That night, she had looked into his face, across the table, and seen his death. There was something behind his pale-grey eyes, something that was dying already. His face, so full, so healthy, was becoming lined. His skin was becoming sallow. And the tests showed nothing, nothing except that he was dying, of some interior wasting, some mysterious canker that consumed the tissue, the fibre, the nerves, the very engine of his being.

After the conversation had fallen into silence, they had gone to bed and made love, slowly, without joy, thinking it would be the last time. They were wrong. For two, perhaps three weeks – she could no longer remember, those days were a blur – he had clung on to normality, and the proximity of death seemed to fire their hunger. In the morning, the afternoon, the evening, he would suddenly take her hand and she would follow. What happened was not simply sexual. It was an act of defiance, their way of spiting death itself. Their way of saying 'do not go gently'. Then the disease, the *thing* fought back. He faded, before her eyes.

104

She could not bring back the memory of how he looked in those last few weeks. Something blocked out the sight of that ravaged face, that skeletal frame, the pale husk of a human being, lying still and lifeless on a hospital bed, eyes glinting dully, like lead, in the pale-grey afternoon light.

Twelve weeks after that evening around the table he died. She had stayed at the bedside for the best part of a day and a night, constantly, holding his hand, feeling the grey, cold parchment that was once his skin. And then he had simply ceased to exist, ceased to breathe.

A week before he died she had sat in the bathroom, looking at her urine in the small, clear plastic container, watching it change colour, tears of rage streaming down her cheeks. He was still lucid then, but she did not tell him. What did you say? Was life something you could pass on, like a game of tag in a children's playground?

After the funeral, the small secular ceremony she could scarcely remember, she drove to the airport, caught the connecting flight to Madrid, queued at the counter for a flight to London, landed at Heathrow, caught the tube into the city, checked in to a hotel. She had seen the ad on the tube station wall, wrote down the number on her wrist, called the moment she got to the room. They saw her the next morning, carried out the 'procedure' the following day. She remembered lying on her back, staring at the powder-white ceiling, trying to will herself into its nothingness, trying not to look at the walls, the red velvet walls. An anonymous face in a pale-green mask bent over her, there was a mild probing inside, too indefinable to describe as pain, and then it was over, in a few minutes, it was over. As she walked out of the room, a little unsteadily, she saw, in a surgical dish, a little pool of blood and tissue, saw the figure in the green mask notice her, then bark something at the nurse who snatched the dish away, poured the contents into a container by the basins. It was over. Two deaths in as many weeks and the rest of that year remains a blur. Save for the dreams: a small pool of blood and tissue lying in a silver medical basin. *Moving.* And in the end that died too. Or maybe it just went to sleep.

The green mask and the red velvet walls

Maria focused on the view again and realised they were now in open countryside. The light was mellowing into the late gold of the early evening. Menéndez was off the phone, scribbling as best he could as the car bounced along a dusty country road. Without turning around, he seemed to have been following her, seemed to have recognised that her reverie was over.

'The bullfighter, El Guapo, has been in the city these past four days,' Menéndez said. 'Quemada and Velasco are looking for him now and checking on the Angel Brothers' contacts. El Guapo's real name is Jaime Mateo. He comes from El Viejo. There may be a connection. Caterina Lucena was taken into a nursing home this morning. There is a chance she has pneumonia. The doctors are looking at her now.'

'Did anything come of the press conference?' Maria asked.

'There are half a dozen calls. Mostly cranks probably. We're looking at them.'

'Castaneda been calling the top brass?'

'Not that I've heard.'

Torrillo laughed. 'Now *that's* interesting. Struck me as the sort who'd be on to his friends in the red dresses every time he got a parking ticket.'

Menéndez thought about it and nodded.

'Nothing forensic?'

'Nothing we don't know already. No prints. Nothing on

the weapons to suggest you couldn't buy them down any market.'

Torrillo shook his head. 'Is this man clever or just lucky?'

'Maybe both,' said Maria. They didn't stare at her now, when she talked. The scene outside Castaneda's office seemed to have bound her to them somehow. Or perhaps they just didn't have the time to think about it, the time to separate her from what they were doing.

'Maybe,' said Menéndez.

'The holiday starts to get really big from now on,' said Torrillo. 'You got twelve, maybe fifteen thousand people out there tonight taking part in the church parades alone, all over the city, over fifteen, maybe twenty different parishes. He couldn't be more anonymous. We'd stand more chance of finding him if he dressed up as a waiter, for God's sake. He's clever.'

'Then let's hope his luck starts to run out,' said Menéndez.

The car bumped off the road and onto a makeshift track of dust and stone. They drove along it for four hundred yards then stopped in front of a small, single-storey farmhouse built of pale-brown stone. On the porch, in a large raffia chair, Maria could make out the figure of an old man in a white shirt and pale-grey trousers, cream straw hat pulled down over his eyes.

Torrillo chuckled. 'You're going to like this. Believe me, you're going to like it. Old Manolo here, in his day, was one of the best bullfighters around. A *bullfighter's* bullfighter, too, not the Hollywood stuff you see today. So let's leave El Guapo to the end of the conversation, huh? I got a feeling we might get some fireworks when that name comes up.'

They climbed out of the car and headed towards the pool of shade beneath the straw-covered roof of the porch.

Abruptly, from nowhere, she thought again: *will this story let me sleep tonight, Bear?*

Manolo Figuera sat motionless in the cane chair on the porch. When they arrived he had gone into the house, returned with a bottle of cold white wine, a glass bowl full of ice cubes, a plate of olives. He had set them down on a small wicker table, then beckoned them to sit down. The house, the chairs, the cracked, white wood porch floor, all seemed brittle and aged. Like Figuera himself. In front of the house grew a handful of tomatoes, a few aubergine plants. A stone water tank was half full, the surface dark green and algaed. Overhead, a party of swifts swooped and sang, high-pitched chitterings against a cloudless cerulean sky.

'You saw me fight?' he said to them.

Maria and Menéndez shook their heads.

Torrillo said, 'They missed something. When I was a boy, my father used to take me to the corrida. Here. In El Puerto, sometimes, Ronda too, once. For the festival. It was . . . something.'

Figuera smiled. 'It was something. It was a long time ago, that something. No one should remember it now. How old do you think I am?'

Maria looked at him and guessed. 'Seventy?'

He laughed. Then spoke very precisely, showing clean, white, artificial teeth. 'Eighty-two. *Eighty*-two. I walk three miles every day. To see my daughter in the village. I keep house. I grow a few vegetables. You live life like you did in the ring *after* you stop, you go on for ever. Well . . .'

He made a small gesture with his hand towards the table, poured four glasses of wine, then dropped an ice cube in his own. Maria almost gasped. The montilla was so chilled it had little taste. Just a hard, flinty feeling on the tongue.

'I was not a star. I was too traditional for that. Even in those days tradition was not something that won the crowds. The purists, the aficionados, they liked me. The crowds, they preferred the handsome boys, who flirted and did the tricks. Not so much as today. But it was there. I made a living. I own my home, which is not sumptuous but you will find no debts when I die.'

'Don Manolo,' said Menéndez, and Maria noted the formality, 'we need your advice.'

Figuera picked at some olives and listened intently.

'There is a crime, perhaps more than one crime, in the city which has some connection with the bulls. My sergeant, Torrillo, hopes that you may help us ... *understand* it better.'

'Understand? If I can. But I am an old man. I go to the city rarely. To the bulls never, except for the *romería* in Ronda and that is more habit than pleasure.'

'Be that as it may. I would still appreciate your thoughts.'

'On what?'

Menéndez played with his glass, swirling the wine around with gentle movements of his hand.

'We have a man who has murdered two people, tried to murder another, using something I can only describe as a kind of copy of the corrida.'

'You mean he kills people in the ring?'

'No. But he uses the weapons – the darts, the lances, the sword. There is a deliberate attempt to make the deaths resemble the ring.'

Figuera's face went blank. The muscles relaxed, making the flesh hang on his cheeks like leather on a frame. He reached for the table, picked up a pair of sunglasses, then put them on. 'It becomes bright for these old eyes sometimes. You were saying.'

'We were wondering, firstly, if you knew of a case in

109

which someone connected with the ring, in whatever capacity, had done something similar.'

'You have no records?'

'Yes. We have records. But they go back only a few years, paperwork is not a strong point in the city. We can see no parallels, but even if they existed they might be hard to find, and if there was a parallel elsewhere it would be impossible. You have travelled throughout Spain in your career. You know many people. What might take us a year to find you might be able to point out for us very quickly.'

Nothing was intelligible behind the sunglasses. The old man drained his glass, poured another one, dropped in two more ice cubes.

'Bullfighting is about honour. Not crime. Even today, even with the fancy boys you see on the TV – oh, I see them still, I have television, a video recorder – even with them, it is a question of honour. Without honour you fail in the ring. This goes without question. You speak of crime. You know, bullfighting is a *legal* thing. The president may, if he wishes, jail any matador who refuses to fight the bull. Now *that* would be a crime, and while I have heard it has happened, I have never witnessed it myself. But talk of the crime that you see in the streets, never. It is inconceivable.'

'But it doesn't need to be the matador,' said Torrillo. 'There are others. Maybe a picador. Maybe an administrator.'

'No one, *no one* who goes into the ring would do this kind of thing. For what reason? As to the hangers-on, well, perhaps, but it does not convince me. There is petty crime. Embezzlement, corruption, a little dipping of the beak here and there. But never, in my experience, any more than this. These are little people, essential people I suppose, but little people. Bank clerks. Accountants. Lawyers. Little people. Do you know what it is like to kill a bull with a sword?

110

No. No one knows until you have done it. It is a question of strength, physical and spiritual too. To kill a man this way ... I cannot imagine. You would need such steel in you. These little men do not have it.'

He paused, put the glass down. 'You say he has killed more than one person in this way?'

'Yes. Two that we know of, one he tried to kill.'

'And you think he may kill more?'

Menéndez drained his glass and poured himself another. 'You read us as well as you used to read your bulls, Don Manolo.'

'A lieutenant in the police force does not come all this way with his sergeant and his charming companion merely to talk to an old man about minor events.'

'We think that this may be linked in some way to Semana Santa and, yes, we fear that there may be some sort of cycle involved.'

'Yes.'

'There is one other factor, too. It appears the man wears the robes of a penitent, as a disguise presumably. Scarlet robes, we presume those of the Brotherhood of the Blood of Christ.'

'Ah.'

They waited, in vain.

'Might this mean something to you, Don Manolo?' asked Menéndez at last.

'I seem to be drinking most of the wine, Lieutenant. It is a hot day, but this is unusual for me. Perhaps the lady would fetch another bottle from the refrigerator. It is in the kitchen, to the right. There is a corkscrew in the drawer.'

From behind the dark glasses he read her expression. 'Do not worry, my dear. I shall wait until you return.'

When she came back, she poured him a fresh glass, then sat down. Menéndez's hand hovered over his notebook, pen poised.

Figuera sipped. 'It is a good wine. From one of the sherry houses at Jerez. You know, they have so many grapes they do not know what to do with them these days. No one wishes to drink fino any more, not even the English. So they turn them into this wine and I, for one, will not complain.'

He removed the glasses, put them on the table, then rubbed his eyes. They were darting: alert, observant.

'There is only one occasion of which I am aware where people, more than two people in this case, were killed in this way. You will not find it in your records. You will not find it in records anywhere, though doubtless there are people still here who will be able to tell you much more accurately than I can what occurred. *If* they are willing, and that I somehow doubt. Besides. This was a long time ago. Before you were born, I imagine.'

'I think we should know about it,' said Menéndez.

'I thought you would,' Figuera replied curtly. 'We have spent the best part of half a century politely refusing to talk about, to think about, the war. And now there are always ears that wish to listen. Now it is too late.'

During the war, said Figuera, the people of the city were divided. Into three: the right, the left, and those who lived in between, the great, hushed majority for whom life was enough of a struggle already, without the need for fighting.

'It is into this category that I fitted. When people ask me where I stood in the war, I look them in the eye and I say "*indoors*". Read that as cowardice if you like but I think I am no coward. It is just that I could never kill another Spaniard for such a petty reason as politics. Of course, if the Germans had invaded, or the British, or anyone, then I would have fought. But for the bandits we had running Spain then, no. I was young, I was newly married, we hoped for a family. I was determined that I would not become involved. But then, so were most of us. The middle was an

112

uncertain place to be. It shifted, almost by the day. As they fought, the Falange and the Communists, it changed so that you became marked not for what you did but for what you did not do. My enemy's enemy is my friend – you know this saying? This was what it was like. However hard you tried to stay aloof from it all, the harder they tried to involve you. I was lucky. I had a little local fame from the ring. It gave me some kind of charmed protection from them, from both sides. Had I been a different kind of artist, a painter, perhaps, or a poet, like Lorca, I would have been a marked man. But I was not and I was lucky. Many were not and became swept up, against their will. And this is why we did not speak of it for so long. You may read of the atrocities today, you may read of the death camps, the assassination squads, and think that these must have been special men, hard, *political* men with fire in their bellies. But they were not, much of the time anyway. They were ordinary men. Postmen, bakers, waiters, shopkeepers. Men in the middle who had been swallowed up by one side or the other and suddenly found themselves in this violent new world. Men who, before the war, would never have hurt anyone, even in anger, became people who would kill a woman, a child even, without a thought, just because of their name or the place where they lived. This was a *civil* war. There is a difference.'

'La Soledad,' said Menéndez. 'You saw this place.'

'Never.' The old man spat out the word. 'Never. We knew it was there, everyone knew. It was an abomination. But no one in their right mind went near the place, except for those whose relatives were inside. They would go to the gates – it was very well protected – and try to pass food in through the guards. I doubt that much of it arrived. At first, La Soledad was simply a prison, you understand. The Falange made it a holding point for those soldiers it had captured in battle. But then something changed. The soldiers went, shipped to the fighting somewhere else probably. Civilians took their place. I remember the time. It was May 1936. For a whole month no one in the city spoke of La Soledad but everyone knew, they knew that something was happening there.'

'For a month only?'

'Yes. When Franco heard the rumours, the gossip, in Madrid, he sent one of his officers to investigate. The entire camp command was changed, the men in charge disappeared. Then it became simply another prison camp. There were executions still, of course. And local people continued to disappear, though I doubt to La Soledad. Madrid had it under control by then and they had their limits.'

'And what happened,' said Maria, 'was that during this month, before things changed, people were killed as if they were in the ring? As we have described?'

'So the street gossip said. And much more. Some, they say, were put into a makeshift ring with a bull which had already been enraged, and forced to fight it without weapons. Others were treated as if they themselves were bulls. The camp people would attack them with darts, with lances, finally kill them, with a sword through the heart. These were the stories we heard that month. At first no one could believe them but then people reported seeing bodies, hearing screams. We knew it was true. We knew.'

Maria shook her head. 'And this was the time that Caterina Lucena's family was killed? When she somehow managed to *escape* from the camp?'

Figuera reached for his glass, took a deep swig.

'Doña Caterina is an honourable old woman from one of the greatest families in Spain. What happened to her family was a disgrace.'

'But how did she escape?'

He toyed with the sunglasses. 'Why ask me? Doña Caterina can speak for herself. It is not my business to spread tittle-tattle about such individuals.'

'We are talking about murders, Manolo,' said Torrillo. 'We need to know.'

'If the good lady herself has chosen not to speak about what happened all this time ago, it is not for me to betray her confidence. I say again, you must ask her.'

'She is old,' said Maria. 'She is frail. Perhaps we should spare her the pain.'

Figuera snorted and it was not a pleasant noise. 'She is Caterina Lucena. She is stronger than any of us and if you ask, she will tell you. If she wishes to do so.'

'We will,' said Menéndez. 'And the brotherhood?'

'The brotherhood.'

His head rolled back on its shoulders. The sky was full of swifts now. Their cries made a skein of noise above them.

'You know the answer, Lieutenant,' said Figuera eventually. 'Why ask? You do not need me to say it.'

'When the war was over, the brotherhood was formed by the leaders of the local Falange,' Menéndez said. Maria watched him, thinking as he spoke, trying to make the connections. 'Among those in the brotherhood were men who had been in the camp. Men who knew about the atrocities, who had taken part in them.'

'And others too,' said Figuera. 'Innocent men. Men who did not *appreciate* what they were doing. Don't forget that. But yes. There were those in the brotherhood who had no place in any organisation which bore the name of Christ. And we all knew that. We all knew that. And did not dare speak a word.'

'I see,' said Menéndez. And wished it were true.

115

13

At six in the evening, as Torrillo's car was bumping along the dusty road to Manolo Figuera's country house, the processions were beginning to assemble across the city. Beneath penitents' hoods and priests' caps, beneath lace mantillas and grey felt riding hats, on foot, on horseback, on the saddles of slow, noisy motorcycles, they came in their thousands, cramming the narrow streets of the barrios, the broader, scruffy thoroughfares of the working-class suburbs. In dark and dusty halls, men shouldered the gilt and silver carriages, grunted, strained and heaved them into the streets, great gaudy magnets for the crowds who pushed and shoved around them.

It was now halfway through Semana Santa and the strain was beginning to show. Tempers rose, between men and women, between parishioners and priests. Beneath the interior cover of the week's relentless blanket of sanctity, passions flared, lives took new courses, vows were made and broken in the unmoving, impassive heat of the night.

In El Viejo, where three different parades, from three different parishes, each consisting of only a few hundred people, would happen this night, the celebrants gathered around the Fountain of the Colt, in white, in scarlet, in plain and holy dress. The excitement was muted, almost guilty. From now on, the pageant would darken, become more intense, until the tragedy of Good Friday, when death would be triumphant, as always, triumphant for two days, until the world was created anew on Easter Sunday. And then the bulls would run, the feria would begin, and life would return, reinvigorated, sanctified again, made whole by the annual ritual of passion and power and love.

From the building on the corner came a cry that was lost in the chaos. It was an hour before the first policeman managed to make his way through the crowds.

14

'Show business,' said Manolo Figuera with obvious distaste. 'This is not bullfighting. This is show business.'

The three visitors sat in the front room of the little house, the curtains drawn, coloured light flickering on a small Japanese TV which sat on top of a video recorder.

'El Guapo. The "pretty boy". It is not a nickname that flatters, you think?'

Maria looked at the figure on the screen. He was between twenty-five and thirty years old, blond-haired, tall, muscular and handsome in the way that male models or minor film stars are handsome. He smiled constantly, he played to the crowd, encouraged and rewarded their attention. He exuded superficial warmth, waved spontaneously to the audience, tossed an ear once, all for the spectators who clearly loved him. Yet there was something artificial too. When the camera focused on his face, grinning, triumphant, after some pass perilously close to the bull, he seemed, to her, almost to be mocking the crowd. The eyes, grey, two-dimensional, reflected nothing, nothing at all. It was show business, the old man was right, show business, or something else altogether.

'Now,' said Figuera, punching the remote control. 'Let me show you this. This is what El Guapo has brought to the bullring. *This* is what makes the crowds love him so.'

The picture flickered and broke up as it scurried across the screen: pale dun earth, flashes of gold and red and shiny brown hide. He punched the remote control again, the screen froze momentarily then began to move.

It was towards the end of the contest. He was hatless, his luxuriant golden hair waved in the light breeze and the motion of the fight. The *banderilleros* danced around the edges of the ring, watchful, waiting for any sudden danger which required their presence. The picadors, seated on blindfolded horses, thick padding under their stomachs, stood rigid at the periphery of the screen. El Guapo was centre stage with the bull. He was radiant in a gold-and-silver suit of lights cut tight to the body. Sweat gleamed on his face. He danced and feigned with the red muleta, swirling the bull around him as if it were a puppet. The creature looked exhausted, but furious too. Snot and saliva dripped from its nose and mouth. Darts, beribboned, pierced its shoulders, blood from the picadors' lances formed a dark red stain across its back. It lunged and stamped and snorted around the ring, unsure of anything except its anger.

'Watch now,' said Figuera. He hung on every move, the old ritual stirring up the memories. 'Watch. You must understand. This is the point at which any conventional matador would kill the animal. Exactly the point. He has already taken it too far for most. It is tired, so tired. There is nothing left there.'

El Guapo danced the animal around the ring three more times and they could see how it lumbered, almost stumbling onto its knees in exhaustion at one point.

'I would have killed it two minutes ago,' said Figuera flatly. 'It was a good animal. It deserved that.'

The figure in the suit of lights carried out one more pass, closer than ever, then walked away, turned to the crowd and waved. He smiled, a film star smile, perfect teeth, hands raised above his head in acclamation. The camera moved to the crowd. They were jubilant. Men, women, girls, they screamed, went crazy. A group of young women, in short dresses, flowers in their dark, long hair, shook their heads frantically, close to frenzy, close to tears. Maria felt utterly detached from them, as if they were creatures from another planet. The sexual charge which so clearly consumed them was quite lost on her. The man, the event, they seemed so artificial, so *wrong*.

He tossed aside the muleta and the sword concealed inside it and walked slowly, unprotected, towards the bull. It stood, stock still, baffled, in front of him, saliva dripping to the ground. He was speaking, words they could not hear, addressing it. They could not hear but they could sense the dark mockery in his words and the thought came suddenly to Maria: you who are about to die salute me.

El Guapo fell to his knees, no more than three feet in front of the bull. The tips of its horns burned brightly in the baking sun. He shuffled forward through the golden dust. The animal stared down at him, senseless. When he was no more than a foot from its face, he reached up. The camera zoomed in. You could see the animal's hot breath, now short, deep punctured gasps of weariness, blowing against his face, making the thick golden locks move gently away from his head. He reached out and, for a moment, it looked as if he was going to kiss the animal. He pulled back his hands, shuffled forward another six inches, reached up and touched the horns. It was an electric moment. The sound of the crowd died completely. With absolute symmetry, he touched the base of each, felt the thick bole as it grew outwards and joined the skull. Then, slowly, he ran a single finger along each side, with the tenderness of a sexual caress. The animal stood motionless, transfixed, panting for breath, its eyes dark and focused, pupils contracted to two tiny, dark points. At the summit of each horn, he paused, brought the tips of two fingers and thumb together, felt the

120

point, *inspected* it, clinically. The camera zoomed in on this moment: the finger, testing the tip, recoiling, theatrically, as it appreciated the strength, the sharpness of the deadly point. The producer inserted a picture within the picture. In a small window, the girls they had seen earlier, with their pretty dresses and tanned, attractive faces, now moaned in ecstasy, long hair dancing in the air as their heads moved from side to side, eyes closed, mouths agape. One seemed to be touching herself through her dress: the camera abruptly raced elsewhere.

El Guapo removed his hands, put them by his sides and stared into the bull's face for what seemed like a long minute. It was meant to be a look of reverence. Still on his knees, he shuffled around, 180 degrees, until his back was to the animal, now some three feet away and showing signs of restlessness. It began to stamp its feet, its breathing had become more regular, but still it stood unmoving, as if charmed into quietude by the ritual to which it had been subjected.

The camera angle now shifted so that it showed the matador face on. He stayed on his knees, waving to the crowd, seemingly oblivious of the creature behind him. On the little TV set its horns and its massive head towered above the small, golden figure in front. They almost appeared to be one: a man-bull, life and death intertwined. Then El Guapo rose to his feet and the audience, which had held its breath for the entire episode, rose in acclaim, rose to its feet, applauding, waving, shouting. Flowers fell from the terraces, handkerchiefs, hats, mantillas joined them. All parts of the arena, *sol* and *sombra*, were in uproar. And still the bull stood impassive.

El Guapo picked up the bright-red muleta, picked up the sword, hid it underneath the cloth, strode over to the bull and, in a single, swift movement, leaned over its massive horns and thrust fast and deep and hard between the shoulder blades. The creature seemed to shiver, pulled back, as if awoken from a dream by some sudden, terrifying shock. The crowd screamed again. Then the animal collapsed, slowly, down on to its right side, one leg bent at the knee. Blood ran from its muzzle, a convulsion gripped the length of its frame.

It fell like a dead weight to the ground and blood, bright red, mingled with the sand of the ring. Unseen, the crowd began to roar, the cheers rattled the tiny, tinny loudspeaker on the TV.

'Show business,' said Figuera and with a look of distaste on his face snapped the remote control. The picture disappeared with a flash. Outside the light was starting to fade and the trill of the swifts had gone. On the little table the bottle was empty. He stared at it. 'That is all it has come to. Show business.'

'Have you met him?' Menéndez asked. 'Personally?'

'Briefly. He will not remember. He is not interested in history.'

'Do you know his background? He is from the city. That I know. He is an orphan.'

Figuera laughed. 'An orphan? This is a new word for it. I must remember. An *orphan*.'

Menéndez stayed silent. He could feel Figuera grasping around at something, wondering whether to let it go.

'A *bastard*. I mean this literally, you understand. He is a bastard, not an orphan.'

'You know of his father.'

'Family secrets, Lieutenant. How they interest you. First Doña Caterina, then El Guapo. How they interest you.'

'I know of no family secrets concerning Doña Caterina.'

Figuera switched off the TV and the video. 'No. It is as well. But I will give you a family secret of El Guapo and I

122

will tell you why. Look up your records. His father is dead now but, some time in the fifties, I cannot remember when exactly, he was a "big man" in our fine city, briefly, for maybe two years, until someone checked the books and wondered where the money was going. Antonio Alvarez. Yes. Write down the name, note it well. He is dead now, dead a good ten years, I think. Unmourned.'

'Who was the mother?' asked Maria.

Figuera shook his head. 'You think I hold a registry of births and deaths in my head? No. I apologise. I get tired, I get bad-tempered. I cannot remember. I said that he was Alvarez's bastard but he was not alone. This man was – let me put it politely for you, lady – *prolific*. From an early age. Ask around the city, search your records, El Guapo has many half-brothers and half-sisters though I doubt he would recognise them in the street.'

Menéndez finished scribbling. 'I am grateful. But I must ask myself. Why are you telling us this, Don Manolo?'

The old man smiled at him. It was a look of respect.

'You are a clever man, Lieutenant. You listen. It is rare these days. Why? Because Antonio Alvarez was a different kind of bastard. He was, for example, secretary to your brotherhood. That is a fact, you can see that in your records. He was a Franco-lover too. He didn't just go for the General because he wanted to make good for himself, because it was the safe thing to do. He *believed* it all too. And that is worse.'

'I will look these things up.'

'Good. You look them up. Records are fine things. There is one thing you will not find in your records, however.'

Menéndez could feel the strain inside the old man as he spoke.

'I did not tell you this. You understand?'

The Lieutenant nodded.

'In La Soledad, Alvarez was there.'

'When the killings occurred?'

'Yes,' said Figuera.

'And you think he took part?'

Figuera stood up and started to clear away the glasses.

'I think I am tired. And I think I have told you enough. Also I believe your sergeant wishes to speak with you.'

Torrillo was at the door. Menéndez had never noticed the Sergeant move. Now he stood by the door, silent, concerned.

'It was the carphone, Lieutenant. I heard it while you were talking.'

Menéndez read his face, dark, pale and troubled, in an instant.

'I thank you for your time, Don Manolo, and hope we may speak again before long.'

The old man said nothing when they left.

15

The Plaza del Potro was full of people, some in costume, some in casual dress, everyone subdued, silent, under the clear, starry sky. Menéndez, Torrillo and Maria pushed their way through the mass of shoulders. Close to the entrance, herded together, stood a group of reporters, from the newspapers and the TV stations. As they entered, it was to blinding flashes of light and shouted questions. Menéndez ignored them all, Torrillo and Maria hurried behind him.

They walked past two uniformed policemen guarding the door and entered the ground-floor office they had left only hours before. From upstairs came the sound of low, male voices. Menéndez started up the steps and they followed him.

The office seemed to be soaking in blood. It lay on the floor, in sticky, dark-red puddles, it was dashed against the walls. The smell, sweetly noisome, hung on the air. Five policemen were inspecting the room; Maria recognised none of them. A man in a white nylon jacket was examining the body. At first glance, it resembled a carcass from a meat market.

Menéndez bent eagerly over the corpse, Torrillo began to talk to the cops who had arrived earlier. She felt torn between the two, wondered what they would like her to do. Then she realised that, to them, she was now invisible. The matter was moving on to a different level. Her work, her original work, now seemed increasingly irrelevant. She wondered why Menéndez had tolerated her so far, whether he would continue to do so, what would happen if she ceased to be useful. When the answer came, almost automatically, she walked over and joined Menéndez and the pathologist as they looked at the mortal remains of Miguel Castaneda.

The pathologist wore white, opaque surgical gloves, now covered in blood, and crouched over the body as if he were tending it. As he worked, he poked and prodded, examining folds of torn flesh, a variety of entry wounds, looking inside the dead man's mouth, lifting each arm to judge the degree of rigor mortis, testing the tightness of a ring on the dead man's right hand. Menéndez and Maria watched in silence. Finally, the man stopped, stood up, then turned to them. He had a thin, slightly neurotic, sallow face, with a pencil moustache that looked as if it had taken a lifetime to grow. He smiled. There were brown tobacco stains on his teeth.

'Lieutenant?'

'Dr Castares.'

'You get the short version now. The long one tomorrow.'

'And the short version?'

'He was killed some time ago. The afternoon, perhaps the morning. Multiple wounds, at least three instruments. One of them has been left here.'

He pointed to a dart, with a red ribbon, enclosed in an exhibit bag next to the body.

'It was on the floor, not in him, but there is blood on it and tissue too. My guess is . . . there is a wound to the eye, here.' He pointed to Castaneda's head. The eye socket was a mass of blood, coagulated fluid and purpling tissue. It did not look human. 'Probably the dart caused the wound. He threw it straight at the man, it broke his glasses – there are traces of glass in the eye – and then punctured the eye. Not a fatal wound in itself, though. What killed him was the blow to the throat. Cut through the windpipe. He couldn't have lasted more than a few seconds after that.'

126

Menéndez's head was swimming. Six, seven hours? 'There are other wounds.'

'Yes,' said Castares. 'Many. I will give you a full list after the postmortem but at a guess I would say at least twenty. Probably inflicted shortly after death. Some may be darts again. Others look as if they came from some larger pointed object. Difficult to say what, though.'

'You carried out the postmortem on the Angel Brothers?'

'Yes.'

'Did they look similar?'

Castares thought for a moment. 'Don't push me, Lieutenant. I'll look at my records and tell you for sure. But yes, I think they probably are similar.'

'So you think the first blow was the dart, and it hit Castaneda in the eye.'

'Yes.'

Menéndez turned round, looked at the door, the office, thought about the way it might have happened. 'Which is not what the killer planned. So he improvised. He is a "practical man". He killed Castaneda with the sword and then carved the body to fit the ritual as best he could.'

'It's up to you the way you read the facts,' said Castares. 'All I can say is there's no reason for these secondary wounds. None of them are life-threatening.'

One of the cops who was working through the office effects behind Castaneda's desk picked up a book, put it down, then said, 'This is meant to be El Matador, huh?'

Menéndez nodded. 'It looks like it.'

'Well,' said the cop, 'there's something funny. I was in the house of those queers and it was, like, *full* of things that were worth something. Just out there waiting to be taken. Yet he didn't take anything? Not so far as we know? There was nothing stolen?'

'Not that we know of,' said Menéndez.

'Well, normally I work burglary, right?' He pointed to the grey filing cabinet at the end of the desk. 'So I guess I look for these things. See here.'

He went to the filing cabinet, pulled out a handkerchief, then opened the top drawer.

'Now mostly this office stuff has the kind of lock on it you could pick with a paper clip. Beats me why they even bother. But this is different. It's got these little padlocks, you see, that clip through the staples?'

Menéndez went and looked at the cabinet.

'Now every one of these little padlocks is open, just off the lock, you know. *Every* one. So I looked inside.'

He pulled open the drawers, one by one, from the top.

'They're all full, all right. All except this one.'

He kicked gently on the bottom drawer. Menéndez bent over, looked inside it. There were a few files, without identification. He picked one up.

'They're all empty,' said the cop. 'Except for this. Don't worry about prints, Lieutenant. Our bullfighting friend didn't leave any.'

He pointed to the last one in the drawer. Menéndez picked it up and looked inside. There was a single sheet of cream office paper, blank, except for the mark in the corner. It looked like a smudged red thumbprint.

'Glove,' said the officer. 'Just a smeared glove print, in blood, I guess. But you see what I mean?'

Menéndez nodded. 'He cleared out the drawer.'

'No sign of what was in it. You look through the others and you see the usual stuff. Records of meetings. Accounts. Membership records.'

'You're sure they're membership records?'

'Absolutely. They're still there.' He pulled out the second drawer down. 'This one, and the one below, all paper records, some of them going back years. And you see this too?'

He pulled up the little card on the front of the drawer. 'These top three ones all have cards that say what they contain. This boy had a good filing system, neat, tidy habits. This bottom one. Nothing. There's a card. It's just blank. Our friend obviously knew what was in there but he didn't want to label it for anybody else.'

'Perhaps it wasn't a record, perhaps it was something valuable.'

'No. I looked in the other drawers. Somebody's been through them too, looking. You can tell, the way the papers get messed up. There's even a few spots of blood in them too. Understandable in the circumstances.'

Menéndez shook his head. None of it made sense.

'Wait,' said the cop. 'These old files. Sometimes they trap things behind the back. I got that tip from an office guy once.'

He reached into the empty drawer, unlocked something from the top, then slowly rolled the whole thing out of the frame. Underneath was a small army of dustballs, several paper clips, a pen top ... and a single piece of paper. Menéndez picked it up and looked at it. Maria came over and looked over his shoulder. It was a list of names, company names. Beside each was a sum. They were quite big sums. There were no dates.

'Donations?' she asked.

'Who knows? You recognise any of these names?'

She shook her head. 'They don't exactly sound like multinationals.'

'No,' said Menéndez then folded the piece of paper and put it in his pocket. She looked at him curiously. His face gave nothing away.

Menéndez asked, 'Did the woman who found him say anything?'

'Not that you'd want to put too much weight on. A real

gentleman, Mr Castaneda, she says. Why'd anybody want to do such a thing? Why'd they ever?'

Menéndez gestured to the filing cabinet. 'Take that to the station when they've got the body out of here. I want every membership record checked against possible connections with the Angel Brothers, records of sex offenders, and anything serious to do with the ring. Get some of the night team working on it. I want a report in the morning.'

'Sure.'

'You know where I am if you need me.'

The three of them went downstairs.

'Lieutenant?' One of the plain-clothes detectives came up to them, a stained handkerchief in his hand. 'Looks like the guy wore some kind of disguise. There are traces of make-up, what looks like hair, in the washbasin.'

Torrillo took his notebook out of his jacket pocket, found the page, scribbled out the name and then tore off the new page. 'Run a check on a name for me, will you?'

'Sure, Bear,' the man said, then walked outside to find the car. The three of them were left alone in a corner of the office, set apart from the officers who scurried around the building.

Maria felt their sad, depressed silence.

'You really think it was him? The one we saw?'

'The one I frisked? The one whose ID I looked at?' Torrillo stared glumly out of the window. 'We'll know when the ID checks out.'

'The timing looks right,' said Menéndez. 'And think about it. Think back.'

She tried to remember, to rebuild what had happened as if it was a photograph, something that could be recaptured and printed to film. She tried, and she knew they were right.

'He didn't mean to frighten me,' she said. 'He was leaning

130

on the door because he was thinking about what he was going to do, he was distracted.'

She thought again. 'His face was too red. His beard was too . . . too black.'

'Yes,' said Menéndez. Looking back now, they all knew. 'It's the old illusionist's trick. We saw what we expected to see, not what was really there.'

'But, but . . .' She struggled for the words. 'You mean, he came here to kill Castaneda, got interrupted by us, and still went ahead with it?'

'Looks like,' said Torrillo.

She shook her head. 'It's impossible. I just can't believe how he wasn't even thrown by it. By being interrupted like that.'

'Intelligence, confidence, impulsiveness, lack of remorse, guilt or shame, as far as one can judge.' Menéndez counted the points. 'Lacking in automatic responses for anticipatory fear or apprehension, callous . . .'

'They teach you these things, in the police?' asked Maria.

'Not necessarily. But that doesn't mean you don't learn them. I read somewhere once that fifteen, maybe twenty, per cent of all crime is related to psychopathy, and that the figure is much larger for violent crimes. Perhaps we should learn more about it, as a matter of course.'

Maria tried to remember what she had read years ago. 'Does this really fit the facts?'

'Yes,' said Menéndez, and she was surprised by the firmness in his voice. 'It fits exactly.'

'But does it *help*?'

He wondered. 'The signs are that this is the work of someone with psychopathic tendencies. We should check the records to look for connections, talk to the hospitals. But in a way it's somewhat depressing.'

'How?'

'For a policeman, the principal problem with psychopathic behaviour is that it doesn't stem from any underlying emotional disturbance. You can't profile these people according to their behaviour except for the moment when they are committing a crime. They may be people who hold down a respectable job, go to an office each day, have polite, occasionally strained, but always distant relations with those they know. Not that they know many very well, of course. And they believe they are normal when they kill too. It makes our job harder.'

Torrillo stuffed his hands in his jacket pockets and let out a long sigh. 'What the Lieutenant is trying to say, Maria, is that when we catch people it is because we know they're driving a red Panda, or they beat up their wife, or they're carrying something they shouldn't be. We can detect our way there eventually but we need a little help. Tell those guys out there we're looking for some ordinary joe who just happens to hate his fellow man, hate him to the occasional point of killing, and you run the risk of looking at a room full of cops shrugging their shoulders and saying: what is this shit? *We* hate our fellow man and get grumpy too sometimes. This is the city.'

'You're off duty now, Sergeant,' Menéndez said. 'Let's see how this looks in the light of day.'

Torrillo grunted and looked at the floor. Maria waited, undismissed.

'It's not a painting,' she said.

Menéndez looked at her and she wished his face was more open, more legible.

'What do you mean?'

'The Angels. He went to such lengths to make it look like the painting. It was as if it was more than a simple killing. Something symbolic. But here, it's just a killing.

132

Deliberate. It's different somehow. I don't know how, but it's different.'

He thought about it. 'There was time with the Angels. He had no time here.'

She couldn't argue with him. 'I know. But it's still different. It *feels* different.'

'But it's the same person. It has to be. No one could copy-cat the MO to that kind of detail.'

'No. You're right.'

She said it in a way that meant, he knew, the opposite.

'Maria,' said Menéndez. 'In the morning, I would like you to do something for me. I would like you to visit Caterina Lucena and ask her, ask her outright, what happened in La Soledad. She may tell you. I know she will not tell me. I will send a car for you. The driver will wait outside the hospital.'

'You don't want to come?'

'It would be pointless. If she is going to tell what she has to tell she will tell it to a woman, and not a policewoman at that. Besides . . . there are other things to do.'

One of the detectives returned with a note. 'That ID's no good, Lieutenant. Reported stolen two months ago. Belongs to some bus driver. It's in the book. We checked with his neighbours. He's on holiday with his wife and kids in Mallorca.'

Torrillo grunted. Menéndez left and they followed him.

Outside, the night was warm and humid. They soon walked out of the square, leaving the subdued, gawking crowd behind.

'Lieutenant?'

He opened the car door for her. Maria thought he looked exhausted.

'I want you to know that I will not be putting down

these details in my report. It's not my job to get involved in that kind of detail.'

'You should write what you want. There is nothing to hide here. I shall make everything clear in my own reports. Don't feel you need protect me or Torrillo from what you think.'

She felt like pinching herself. 'That was not what I meant. I just wanted to say . . . that I don't think you need blame yourself.'

'No. Perhaps not. Ask me tomorrow.'

Menéndez drove her home in silence, walked her to the door of the house, watched as she went in and waited until he heard the door bolted. She went straight upstairs, rifled through the bookcases in the living room, chose five different titles, went to the bedroom and threw them on the bed. She took off her jacket and let it fall on the bed, then picked up the first book. It was called *The Mask of Sanity*.

16

The man wore a Zapata moustache and a red satin dress cut to just above the knee. He was way overweight in the kind of way that thin people become overweight when they just can't stop themselves. Hairy, tanned legs poked out of the bottom of the dress and ended in brown patent leather shoes. He was about forty years old and smoked a cigar that emitted bursts of acrid smoke every time he puffed on it. In the little room, off the corner of the barrio where the sex shops operated behind blacked-out windows, the atmosphere reeked of tobacco, sweat, and amyl nitrate.

Quemada and Velasco looked at their interviewee, then looked at each other. They were not happy.

'I'm a businessman. That's all. You got no need to hassle me. I know my rights.'

The trouble was, when they tried to imagine Felipe Ordoñez without the dress, he looked exactly like someone who *did* know his rights. A lawyer, a civil servant, someone from the bus company.

'No one's trying to hassle you, Señor Ordoñez.' Velasco tried to make his voice sound as reasonable as he could. He thought he was doing quite well, all things taken into consideration. Velasco felt like shit. His sinuses were starting to congeal into some kind of mucus mess. The weather was making them worse. Inwardly he had a growing conviction he had hay fever, Chinese flu and typhus coming on simultaneously. His face was a sickly parchment colour, the colour of the old books he liked to peer at in the museum when he wanted to waste a couple of hours' duty on a dead day. And all the outside world could see was someone sniffing. He sweated inside his polyester suit, feeling more uncomfortable by the minute, and tried, tried very hard, to be as reasonable as he could.

'We're not here to interview you about what you do. We're just trying to get some information on people you might know. People who have met with some very unfortunate happenings, that's all.'

'I'm a businessman. This is all legit. You go down the companies office, look at the forms. I pay taxes, more than you do probably.'

'We're not arguing with you, *sir*,' said Quemada, staring at the pictures on the wall. They were of young men in a variety of poses: wearing jock straps, reclining on a beach, pouting for the camera. He didn't like looking at them but he liked looking at Felipe Ordoñez even less. Every time he tried to look the guy in the face he found himself staring at the dress. 'All we're trying to do is find out if you fixed up a date for these two people who got killed. You did, that's fine, we're easy. We're just talking to everyone in your line of business. Nothing specific. We'd just like you to cooperate.'

Ordoñez looked as if he was trying to make his face match the colour of the dress. He was getting angry.

'I do not – Jesus, the ignominy of it! – I do *not* fix dates for people. Can't you understand that?'

Quemada picked up a colour brochure on the desk. It bore the name and address of the office they were in. The cover was a photograph showing a group of young men on the beach. They were tanned, lithe, muscular, grinning for the camera. Underneath it said, 'Abraxas Introductions: Select Partners for Select Males'.

Quemada stared at the brochure in his hand. 'So what you do for your guys then? Sell them tickets to the opera? Rounds of *golf*? I mean. What we talking about here? Charity work?'

Ordoñez put down the cigar. A little tic appeared above his right eye and the man prodded at it with a fat forefinger. Quemada and Velasco looked at each other. This was someone who had been rousted before and didn't like it. This was someone they could bend.

Ordoñez finished poking at his eye, controlled the tic and said, 'I run a contacts agency. You know what that means?'

'Kind of like a brothel, only you turn your head to one side when they start fucking each other?' asked Quemada.

'Jesus.'

Ordoñez sat down hard on a metal-framed office chair behind the desk. 'Why can't you just leave us alone? Why do I get this two, three times a month? You do this to the straight people? Is it money you want?'

Velasco bent over and looked him in the face and sniffed very hard. It sounded like a camel trying to clear its throat. Ordoñez shrank back visibly. 'You offering us money? You *offering* us money? I'm gonna pretend I didn't hear that 'cos if I did we'd be taking you down now. What I want you to do, Señor Ordoñez, is listen to what we've been saying to you. We're not interested in what you do here. We don't care you got chickens, goats, sheep on your books. We don't *care*. We're just interested in who's been through your books and seeing the Angel Brothers. You tell us that, you give us the names, we'll leave you alone.'

'I never supplied any names to the Angel Brothers.'

They didn't say anything for a while and watched him sweat.

Finally Quemada toyed with the brochure. 'You're the second biggest gay agency in town, right?'

'That's right.'

'And there's only three of you agencies operating, like, legit. Right?'

'Yes. But a lot of people don't use agencies. You just look at the personal ads in the papers. A lot of people don't use us.'

'Yeah, well, maybe that's the case. But you see, we've been to see both your rivals and we seen their books. They didn't give us all this shit. They showed us their records and we *know* the Angel Brothers didn't use them, or if they did they didn't keep any record at all of it.'

'Which we think is unlikely,' added Velasco, 'seeing as how some of the names on the books they *did* show us in the end could have filled the front page of *El Diario* for several weeks on end, so we figure it most unlikely they kept a separate, private list, for people like the Angel Brothers who didn't make any secret about which way they buttoned their pants.'

'So we figure also,' said Quemada, 'that if the other two guys say they never spoke to the Angel Brothers, maybe they spoke to you. Or maybe they didn't. Either way, we'd just like to know and, excuse us if it seems rude, but we'd just like you to *prove* it when you say you never gave them any names. You got a nice little personal computer over there. You got no big filing cabinets. My guess is all you got to do is sit there, call up some program or something, then type in the word "Angel" and just *show* us something don't come up.'

'Yeah,' said Velasco. 'That would do it.'

Ordoñez shot a glance at them, then looked at the computer. He stayed put in the chair and rolled it over on its wheels to the side of the desk where the PC sat. The move had the familiar, easy casualness of a secretary working her

way around the office. Velasco shook his head. Ordoñez
didn't spend his time oiling the bodies of suntanned youths,
like the brochure promised. He punched keys on an office
PC like any secretarial temp.

Ordoñez pushed the power button on the front of the
machine, then it booted up to a Windows desktop. He
pointed at a little folder, opened it, clicked quickly on the
mouse. The computer paused for a moment, then the
window changed and a form came on the screen that looked
like an address book. There were spaces for first and last
names, addresses, a postal code, telephone number, fax
number.

'There. You want to try for yourself, *officers?*' Ordoñez
glowered at them. He was moist around the eyes.

'Naw,' said Quemada. 'You type it in.'

Ordoñez's fingers flashed over the keys with the speed of a
touch typist. The word 'Angel' appeared in the name field.

'OK?'

'OK,' said Quemada.

He slapped the return key, the PC whirred for a moment,
then the message 'Name not found' appeared in the centre
of the screen.

'Satisfied?' said Ordoñez, not looking at them.

'Señor Ordoñez,' said Velasco.

The man continued to play with the PC, pushing the
mouse around, closing windows.

'*Señor Ordoñez, will you look at me for God's sake?*'

Velasco could feel his throat going as the volume rose
and a broad, dull line of pain was starting to make its way
from one temple to the other.

Ordoñez brushed his eyes with his sleeve and turned to
them.

'Señor Ordoñez, do I look as if I have shit between my
ears? Huh?'

Velasco pushed him out of the way and started to run the mouse around the desk.

'Do I look like I'm stupid? Huh? My kid has this stuff at home. Sometimes I use it too. Do I look like I'm stupid? You resent the fact we look at you thinking: who's this fucking queer in the red dress? Let me tell *you* something, I resent the fact I come through the door and you think: here's some fucking cop, must have shit between the ears. Look. Look here. This is what I'm talking about.'

Velasco had leaned over, quit the application Ordoñez had opened, gone to another folder on the desktop, opened that, and was looking at an icon named 'Customer Database'.

'What you were showing us, that was just some shit you use to keep names and addresses case you want to write letters or something. I *know* that, Señor Ordoñez. My kid uses it. *I* use it. You want to run a business, you don't use this crap. You want to record times and places and *money*. You know that word, Señor Ordoñez? *Money*. Stuff you get from people you call "customers". Like this.'

He double-clicked on the icon, the computer clicked and whirred, a new application started. Some text appeared on the screen with the instructions, 'Type password'.

'Yeah. A password. Sounds a good idea, all things considered, Señor Ordoñez. Now be a good boy and type it. Sooner you do, sooner we start talking, and sooner we'll be out of your office.'

Ordoñez reached for his cigar, relit it, took a few puffs and waited for them to say something. Quemada and Velasco sat silent, waiting.

'You guys straight? This goes no further? No footprints to me, where this stuff came from? No charges or nothing?'

'Señor Ordoñez,' said Quemada wearily, 'do we have to keep on repeating ourselves?'

'OK,' the man said. 'OK. That's fine.'

He typed in a word. It appeared as asterisks on the screen, then the application opened, names and addresses came into view. He pulled down a search screen, typed in the word 'Angel', pressed a button marked 'Report' then one named 'Print'. A few seconds later, a little laser printer in the corner of the office began to whirr.

'Those boys were shits,' said Ordoñez, puffing on the cigar. 'I'm surprised it didn't happen to them sooner.'

The smoke curled silently through his moustache and twirled around his cheeks.

'You know what?' said Ordoñez. 'When they first came here, when they first rang me, I thought it was an honour. Can you believe that?'

He had pulled out a bottle of Soberano brandy from the desk and was now handing it round in paper cups. Velasco declined at first, but took a big one when he saw Quemada said yes. It stung on the rawness at the back of his throat but it felt good all the same.

'Two years ago, must have been. They phoned first, then came round the office. These *were* famous people, right? Well. We've had them before but never like that. Open, up front. They just didn't care.'

'I don't understand,' said Velasco. 'Why'd they need to go to an agency to find boyfriends? I'd have thought they'd have them falling over each other, what with the parties and the rest.'

Ordoñez smiled. 'It's not as easy as that. Not when you want what they wanted.'

'They spelled it out?'

'Not in so many words. If I'd known at the start, I would have said no right then. But I didn't.'

'So this list of names.' Quemada glanced over thirty or

141

so names and addresses printed out like envelope labels from the computer, a set of dates beside each. 'They didn't know either?'

'Precisely,' said Ordoñez, then filled up their cups with brandy. 'The brothers just said they wanted to meet other guys, about their age, maybe younger, sense of fun, love of art. You know the kind of stuff.'

'Not exactly,' said Quemada.

'Yeah,' said Velasco. 'I seen it. You get that kind of language in the little ads you see in the paper.'

Quemada gave his partner a little sideways look.

'Yes, officer, you do,' said Ordoñez. 'Most people are more specific. To be honest, and you won't believe me, most people just want company for the evening. If they like each other, fine, if they want to take it further, that's nothing to do with me. Most of the people who phone are just here on business, a little lonely, looking for someone to have dinner with. Someone sympathetic.'

'And the Angel Brothers?'

'The Angels were looking for S & M. They didn't say so. I just found out when people started to complain.'

'That's sado-masochism, like beatings and stuff?' asked Quemada.

'Yes. But the Angels went beyond that. You've got the list. You ask these people' – Ordoñez reached over and put a tick by ten or so names – 'they were the ones who complained the most. It was like it was some kind of game for the Angels. They'd be very charming with every couple they met, they'd take them to a very expensive restaurant, invite them back for coffee and drinks . . .'

'And then?'

'Then . . . things wouldn't be consensual.'

'Meaning?' asked Quemada.

'They'd try to beat them up and then rape them,' Ordoñez

said flatly. 'Sometimes they met their match. Sometimes people beat *them* up pretty badly too, but maybe that was part of the idea.'

'Why didn't anyone call us?' asked Quemada.

'Are you serious? What would you have done?'

'Talked to them. Arrested them. Beating people up is a crime, doesn't matter who the people are.'

Ordoñez took a swig of the brandy. 'It doesn't really work like that.'

'Anyone on this list might have a particular grudge against the brothers?'

He thought about that one. 'No one stands out. They all complained. Maybe some of the others had the same treatment but didn't complain.'

'Maybe they liked it,' said Quemada.

Ordoñez looked at him wearily. 'Maybe.'

'You go there yourself, Señor Ordoñez?'

'No.'

'You get invited?'

'Yes.'

'So why didn't you go?'

Ordoñez lit another cigar. 'I'm married.'

Quemada's mouth fell open.

'To a woman. Before you ask.'

'You mean this is ... this is just business?'

He nodded. 'Business. And a little pleasure too, sometimes.'

Velasco looked up from his notebook. 'You a fan of bullfighting, Señor Ordoñez?'

He shook his head. 'I am not just *not* a fan, I positively hate the thing. Barbaric and cruel.'

Velasco asked, 'You ever belonged to any of the brotherhoods? You know, the religious ones?'

'No.'

Quemada thought. 'Is there a gay brotherhood? You know, kind of a penitents' one?'

Ordoñez shook his head. 'Not that I know of. There's a gay ecclesiastical movement, of course. But I don't think there's anything separate.'

'Right,' said Quemada.

'And this list? Any of these people on it fans of the bulls, into the brotherhoods?'

'I have no idea. They phone, I make a booking. Most of the time I don't even meet them. Just a phone call.'

'And this is it. Nothing more?'

'Nothing. When I got the last complaint, maybe three, four weeks ago, you have the dates there, I told the Angels I wouldn't have any more dealings with them. It wasn't worth the trouble.'

'How did they react?'

'They said they'd come and burn my house down.'

'Nice people, huh?'

'Nice people.'

Velasco scribbled something, then said, 'Thanks, Señor Ordoñez. We'll look into these names and if we need more we'll get back to you.'

Quemada looked him up and down, then reached out for the door handle. 'Nice dress,' he said. 'But the shoes clash.'

17

Maria found herself drowsing over the pages. They made a little sense, reminding her of things she had learned as a student, learned then forgotten, since they seemed so unreal, so distant from her life. But she understood Menéndez's depression. Psychopathy was a condition that could provide a perfect disguise in the city. There was a cluster, a cocktail, of traits and behaviour patterns which fell under the general heading. The condition was common, but misunderstood. Psychopathy was more likely to reveal itself through thoughtless, anti-social behaviour than outright crime. But once the momentum took hold, the tendency to violence was often unstoppable. The difficulty, for the doctors and for the police, was that the usual signs of mental illness – psychosis, neurosis, mental deficiency – were absent. Psychopathy did not stem from some underlying mental disorder; it was not a tendency that could be picked up from being brought up in a criminal community, handed down from father to son by habit. 'Normal' criminals could commit offences and feel guilt and concern. They were capable of conventional, loving family relationships, even while they were pursuing careers as criminals. For the psychopath, this was impossible. Affectionate relationships meant nothing. Crime, if the condition manifested itself in this way – and it was just as likely to manifest itself as hedonism, professional intolerance, impulsiveness or general anti-social behaviour – crime was simply something that occurred. A deliberate act born of nothing but the desire to commit it. There was evidence that suggested triggers existed for intense psychopathic behaviour, but these were everyday events: a car crash, an insult, a headache. To the psychopath these lacked the sense of scale which limited and defined the responses of 'normal' people. So, if he were cut up on the road and received the single finger in response, that single event might escalate into a serious assault or even murder. And when asked about it afterwards, he, or she, would express amazement that anyone could question his actions, could feel they were out of proportion to the original insult.

They were like people, ordinary people, with monsters hidden inside themselves, and just a few sores on the surface. Prick the sores and the monster appeared, did its worst, then went back to slumber, lightly, until the next time.

Maria shuddered, closed the book and rolled over on the bed. This man would not reveal himself by going berserk, locking himself in a house, daring the police to force him out. He would not reveal himself by escalating the violence until it became so large that even the most stupid of police forces would stumble on the act in progress. One passage she had read came back to her: 'Attempts to modify the behaviour of psychopaths have not been successful, probably because they do not suffer from personal distress, see nothing wrong in their behaviour, and are not motivated to change.'

This man would think about what he wanted to do. About who he wanted to kill. Then, when the time was right, he would go out, commit the act, return home, wash, change, turn on the TV and wait for it to appear on the evening news. Like waiting for a football result: detached, interested, patient. And in between times, he would sit at home or go to work, quiet, inconspicuous, maybe noted only as a little introverted by his neighbours, his acquaintances (for there surely would be no friends). Menéndez was right. All he could do was to check the facts, to try to pull some link, some crossover, in the details. And to wait.

She got off the bed, walked through the living room into the little kitchen and poured herself a glass of mineral water from the bottle in the refrigerator. Then she went back into the living room and sat on the low leather sofa. Maria felt the arms, shiny tubular metal, and thought: just the kind of thing a man would buy, all appearance, no comfort. Outside she could hear the sound of crowds: shouting, some of it drunken, singing, the blare of car horns echoing around the narrow stone streets. It was not yet midnight and the noise would go on until the first light of morning.

The flat occupied the first floor of a two-storey building, above a small optician's shop, reached by a private door next to the shop window, with its huge glasses and ads for contact lenses. You opened the door, walked forward a pace, then walked up the flight of stairs to the second, locked door. It opened straight into the living room: three times as long as it was wide, decorated with low-slung Italian furniture in cream and brown. Bookshelves lined the opposite wall, a blocked-up fireplace in the centre. Two doors led off the living room, one to the small kitchen, the other to the bedroom, with the bathroom adjoining it. A bachelor flat, a world for one person, enclosed, private, apart.

Maria thought briefly of the owner for a moment. When they were students together, in the city, so long ago, briefly, for a month or so, they had been lovers. She remembered wandering around El Viejo drinking cheap wine, living off tapas, hot evenings in a tiny student apartment, a single bed with a metal frame and springs that groaned like wayward, metallic tom cats. And then it had all dissolved into simple, slightly dull, friendship, gradually, unconsciously, naturally. The passion, if passion it was, had dissipated as if it had been possessed of a life of its own, a life finite, tied to a set period of time, like a mayfly. After which it died, quietly, unheeded, unmourned.

'Paolo,' she whispered and even his name sounded different after all these years, summoned up a different person, someone who was not the quiet, bookish young man she had once taken shyly to bed.

Maria sipped the water, stood up and took off her clothes. She looked at herself naked in the full-length mirror set in the back of the apartment door. Her hair was as wayward as ever. There were bags, pink and wrinkled, beneath her eyes. Her flesh sagged. At thirty-three, she felt old. She touched her left breast, squeezed the nipple gently until it hardened and thought: was this the same flesh that felt such fleeting excitement in this same city more than a decade before?

It seemed wrong. The bright, naïve, reticent person she was then seemed to be a player in some minor, forgotten drama, speaking lines she could no longer hear, driven by motives, desires which no longer made sense. She had no perception of having been that person, no interior memory of a link between the Maria of then and the Maria of now. They were separated, irrevocably, by the intervening years, the years when she had buried herself in the dry, passionless ambitions of academia and that brief, incomprehensible flowering of light that was her time with Luis. It was a chasm she could never recross, a chasm into which some vast element of her life had fallen, with nothing to touch, nothing to show for the effort.

She looked at herself in the mirror, left hand on her breast, the nipple half-heartedly stiff, the glass of water in her right hand, watched herself naked in front of the mirror, trying to ask herself: am I still attractive? And do I care in any case?

Then, with a sudden, harsh sound, the phone rang. She shook, an involuntary spasm, felt the glass slip from her hand, watched, stupidly fascinated, as it fell, seemingly in slow motion. It hit the stone floor and shattered into shards of bright glass and liquid.

'Shit,' said Maria, and stepped back from the mess. Then she walked over to the low table, wondering why it felt so uncomfortable being naked.

She picked up the phone and waited for someone to speak. There was nothing except low, controlled breathing.

'Is there someone there?' She looked at the clock by the bed. It was nearly midnight. Automatically, she checked again that the curtains were closed.

'Is there anybody there? I'm about to hang up.'

There was what sounded like a laugh, cold and dry.

'You don't even know you've lost it,' said a man's voice. It sounded like someone young, a little drowsy, maybe even drunk.

'I think you've got the wrong number.'

The laugh again.

'Really?'

'Really,' said Maria and put the phone down. She sat for a minute, waiting for it to ring again. When it didn't, she went to bed and fell into a deep, dreamless sleep where the night world was nothing but a wan, grey, lifeless landscape of two inescapable dimensions.

18

Velasco and Quemada sat together at their desk in the station. It was well over halfway through the night shift. The room was almost empty. From along the corridor came the racket of a drunk being escorted to a cell with a minimum of delicacy.

'How the fuck you supposed to think in this place with that row going on?' Quemada asked.

'That's a rhetorical question, I guess,' said Velasco.

'Huh?'

'Never mind.'

'You OK? You look a little peaky. Normally you just look kinda dead. But I'd say you're deteriorating. Fast.'

Velasco closed his eyes. He gave it a couple of days at the most. If the cold wasn't over by then he'd take some time off. Really he would. And that was one idea he hated. This was one giant, one monster of a case, the sort of thing you only got come along once in a lifetime. And there was no way he was going to miss all the fun.

'They should give me an allowance for working with you. Really. They should. Like you get for looking after orphans or keeping cripples.'

'Just don't go giving your diseases to me. That's all. And quit sniffing so much.'

'It's a human disease. How *could* I give it to you?'

Quemada nodded. It wasn't a bad one. Then he gulped

down some coffee and looked at the list they had got from Ordoñez.

Velasco watched him, then said, 'Way I see it is we just work our way through the list and see what they got to say.'

'This time in the morning? You want the Captain's desk to be knee-deep in complaints when he wakes up? Half these guys are probably married in the first place. We wake 'em up at two in the morning, say "Mr Sanchez home, we'd like to ask him about his boyfriends?", you're talking law suits.'

'Like someone keeps saying, this *is* a murder inquiry.'

'Yeah. But that doesn't mean we don't use our heads. Sure, someone needs to check this list out, but I think we'd best leave that to the Captain to decide when and how.'

'We gotta do something with it.'

'Yeah.' Quemada picked up a phone book, weighed it in his hand. 'If the guy we want *is* on this list, you think he's going to use his real name?'

Velasco pulled a face that said: maybe, maybe not.

'Why don't we just go through these names and see maybe whether any of them aren't real?' he asked.

'OK,' said Quemada. 'On the other hand, if you were going to use a place like this just for the usual stuff – you know, the fistfucking, the oral things, all that kind of stuff – would *you* leave your real name? I mean. *Would* you?'

'Yeah. But let's do it anyway.'

Quemada shrugged and picked up the A–M phone book. 'I'll start at the beginning, you start at the end. Race you to the middle.'

Velasco grunted, picked up the N–Z phone book and began looking.

Thirty minutes later, Quemada stopped and stared at the list. He'd been ticking in red, Velasco in green. Every one had a tick mark by the name, bar one.

'I don't believe it,' said Quemada. 'These guys ring up

151

and say "send me a new boyfriend, the old one burst", and just leave their names and addresses, just like that. Shit, half of 'em leave their credit card numbers too. I can just see old Felipe: "American Express, sir, yes that will do *nicely*." Unbelievable.'

'You oughta get off this queer thing, Quemada. They say those who bitch the most got the most to hide.'

'Yeah?'

'Yeah.'

'Well, they best not fucking say it to me, not while I'm hearing.'

Velasco looked at the one cross. 'Some joker. Miguel Ratón, Hotel Inglaterra.'

'Maybe he was just passing through without Minnie and got to feeling a little lonely.'

'Disney ought to sue.'

'Yeah. You know, they once did a cartoon where Mickey and Minnie were doing it. For real, you know?'

'For *real*?'

'Yeah. It was a joke.'

'You don't say.'

'It was a joke. They did it for Disney's birthday or something. Screened it at the party, Mickey humping Minnie. I read it in a magazine.'

'Really?'

'Disney watched the movie, asked who did it – apparently the drawing was real good – then fired them all. After the party, after he got the presents.'

'You read some crappy magazines.'

'Thanks, partner,' said Quemada. 'Thanks a lot.'

He scanned the list again. 'Nothing. Every one checks out, right address, right phone number.'

'Yeah,' said Velasco. 'Old Felipe's not so great at typing in the phone numbers though.'

Quemada waited.

'Like this one here.'

He pointed to an entry with a tick beside it. It read: Luis Romero, 3 Calle de Calderon, telephone 5167678. It showed a contact with the Angel Brothers four months before.

'The number's wrong. Way wrong. I made a note of the right one. It's 5123397. Bad typing.'

'Maybe it's a different number for him. A work number or something.'

'No. Don't you know anything about telephone codes? There isn't a local exchange that begins 516. It's all done on an area by area thing. I know. I had to try to get some phone fraud guy once. Believe me, it is not easy. But there's no way that number can be right. Watch.'

Velasco popped the hands-free button on the desk phone and listened for the dial tone. Then he dialled the number. All they got was a long low continuous whistle. He dialled the number again. The same thing happened.

'That is *not* a real telephone number, and it never was. Maybe it was a mistake,' Velasco wondered.

'Maybe. But the guy couldn't have deliberately left the wrong number to disguise who he was. Otherwise why would he have left his name and address? He must have done it when he booked, make sure no one rang back or something.'

Quemada thought for a while, then began flicking through his notes.

'You remember when Felipe said he closed down the office? What time?'

'Three. Three in the morning,' said Velasco. 'Lot of late trade, I guess.'

Quemada looked at his watch. It was 2.30 am.

'There's something we should have asked,' he said, dialling the number. Ordoñez answered immediately.

153

'Señor Ordoñez, it's Detective Quemada, we spoke earlier, you have my card? Yes, sir.' Quemada silently echoed the word 'sir' to himself incredulously across the empty office. 'I'm sorry to have to trouble you again. But there is one thing; I'd be grateful if you could look it up on your computer. It won't take a minute and then we won't disturb you again.'

Quemada waited. He could hear the office chair shuffling across the office, the beeps and whirrs of the computer.

'You got your database in front of you? No. OK. I'll wait. Fine. No problem. That's OK now? What I was wondering, sir, was whether you had any entry for someone called Freddy Famiani, an American.'

Quemada listened, nodded, then put his hand over the mouthpiece.

'He's looking Famiani up. He remembers him. Remembers the American.'

'Jesus,' said Velasco. 'You never can tell . . .'

'You had one booking for Mr Famiani? Yes, sir. He asked for his money back because the guy never showed? Fine. And the name. Is this someone you've met, sir, someone you've spoken to? No. I see. Always pays cash, by post or through the door, always books over the phone. Fine. I am very grateful. Have a nice evening.'

Quemada put down the phone, scribbled something on the pad then looked at his partner.

'Friday night, Freddy Famiani fixed a date with Luis Romero. Says Romero never showed.'

Velasco tapped his pen on the table and gave a little grin. 'You want to wake that shit Menéndez or should I do it?'

19

An hour later, four police cars were speeding across town into what passed for middle-class suburbia. The streets were still not empty. Crowds, dull from drink and sullen from tiredness, hung around street corners. The gaiety had gone. Now it was just late. Menéndez was in the first car, with Velasco and Quemada. In the three other vehicles were twelve officers, all in uniform, all armed. Four of them were from the special services squad. They had specific training in dealing with armed sieges. Two were from the police shooting team that, a year before, had won the national rifle trophy in Valencia.

Quemada asked, 'What do we do, Lieutenant?'

Menéndez watched the streets roll by, high walls, lit by wrought-iron lamps. 'We knock on the door and ask. What else would we do?'

Quemada grimaced out of the window, into the night. 'This guy, he's not exactly the sort to let us cuff him and walk away, is he?'

Menéndez disagreed. 'Maybe. If we come upon him out of the blue, he's exactly the sort to do that.'

'You mean, all that psychology stuff.'

'If that's what you want to call it.'

The car turned right, into a dead-end avenue, then drew up outside a drive guarded by a high iron gate. They got out and waited for the cars behind.

'Yeah,' said Quemada to his partner, 'if he starts chucking

them darts around I for one don't intend trying to *psych* him into surrendering. Those boys can sort it out. That's what they're paid for.'

Velasco shook his head. 'Just leave it to the Lieutenant, huh? He knows what he's doing.'

'Yeah. Leave it to the Lieutenant. One of us gets killed maybe he'll make Captain even sooner,' Quemada said sourly and kicked at the gravel in the drive.

Ten feet ahead of them Menéndez felt for the latch on the gate, found there was no padlock, opened it and walked through. The rest of the team followed him. The house was a modern two-storey villa surrounded by a large garden. A kidney-shaped pool shimmered under the light of the moon at the far end. The garden was overloaded with the night perfume of flowers. Under a scummy lean-to sun cover set against the house stood a Mercedes four-door saloon.

Quemada looked at it and whispered, 'Guy's got money, OK. Could afford a few boyfriends if that's what he wanted.'

There were no lights on inside the house. The front door and all the ground-floor windows were covered by wrought-ironwork frames, all closed. Menéndez gently shook the one on the front door. It was locked. He turned to the officer from the special services unit carrying the sledgehammer, saw the reaction, and shook his head.

Quemada looked at the armed men and said to Velasco, 'Shit, you see they're wearing vests. How come they get vests and we don't? How come?'

'Because if there's shooting they're the ones who're going to have to deal with it.'

'Too right,' said Quemada and started to wonder about how much the Mercedes was worth.

Menéndez reached forward and pressed the illuminated doorbell. From inside the house came a long, metallic sound, like a gong. They could hear it echoing down long, bare corridors, searching for a response and failing to find it. Menéndez pressed it again, then once more, and waited. Velasco and Quemada wondered what was going to happen next. There was no easy way they could get in, not in the night, not without knowing what was in there.

Then, on the second storey, a light came on, low and yellow. A bedside light, just an ordinary thing. They heard noises from inside, someone moving. More lights, more sounds, coming closer. With an abrupt, loud rattle the door was drawn back. Quemada and Velasco unconsciously stepped backwards, behind the uniformed team. They watched the uniformed men, hands on the hilts of their guns, tense and expectant in the dark. The armed team stood a good three yards behind Menéndez who was leaning on the iron doorguard, looking for whoever was inside. Then the porchlight came on, the door opened and a tired, female figure, in a long, drab dressing gown, confronted Menéndez.

Quemada and Velasco relaxed a little, moved forward and, without thinking, found themselves between the armed team and Menéndez. They wanted to hear what came next.

'Mrs Romero? We are police officers,' said Menéndez.

The woman peered at him, nodded, then tried to see beyond him, into the dark. She looked as if she needed glasses; she was squinting to try to make out who was beyond the Lieutenant.

'What do you want?' she said quietly. 'What time is it?'

'We would like to speak with your husband. I am sorry about the lateness, but it is important.'

She stared at him and Velasco found himself patting the gun in his holster just in case. She looked more than a little crazy.

'You want to speak to my husband? You are police, and you want to speak to my *husband?*'

157

'Yes.'

'Is this a joke? Some kind of a joke you are playing?'

Menéndez was silent. Something had been nagging him ever since Quemada and Velasco had woken him up. Something had been stirred, something about the name: Luis Romero. He tried to think: what? He thought of the reports, the incidents that had crossed his desk, incidents he knew intimately. Then, there was a hiatus. He had taken a holiday: a brief week spent driving along the coast. He had returned, run through the log to check what had happened while he was away, looked to see if anything had required his attention . . . and it was there. Luis Romero was there, buried, quiescent, half forgotten.

He looked at the pale, sad woman and said, 'I am sorry. There has been a mistake. I can only apologise. But I must speak with you. Please.'

'Now?'

He nodded and she started to unlock the doorguard.

The Lieutenant turned to his men and dismissed the uniformed team. They disappeared into the night, disappointment hanging over them like a cloud, leaving Quemada and Velasco alone with him.

'Isn't he at home?' asked Velasco. 'There some problem?'

Menéndez thrust his hands into his jacket pocket, waited for her to push open the ironwork frame, then headed for the house.

'Luis Romero committed suicide two months ago. It was in the reports. I should have remembered.'

'Two *months*?' said Quemada.

'Shit,' muttered Velasco, then followed Menéndez into the house.

Teresa Romero sat on a cream sofa in the living room underneath a broad, modern canvas. Menéndez felt he ought to recognise it but the name escaped him. Quemada and Velasco occupied dining chairs to one side, silent, making notes. The woman looked as if she were on the edge. Her hair was lank, long, stringy. It hung down lifeless to her thin shoulders, her tan was pale and dun. She was, perhaps, fifty, thought Menéndez, but her features, burned away by what – anguish? fear? life? – seemed much older. There was something both haunted and haunting in her eyes.

'I am sorry,' Menéndez repeated. 'We did not link your husband's name with the information we had. That was a mistake. I apologise.'

She clutched a glass of brandy. It was close to four in the morning.

'What do you want to know?' It was as if she feared the question.

'Mrs Romero . . .' Menéndez struggled for a beginning and found himself wishing Maria were with them. 'We are investigating some serious crimes and we came across your husband's name.'

Nothing changed in her face. She didn't want to ask the question.

'Clearly, at least one occasion when someone used his name it was a deliberate lie, since it was last week. But I do need to know if that was always the case. I need to know what kind of company he kept.'

She drank some brandy. 'Do you know who my husband was?'

'Something at the university? I'm trying to remember.'

'He was a history professor. He was "the history man".' She looked at him to see if he got the reference, then laughed dryly when she saw it was lost.

'He was a popular professor?'

Teresa Romero laughed again, drank some more brandy. 'Oh, yes. He was *popular*. Every day, every evening. He was there or somewhere else, being *popular*. Here.'

159

She got up, walked to a side table, picked up a photograph and gave it to Menéndez.

'Here. What do you see?'

It was a portrait, slightly posed, of a man in his late forties, wearing an open-necked shirt of a floral design, raising a glass to the camera. There was a gold bracelet on his wrist, a gold chain around his sunburned neck. His hair was brown and frizzy. He had a moustache and a broad, sunny smile.

'A professor of history?' She leaned over him and he could smell the drink. 'Or some little play actor trying to pretend he's still twenty-five years old?'

She stumbled over to the sofa and sat down.

'Was your husband a homosexual?' Menéndez asked.

'No,' she said straight away. 'Not that. He liked women, he liked history. There are plenty of people out there who can tell you. I was just married to the man. I have no idea.'

'Do you know if he used gay dating agencies? We found his name in the records of one.'

She thought about the question. 'No. I can't believe that was him.'

She spoke in a dreamy, disjointed way.

Menéndez pulled a sheet of paper out of his pocket. On it were the names from Abraxas. He passed it to her.

'Do you recognise any of these people?'

She went down the list, one by one, then said, 'No.'

'Was he interested in bullfighting?'

'Oh, yes. Blood, thunder, passion. He loved that. He used to follow one in particular. You know, the pretty one, with the blond hair.'

'El Guapo?' asked Velasco.

'Yes. Him. Every fight. I think Luis knew him slightly.'

'And religion?'

She stared at him. 'Are you serious?'

'Was he involved in any of the Semana Santa activities? Did he belong to any of the brotherhoods?'

'My husband was an anarchist who hated everything to do with the church, Lieutenant. The only thing he liked about Semana Santa was the corrida at the end.'

'I see.'

Menéndez rose from the chair. 'It's late.'

'Is it?' she asked.

'Mrs Romero?'

She was drifting away somewhere, the questions were starting to go past her.

'Why do you think your husband killed himself?'

She snorted, spilling brandy down the front of her dressing gown.

'Why?'

'He seemed a happy man. His lifestyle may have been unconventional. But, from the picture, he didn't look unhappy.'

She gazed out of the window. There was a hint of dawn in the sky.

'I don't know,' she said. 'For the last ten years I didn't know Luis. He was not the man I married. He became someone else, someone chasing this *youth* he never had. I never knew *what* was happening in his mind. And besides . . .'

Menéndez watched her hesitate, then overcome her reluctance.

'Besides?'

She put down the glass on the table with a look of distaste on her face. 'I drink this shit. God knows why. I blame Luis and it is not his fault.'

Teresa Romero pulled her dressing gown around her and gazed at him. 'They came, Lieutenant, they came and told me that one night my husband drove his car into the Alfabia

161

park, drank half a bottle of whisky, took out a penknife, then cut his own wrists. Then they say what you say: "Why?" Lieutenant, I may not have known my husband well these past few years, but some things never change. Luis was a coward. I couldn't get him to take a shot when we went abroad. He hated the idea of blood, of cuts, of anything surgical. He could have killed himself, he had something inside him that made him capable of that. But not this way. Not Luis. It would have been pills, something like that.'

'So what do you think happened?'

'You ask me, I say exactly what I told your people before. I don't care what you think, someone killed him.'

Menéndez said nothing.

'I am not a hysterical, bereaved widow, Lieutenant. I was not when this happened. I am not now. But I knew enough of Luis to know that he would *not* do this to himself. Many other things, but not this.'

'I see.'

'Do you?'

She picked up a packet of cigarettes, opened it, thought better of the idea, then put it back on the table.

'What happens between a man and a woman when they are married, married for years, no one sees. No one sees that, Lieutenant. Not even the people themselves. It all happens invisibly, behind, around us, and if we notice it we are too polite to mention it.'

'Why would anyone *want* to kill your husband?'

'I have no idea. No idea at all.'

Menéndez pocketed his book, racked his brain for more questions. None came. He got up to leave and the detectives moved to follow him.

'Mrs Romero,' said Menéndez, 'you say your husband was a professor of history?'

'Yes.'

'What was his speciality?'

Teresa Romero changed her mind, picked up the cigarettes and lit one. 'Luis was a fine historian, Lieutenant. No one can take that from him. He began as a classicist but for the past decade he really has had only one subject area. His field was the history of the Civil War.'

'In the city?'

'Why, yes. Without the city there would *be* no history.'

'No,' said Menéndez flatly. 'I suppose not. But he was particularly involved in the history of the war in the city? What happened here? This may be important.'

She stared at him, surprised by the pressure behind the question. 'I think so. You should ask his colleagues. I was never privileged to hear the fine detail of what interested him.'

'No,' Menéndez said and signalled to Quemada and Velasco to leave. When they had gone, he said, 'I will let you know what happens.'

'About what?'

'Your husband's death. The causes.'

'Lieutenant,' said Teresa Romero, 'you do not understand. Luis may have been killed. No. He *was* killed. But I do not *care*. It is a matter of no importance to me. He is dead and my life has not changed.'

Menéndez nodded and looked once more at the canvas: Miró. Now he could make out the imagery: sun, bulls, blood, death.

'No,' he said and walked outside into the fresh morning air.

20

The phone rang on the bedside table. Maria was dragged abruptly from a bottomless slumber, spent a moment trying to work out where she was, then picked it up. The little green digital clock by the bed said eight: she felt she could have slept for ever.

'Good morning, Maria.'

It was Torrillo. For a moment she wondered why she thought it might have been somebody else. Then she remembered the curious call the night before. She tried to assemble her thoughts. It wasn't easy.

'I'm sorry, Bear. I overslept. It's not like me.'

'No problem. There are plenty of people here going to oversleep too. It's been a busy night.'

'Has there been another killing?' She winced at the sudden excitement she felt. It seemed improper, it had a prurience she felt did not belong to her.

'No,' replied Bear, 'but it's been busy all the same. Some of the night guys picked up a lead. We're starting to get some names to chase and that always makes people happy.'

'I'll be there in fifteen minutes once I've got dressed.'

'Lieutenant says not to bother. He'd like you to go straight to Caterina Lucena, visit her in the hospital. See if you can get her to talk about the war. We've got some things to chase this end. He'd like a conference at twelve noon; we'll try to get down to things there.'

'He really does want me to go on my own?'

'Seems to think it's essential. That old bird won't be talking to the likes of us.'

Maria wondered what simple instinct told them she would fare any better.

'You can get there OK?'

'I can walk from here.'

'If you like. When you need a car, call and we'll send one.'

'I will.'

'And good luck.'

Torrillo rang off. She marvelled at his brightness so early in the morning. It was not an academic habit. She pulled herself out of bed, showered, ate a little breakfast in her dressing gown, then changed. A simple pair of dark slacks, a white blouse. She remembered the way Caterina Lucena had looked at her jeans.

At twenty to nine, she walked downstairs, let herself out of the front door, and set off on the ten-minute walk to the hospital.

At nine thirty, when the opticians opened, a young man in a light-blue uniform with the name of the city's electricity company embroidered on the left shoulder, finished his coffee in the corner café opposite the apartment, crossed the street and walked into the shop. The optician, an aloof, patrician figure in a white nylon jacket, stood behind the counter. He wore expensive tortoiseshell spectacles and the officious air of the semi-professional. He stared at the visitor with faintly disguised distaste.

'You want some glasses?'

'No,' said the man in the uniform. 'Miss Gutierrez rang us from her office. Said she thought she had a problem with the power supply and it was urgent we should have a look at it. She was out and couldn't hand over the keys herself. Said you had a spare set and would let us borrow them.'

The optician stared at him.

'She said nothing to us.'

The workman shrugged. 'Nothing to do with me. You want to let me in, you don't want to let me in. Either way. But you'd best ring her first. We have to come out a second time there's an extra charge. All I want to do is look at the meter. See it's running properly.'

The optician polished the glass counter with a small yellow duster.

'I'll send in one of the girls. She can watch you.'

'Fine,' said the workman.

'You got some tools?'

'Like I said. All I need to do is read the meter. See it's OK.'

The optician reached beneath the counter and pulled out a set of three keys. Then he put them on the counter.

'Gina?'

A pretty teenage girl with shoulder-length auburn hair came out from a back room. She was wearing a pink overall and, in her hand, carried a wire-framed pair of spectacles. The optician nodded across the counter.

'He wants to check the meter on the flat. It's at the bottom of the stairs, just behind the door. He doesn't go any further.'

She looked at him and smiled. He looked nice.

'It's the brass Chubb,' said the optician as he handed her the keys.

They walked out of the shop door, turned left and she turned the key in the lock.

'He always that cheerful?'

She giggled, said nothing, then pushed the door, and they were inside. The entrance hall was dark. She pushed the light switch; it was on a timer. He could hear it clicking away the seconds as he closed the door behind them.

'It's in there.' She pointed to a cupboard held by a single latch. He opened it, then looked at the dials and switches inside: ordinary stuff.

'Is it OK?' the girl asked. 'We're on the same circuit, you know. Once, they cut the flat off and we had to close the shop too.'

He stood up and said, smiling, 'No problem. Just a false alarm.'

She wondered how old he was: thirty, maybe older. The moustache didn't suit him. His hairstyle could be improved too.

'OK. I got to go back to the shop now.'

The workman scribbled something in a pad he'd taken out of his pocket.

'Yeah. Let me lock up for you.'

He took the keys from her hand, briefly put them inside the big wide waist pocket, put a hand on her back and they walked out of the door. The light switch was still ticking: at least two minutes. He pulled the door shut, put the brass key in the lock and gave it a half turn.

'You need to do that?' asked the girl.

'Yes. Some of these locks need an extra turn,' he said then tried to pull the key out. It didn't come.

'Shit,' he said. 'It's stuck.'

She looked at him doe-eyed and mute.

He reached into his toolbag and pulled out a screwdriver. 'Won't be a moment.'

She watched him unscrew a panel at the back of the lock, move some levers with the blade, waggle the key around, then pull it out from the front.

He wiped the key with his hands then took a good look at it. 'No damage done. Just a bit stiff, that's all.'

Then he handed her back the set.

She walked back into the shop under the baleful gaze of the optician. He felt, in his pocket, the wad of putty, knew the impression would hold, then set off home.

21

Caterina Lucena sat upright in bed in a tiny private room of the Hospital of the Sisters of Mercy. Maria had only seen her before on the day after the discovery of the bodies. It was natural, then, that she had been distressed. Now, in the hospital room, she seemed a changed person. Her skin had taken on a grey sallowness it had not previously possessed, yet there was also a calm about her Maria had not expected.

Sunlight streamed through an enormous window by the bed. The room had a high ceiling, with plaster ornamentation almost hidden by years of rough painting. It felt like what it was: an old servant's room in a mansion now given over to the public good. A nun, dressed in grey and white, brought the drinks they had asked for: a lemon tea for Maria, hot water for Caterina Lucena. She smiled at them, then left and Maria searched for a way to begin, until she was saved the task.

'Tell the policeman I am grateful.'

'I am sorry. I don't understand.'

'The nuns told me. This room, it is from some police charity. I could not afford it myself. Tell him, I am grateful.'

'I will.' She nodded and sipped her tea. It was lukewarm and had a metallic taste. 'How do you feel?'

She smiled. 'I am old. I always feel this way. They call it the onset of pneumonia. Perhaps. I feel no better, no worse, than I would usually, except that they do not allow me my manzanilla, which is, perhaps, for the best. In any case, I do not miss it. They are kind. They do not ask questions. They accept me for what I am: a lonely old woman near the end of her life. Their faith in God is touching. I wish I had it.'

Maria listened to the birdsong outside the window and thought there could be worse places to end one's life. 'I am sure you will get better.'

'Yes,' she said. 'You are trying to be kind. The young always do this with the old. Treat us like children. But you want to ask questions too. Or you hope to.'

Maria put down the tea and looked at the old woman on the bed. There was a strength to her, an inner steeliness, however frail the body that enclosed it.

'I am not a policewoman. I am not a professional interrogator. I imagine it shows.'

'It shows,' she said. 'And that is why they sent you. The Lieutenant is no fool. He does not know as much as he thinks he knows, but he is no fool. There are more killed?'

Maria nodded.

'I thought so. They do not give me the newspapers. They treat me like a senile old woman. But I knew, if there were more killed, you would be back.'

'What is it that the Lieutenant does not know which he should?'

Caterina Lucena seemed to be looking right through her, eyes burning deep in their wrinkled sockets.

'They are excluded from this. Men. They cannot belong.'

'From what?' asked Maria and, from nowhere, an image she had seen once before crossed slowly, tentatively in front of her vision: an image of a white bird, headless, descending slowly out of a pure blue sky, blood pumping droplets of scarlet from its severed neck. She shook her head and it disappeared.

'From the flow of life and death that runs through the

world,' said the old woman and Maria felt the room turn deathly cold. 'It flows only from us; when it is taken away, it is owed only to us.'

Maria was shivering. The room looked smaller than before, the light had turned from a golden warmth to a different colour, bright, cold, harsh. There was a craziness about the woman that frightened her. 'I'm not sure I understand . . .'

'You will. They will hurt you, they will dominate you, but in the end you will understand. And you will defeat them, through the pain. That is the gift we have, the gift they hate us for because they can never take it away.'

Maria looked at her hands and saw they were shaking. She held them together and they steadied, slowly. The blood returned, warmth returned, the room resumed its earlier appearance.

'He has sent you here to ask about the war,' said the old woman on the bed in a voice that sounded centuries old. 'He knows I will never tell it to him. He knows I have *never* told it to anyone else. He believes you can unlock the secret. Why does he believe that of you?'

'I don't know,' she said.

'Because he knows that they have marked your past too. He can recognise the scars.'

Luis? she thought. Were the scars so visible? Or were they simply records in a file somewhere?

'To be hurt by someone you love, that is more painful than being hurt by someone you hate,' said Caterina Lucena.

Maria dug her nails into her palms, summoned herself. 'How do you know these things? Where does it come from?'

'I look, I see. '

She laughed. It was the sound of dry leaves crushed softly underfoot.

'So,' said Caterina Lucena, 'you would like to hear about La Soledad?'

No, thought Maria, no, no, no. I would like to hear of anything else. I would like to hear of music, of flowers, of sunshine, of cool patios, running water, the sound of laughter, children, the light. I would like to hear a conversation that inspired me, that filled me with life. I would like to hear of life, of kindness, of gratitude.

The green mask and the red velvet walls

'Yes,' she said. 'I would like to hear about La Soledad.'

And for a moment the dove returned, ten feet tall, in front of her face, blood pumping relentlessly into the air.

When she recovered, when the scream deep within her had faded towards nothingness, she looked at the old woman. There was a sense of triumph on the grey, wrinkled face.

22

When the war began, she had just turned fourteen. The Lucena family lived in the old family mansion in Carmona, then a suburb of a scant few upper-class homes, set on broad, dusty streets lined with palm trees, marked, sporadically, by dark-brown piles of dung left by the carriages that people still preferred, even though most could afford a car. She was the youngest: three brothers and a sister stood over her, from sixteen to twenty-one, and took care to define her position in the household, which was that of the infant. From as far back as she could remember, they had kept her apart. Caterina would be too *young* to understand something. She would not be ready for the games they played, the circles they moved in. When Papa's important friends came to visit, she was the first to be told to leave the room. *They* were allowed to stay, at least for a little while, to be privy to the news and gossip that came, from Madrid, from Barcelona, from Palma. She would sit outside the room, listening to the whispers beyond the door, like the fluttering of moths' wings in the dark; anger, injustice, burning her face.

She was the youngest, the baby. Yet weeks before, as she lay on her bed, hot, covered in sweat, in the sweltering afternoon, she had felt a burning pain in the pit of her stomach, had looked down at her light afternoon shift and seen the dark stain of red at her groin. She had held herself, through the fine cotton, felt the thick dampness seep through the fabric and stain her fingers, watched the mark grow until it streaked the dainty, embroidered coverlet of the bed. Then she had carefully removed the shift, folded it on the bed to leave the stain facing uppermost, bathed, cleaned herself and changed into fresh clothes. She left the shift there as a sign. To say: I am growing, I am becoming like you. Then she went downstairs and walked from room to room, her face shining, eyes radiant. When finally she returned to her room, the shift was gone, the coverlet had been changed. She waited for someone to speak: her mother, her father, her sister. Even a maid. But it was as if the thing had never existed. Three times it had happened, once each month, with the same brief, aching pain, the heat, the sweat, the tremors, and then the blood. Three times she had left the sign of her change on the bed. Three times it had been removed without a word. And there was no one she could ask, no one she could speak to. The family was growing more apart, retreating from her, retreating from each other.

She did not understand.

As the summer wore on, Papa ceased to leave the house, except on rare occasions when he needed to see the bank. He spoke to her only rarely. He seemed preoccupied, his reserved, handsome face now looked gaunt and worried. There was an affliction there that she could not recognise, an interior, wasting concern that seemed to be without cure. Her mother, who now retreated into herself more than ever, scarcely seemed to acknowledge what was happening. Daily life became disjointed, a routine of meals, taken in silence, or interrupted by minor items of news, of gossip. Then vast, empty hours in which she was left to roam the house on her own, reading books, talking to the servants.

It was like being in the garden during the approach of a great storm. She could feel the pressure building, the change

in the atmosphere, the close, clammy approach of catastrophe. Yet all around her, the family seemed to wish to
pretend that nothing had changed. Life was a parody of
what it had been before. The same events were enacted as
if by rote, as if by reliving the ritual, the past – was it a
happy past? she wondered – could be magically revived and
made real in the present.

One night, when the heat was so strong that she could
not sleep, she sat upright in her bed, alone in the room
that overlooked the garden, listening, waiting. Outside, the
world seemed disturbed. There were sounds, foreign
sounds, of soldiers and horses, heavy, unfamiliar carriages,
and, all around, that strange, aggressive voice that men used
when they were trying to prove that they were men. From
downstairs she could hear shouting, getting louder and
louder. It was her mother's voice, high and hysterical and
accusatory, and the words seemed to go round and round
in an everlasting circle: 'Why did you have to take sides?
Why? Why? Why?'

She listened, but there was no reply.

There had been premonitions before. When a cousin had
written her a letter, she had foreseen its arrival even before
the postman arrived in the drive. When her father had left
for the office without his umbrella, she had been able to
tell why he had returned prematurely, even before he spoke.
Her father had recognised this too, in his way. He called
her 'our little gypsy' and looked at her through those
troubled, brown eyes as if apologising. As if he were trying
to say: I am sorry, this is the best I can offer in the circumstances. It is not enough. And for that I am sorry.

That night she did not know whether she was asleep or
awake, whether the terror that gripped her was the product
of a dream or a real, deadly premonition of the darkness
that was about to engulf them. As the light began to fail,

she lay on her bed, straight, rigid, hands behind her head, staring at the ceiling, listening to the voices downstairs subside. She thought she heard the sound of her mother sobbing, and wondered if that could be true. Her mother did not cry like this. It was not what was expected of a Lucena, even one who had married into the line. But then it became unmistakable, a rhythmic, breathy sobbing that sounded sadder than anything Caterina had ever heard.

Outside, in the hot, thick, semi-tropical dark, there was the brief sound of a gunshot and, on her big, iron-framed bed, comfy on the feather mattress, Caterina shivered. The beads of sweat turned icy on her skin and, for a moment, she felt she was quite alone in the world. Nothing stood between her and the stars. God was now absent from the universe and in his place was a great, all-enveloping blackness, cold, inhuman, capable of flicking away her tiny existence as if it were a mote of dust floating idly in a sunlit room.

Caterina shivered again, closed her eyes and tried to sleep. The night gave way to vague shifting shapes of deep, dark red, shapes that lumbered and twisted through her consciousness, unformed, unspeaking, unremitting, like huge faceless phantoms of living tissue, dancing through the night. They had no eyes, no faces, yet somehow they were human. And they did human things too, things she only half understood. Limbs formed from the red, bleeding tissue, formed, then opened and closed on each other. Huge torsos rose and fell, pushing, twitching, writhing against each other, blood spurting from dark cavities that appeared then vanished. This was the world, an endless procession of blood and tissue and muscle, intertwined, intertwining, ever restless, ever in agony. And behind it there was a sound, a deep low moaning that mixed pain and ecstasy with animal grunts that hovered around the edges of words, real words,

words Caterina only half began to comprehend. Words she feared, for the effect they might have on her.

She watched two phantasms writhe to the centre stage of her nightmare, grip each other, sometimes half human in form, at other times a mass of sinew and flesh. Then they separated and, briefly, took on a dimly recognisable shape. Arms formed from the trunk, large and fleshy, each ending in a reddened point streaked with veins and arteries. There was a head, a body, and then legs, fat as tree trunks. From somewhere came a sound like high-pitched laughter, but wrong. It was too forced, too rapid, too mechanical. There was something *liquid* about it too, she realised, and for a moment she thought her sanity would leave her. Then the creatures embraced, shockingly. One fell onto its back, the huge tree legs opened to reveal a vast, blood-red cavity in the crotch, and its mate changed shape, transformed into something massive and threatening. It bent down, towards the cavernous hole, entered it, pushed, joined with the flesh, pushed and shouted in joyous, ecstatic screams. The world shook. It comprised nothing but this image, of two things consuming each other. She watched as the one below divided, was split in two by its partner, then they joined in a single, twisting mass of meat, rolling in the waves of blood that gushed around them, a vast red ocean possessed of a heat she could feel on her skin, with a smell that mixed blood with something more fundamental, some base human essence.

Caterina closed her eyes but the obscenity was still there, still real in front of her. She looked up, to the sky, to God. It was a clear, cloudless night. The stars were bright against a deep blue darkness, unfamiliar shapes, constellations she did not recognise. She was beyond the world, beyond the universe.

There was a light in the centre of the sky and it came

closer. As it did, she recognised the form. It was a dove, pure white, a radiant, iridescent white that made her want to shield her eyes from the ferocity of its pureness. As it came closer, she heard a single, monotonous sound: an unchanging, high-pitched musical tone from an instrument she could not recognise that seemed to come from every direction simultaneously.

The dove drew nearer. It was flapping its wings with a lazy, slow regularity. She could see every feather moving gently in the air, backwards and forwards, the wing tips translucent, the stars shining through them.

It came closer, closer, until it was hovering, still with an impossible slowness, only inches from her face, staring at her with a single eye. She could feel the air being gently displaced by its tiny, beating wings. She could examine every inch of its unblemished body. It *shone* with a blazing, chaste light that had a preternatural intensity, shone inches in front of her face, dazzling her with its radiance.

Caterina looked at its head. The half-open beak was yellow, the colour of newly ripened corn under the sun. It held its head still as its wings beat slowly in the air. There was a nobility, a majesty, about the creature which filled her with awe.

She looked into its eye and this alone seemed wrong. It was dark, with a faint white circle of iris near the rim. She stared at it, then, with a shock she could not explain, realised that the bird was blind. If this was God, it was a God that could not see and this seemed more terrible than anything else in the nightmare. She gazed into its deep black eye, searching for recognition, but there was none. Then something changed. The black centre seemed to alter shape, its colour turned darker. It was a swirling tiny mass of liquid that shifted tone the more she stared at it.

Caterina watched, unable to look away, as a pinpoint of

bright blood appeared in the centre of the retina. It grew, like a tiny scarlet whirlpool, grew larger and larger. A drop fell from the bird's beak and stained the perfect feathers of its chest. She began to scream, but no sound came out of her mouth. The bird was now no messenger from God. Its eyes were red pits. A steady stream of blood dripped out of the corn-yellow beak, luminescent red pearls against the velvet sky.

Caterina tried to cover her eyes with her hands but the vision remained. It was there, always there, always demanding to be seen. She looked at her fingers. They were covered in blood. Its blood. The bird opened its beak. Wide. Wider than was possible. Its throat was a pool of vivid, eddying red.

There was the sound of wings, larger wings. Black shadows hovered over her and the smell returned: fetid, miasmic yet somehow terribly human.

This time the dove screamed and it sounded like a child in agony, in terror. She watched as its head exploded in a cloud of gore that erupted everywhere. It spattered her face, it flew into her mouth. She could feel its brains on her tongue. The world went black, then white, then red. She felt herself turned upside down, flung down a long, narrow tunnel into hell.

White light. Bright white light. She was awake. In her room. It was morning. The sun streamed through the open window. Outside came the street noise, loud, unfamiliar, threatening. She looked down at herself. It was the heaviest she had known. It did not seem possible. A huge pool of dried blood soaked her nightdress from knee to waist. The coverlet beneath was ruined. She felt herself. The blood was warm and sticky but it had ceased to run. This was not sickness. This was *normal*. She looked at it on her fingers, dried in brown clots. She sniffed it and felt a sense of awe.

179

The room was no different. The world was only a little different. She had survived. There had been screams, there had been shouts, of that she was sure. And no one had come. *No one*.

Caterina looked at her fourteen-year-old fingers again and thought: I have met God and he failed me. I have loved my family and they have failed me. I bleed and I alone notice. But I am a Lucena and I shall not be defeated.

She poured herself a bath, stayed in the water for a good half-hour, came out clean, smelling of strong soap and talcum powder, wore a freshly pressed white dress, went down to breakfast, then walked through every room. Listening to their conversations, so full of fear and trepidation. Watching them look at her through a haze of condescension. They did not know, they could not see.

At ten in the morning she had returned to her room, tired of the tense wave of near-hysteria which seemed to have gripped the house, ashamed of their fear. She had changed into her favourite white and pink cotton dress, sketched a little: the courtyard from the window, light dappling the trees, the golden stone of the wall. She had ignored the noise from the street. It was irrelevant now. She had started a new book, *Kidnapped* by Robert Louis Stevenson, and entered a different world between its burnished green leather covers, with the title blocked in gold lettering. She had dozed, she had dreamed.

Somewhere close to midday a noise had woken Caterina Lucena. She had walked downstairs, looked into the courtyard, stood back in mute shock as another, louder noise ripped through the fabric of her world.

When she saw the dove fall in a flutter from the sky, headless, blood pumping from its neck, she realised, with a start that made her feel physically sick, that this time the nightmare would be real.

23

There were at least a dozen men. They wore coarse country clothes: rough jackets, heavy cotton trousers. They carried rifles over their shoulders or held them, threateningly, over an arm. Violence hung around them like flies around a dead animal. When Caterina tried to look into their eyes she found nothing there except the hint, distant and ominous, of dull, mute hatred.

With a start, she realised what they reminded her of: a hunting party.

They motioned the family into the back of a delivery van. Inside, in the airless darkness, Papa could not bear to look at anyone. He stared at the metal wall, his face lit haphazardly by a grilled window on each side. He seemed to be somewhere else. One of the boys, Fernando, she thought, said something and a man screamed at him, waving the gun. After that they were silent as the van bounced and lurched through the streets, silent except for the faint sobbing of her mother who sat with her hands over her eyes.

Caterina thought: if they were going to kill us, why didn't they kill us at the house? Why take us somewhere else?

It didn't make sense. But then, killing people didn't make sense. She found herself filled with a quiet, internal feeling of outrage. Not for what was happening, or might happen, in itself, but for the outright, naked *stupidity* of it all. 'Men's games.' She had heard her mother use the phrase during the night, when she had been berating Papa for 'taking sides'. These were 'men's games' and they were indescribably, ineffably stupid.

The van threw them around for what seemed like hours. She could sense the change in the air as they left the city and found the countryside. The smells of horse and car fumes disappeared, to be replaced by fields, manure, the dry dusty tang of crops waiting to be harvested. The sounds changed too. The birds were different; the space between their songs more pronounced. Gradually, the birdsong disappeared completely, then, with a bone-jarring lurch to the right, the van turned off the road, jounced over some rough ground and came to a stop.

Please, thought Caterina. *Do not open the doors. Make this a joke. Leave us here, rotting in our fear. All night if you wish. Let us stew in our own terror. Have your fun. Your men's fun.*

Then the doors opened, light spilled into the van, harsh and cruel and golden, and they looked out onto a landscape of utter desolation. Caterina heard her mother release a cry so desperate it made her shiver and she felt a collective dread enfold them like a soft, consuming cloak.

La Soledad.

The wilderness.

The grieving.

The camp had been built in a flat, shallow depression on dun, infertile ground just outside the city boundary. The landscape was bare and forbidding: dry rock and dust and sand. There was not a blade of grass or a sign of water anywhere. They were outside the twin main gates which were now opening to receive them. A little way off to the right was a single-storey white farmhouse, next to it a bull enclosure, then, a little further along, one of the training rings where the farmers tested their animals, sorting the fast from the slow, the brave from the cautious. A meagre herd of bulls stood motionless in the enclosure, mouths open, panting in the still summer air. They did not look like the creatures of the ring. They were thin and listless, bones jutted out from their haunches.

No sport there, Caterina.

The thought came from nowhere and she found herself shivering. She was damp again and didn't dare to see if it showed. Before they were shoved through into the camp, she turned and looked again at the farm. In the little practice ring, hung on the rickety fencing, stood the trappings of the corrida. Pikes, horse guards, darts with fading ribbons casually stuck into the woodwork. There was a stain in the sand too that looked recent. She shook her head, tried to look again, but an arm pushed her towards the gate and she obeyed.

La Soledad looked as if it had been made out of flotsam and jetsam collected from the beach. The enclosure was roughly the shape of a horsetrack: an oblong, rounded at each corner. The perimeter seemed impenetrable: a picket of wooden stakes, at least twelve feet tall, with ramshackle lean-to guard posts at each corner reached by ladders. From each guard post poked the long, silver-grey nose of a machine gun, with a khaki figure behind it, guarded from the sun by a makeshift palm roof. Beneath the post nearest the main gate was a small hut with the flag of the Falange fluttering idly from a window. Around the enclosure, in haphazard arrangements, were scattered simple low buildings, perhaps twenty, dilapidated hovels of scrap metal and wood, straw and occasional brick. A few had palm fronds extended at the front, on bamboo sticks. In the shade, men and women lay silently, still, without life. There were no chairs. There was no sound. She registered the smell of sewage. From behind a flimsy fence came the stench of an open latrine.

The family had entered together but soon they were split apart. The men with guns ordered her mother and father to a low, brown hut close to the latrines. The rest of the children were ordered to the opposite end of the camp, to a hut that looked like a converted sty. Caterina discreetly felt herself, felt the dampness between her legs and wondered, inwardly: how would she cope? There were no servants, there was no sign of water.

They were halfway across the dry dusty ground that formed the centre of the enclosure when she saw him. He was sitting on a chair in front of the guard post with the flag. He looked as if he had some kind of authority, just from the way he sat on the chair, idly, casually, rocking back and forth, a cigar in his mouth.

She saw him look at her, felt the unpleasant attention of his eyes, then turned away. He was behind her now. She could pretend he did not exist, follow her brothers and sisters to the hut, keep quiet, do as she was told, whatever. She could do it.

One of the guards leading them motioned the group to stop. She looked up. Overhead, black shapes were circling in the sun. She felt terribly thirsty. She blinked and when she opened her eyes he was standing in front of her. Looking. Smiling. The silence boomed all around her.

The man asked the guard for their names. He smiled when he heard.

'How old are you?' he asked Caterina.

She swallowed. It was hard to swallow in the heat.

'Fourteen, sir,' she said.

'Ah.' He towered over her, blocking out the sun. She wanted to look at him but found she could not.

'You don't look well, Caterina.'

She tried to swallow again.

'I would like a drink of water, sir. If that's possible.'

He laughed. 'It is possible. Come.'

The guard was glaring at him. 'Antonio . . . ?'

The man turned on him and Caterina could see his face for the first time now. It was caught by the full blast of the sun and quite astonished her. Antonio Alvarez looked like a film star: fine, high cheekbones; clear, lightly tanned skin; dark, intelligent eyes; a thin, dark moustache that almost seemed as if it had been drawn on his face, the line was so neat and straight and proper. He looked like the men she had seen in the cinema, men who had seemed more than human. Brave, dashing, honourable men. She could not take her eyes off him.

'Remember your place, *amigo*,' Alvarez said coldly and the guard was quiet.

'Come.'

They walked across the encampment, he in front, she following behind, a bewildered young girl in a pink and white cotton dress. He barked at the guards at the entrance. The timber gates swung slowly open. She followed him to the little white cottage, keeping the same distance behind all the way. When they reached the porch, he took out a key, opened the old, wooden door, painted a fading shade of deep blue, and waited for her to walk inside. It was cool and dark. Antonio Alvarez walked to one side and opened a ragged curtain. Light flooded one side of the room. She saw a desk with papers, a few chairs, an old sofa, a water basin with a jug on a low table beside it. Leading off to the left was a door that was ajar. Beyond was what looked like a double bed, unmade.

He walked to the little table, lifted the jug and poured her a glass of water.

'We have wine too here, Caterina. And brandy.'

She shook her head, gulped at the water, and said nothing. The room seemed to be boundless, with deep shadows at every corner. There was a smell, stale and organic, which she could not place.

'Are you ill?'

'Sir?'

She looked at him, trying to be as young as she could.

'You look ill. There is blood on your dress.'

She shook her head.

'It is nothing, sir. I am not ill. I would like to go back to my family.'

Alvarez looked around the big desk, found an oil lamp and lit it. A smoky yellow light fell on the unlit corners of the room.

'Before the war, you know what I did?'

'No, sir,' she said.

'I worked in the hospital. I helped sick people. People who were bleeding. Like you. I still help people. This is a good thing. Everything I tell you about, Caterina, *everything* will be a good thing.'

'I am not sick, sir. This just happens. It is not a sickness.'

'No,' said Alvarez. He drew the curtain closed, walked to the door and bolted it. 'But you should always do as the doctor tells you, Caterina. Didn't your mother tell you that?'

She could not see properly in the light. He shifted about in front of her in the dull yellow rays of the lamp. Then she felt his arms on her. And his breath.

'Do not be afraid,' he said.

She could feel the dress being lifted from her, mutely let him lead her to the bedroom.

'The only things I will show you will be good things,' he said.

But she screamed in agony at the pain that he brought,

186

screamed until he clamped his hand over her mouth, rocking, rocking above her, thrusting, filling her body with a brutal agony that seemed endless.

Then he screamed too, the world turned dark, revolved, seemed more dream than reality. They were in a place where good and evil coexisted hand in hand, were indivisible. They had gone there together.

He looked spent, the handsomeness had disappeared. His breath came in short, desperate pants. She felt down with her hand, felt between her legs, where the blood now lay like a soaking rag between them, felt this stiff thing that was still inside her, wondered what she had done to make this happen.

He pulled himself from her, rolled over on the bed, wiped the sheet against his groin, automatically, without thinking. She looked down, trying to see in the dim light what had happened to her. It was impossible.

His breathing became regular, he stared at the ceiling. Then he sat upright, swung his legs over the side of the bed, started to pull up his trousers. She wanted to say something. She wanted to apologise. She found herself bound to him in a way she did not understand.

He stood up, fastened his belt, put his hands in his pockets and looked at her, grinning. She could not read the expression. Suddenly, from nowhere, a terrible ache, a terrible soreness gripped her. She put her hand on the place, pushed gently, started to cry.

He leaned over and held her by the chin.

'Do what I say, Caterina, and only good things will happen to you. And your family too. This is a war. We walk a narrow path, life one side, death the other. We can both keep each other alive. If you do as I say.'

She nodded, then wondered if the movement of her head was of her own making or simply the force of his hand, holding so tightly it hurt. The tears stung her eyes. She wiped them with the sheet.

'There is a bath in the next room. Use it. I will lock the door behind me. That way you will not be disturbed. While I am out, I will see that your family is well looked after.'

He looked handsome again now. A little like someone she had seen in the movies, an American. He was a pirate in the movies.

The door closed. The room was now in almost total darkness. Only a dim light came through the closed curtains drawn against the small, square windows on either side of the room. She staggered to the bathroom, poured cold water in the tub, washed, slowly, mindlessly. Then she crawled back into the bed and fell asleep.

24

It was early evening. Outside, she could hear the sound of animals. Was it just animals? No. There were human voices too: an excited undercurrent of men, talking some way off. She could not make out the words but she could sense the tension in their voices.

Caterina got out of bed, put on her pink and white cotton dress, and started to try to make sense of the house. It was a tiny peasant's cottage: one bedroom, one living room, a small bathroom, a small kitchen. There was a door to the front and one at the back leading from the kitchen. Both were bolted from the inside. She did not dare try to see if they were locked.

Every window was covered with a ragged, heavy curtain that blocked out both light and heat. She pulled one back at what she thought was the rear of the farmhouse. It opened onto nothing: just a bare rock hillside rising behind her, a few prickly pears struggling through the ochre earth. The light let her see the living room a little better. There were some men's clothes strewn around the room on cheap wicker chairs, on the floor. The furniture she had noticed before. Some bottles of wine on an old, dusty sideboard. This was not some general bunkhouse. One man lived here, one man who had some kind of hold over the others outside.

The pain had now turned to a dull, low ache. In some way she almost felt proud of it. What had happened was something outside her old life, with its narrow confines, cosy prettiness, its antiseptic regime. The old life could *not* have continued. She was bleeding, she was becoming something new, although her family, even her mother, refused to acknowledge the fact.

Only Antonio, alone in the world, had recognised this change. He had seen it, appreciated it for what it was, and then taken her, introduced her to a new, savage reality, of pain and blood and dark, raging feelings. A new reality that intrigued her, for all the hurt.

She wanted to think of her family. Try to help them. But she could not shake the image of this man from her head, so powerful it was. And the image of the act they had performed together, something so strange, so fundamental, so real. Thinking back on it now, reviewing it in the jumble of pictures and pained sensations in her head, she saw it was some kind of door into a new reality, a world more solid, more substantial than the one she had left behind for ever that morning. She held her hands in front of her face. They did not shake. She was a Lucena.

Outside, the voices grew louder. Caterina looked at the front window. It was long and deep, the frayed curtains blocked out everything. There was a simple wooden chair at one end of the window. She dragged it into the middle, by the gap in the curtains, kneeled on it, leaned forward and opened a tiny chink of light between the two pieces of fabric. There was a musty smell there, old and dry and dusty. She looked for a cause then realised it was the curtain itself. Years of dirt, damp and neglect were woven into its fabric. She peered through the chink and saw the sun low and quiescent in the sky.

The view gave directly back towards the camp. The gates were shut. She wondered what the rest of her family were doing. Whether her parents had been allowed to see the others. Whether they were even thinking of her.

In front of the camp, close to the bull pen and the practice ring, groups of men stood, chatting to each other in the low, tense voices she had heard when she first awoke. They were still too distant for her to distinguish the words. Far away, beyond them, she could make out movement in the practice bullring. Someone was pushing the machine she had seen before, on a holiday trip somewhere, on a bull farm. The machine she thought of as the 'chaser': a set of horns on wheels she'd seen used when they were training. Some people were in the ring, moving slowly around. It was impossible to make out what they were doing.

Caterina closed the curtains slowly and got down off the chair. Suddenly, she was hungry. A big, aching hole had appeared in her belly. She searched through the kitchen. There was a loaf of dry, hard bread, some cheese, some old ham. She looked in the drawer set into the battered wooden table, found a sharp little knife and carefully cut away at the corners of the food, paring a shaving of cheese, a shaving of ham, a thin slice away from the bread. She rolled the meat and cheese together, put them on the bread and folded it over. The food was so dry it almost made her choke. She found the jug and drank some water. It was lukewarm and tasted of dust.

Then she sat down and waited for him to return.

Afterwards, when she was recovering in the nervous calm of the house in Jerez, wondering if the climate might change and whether she would have to return to La Soledad, she tried to count the days. It may have been thirty, it may have been more. Each ran into the next, seamlessly, as if melded together, day and night transformed into one. She would wake up and eat. He brought food, left it on the table. More bread, more cheese, occasionally oranges. His own life did not run on some conventional path. She had soon come to realise that. Sometimes he would be there

191

when she was woken by the sunlight illuminating the bedroom window. He would be there naked, stubble on his chin, his cheeks. She would look at him asleep and remember how the bristles hurt, chafing at her face, her shoulder, as he strained and pushed above her.

When he slept, he slept so soundly that she thought nothing would wake him. If she went into the kitchen, took the little knife from the drawer, returned, then cut his throat, from ear to ear, watching the blood flow on the sheets, would he wake to see her standing over him, the little blade flashing in the sun? No. She did not think so. It was possible. But she did not do it. She could have killed a man. Of that she was certain. But not him. There was a bond, she recognised. He protected her and if, in the beginning, it had started as rape, then the act had changed, over the days. Now she welcomed him, she expected him. He taught her, looked after her, was both guardian and lover, and for this she was grateful. Sometimes he did things – touched her small breasts, kissed the nipples and watched them grow and stiffen – things that made her feel different, grown up, like a woman. There was a moment, and it had not taken long, when she realised that she wanted the thing to happen, would be disappointed if he simply rolled over and went to sleep (as sometimes he wanted to, since he seemed to be tired, worried, distracted so often). When this had first happened she had touched him on the chest, felt the soft, black hairs there, the warmth of his skin, explored his body, reached down to touch between his legs and, to her astonishment, felt it grow and harden between her fingers, heard the pattern of his breath change, and then, without thinking about what she was doing, kissed him there.

It was an act of complicity and, once performed, there could be no turning back.

He told her never to leave the house. He locked it each time he went out. She heard the key in the door and never tried to escape. There was nowhere to go and, in any case, she did not want to leave him. The dark interior of the farmhouse became her world, her universe. The days seemed endless; it was rarely he returned from wherever he visited before the light was fading. The nights were spent locked together, sweating, panting, entranced by the harsh, rough sweetness they found there. She started to look after the house, to care for his clothes. Each morning, before he left, he brought water in for her to wash things, some food. She learned how to fry eggs he brought, warm from the coop she could hear outside.

It was at least a week before she asked about her family. His face grew dark. He looked away. She hated herself for asking the question.

Eventually he said, 'If you stay quiet, if you do as you are told, I can keep you alive, Caterina. There are crazy men here, in La Soledad. They do things I cannot stop. If I tried, they would kill me. Be patient. When the fighting subsides in the city, and that will not be long, then things will be safer, more secure. But do not press me. Do not ask questions. Above all, *stay inside*. Do not remind them of your presence. I will do my best for your family.'

She marked the hesitation in his voice. 'And for me?'

'And for you. Always.'

She smiled. It was true. They were two against the world. She had sensed this all along and now he had confirmed it.

'Your pact is with me. Not my family,' said Caterina, eyes glittering in the dark.

Antonio Alvarez looked at her and wondered what key he had turned to begin the transformation he had witnessed. She now looked older. She was dressed in a peasant shift he had brought one day. She was still slim, but her breasts were growing and she could pass as a farmer's young wife, pretty, full of life, any day. He thought of his own life, back in the city, and wondered how his hunger could have led him so far. Then he thought of the night, their limbs moving together on the stiff hay mattress, her face in the moonlight, eyes closed, mouth half open, the gentle, bird-like sound of her moaning. It was not possible and he hated to face the thought.

'Stay inside. Stay silent. Stay away from the windows,' he said, then rose from the table, gathered his jacket and unbolted the door.

In the brief sunlight of his going she had nodded and said, 'Yes.'

But she was still a child and she did not mean it.

25

Something had changed outside, something she sensed in his eyes, in the way the voices had shifted beyond the locked door, in the air itself. The atmosphere had become more taut. Antonio spent longer away from the house. She missed him. Sometimes in the evenings he was so tired that he fell asleep straight away, and woke only when she mounted him, legs around his belly, hand feeling gently at his groin.

But the act had changed. His excitement had dwindled, had been diverted elsewhere. There was a look on his face she did not understand, did not like. And she did not dare ask what had put it there, what was happening outside, in La Soledad.

One evening he was even later than usual and she was bored, resentful, feeling neglected. She had washed his clothes, she had made some food. Half of it was uneaten. She had drunk some of the harsh red wine he had brought, in uncorked green bottles. It made her head spin, made her think wild thoughts. When she drank too much, she sometimes felt ill. But not this night. This night it filled her with curiosity, with bravery, with impudence.

She went to the big front window, kicked the chair aside and slid in front of the curtains. It was night but there was a full moon, glorious and silver in the starry sky. She could not remember such a beautiful evening, ever. Everything was clear and still under the pure white light. Even the barren land of La Soledad, the cheap little buildings, the picket fence of the encampment, they all seemed *right*. She remembered a phrase she had heard her brothers saying when they played soldiers: all present and correct. This was how the landscape in front of her now looked. Everything in it, scrubby rock outcrop, straggly clump of prickly pear, rough iron outhouse, everything was in its place.

She stared happily at the scene, rapt, dreaming, hoping it would never end. Then came a sound she would never forget. A sound of human agony, so loud, so tortured, she thought she could feel the pain itself. It went on and on, like the cry of a beast being slaughtered and a distant inner voice said to Caterina: *Get down, get away from the window, forget, go to sleep.*

This was not possible. Not without knowing. The screams came again, she shivered in the heat of the night. Caterina got down from the window, went to the table where Antonio kept his papers, opened the little leather attaché case and pulled out a pair of field glasses.

The sound came again and she walked back to the window. She had never used the glasses before but she had watched him playing with them, focusing on the horizon as he stood at the curtains, watching, silently, for something she could only guess at. The eyecups were sandy and hurt her skin. She took the glasses away from her face, scrubbed them with her sleeve, then tried again. It was hard at first, but soon she got the idea. The focus was fixed and her eyesight was good. Soon she could make out the detail of the gates, the shape of the rocks and terrain in the distance. Then she returned to the camp, tried to see if there was a gap somewhere that would let her peer in, beyond the picket fence. But there was nothing.

The screaming was becoming more faint. She gave up on the perimeter fence and ranged left, to the bull pen, where a few dark shapes stood immobile. Then she ranged further left, to the practice ring; the shapes of men, and other things, began to form in her line of vision, and she felt herself make an involuntary gasp. The inner voice spoke again. Again she ignored it.

She could see Antonio, silver grey in the moonlight, seated on the top row of the three-tier benching. In front of him, on both sides, were ten or so other men, all seated, all watching what was going on in the ring. She could not read their expressions at this distance; she was grateful for that.

Caterina moved the glasses slightly and turned to look in the ring. A man was tied to the practice chaser, hands bound to its handles. From the way the moonlight shone on his back she guessed he must have been stripped to the waist. He slumped over the handles, almost as if asleep. Then, from behind, a figure appeared, with small things dragging ribbons in his hands. He walked towards the man, pulled back his arm, threw something. It flew through the air and stuck into the man's back. Caterina watched as the head went up in agony, braced herself for the scream that now came thin and terrifying through the night air.

From the side of the ring came someone on a small horse. He had a lance in his hand. It stuck out comically in front of the animal, too big, too ungainly. She heard, dimly, laughter from the men seated on the benches. The horseman jogged slowly towards the centre of the ring. He looked bored. He looked as if he had done this too many times. With a lazy sweep of his arm, he lifted the lance, then thrust two, three times into the man's side. The wheeled frame moved a few feet. The men at the side shouted abuse. The lance rose and fell again, and the frame shifted once more before the figure bound to it slumped again.

The shouting was now getting louder, impatient, annoyed. The spectacle didn't seem to please them. Caterina looked at the men again. They frightened her. Then she saw Antonio, still seated above them, raise his hand, make a gesture she did not understand. There was a small cheer. One of the men at the front stood up and walked into the ring. He was carrying something long and thin in his hand. She closed her eyes, then found she had to open them. It was a sword.

They were yelling now, really yelling, but the figure strapped to the frame remained motionless. Maybe he was dead already, she thought. Maybe it would be better if he were dead.

The man with the sword reached the frame. He looked at the body, shook his head, prodded the torso with the sword. There was some small movement. He shrugged his shoulders. Then he lifted the head, looked into the face, let it drop back hard onto the frame, lifted the sword, lifted it so that the moonlight glittered like ice along its length, shouted, then stabbed, again and again, stabbed the head, the back, the sides, madly, in a frenzy, yelling, yelling, yelling.

But Caterina registered this only dimly. She was screaming already, a scream that sent two guards racing towards the house, pistols drawn. She had seen the face, pale under the moon, the face of the man dying in agony in the ring. It was the face of her father.

As they hammered on the front door, screaming at Antonio for the key, she retreated slowly, as far away as possible, into the kitchen, where they found her, face bloated and swollen with tears, cowering on the floor, hands around her knees, speechless with fright.

They dragged her out of the house screaming, a young girl in fear of her life, not suspecting, not remembering that this was Caterina Lucena, not thinking that she might have had the presence of mind, before they arrived, to reach into the drawer of the kitchen table, take out the sharp little knife she had once used to prepare his meals, then hide it deep down in the pocket of her plain, coarse peasant shift.

Antonio still sat on the top tier of the seats, his back to the moon which was now huge, placid in the night sky. It cast his face in shadow. She desperately wanted to see his face, to read it. She *could* read it. She knew that now.

'Let go of her,' he said, from the shadows. 'She has nowhere to run.'

Then he got down from the stand and turned to look at her. She saw his face now, cold, expressionless in the moonlight. It came to her in an instant: there were two of them, two Antonios sharing the same skin. Twins: one light, one dark. Inside, in the house, where there was love and warmth and passion, lived the light one. Out here, next to the ring, the place of torture, the dark one ruled. And looked at her now, without pity, with nothing in his expression except a faint air of disappointment.

The men gathered around her. One spoke, in a rough, peasant voice: 'She saw it, Antonio. You got to kill her too. We could all die if she goes blabbing this around. You had your fun. Now's the time.'

He kicked at the ground, ignoring them. He had a power over them. It was obvious, tangible. 'I am the leader. *I* say when it's the time.'

'She saw. She could get us into big trouble. We get caught, for some reason they hear about this, we're dead men.'

He laughed. 'You think we aren't already? Leave us. Take the body away. I will talk to her.'

They walked away, grumbling, walked to the centre of the ring and the husk of a human being slumped in the moonlight.

Antonio bent down to her, stroked her cheek. She shivered.

'Child, child, child. I told you. I *told* you. Why did you not listen?'

She was crying now, the tears filled her eyes and slowly dampened her face. 'That is my *father*.'

She wanted to hear him deny it but knew he would not.

'Yes. They are all dead. Except you and you are very lucky. The last Lucena. This is a death camp, Caterina. Do you know what that means? Do you understand? We remove our enemies to ensure we do not have to fight them again. They do it. We do it. As I said, this is war.'

She could feel the fury building inside her. 'Enemies? My brothers? My sister?'

He shrugged. 'Perhaps not today. But this is a war that will dictate the future. Tomorrow . . . who knows?'

'Am *I* your enemy?'

She saw that he could not face her, could not look into her eyes. Antonio half turned away and stared at the low rocky hills, gaunt in the moonlight.

'You are . . . I do not know what you are. You are . . . a source of comfort.'

'Your whore?'

Then he faced her and she saw anger in his face. 'Such words, from a *lady* of your age.'

He grabbed her roughly by the dress and tugged her along with him.

'Come. I will show you.'

They walked behind the ring. A group of men were loading her father's body onto a cart. She turned away, he let go of her. She followed, in silence. It was another minute away, announced by the stench. She had never smelled anything like it. Her stomach turned. She thought she was going to throw up.

'No further.' He stopped her with an outstretched arm and, in a moment, he seemed changed. This was the inside Antonio again, she thought. His voice was softer. His manner seemed gentle again.

'Look.'

He pointed down. It was dark. A black line stretched in shadow in front of them, deep and foreboding. The stench came from there.

'Here.' He reached into his jacket pocket and passed her something. It was the light from the front of a bicycle, a tin battery torch. She fumbled for the Bakelite switch, found it, turned it on, cast the light in the direction he was indicating, gasped, then turned it off.

'Did you see?'

She clutched a hand to her mouth. She felt sick.

'*Did you see?*'

'Yes,' she said and that momentary flash came back to her. Body piled upon body, limbs askew, twisted into crazy, impossible angles, dull, blank eyes glistening in the dark, and dead, open mouths. It was a burial pit, the place they hid their carnage.

'I want to go,' she said, quietly, in a calm, unhurried voice.

He turned around and she followed. They walked almost back to the ring. The stench diminished, but it never disappeared. Afterwards, she thought she could smell it for weeks. Perhaps even years.

'There are sixty, perhaps seventy people in there. I don't know how many they put in before I came here.'

She coughed, then vomited, quietly weeping, into a clump of dry brush. When she had finished, he gave her a handkerchief to wipe her mouth. It tasted of gun oil.

'Why?' she said.

'Because . . .' He searched for a reason. 'Because it can

201

be done. These men are not fighting a war, they are fighting the world. They would bury the world there if they could. I try to stop them, as much as is possible. But I cannot *change* them. If I tried, they would kill me as surely as they would like to kill you. My power here is very tenuous. But I do what I can. They have not killed everybody. They have not killed you.'

'Yet.'

'They will not kill you.'

But this was the inside Antonio talking, she thought. What would the outside Antonio say?

She wiped her mouth again, then stuffed the handkerchief into her pocket.

'When you first ... when you first took me, you said you were a doctor. Was that true?'

'I said I worked in the hospital.'

'You ... you made me think you were a doctor.'

'I was a porter. I carried sick people around. From room to room. Dead people too sometimes. Someone has to do it. Someone has to do this.'

She sensed his pain, sensed his realisation that he was not untouched by La Soledad.

'You belong to me,' he said, in a dull, metallic tone. 'You are mine. Understand that. Then we will both survive.'

'In the city,' she said, 'you have a wife.'

'She is in Madrid. With her parents.'

'Is she pretty?'

He watched the expression on her face, trying to see what she was thinking. 'She looks a little like you. Like you are now. Not before. Yes. She is pretty.'

'You have children?'

'No. No children.'

'And us? Afterwards? When it is over?'

He laughed. 'Afterwards? How can any of us think "afterwards"? There is here. There is now. Stay alive, Caterina, stay alive. Without that there is no "afterwards". Come.'

She followed him back to the camp and the group of men now grouped around the picket gate.

'Remember what I said, Caterina. You belong to me. You are mine. Remember that and we both survive. These men are angry. They would like you dead.'

She could hear the new harshness in his voice. It was as if every step he took towards them, every step he took away from their own, self-contained intimacy, was a step to the other Antonio, the outside Antonio.

They stopped by the men and Antonio smiled at them. 'Juan,' he said.

A youth, squatting on the ground cleaning an old rifle, looked up. Caterina thought he could be no more than seventeen. He was filthy. His hair was ragged and uncut, his clothes looked like rags.

'Stand up, Juan,' said Antonio. She could feel the other men looking at her, wondering.

The youth got up. He was astonishingly thin, with a sunken chest and hunched shoulders. He flicked a greasy hank of hair from his face and said, 'Sir.' The voice was bucolic and simple. Caterina could smell him: sweat, old clothes, urine.

'Juan,' said Antonio. 'Have you ever seen something like this before?'

He lifted her dress. Her legs were pale, carved images lit by the moon. Juan looked shocked.

'Don't be frightened,' said Antonio. 'Look.'

He lifted the dress higher, above her knees, higher still until they could all see the small dark triangle at the top of her legs. Caterina was trembling with fright and shame, her eyes closed, tears brimming in them.

'Have you been with a woman, Juan?'

The youth shook his head. He looked imbecilic.

Antonio let go of her dress. She felt the hem fall back around her ankles.

'Take her. Over there. In the stable. Take her. She knows what to do. She can show you some things.'

They laughed, a grim, animal sound.

'Go. When you have finished, put her back in the house. Lock the door. Perhaps next time she will do as she is told. If not . . . then someone else may have the pleasure. *Go!*'

The youth came to stand in front of her, then grinned. His teeth were yellow, uneven and rotting. The fetid odour that came out of his mouth in taut, excited gasps made her want to stop breathing.

She reached out for Antonio but already he was walking away, barking orders to the others who hung back, grinning at the youth, making obscene gestures. Juan laughed back at them, clutched at his groin with his hand, then pushed her in the back. She walked in front, towards the stable by the house. The moon was bright over the distant hills but clouds were beginning to scud across its face.

He patted her backside as if she were a piece of livestock, opened the stable gate, then pushed her in. There were no horses. Just straw and hay, strewn around, a manger, a water trough. He pushed her again, towards a corner protected by a ramshackle awning.

'You go over there. I don't want none of those dirty bastards watching.' His voice sounded coarse and guttural. Small pearls of spittle flew from his mouth as he spoke.

Carefully, she patted her pocket, walked over to the hay on the ground, kneeled down, turned round, then lay on her back. He motioned to her. She pulled up her skirt until he nodded, parted her legs a little.

Juan laughed, a banal little noise, fumbled with his pants, then dropped them to his knees. His penis stood pale and half erect in front of him. Then, laughing, he went down on his knees and shuffled in front of her. She opened her legs wider, he came forward. She could smell his breath, his body reeked. He stared at her, half in despair, holding his penis. He looked lost.

'You put it in for me,' he said. 'You know what to do.'

She nodded and gently pulled her hand out of her pocket. Juan felt the warm pleasure in his penis, grinned and looked at her. He was still grinning when the blade flashed, a sudden silver light across his line of vision, and then Juan wondered what had happened to his throat. There was a sudden warm feeling there, as if he had been pricked. He put his hand to the flesh, pulled it away. Something warm, something viscous, ran through his fingers. He could feel his stomach rising. When he realised what was happening he started to shout, but Caterina recognised the moment, recognised she was not finished. She rolled out from underneath him, brought herself upright with her elbows, then thrust the little kitchen blade deep into his throat. He bent over, clutching his neck, life flowing out of him, slowly, like a thick, red river. He choked for a few seconds, then lay silent at her feet.

Caterina wiped the blade on her dress and listened. The only sounds were the sounds of the countryside: a distant owl, dogs barking, the chirruping of crickets. She unfastened the boy's boots, pulled them off his stinking feet, and put them on her own. They were too big for her, but she could not run barefoot, not through the countryside. Then she vaulted the wall, pausing momentarily to look around. The distant group of men were working near the ring, the far-off red winking of cigarettes marking their presence.

Without a thought in her head save survival, she turned in the direction of the hills and ran and ran and ran.

26

They did not follow her, not as far as she knew. The next day she woke by the side of the road, half hidden in a ditch filled with rough scrub. Her feet, her legs, her entire body ached, in unison. She was thirsty and starving. She did not know where she was, what day of the week it was. Caterina pulled herself out of the ditch and started to walk to the distant low mountains. They looked familiar, like the ones on the road to Ronda. And they led away from the city.

La Soledad proved a good school for what happened during the next two weeks. She soon realised that she could not survive on her own. Occasionally, there was a trickle of water in a mountain *arroyo*. Occasionally she would eat herbs, strip a fattening prickly pear, trying hard to keep the tiny, niggling spines out of her skin. But she could not survive without the help of others and that help had to be found one way or another.

These were not people who were directly involved in the war. They were outside the conflict, somehow, working with anyone who provided the most profit, mountain people, solitary, silent, suspicious. As she walked the hillsides, from one small white *pueblo* to the next, she learned how to touch them. Sometimes there were small kindnesses which came unbidden: water, fruit, some hard, fatty sausage. Sometimes she could earn a meal, even a night in an out-building, by doing whatever work they needed, or would pretend they required, sweeping out the stables, hosing down the sty, threshing dry dusty corn in the midday sun. She became practised at asking in the right way, asking not for charity but for payment. She wanted them to know that she was no mere beggar and when they looked into her eyes, saw the grey, steely stare that now lived there, usually they appreciated that.

Sometimes she got what she needed in other ways.

The distances were not small, and the weather was hard: hot and dry with a scorching sun. Soon she had the geography of the mountains fixed in her head. She knew where she was, she knew where she wanted to go: west, until the *sierra* fell down to the plain and Jerez was only a few miles away. It would take weeks to walk all that way. So one morning, after she had earned a bed and some food washing an old woman's laundry in the *pueblo* spring, she walked beyond the last house, sat down by the roadside and waited. Half an hour later a rusty old truck came past, the driver looked at her, grinned and waved to her to get in.

She knew there was usually a price. With Antonio she had learned things she could show them, with her lithe, deft fingers, things that brought it all to a swift, messy little conclusion and then they could get back onto the road, the man bemused, marginally happy, puzzled by this girl beside him, who seemed so young and so old at the same time.

Sometimes they tried to go further, further than she wanted. Only one man had known her that way. Only one man ever would. And if they tried too hard she still had the knife, worn and tiny, but sharp as a dagger, and was not afraid to use it. They backed off when they saw her pointing it at them, when they saw the look of deadly intent in her eyes.

The girl of fourteen, in her pink and white cotton dress, living in her own private world in a tiled mansion of marbled pillars and cool patios shaded by palms, this girl was buried, gone. In her place was someone infinitely older, someone marked for ever by the darkness of the world.

A month after the old Caterina died, a young woman dressed in a faded country shift, her face lined, tanned and leathery, hitched a lift in Medina Sidonia. She had slept in the churchyard, in the shadow of ancient, Arab battlements. When she woke, she felt strange: drowsy, ill. She had vomited on an empty stomach, then, suddenly, felt much better. The truck driver was a farmer, going to buy wine in Jerez. A man in his twenties, worried about the journey, worried that the fighting in the plain might not have stopped, as all the town gossip insisted it had. He asked nothing of her, nothing except that she listen as he recounted his fears, told anecdotal tales of the terrors of the war, the blood, the battles, the massacres. When Caterina jumped down from the front cab, on the outskirts of Jerez, she felt nothing for him but contempt, and did not pause to wonder why.

The streets of the town were deserted. It was mid-afternoon, but the torpor went beyond this. Jerez was in waiting, hoping it had seen the worst of the war, hoping that it would not return.

She sat down on the kerb, tried to work out her bearings, failed, then asked the way of a lone postman walking down the street. He looked at her, told her what she wanted, then was glad to go on his way.

Caterina skirted the centre of town, followed a leafy avenue, turned into a side road, then recognised the house. It had been three, perhaps four, years since she had seen her aunt and uncle. The house, a middle-class two-storey villa covered in bougainvillaea, jacaranda trees blooming in the front garden, seemed much smaller than she remembered it. She saw it with the eyes of an adult, recalled it with the memory of a child.

Caterina opened the iron gates and walked down the

drive. A man came from round the back of the house, looked at her and started shouting. She stood her ground. It was her uncle, Ramón.

'Go,' he said. 'We have nothing for you. The town is full of beggars. We cannot feed them all.'

Caterina almost obeyed. She felt strange. The world was swaying in front of her. She thought she was going to be sick again.

'I need a glass of water,' she said. Ramón held a hoe. He clung to it like a weapon. From her left, she heard the sound of another person. Her aunt Francesca walked up. She was wearing a flowered smock, the kind women wore when cleaning. There was a glass of water in her hand, a curious, seeking expression in her eyes. The colours danced and swam in front of Caterina.

'Thank you,' she said, and lifted the glass to her mouth. It was cool and fresh and wonderful and still she felt sick.

Francesca was staring at her, trying to work something out.

'They are dead,' said Caterina. 'They are all dead.'

Ramón came closer, tried to see what his wife saw.

'Who are dead, girl?' said Francesca.

'Papa. Mama. Everyone. They killed them. At La Soledad.'

Francesca put a hand to her face, felt the skin, its dryness, its harshness. She looked at the girl in the dirty dress. She looked twenty, at least.

'Caterina?' Francesca asked, incredulous. '*Caterina?* Is it you?'

But the world was turning black, black and dizzying. It came down in front of her, a falling curtain descending over her vision, and she was unconscious before her body hit the ground with a sound that made them wince.

27

The early days were a blur. There was a bedroom which became her universe. She could fix the point of every candle, every ornament, remember each flower on the wallpaper, each crucifix, every religious painting hanging there, still and eternal in the shaded interior light. Francesca and Ramón came and went. She would look into their watchful, worried faces and wonder: do they believe *now?*

But they believed. They believed more and more each day as the dirt and grime of the road disappeared, the lines on her face faded imperceptibly, and they could see a little of the Caterina of old. A little.

Ramón tried harder and harder to win her over, to banish the coldness he had first shown when she had walked through the gate, looking just like any other street beggar asking for food. There had been so many since the war. Some were orphans, some were simply abandoned, left to fend for themselves. When the battles began, he had taken Francesca aside, they had talked, they had agreed: we look after our own. Which they did. And to find out that he had nearly rejected one of his own was something akin to a sin, something Ramón tried hard to atone for.

She remembered them from childhood visits to Jerez, and family parties in the city. In the old days, before the war, Ramón almost seemed like another kid. He joined in their games. He spent time with the children when all the other adults simply wanted to forget about them. Why? She had wondered at the time, and Mama had simply said something about 'their tragedy'. Later, she had found out. They had had a child who died young, little more than an infant. They could have no more. The chance to play with children, to be near them, was something that let Ramón enter, even for only an hour, a world from which life had excluded him, excluded them, before they had even reached the age of thirty.

The blur began to fade, to make sense. The days began to have a rhythm. She still felt ill. There was sickness, sudden, incapacitating, normally in the morning. But once she had been sick, she recovered. After a while, she felt well. No, more than well. She felt fit, full of life. The blood coursed through her with a strength, a vitality she could almost measure. She felt *alive*, felt invigorated by the sheer physicality of her body, the very act of being. This was not the same as happiness. She was not happy. She did not believe she would be happy again. She was not sure she had been happy in the past. Whatever happiness was, it was something which had been taken outside her circle of experience. Just as some people could not whistle, Caterina, she realised, could not feel simple, sudden elation. This had been removed from her and she did not miss it. Survival, strength, fitness, mental and physical, these were things that mattered. These were things that were within her grasp.

Her appetite was huge. Ramón and Francesca joked about it for a while. Then they began to exchange glances when they joked, and Caterina followed them, secretly, followed their eyes, wondering what hidden messages were being exchanged there. She would eat whatever they brought: milk, eggs, pork, sausage, chicken, potatoes. Whatever the state of the war, they had no difficulty in finding food. Either that, or they gave her the best part of what they had. Later, when she started to leave the room, to walk around the house, spend hours resting in the cool, shady lounge, she realised it was the latter. They had what they could buy, but it was not much. Secretly, without letting her know, they gave most of it to her.

One morning, when the threat of sickness came briefly then disappeared as inexplicably as it had arrived, she lay on the bed, in her nightgown, and felt her stomach. The shape was changed. There was a fullness that had not been there before, a warm bulge above the hair that was comforting to the touch. She put her hand underneath her nightdress, rested it on the flesh and felt a shiver of contentment run through her, though she still did not know why.

The day was overcast. Autumn was on its way. Ramón and Francesca said that the local fighting was now over, what remained was now so distant that the farmers felt brave enough to collect their crops. Soon everyone would be out in the fields, bent over the vines, heads bowed, straw hats to protect them against the sun. The old ritual would be under way. If they practised it enough, perhaps it would work its magic, the wounds would heal, the country would return to peace, the war itself would be over.

Caterina stroked the bulge, wondered if she should stop eating so much, then thought, out of nowhere: *I do not bleed*.

This meant nothing to her. The connections were too hazy, too unexplained. But connections there were.

I do not bleed.

She felt the hot flesh underneath her hand and it almost seemed as if something was there, something moving.

Caterina saw her vision narrow. It was as if walls closed in from the periphery of her sight. There was now nothing for her to see but her body on her bed.

She pulled up the nightdress, pulled it above her hips, felt it ruffle underneath her back, then relaxed back onto the bed. She looked down. There was a distinct shape there, at the base of her stomach. It was real. It curved down from her navel with a growing fullness that seemed so natural, so adult. A year ago, she had only had the beginnings of hair. Now, as she looked at herself, she looked like a grown woman, like a torso from a museum, the kind of carving they had always hurried past, the children sniggering on the way.

Caterina put her hand on her stomach again, felt the heat of her flesh, and felt, though she knew it was impossible, a distinct, a real movement beneath her fingers.

She squeezed her eyes shut, held her breath for as long as she could. But when she could stand it no longer, when she looked at herself again, regained her breathing, it was the same. This was real. This was Antonio's parting gift.

She got up, walked out of the room, found Francesca in the kitchen. They looked at each other and Caterina realised she knew, she knew already. There was a look in her eyes that mixed sympathy and pity. Perhaps even a little envy.

Francesca walked over to her, put her arms around her neck. Caterina felt her aunt's tears damp upon her skin but she did not cry. She would be a mother before her fifteenth birthday. There was no room, no *space* for tears.

Close to midnight on Good Friday, 1937, the child was born in the bedroom of the little house in Jerez. Caterina had stared at the flowers on the ceiling. She had refused to scream, refused to cry out, but in the end that was impossible. The pain was too great. She felt she was being torn apart. Nothing in La Soledad or on the journey through the mountains could compare with the intensity of this sheer physical agony.

She could see the concern on the doctor's face. This was not ordinary. This was not normal. Something, the baby, moved inside her, moved *wrongly*, to a position which made no sense. She could feel it – *he? she?* – inside her, not knowing how to prepare itself, struggling to be free of her. When she pushed, nothing happened, except that the blockage, the agonising hindrance inside, became more solid, more fixed, more tormenting.

She bit hard on the leather strap they had pushed between her teeth, pushed again, found herself going nowhere. Then she looked up and saw the glint of silver in the dim electric light, two arms, like horns, a shape that was dimly familiar, like something out of a toy chest.

He went back down the bed. She strained forward, trying to peer over the vastness of her belly, sweat running down her forehead, stinging in her eyes. The doctor looked deathly pale as he held the forceps. Then he crossed himself, the silver arms bent down, below her line of vision, and a pain began that was like no other pain she had felt or would ever feel again.

Caterina opened her mouth, felt the leather strap fall away from her, and felt the scream tear through her head, become everything there was in the world, a red slash of pain and fury. And then it ended. A crimson haze fell in front of her eyes, the room dissolved and with it the pain. The last thing she heard was a tiny, high voice, crying, as if in sympathy. Then the world disappeared, abruptly, and all she could hear in the darkness was the rushing of her blood through her veins.

It was a week before she felt strong enough to ask. A week in which the past had risen to haunt her. A week of ghosts and spectres, a week in which the dead, her dead, had walked, had looked at her, shaken their heads then faded away into the dark. They talked about fever. But it was more than that. During that week, Caterina knew, she had flitted between two worlds, never quite fully in either. She did not want to think about what the dead had said to her. She did not want to remember their urgings. When she finally did wake up, she wanted it to be in her world, not in theirs.

There was still bunting over the window. They had not time, had not thought, to take it down. The war was now distant enough for Semana Santa to be marked, albeit in a muted, slightly impoverished fashion. The doctor now came only once a day. Ramón and Francesca looked after her constantly, bringing bread and soup and fruit, water with a little wine in it. She was young, she was recovering quickly.

She waited until Francesca was alone and then, in a flat, insistent tone, asked. Her aunt could not look at her. She turned to stare out of the window. Caterina did not need to see her to know there were tears in her eyes.

'The baby died, Caterina,' she said, her back still to the bed. 'There was nothing the doctor could do. It was a breach birth. It was impossible.'

She turned, walked to the bed and hugged her niece. Caterina felt oddly detached from the scene. The light was grey and diffused. It did not look real.

'It was a boy,' she said. 'A little boy. He was strong, but not strong enough. But be brave. The doctor says you are young, you are strong too. There is no reason, when you are married, why you should not have more children.'

Caterina smiled to herself. But there *was* a reason . . .

'And besides, Caterina . . . Had he lived . . . you are not yet fifteen. You could not have hoped to support him.'

Immediately Francesca wished she had never said the words she was thinking. The girl looked at her with a ferocity which was frightening. Hers was not the face of a fourteen-year-old. There was more pain, more experience, more hardness there than Francesca would have wished on someone many times her age.

'He was my child,' she said. 'He belonged to me.'

Francesca picked up the tray with the empty dishes on it, then looked at her niece.

'Yes,' she replied. 'But this, all of this, is something you must put behind you now. Next week, we have arranged for you to go to Cadiz to recuperate. There is a good hotel, run by friends of ours. We will pay. They will look after you well. The sea air, the food, it will get you back on your feet. We have relatives there too. You may not remember them, but they will visit you.'

Caterina shook her head. She did not understand. 'You want me to leave?'

Francesca tidied the plates on the tray. 'This has all been a strain on Ramón and myself. We need some rest from it too, Caterina. There is a house in Melilla, we bought it some years ago. It is by the sea. When you have gone, we will take the ferry from Algeciras. It won't be for long. We have spoken to the solicitors. You inherit the estate in the city. It is quite valuable, but you will not control it until you are twenty-one, of course.'

'And until then . . .'

She could feel her temper rising. Francesca would not, would *not* look at her.

'Until then . . . we must see what happens. When we have all had time to think of these things.'

Precisely seven days later a car arrived to drive Caterina to Cadiz. She lived there, in the same apartment room, with the same quiet, distant family, for the next six years, unvisited by anyone except the lawyers trying to settle the estate. From Ramón and Francesca there was an occasional letter, postmarked Melilla. To the rest of the world, she no longer existed.

Then, when the papers came through, she returned to the city, and was driven to the mansion. Feeling like a returning ghost, she turned the key in the door and walked into her home, her own home. It was thick with dust and the corpses of moths, there was some bomb damage to a corner of the first floor. When she went into her bedroom, she felt, for a moment, fourteen again, she could hear their voices, quiet, tense, and ready to argue downstairs. She sat down on the bed. Clouds of dust rose from the sheets. On the pillow, now a dingy grey, lay a book, bent at the spine, pages uppermost. She picked it up and, with a clarity that astonished her, she recalled it, remembered it precisely, remembered the part of the story she had reached, where the characters were, the phrases, the very words on the page.

She turned it over and looked at the cover, though she knew what it would say. The gold blocking was now dull and peeling but still it read, in bold, serif capital letters: *Kidnapped*.

28

Caterina Lucena lay back in her hospital bed, drained, but somehow satisfied. Maria tried to decode her expression. Beneath the lines of age, beneath the grey pallor, something pleased her. What? Maria tried to examine her own feelings. It was as if something had been transmitted, passed on, and in the act a burden had shifted. She did not fully understand what had taken place between the two of them, what the exchange of this ancient tale meant. Except that it made her uncomfortable. She felt prurient, she felt somehow soiled by being a distant witness to events that still had their currency within the city. She felt marked.

Maria drew a long line underneath her notes, in broad blue ink. What to make of it? What to *believe*? She looked at her watch. Three hours had passed since she arrived and she had scarcely noticed. She tried to see beyond the shield which Caterina had drawn around herself, tried and failed.

'You must be tired,' she said.

Caterina closed her eyes. 'Age. Just the weariness of old age. I hate it.'

Maria poured some water for them, then helped Caterina to sit up in bed to drink it. Outside was the noise of a brass band, cheap and tinny, making an unsteady progress down the street. The squealing sound of an ambulance whined towards the room, steadied its tone, then descended into the distance.

'Antonio is dead?'

She closed her eyes again. 'More than a decade ago. He was ill.'

'So you saw each other again?'

'No. I saw him. He was not aware of me.'

Maria waited. It would come.

'It was three years later. In the ring. By then he was becoming something in the city. The scandal around La Soledad had faded, others had taken the blame. And Antonio knew how to please people. He knew how to give them the "good things". They liked him. They warmed to him. He was rising in the Falange. Working in the city hall. He did not have to push hospital beds again.'

She said the words with a slow, methodical precision.

'I had thought about it for a long time. I still had the knife, that little knife from the house in La Soledad. I *still* have it. Somewhere in the house. I waited until the end of Semana Santa, the great bullfight. Franco was there, he was the special guest. There were thousands of people, all fighting, screaming to be nearest the president's box. This was when the Falange were really the victors, before the bitterness, the fear had set in. There was no middle ground. They were all for them then. Everyone else did not exist. So I stayed in the crush, I went with them. After the last fight, we scrambled around the box, jumped into it, people were kissing El Caudillo, kissing his hand, blessing him. And Antonio stood there silent, looking into the ring. I was behind him. I could have killed him. It would have been very simple.'

Maria watched her pause. Watched her searching for the words.

'But I did not.'

'Why?'

'You ask for reasons so glibly, so easily. Do you think that life is run on reasons? For this reason we do something, for another reason we do not. No one's life is run like a machine, an engine. Not even yours.'

Maria found herself disliking Caterina Lucena, with an intensity that made her guilty.

'It's not my life we are talking about.'

The thin lips puckered. 'No. Why? Perhaps, in a way, I loved him. At least I was aware that he was the only person I would be capable of loving in this lifetime. I no longer wanted him. I thought about him, true, I thought about our time together. The *realness* of it. But it was gone. Killing him would not bring it back. I felt the knife in my dress. I could have killed him. But there seemed . . . there seemed no point. Had I been a man, of course, I would have done it. Men are driven by baser things – jealousy, revenge, hatred. I felt none of these.'

'What did you feel?'

Caterina looked at her with an expression that came close to contempt. 'I felt he failed me. What else?'

'And afterwards?'

'Afterwards, I saw him around the city. Always by accident. We were never face to face. I suspect he would not have recognised me in any case. I looked very different from the girl he would have remembered. I watched him, noted him over the years. His face was in the paper a lot, then there was some scandal, he left politics. The next time I saw him, he was dying. It was obvious. This was a man who had always seemed so full of life, of vitality. Then one day I saw him near the city hall and he was dying. It was written in his face. There was something, some kind of cancer, that was eating him from within. A year later I read about his death in the paper. There was a short obituary. "A loving family man."'

Caterina sniffed. It was an unpleasant, dismissive gesture. Maria wanted to get out of there without having to ask the question. She could not. When she went back to the station, they would demand to know. If she did not ask, someone else would.

'Caterina.'

The old woman was tight-lipped now. She looked gaunt and faded, as if she were part of the bed itself, a thin sheet of humanity in the midst of folded, bleached cotton.

'Did you see the grave of the child? The boy? Did your aunt and uncle take you there, tell you where it was?'

She snorted and now Maria could see it for what it was: pure contempt.

'Grave? *Grave?* There was no *grave*. Do you think I am a fool?'

'No,' said Maria softly. 'No, Doña Caterina, I do not.'

29

They were sitting in the little office, now stuffy with heat and perspiration: Rodríguez, Menéndez, Maria, Torrillo. She looked at Rodríguez and remembered what Torrillo had said about him, remembered the unspoken, unshakeable confidence they all appeared to have in him. His distance, his reluctance to become involved in the case seemed to be disappearing, dissolving by the hour. They were waiting for him to move, waiting for his insight. And in recognition of that, his levity and, to a degree, his politeness had disappeared. She wondered how she could ever have mistaken him for an academic. It was an act, one he performed well, with subtlety, but at heart Rodríguez was a cop. She watched his eyes scanning the pages in front of him anxiously. A worried cop, too.

Quemada and Velasco joined them part way through the conference, having accepted the inevitable: this was one case where you worked when you worked, and the shift thing just had to wait. It was just after one. The blackboard was covered in white spidery scribbles. Maria could feel her head swimming. In the space of a few hours they seemed to have moved from darkness into light, but a light that blinded them. There was too much information for her to absorb, too many possibilities to be sorted into some kind of sense.

Menéndez led the discussion, writing on the blackboard what he called the 'known points' of the case.

She read his shaky handwriting.

1. The killings were not random? Some link – possibly a homosexual one?
2. Luis Romero, a professor of history, possible victim.
3. The Brotherhood of the Blood of Christ – grudge? Other link?
4. Antonio Alvarez?
5. El Guapo. Links to Alvarez, Angel Brothers *and* Romero.
6. Caterina Lucena's son – who? Still alive?

There was a lull in the conversation. So much information, so many roads to explore ...

'It can't be the son,' she said.

Menéndez agreed. 'No way. He'd be too old. Pushing sixty now. All of the information points to someone younger.'

'He *is* too old,' said Maria.

'Yeah. Well, you seen him,' Quemada mumbled.

She felt the hidden accusation roll off her, barely noticed.

'We still need to know,' said Menéndez. 'Is he still alive? If so, where does he live? You two can check with Melilla. Start there.'

Velasco wrote on his notepad then grimaced. 'Sure. Trouble is – and you'll excuse me for telling you your job, Lieutenant – you know what it's like trying to get back this stuff from the war. They didn't keep such good records then. I tried before, other cases and things, and like everything you get is anecdotal. No paperwork. Nothing.'

Rodríguez looked at Velasco and Quemada for a moment, then said, 'You keep pursuing this line till it gets us nowhere. Bring it to an end. Talk to the police in Melilla. See what they can find. If necessary, fly there yourself. You could do it in a day. I want it out of the way so we can concentrate on something more material.'

The two detectives glanced at each other, nodded, then scribbled some more.

Menéndez asked them, 'Is there much more to be had from the records you took from the dating office?'

Velasco didn't look hopeful. 'Don't think so. We got some people running through the names now. Lots of interesting ones there but no contacts with Romero, so far. Seems the only people Romero met were the Angels, then he fixed the date with our athletic American friend. Except of course it wasn't Romero. It was our matador friend.'

'You know that for sure?'

'For sure,' Quemada said. 'Ordoñez says he never met "Romero" but he spoke to him whenever he phoned up. Said the guy had a young voice, *definitely* young. He was adamant on that.'

'Why was he so sure?'

'Romero didn't pay by credit card or anything like that. He used to put cash in an envelope, then put it in the post or push it through the door when the office was closed. Sometimes he wouldn't do that until *after* the date. So you see our friend Ordoñez had good reason to make sure he could trust him. He wanted to make sure he got paid. He *listened* to that voice.'

Maria asked, 'Who else did Romero, or whoever, date?'

'That's the funny thing,' said Quemada. 'He booked dates with three other guys, paid for them too, but never showed. We got the names. They're just regular guys, nothing special, no connection with bulls, the war, the brotherhood, nothing like that. We got people looking at them more closely but they never even met the guy.'

'You mean they *think* they never met him,' said Maria.

224

'I guess so,' Quemada replied. 'What you getting at?'

She looked at the blackboard, tried to sort truths from the tangle of facts there. 'What I mean is . . . there's nothing to say this is anything to do with the gay side of the thing. If he *is* gay, surely he's going to go through with it with at least one of them? It's as if he isn't after sex at all. He's after something else.'

'Looking at them,' said Menéndez. 'He's booking dates so that he can look at them. Presumably without them knowing. When he's checked them out, he makes his decision. Something about the Angel Brothers triggered him. Something about Famiani too.'

'Except there's no link with our friend in the brotherhood office,' said Quemada. 'He killed him and he sure as hell didn't get that date through some agency. Castaneda was as straight as they come.'

'He didn't need to check Castaneda out,' said Maria. 'He *knew*. He knew he was the man he wanted.'

'Which brings us back to the brotherhood,' said Quemada gloomily. 'And all this history stuff. I *hate* history.'

'So what we have,' said Menéndez, 'is someone who has some direct link with these events in the war, maybe even La Soledad itself, who is now taking some kind of vengeance.'

'Except he's too young to be linked directly,' said Velasco. 'It must be some second generation kind of thing. So why should that start happening *now*? Why didn't he start killing people years ago?'

'Because he didn't have the trigger,' said Menéndez. 'No one had pulled it.'

'Maybe he was just too young,' said Torrillo. 'Maybe he was waiting.'

'El Guapo,' said Quemada. 'We just *got* to pull him in. He met them all, except Castaneda maybe, and Castaneda sure knew him. He's got the bullfighting connection, he'd sure know how to kill people. If it's true, like your old guy says, he's Alvarez's son, then maybe . . .'

He stopped. The train of thought clouded his face.

'Maybe?' asked Rodríguez, barely disguising his temper. 'We don't build a case on maybes.'

'Shit,' said Quemada. It didn't make sense. 'Maybe he's next on the list. I don't know. We've gotta talk to him anyway.'

'I agree,' said Menéndez. 'We have the appointment fixed at his apartment for eight, Sergeant?'

Torrillo nodded.

'Good.'

Something buzzed around Maria's head, nagging her, tugging just out of reach. She stabbed her hand in the air, looking for some purchase.

'But why, why . . .' She could feel the tone of her voice rising, close to hysteria. Caterina Lucena's face, grey and pallid, flitted in front of her for a moment. '*Why did he pick Luis Romero?*'

Quemada shrugged. 'Why not? It's not an unusual name. The guy liked history, civil war history. Maybe he read his books. Maybe he met him some time, gay date or something. I'm not sure I buy your idea this isn't about sex.'

'But he knew Romero's address,' Maria said. 'He was giving his address out to the dating agency *before* Romero died. It wasn't casual somehow. He *picked* Romero as the identity he wanted to use, and he picked him for some specific reason.'

Menéndez looked interested. 'What might that be? What reason could he have?'

She shook her head. Her hair looked more of a mess than ever. 'I don't know. In universities sometimes people play jokes. Students. Other lecturers. They order things in somebody else's name. Maybe . . .'

226

Quemada waved a big tanned hand in the air. 'Come on. He picks someone else's identity to go kill people with but picks the identity of someone that's *that* close to him? This guy's too clever for that.'

'We should check it,' said Torrillo. 'We should run through the students he taught, the people he knew at the university.'

'Sure,' said Velasco. 'We'll get it done. But you can see his point. Why use someone else's name if you're that close to them? Doesn't add up.'

'Nothing in this case adds up,' grumbled Quemada. 'The whole fucking thing is nutty.'

'No,' said Maria, and she could feel inside that she was right, could feel the certainty behind her words. 'It all adds up except we don't see it. There's something cold and straight and logical all the way through. That's the way he sees it.'

'Maybe the cold and straight and logical thing is that he just likes killing people now and again,' said Quemada. 'You know, some of us play golf, some go to the football, but our guy just puts on his red gown, tools up for the evening and goes out and kills someone. Simple as that. What possible reason could there be for that Famiani guy, the runner? He didn't even live here. Had no connection with Spain even. Just happened along on some queer date, no one showed, the next thing our man's trying to stick him. Where's the logic there?'

Maria fought to shed light on it. Quemada was right . . . and wrong. She couldn't find the words.

'Maybe,' said Torrillo, 'maybe it started off like Maria said. Cold and straight and logical. Then, when he kind of got into the swing of things, it changed. He found he *did* like it. Not just killing the guys he wanted to kill, but killing other people too. Maybe it's a little fuzzy in his mind now too. He doesn't know whether he's killing people because he's got a reason or because he feels like it.'

'That's a cheery thought, Bear,' said Quemada. 'If you're right there we *really* got trouble on our hands.'

Maria stared out of the window. The light was constant, unremitting, the sky a sheet of perfect blue, punctuated by the darting flight of swifts.

'You're right, Bear,' she said. 'You're absolutely right. He just doesn't know any more. He can't differentiate.'

Something akin to sympathy hovered around her head like a moth attracted to a candle. She shook it away faintly, trembling.

'So that's it,' said Menéndez. 'We'll go see the bullfighter. You two chase Melilla. And try the records too. On Romero. Ordoñez. Whoever.'

'Whoever,' echoed Quemada.

'What about Alvarez?' asked Maria and the words came out dreamily, the opposite to how she intended. 'Might there be any records on him?'

The two detectives exchanged glances. They didn't like chasing records. They didn't like rooms of dusty files, tedious pieces of paper.

'He's dead, lady,' said Velasco. 'Long dead.'

'All the same . . .' she said.

They looked at Menéndez. He nodded, and, grumbling, the pair shuffled out of the room.

'And those company names you found? At Castaneda's?' Maria asked.

Menéndez sat silently on the other side of the room.

'Company names?' Rodríguez looked puzzled. 'You didn't mention company names. I have nothing in any report from you at all about company names.'

'Nothing checked out,' said Menéndez. 'Nothing at all.'

The Captain grunted and said, 'Nothing checked out for

you, Lieutenant. All the same, I'd like to see them. When you get back to your desk.'

Then he looked at her across the room, a look it would have been hard for the rest of them to miss.

I am *not* your accomplice in this, Maria thought to herself. I am *not*.

'I'll bring the file round straight away,' said Menéndez.

Rodríguez rubbed his eyes and said, 'I am not giving you the support you deserve on this, Lieutenant. It is not your fault. This holiday, this year, it seems so big, so huge. We have more visitors than ever, every room, every inch of the city is full, and we do not have the manpower to deal with the ordinary tasks, let alone something like this. I cannot – *cannot* – change this for the next few days so I have to rely on you to proceed on your own for the moment but it is essential, *essential* I see every piece of paperwork that comes through on this.'

'Yes, sir,' said Menéndez grimly.

Maria pinched herself. She suddenly got the impression that the coolness Menéndez felt towards her had plummeted several more points towards zero.

30

The streets overran with people. Their voices, high and tense and everywhere, flooded the car as it struggled to find a way through the mass of human flesh. Maria sat in the back, silent, listening to Bear talking to himself in the front. Menéndez was silent too, in a way that seemed new to her. Something disturbed him, something she could not begin to guess at.

They rounded a corner, passed a procession waving banners, red, yellow and green against the golden stone of the cathedral. It was still hot, hotter than she could ever remember for this time of year. She opened her bag, pulled out a tissue, wiped her forehead with it. When she looked back in the bag before closing it something registered. Something was missing. There was a dull, infuriatingly stupid ticking at the back of her mind. She closed the bag and looked out of the window. The lurching of the car was beginning to make her feel sick.

'Big money, these bullfighters,' said Torrillo, and he wheeled the car into a broad gravel drive. The high iron gates were open. They drove up to a three-storey house in pale stone, with long, impressive windows facing on to the arid, plain garden. A patrician's house. Jaime Mateo had come a long way from El Viejo, thought Maria, and then she reached for the handle and stepped out into the close evening air.

A manservant, with downcast eyes and a tanned, pockmarked face, answered the door, then ushered them to a cool, formal room, with elegant furniture finished in pale-green satin, matching curtains, and a few neo-classical prints on the walls. Maria stepped closer to take a look at one of the paintings: it was a Murillo Virgin and Child. Then she looked at the rest in the room. Every one was of the Sevillian School.

'What do you see?' asked Menéndez.

'The paintings. There isn't a Valdés Leal among them. But this is the same period, the same kind of style.'

Torrillo looked at the Murillo. It was not one of the artist's best: hack work, the flesh too full, the faces spoiled by oversentimentality, the sort of thing that paid the rent.

'You mean someone who liked this stuff would know about the painting you showed us? The one that was used to pose the Angel Brothers?'

'I imagine so. Lots of people like this kind of thing, particularly the Murillos. But *everything* here comes from that period. You wouldn't find that by accident.'

'Huh,' Torrillo mumbled. 'Looks like the kind of stuff my mother used to hang on the wall. You got it free with soap powder – ten packets, one Virgin. These people from the barrio, they like this kind of stuff.'

'Yes,' she said, too tired to object.

The door opened and Jaime Mateo walked into the room with the exaggerated theatricality of a second-rate actor. Maria could hardly take her eyes off him. He wore a newly ironed white shirt and cream linen slacks and carried a china teacup. His hair was a brilliant artificial gold, his face a deep, brown tan that seemed too perfect to be real. In the ring, even seen with the relatively close eye of the television camera, Mateo looked as if he deserved his nickname, El Guapo. In the flesh, seen from a few inches, the glamour disappeared and in its place was something wholly artificial and exaggerated. Maria thought of the theatre, the times when she had watched actors perform apparently naturally on the stage, without overstatement, without artifice. Then, when the play had ended, the masks would drop, they would walk to the front and take their bows. And the artifice would be revealed: they would be unreal creatures, plastered in make-up so crude that it seemed inconceivable any-one could have been deceived into thinking it was not there.

This was Mateo's skill: to seem so handsome, so natural from a distance. The price he paid for it was to strut, permanently, like a peacock, once the corrida was over. Far from being handsome, he was, in fact, grotesque. The golden hair, the flawless skin, the blue eyes of the posters seemed, to Maria, to resemble the kind of primary colour portraits a child would paint – too simplistic, too overstated to be genuine.

'The police, how wonderful,' he said, in a curious, flat voice that mixed the accent of the barrio with a deliberate attempt at affectation. Then he sat down in a high-backed green satin chair and looked at them with undisguised amusement.

'You know why we are here, Señor Mateo.'

Maria tried to read the expression on Menéndez's face. He seemed to be as shocked by the man's appearance as she was.

'They say something, when they phone, they say some-thing about some case. I don't know.' Mateo waved his arms about as he spoke. She could see Torrillo peering into his face, looking closely at his eyes.

'I don't know. You people. Why bother me? What you want with me?'

'You OK?' asked Torrillo.

Mateo bristled, in an uncomfortable, twitchy manner.

'Huh?'

'I said, you OK, sir? Just that you don't look too well to me.'

Mateo blinked and Maria thought – the eyes. Bear can see something in the eyes, and he's letting the man know it.

'I'm fine.' He wiped his mouth with the back of his hand.

'Yeah. You don't look it,' said Torrillo. 'You look like a man with a medical problem to me. You know what I mean?'

Mateo tried to get angry. There were flecks of white on his lips. He gestured to Menéndez.

'This what you're here for, Lieutenant? To hassle me? I got friends, you know. I could pick up that phone and speak to people you wouldn't want to talk to.'

'Yeah,' said Torrillo, quietly, then looked at the paintings on the wall.

'Some people you know have died, Señor Mateo. We just need to find out what you knew about them. When you last saw them. That's all.'

Mateo gulped down a swig of tea. It was an ugly gesture.

'You mean the Angels?'

Rodríguez paused, then said, 'Yes. To start with.'

'I last saw the brothers three months ago. In Madrid. Some party or something. I hardly knew them, if you must know. They weren't friends or anything.'

'What were they?' asked Torrillo.

Mateo chewed on his lip then answered. 'People I knew. Just that. I get to know all sorts of people. They parade me around their parties like they own me. It's good for business, I guess. The Angels . . . I just met them from time to time. They were interesting people. They were *stars*.'

'You go out with them?' asked Torrillo.

'*Go out?*'

233

'Yeah. You know. Sex. That kind of stuff.'

Mateo's tan was turning a deep, suffused brown.

'Did I have sex with the brothers? You really asking that? You really asking if I had sex with them?'

'Yeah,' said Torrillo. 'I'm asking.'

'Jesus.' Mateo looked incredulous. 'Look. The circles I move in you meet a lot of queers. Personally, I don't like it. I come from the barrio, you know. But you meet them, you shake hands, you say hello. That's how it goes. It's a business thing.'

'So you didn't meet them socially, outside of parties. With other friends, so to speak.'

'So to speak what? You think I'm queer? Jesus. When I fight in that ring I can look into that crowd and pick any woman I want. You know that? You understand that? Once that fight's over, I just pick whatever I want and take it. You go home to your quiet little wife, policeman, I just take my pick for the night. End of story.'

'Goes with the job, huh? Not being queer and all that.'

'Yes,' spat Mateo. 'Goes with the job. That's the way you want to look at it, that's your choice.'

Menéndez looked at some notes on his pad. 'I looked at your records before we came here, Señor Mateo.'

'Wonderful. Why don't you just read the papers?'

'Some petty theft when you were young.'

'I got caught. Most of us didn't in the barrio. I did. You think this is new? You read *Hola!*? It's all in there, week in, week out. Good copy – ghetto kid makes good.'

'Two years ago in Cadiz, there was a complaint. From a girl.'

'Sure. And your records show nothing happened. The police there didn't do nothing about it.'

'Why was that?' asked Torrillo. 'You get on the phone to your friends?'

'No need. Stupid bitch makes up to me after the fight, comes on like she knows what it's about. We get to the room and she changes her tune. Later. When she thinks about it.'

Menéndez went through his notes. 'She says you raped her. Held a knife to her throat, then raped her.'

'She's a fucking liar. You go to someone's room, two in the morning, what do you think's going to happen? You play cards?'

'She was fifteen.'

'Yeah, and you saw her that night you'd think she was twenty-two. It's only after, when she realises what Mama might say, that she starts screaming rape. Only afterwards. That's why the cops let her go.'

Menéndez wrote on the pad, then turned the page.

'Did you know Luis Romero?'

Mateo stared at the ceiling for a few moments. 'Doesn't ring a bell. Should I?'

'Professor at the university. This is his photograph.'

He passed over the college portrait. Romero was smiling for the camera.

'Well?' asked Torrillo.

'Don't rush me,' said Mateo. 'You want the truth, don't you?'

He held up the picture to get the light on it better. 'I've seen him before. Don't know his name though.'

'Where have you seen him?' asked Menéndez.

'Shit, I don't know. Some party. Some hanger-on. You know how many people there are like that? Hundreds. Maybe thousands. They follow you around, pat you on the back like you were an old buddy or something, then go home and tell their friends how they been out partying with the famous man. Sure. I've seen him before. Hanging out at some party. Don't ask me where.'

'A party at the Angels' apartment?' asked Maria. 'Did you go there? Did you see him there?'

Mateo thought. 'Could be. The brothers threw a party four, maybe five months ago. I went because they promised it wouldn't be just the queer crowd they hung around with.'

'Was it?' she said.

'No. It wasn't. For once they actually told the truth. It was pretty normal really. Some women, some business people. They could lay things on well if they wanted.'

'And you think Romero might have been there?'

'Maybe. I don't know. But maybe. I go to these things all the time. Maybe two, three times a week. I can't remember who was at each one. It's too much.'

'I can understand that,' said Menéndez. 'What about Miguel Castaneda? Was he a hanger-on?'

'No,' said Mateo, firmly. 'You know who he was. The guy who ran the brotherhood. Sure, there were social events with the brotherhood from time to time and he'd be there. But I don't remember seeing him hanging around. That old guy was too snobby for that. He didn't like mixing with the riffraff.'

'Was,' said Torrillo. 'You said "was".'

'I can read, you know. It was all over the front page how he got killed in that little office of theirs.'

'You knew the place?'

''Course I knew it. I was a member for God's sake. Didn't you look through their records and find that out for yourself? I used to have to go to their crappy evenings from time to time. Do the tradition thing. They expected it.'

'Why?' Maria asked. 'Why did you have to be a member?'

Mateo looked into the empty teacup. 'Let's just say it was kind of bequeathed to me.'

'By your father. By Antonio Alvarez,' she said.

He went blood-red in the face and gripped the cup so hard she thought it might break.

'My, we have been doing our homework, haven't we?'

'Your father found you a place in the brotherhood. He made it a gift?'

Mateo laughed. 'A gift? A *gift?*'

The shine, the energy had left his face. His eyes now looked dull and blank, the pupils like pinpoints, unfocused, uncaring.

'I didn't get gifts from my father. He gave us money. To keep us alive. He paid for my lessons in the ring. He left me what he thought was the right ... the right *framework* for me to live in when I grew up. I don't think it was a gift. When you put up fences to pen in your cattle, when you inoculate them to keep away diseases, these things aren't gifts, just housekeeping. The kind of thing you do out of duty, like putting a dog in kennels when you want to go on holiday.'

They paused, waiting, in vain, for him to say more, then Maria asked, 'Did you meet him? Was he a visitor to your house?'

Mateo closed his eyes. His face looked like a death mask. 'Once. When I was small. I remember a man, a tall man, dressed in white, coming to the house. Talking to my mother. They went upstairs. There were sounds. Things I didn't understand then. Then they came down again. He patted me on the head. I remember this big, brown hand in my hair, a wasted, thin face, yellow teeth. He left money on the kitchen table and my mother said that I must never, *never* tell anyone that Don Alvarez had visited us. I thought, then, that my father had died before I was born. That was what my mother had told me. It was only later, when she was dying herself, that I found out the truth. I think I was the last to know. At school, they would taunt me, call me

237

"Antonio's bastard", but I didn't know what they meant. Then, when I found out, he was already ill. He refused to see me, but the money kept on coming. I used it to learn the ring. To fight. I used it to escape.'

Maria found herself wondering: did anyone ever really escape Antonio Alvarez?

'When he died, he was in some kind of disgrace, but there was a public funeral. I went to see the coffin. There was this face I did not recognise. It was so thin, so *wasted*. I couldn't . . . I couldn't feel anything. I still don't.'

'So your father bequeathed you a place in the brotherhood?'

'And a few other things too. Some money. Some paintings. I was not the only bastard, you understand. There were many crows pecking at the cake. But I got more than most. For some reason, I don't know, I think he favoured me over the others.'

'Do you know Caterina Lucena?' she asked. 'Does the name mean anything to you?'

He shook his head slowly. 'Nothing. Nothing at all.'

'You like art,' she said.

He shrugged. 'I got money. I like to buy things.'

'You know what you're buying? All of these pictures, *most* of these pictures here, they come from the same period. The same place.'

'Yeah,' he said. 'And the same gallery too. I buy these things in job lots. You think I got time to decorate the place myself?'

'You know who they're by?'

'Jesus. What is this? Some kind of test? No. They are pictures. Like the pictures we had on the wall when I was a kid. I like that. You think I should buy the sort of shit the Angels turned out?'

No one answered that.

Torrillo said, 'You're a member of the brotherhood, presumably you've got a cloak?'

Mateo said, 'Yes. Somewhere in the house. It's a long time since I wore it.'

'We need to take it away with us. We need to look at it.'

Mateo shrugged, went to the door and barked orders to the manservant. A minute later he returned with the robe, folded over his arm. Torrillo snatched it from him and examined it on the spot. It was slightly faded and smelled of dust and mould.

'You remember when you last wore it?'

'No,' said Mateo wearily. 'You don't need them for the social functions. It's just Semana Santa, and the rehearsals, you use them for, and I don't go out then.'

Torrillo threw the cloak down on a chair. 'We don't need to take it away. There's nothing there.'

'Whatever you want,' said Mateo and he slumped back into the chair. 'Is this going on much longer?'

'You going somewhere?' asked Torrillo.

'No. I'm just tired. I like to get to bed early the week before a fight.'

'Yeah,' said Torrillo. 'Makes sense.'

Menéndez got out of his chair and said, 'We don't need any more from you tonight, Señor Mateo. But we may need to speak to you again.'

'I stay here until next Tuesday. Then I go to Malaga for a fight next weekend.'

'Fine. Then good night.'

He barely saw them leave. Torrillo led the way out of the house, unlocked the car, then opened the doors for them to get in. As they drove out of the gate he turned and said, 'My guess is he's shooting up right about now. You see those eyes?'

Maria nodded. 'What do you think?'

'Heroin. Most likely. Who knows? You believe that? A man brave enough to go fight bulls but can't get through the day without some kind of dope? Doesn't make sense.'

'To him it does,' said Menéndez.

Maria thought: it's not the corrida that frightens him. It's something else, something old. Something bequeathed.

She looked at her watch. It was fast approaching ten. 'I'd like to go home,' she said. 'I feel dog tired.'

'Drop me at the station,' said Menéndez. 'I want to look up some paperwork.'

Then he stared silently out of the window, watching the evening crowds on their rounds, blankly listening to the sounds of the night.

'He didn't kill anyone today,' he said to no one in particular.

'Not that we know of,' said Torrillo.

'No. He didn't kill anyone. He lets us know when he's done it. He doesn't try to hide things. If he'd killed someone today, we'd know about it.'

Torrillo glanced at his watch. 'Still two hours to go. Maybe he's working late tonight.'

In the back of the car, in the still, humid air of the night, Maria shivered.

31

'The way I see it,' said Quemada, 'it's kind of this female thing. The women you know.'

The two detectives sat facing each other across the flat, ink-stained top of the green metal desk in the office. It was approaching eleven in the evening and the place was empty. From far off, down the long corridor, came the usual echoing sounds – drunks getting dragged, complaining, down to the cells, pickpockets protesting their innocence, whores trying to talk low and persuasively. Velasco looked across at his partner and raised his eyebrows.

'This *female* thing?'

'Yeah. With women and that stuff.'

Velasco shook his head, tried to clear the sea of mucus that had settled in for the duration between his ears, and blinked very slowly. 'Women stuff. *Women stuff?* How long is it since you got divorced? Huh? What you know about women, what you *understand* about women, you could tattoo on the end of a roach's dick and still leave space for an ID.'

'That so?'

'Yeah.'

'Well, let me tell you something, *partner*. I know enough about women to know they can be real weird. Not like men. I mean *real* weird. Like, take Dolores. You know what made her leave me in the end? You know what did it? This you won't believe. I promise. Like, she been moaning at me for months about the way I dress. "Your suit looks like it came from the charity shop. It got more shiny parts than a new Datsun." All that kind of stuff. So one day I walk past the Galeria and I see they got a sale on. I go in and I buy this new suit. Kind of a cottony lineny thing. You know, pale stuff, like the politicians wear. Gotta be careful when you take a piss in case you get drip stains down the front of the pants but apart from that real smart stuff.

'So I get a real good deal on the thing. I come home, I put it on, she takes one look at me and says, "Since when did your girlfriend start buying you suits?" I ask you. So I stay nice and cool and don't blow my top and explain how, like, I just bought it so's to please her, seeing as how she spent the best part of the previous six months telling me I dressed like some bum from the gutter. Eventually she calms down a little and I'm getting to thinking that maybe, just maybe, I'm going to get out of the room with my balls intact.

'Then she says to me, "So how do you wash it?" I look at the ceiling and think: *am I hearing this?* "Beg pardon," I says. "How do you *what?*" "You didn't even look, did you?" she says. "You didn't even look on the little label inside, see how you wash it when it gets dirty. Which won't take long with you. But that don't matter. You just go buy it – that's that. Washing, that's somebody else's business."

'So I look at her and I say, "Sure, Dolores, sure I looked. I looked real good, I pulled the label out in the store and it says: 'Washing Instructions – give the suit to your wife and say *fucking wash it!*' " Then you know what she does?'

Velasco looked at his partner from under wilting eyelids. 'Let me guess. She says, "God, I just love being married to this witty and charming hunk of manhood, let's go buy two seats for the opera."'

'Yeah. Like hell. She packs her bags and she goes. You beat

that? I gave her plenty of reason before, mind. I had a couple of girlfriends from time to time, who doesn't? Once or twice I pushed her around a little, and I don't feel proud of that. But still she stays. Until I buy some dumb fucking suit and don't look at the washing label. You believe that?'

Velasco doodled with his pen on the notepad. 'Maybe it was sort of the *culmination* of things, lots of other things. The straw that broke the camel's back like they say.'

Quemada stared him straight in the eye. Sometimes, thought Velasco, just sometimes, he scares me a little.

'That, my friend, is precisely the fucking point. *Precisely*. You live with 'em in the same house, the same bed, you think you know them, then some little thing comes along out of the blue and . . . *pow!* You find the person you been sleeping next to these last ten years turns out to be the Creature from the Black Lagoon.'

'Maybe they switch 'em. Like, after the ceremony. After the wedding. They take away the one you married and put the new one from Mars in its place. And you don't even notice. 'Cos you're drinking all the father-in-law's booze.'

'Yeah. Very funny. Point I'm making . . .'

'Point? *Point?* You mean there's a point to this whole fucking thing?'

'. . . point I'm making is. You got men. They get bad moods. They get mean. They do something about it sometimes and that's wrong. But usually it's kind of predictable. Village priest don't usually turn out to be a cat burglar in his spare time. Don't go around murdering people, unless there's something wrong with him. Women. They're different. All of 'em. One little thing, something you don't even know, it just triggers 'em. They go from dumb little wife sitting quiet at home waiting to make your dinner direct to Creature from the Black Lagoon all in one go. Straight to jail. Do not collect your money when you pass Go.'

'Meaning?'

'Meaning this aunt of the Lucena woman. She could have done all that stuff with the kid. Pinched him. Brought him up. Just 'cos she felt like it. She looked at the girl's belly, the curtains were green, there's beans cooking in the kitchen, it's her time of the month, whatever, she could turn from Mother Teresa to Bluebeard just like that.'

Velasco thought about the proposition. 'I can buy that. That could've happened, for sure.'

'Yeah. For sure. *Equally . . .*'

Quemada let the words drift off into nothingness.

'Equally?' asked Velasco.

'Equally the Lucena woman could be telling us one huge heap of shit.'

'The whole thing?'

'No. Not the whole thing. Just the details. The parts. The parts that matter.'

'You mean, maybe the baby did die? Maybe those people just got sick of the sight of the Lucena girl and decided they'd rather be on the other side of the sea than listening to her go on and on about how this dashing devil killed her family and did unspeakable things to her?'

'That kind of thing.'

Velasco looked at the pile of folders on the table. They were old, faded manila with titles written with fountain pen ink in a flowery, flowing script. He picked up one marked 'A. Alvarez' and threw it across the table. When it landed, a faint film of dust blew out from its torn and grubby mouth.

'I guess that's what we're supposed to find out. Now shall we start?'

Quemada hated paper so he threw the folder back to Velasco, then placed the call to the local police in Melilla.

He wasn't expecting wonders. He wasn't disappointed.

'You want *what*?' asked the voice on the other end of the line. The officer had introduced himself as Sergeant Flores with the same kind of warmth and enthusiasm Quemada expected from a town hall clerk at one minute to lunch break.

'It's important, Sergeant. We got a murder inquiry on here. A *multiple* murder. We need some help.'

He could hear Flores fuming on the other end of the line.

'You want me to track down two people who lived here just after the war? Find out what happened to them? Who their family was? And you'd like me to do it all now?'

'I appreciate the timing's not great . . .'

'You appreciate nothing, detective. You ever been here?'

'No, sir,' said Quemada, and heartily hoped his personal ignorance of Melilla was not about to disappear. 'No, sir, I have not.'

'Well, let me tell you something. I came here from Galicia, God knows why, and this is not what you think. This is *Africa*. You understand.'

'I hear you, sir.'

'No, you don't. This is *Africa*. Not Spain. Not in any real way, anyway. *Africa*. You know what that means?'

'Let me guess, sir. Your filing systems aren't too good.'

'Jesus. They don't even exist. I can't push a button here and tell you that kind of information about people living here right now. Let alone forty, fifty years ago.'

'I understand that, sir. But you must have some kind of records.'

'Yeah. A basement full of them covered by a couple of thousand dead beetles. You want to go through them yourself, you're welcome.'

Quemada did not want to hear this.

'Not sure I would know where to start, sir.'

'Me neither. And I got better things to do. Like chasing drugs and stuff like that. You know. Real policing.'

'Finding someone who goes around killing people is real policing too, sir,' said Quemada with an edge to his voice. 'I appreciate he isn't killing people where you are but he is right here and we're concerned about that all right.'

Even if *you* aren't, you provincial little pen-pushing fucker, Quemada said to himself.

'Yeah, well. I appreciate that.' Flores took the criticism. He went silent for a moment then came back sounding marginally more amenable. 'But you gotta understand, I just don't have the human resources to go chasing these things.'

'That's the same thing as people, right?' said Quemada. He talked just like the ice queen: straight out of some university handbook.

'Right,' said Flores. 'And the point I'm trying to make to you is, you want to go through the records we have, fine. You come here and do it. No problem. But we're not doing it for you.'

'I will pass that message on to my captain, sir.'

'You do that. He got a problem, he can talk to *my* captain. Meantime . . . if you want to come out, let me know. We'll fix a room for you. I may even buy you a beer.'

'Yes, sir,' said Quemada. 'I would look forward to that. One more thing, sir?'

'Yeah?' said Flores.

'There must be some long-time residents. People from the mainland who've lived with you for years. Maybe you could put me in touch with them. I guess it's quite a small community you got over there. Maybe we could all save ourselves a lot of time if you give me a phone number and I just call them, see if they remember these people.'

'That's an idea,' said Flores.

'Yes.'

'Let me think on it. I'll call you back.'

'Thank you, sir. Any idea when?'

'When I've finished thinking on it. And the sooner you get off the line, the sooner I can start doing that.'

The line went dead. Quemada thought of the dirtiest curse he could muster and threw it at the handset.

'Our guys in the colonies not so helpful?' asked Velasco.

'Man's a complete asshole,' spat Quemada. *'We just don't have the human resources ...* where'd they get shit like that?'

'Courses. The training courses. I did one myself a couple of years back. It's easy. You just got to remember to use the right lingo. Human resources. Goals. Strategies. That kind of thing.'

'Really?'

'Goes down real well with the management these days.'

'Fine. Well this human resource would like a strategy that would give him the goal of a nice cold beer in the space of the next hour or so. You got one?'

Velasco looked at the pile of paper in front of him, picked out a couple of sheets, then threw them across the table.

'Funny you should say that,' he said. 'Yeah. Maybe I have.'

Quemada finished looking at the last piece of paper Velasco had thrown him and let out a long, low whistle.

'This guy ... when did he die?'

'Nineteen years ago. Cancer of the throat.'

'Well, can't say it happened none too soon. This was not a nice human being. Maybe that Lucena woman saw something in him but I'll be damned if I can see what it was.'

'People change. Things change people. Maybe the person she met wasn't the person he became. Maybe . . .'

'Maybe, maybe, maybe . . . No relatives, right?'

'No legal relatives. Not so far as I can see. His wife died five years before he did. No kids. Neither of them had a brother or sister either from what we got here. There's some good filing here. Even down to a couple of newspaper obituaries and the funeral report. No mention of relatives.'

'Yeah,' said Quemada, sifting through the pages. 'Plenty of little Antonio spawn around town from the other side of the blanket, though. Least, if the internal stuff is anything to go by.'

The file began in 1947 with the first complaint. It ended in 1964. In all there were thirteen separate reports. Twelve of them were sexual, all but one involving minors.

'These kids. They were all girls, all aged between fourteen and sixteen. You think that's what he liked?'

Velasco nodded. 'Seems so. Goes along with the Lucena woman's story too.'

'This guy must have had some friends somewhere. Good friends. There's different detectives on every case, different names, same conclusions. And none of 'em ever went to court. Now one false accusation of rape I could believe. Two maybe. But twelve?'

Velasco blew his nose, couldn't stop himself examining the contents of his handkerchief, then said, 'Maybe people just misunderstood his intentions.'

'Sure,' said Quemada, and pulled out a sheet of paper. 'Inma Cuellas. Fourteen at the time of the complaint. Says Antonio paid her once a week to come to him. Did most anything he liked with her. Medical evidence of anal bruising. Eye witness saw her sucking him off in the park. Pregnant. Jesus. *Six* of them are pregnant when they make the complaint. Maybe they misunderstood something too.

Thought he was playing pat-a-cake with them or something.'

'Look at the addresses. All in El Viejo. These could have been young whores. Maybe he paid them, they made the complaint when he didn't want them any more. When they got pregnant. You don't know who else they might have been fucking.'

'Don't matter if they was whores from the barrio or trainee nuns with an address in heaven. The law's the law. He should have been in court on this. He should have been in *jail*.'

'Maybe they gave people a little more leeway in those days.'

'Leeway? *Leeway?* This look like leeway to you? The guy got influence. That's all. Look at the way the case notes are signed off . . . "Insufficient evidence", "untrustworthy witness" . . . *all* of them? They all got knocked up by the local school stud and suddenly decided to blame it on poor old Antonio?'

'You don't know what happened. You're talking about a long time ago.'

'No? My guess is this is just the stuff we know about. The tip of the iceberg. Old Antonio was probably poking half the school population of El Viejo in his heyday and you know it as well as I do.'

Velasco looked at the sheaf of paper, the thin black lines of fuzzy typing. He liked the work. He liked being with Quemada. The man could be a pig but he could see into things sometimes. When he had a hunch it was usually a good hunch.

'Yeah,' Velasco said. 'I guess you're right.'

'And that probably means there's a whole generation of Antonio offspring out there with every reason in the book to feel somewhat cool towards him and his memory. Not just the Lucena woman. Kids he fucked. Kids he fathered.'

'That's an enchanting thought.'

'Yeah,' said Quemada. He turned up the last set of notes, which Velasco had set apart from the rest.

'And this is what they finally get him on? Except they don't get him at all.'

'He was creaming the brotherhood. They made him treasurer, he cooks the books. It's vague in there but looks like he got away with the best part of two million pesetas over some two, three years.'

'Wonder what he spent it on. Church donations? Mickey Mouse T-shirts for his little harem?'

'They could have prosecuted him on that one. For sure.'

'They could have prosecuted him on *every* one. What's it say here?'

Quemada squinted at the fine writing at the bottom of the report. The black ink was old and fading. He read out the words.

'"Señor Alvarez has resigned from the brotherhood. Recommendation: no action." No action. Well, isn't that a surprise?'

Velasco said, 'What do we do next? We got to show this to Menéndez. He's going to want us to trace every name in those reports.'

'He's going to want to know about the couple in Melilla too. He's going to want to know *everything*.'

Velasco sighed and looked as if the world was about to come to an end.

'Guess that settles it then,' Quemada said. ''Scuse me for a moment.'

He got out a comb, leaned over the desk, stared into Velasco's suit, and made out he was using the mirror of its fabric to comb the long greasy swatch of hair on the side of his head. Then he looked at his watch.

'Thanks, partner. You come in real useful sometimes. Those people out there are having a big time tonight, some extra big procession or something. Some parade, some heavy audience participation stuff. I read it on the detail. We got more men out there trying to keep the drunks upright than chasing our guy in the red jumpsuit. I guess God's out there, putting in a guest appearance on the pavement or something. We get a move on, you never know, we might meet some ladies full of the Holy Spirit.'

'Sure,' said Velasco and wondered why the hell he took it. 'They gonna go from God to us in five seconds flat.'

Quemada nodded and it made the little dewlap under his chin shake. 'Point taken. I guess we got an hour – how many beers we normally drink in that time?'

Velasco stood up, put on his jacket, and thought about the cold metallic taste beer makes on the back of your throat when you're coming down with a cold.

'He who counts is lost,' he said and walked out of the door.

32

Menéndez got out of the car at the station, said the Captain expected them all at eight the next morning, then went inside. The night was now black and velvety. Even the floodlights on the cathedral seemed powerless in front of it. Their deep yellow rays were swallowed up by the darkness. Only a faint aurora of light glowed beyond the surface of the city. Above the crowded streets and the tinny, local clamour of the parades the world was silent and still.

Torrillo put the car into first and pulled slowly away from the kerb. There were too many people around to go much above a crawling pace.

'What will he do tomorrow?' asked Maria. 'Where do we go next?'

Torrillo thought the question over.

'We got leads,' he said. 'We got Caterina Lucena. Alvarez. Romero. That painting thing you came up with. We got things to chase. And the Captain's getting more involved. You could see that today. He's a busy man, but he's on top of things.'

She listened for doubts in his voice and thought she could feel them, just creeping in at the edges. Torrillo, of all people, had seemed impervious to the ups and downs of the case. Now even he was beginning to wonder what would happen next.

'We're waiting, aren't we? All of us.'

He turned round from the driving seat, puzzled.

'Huh?'

'We're waiting for something to happen. Another killing. Because that's what might bring us closer to him. We need him to fall because that's the only way we're going to catch him.'

Torrillo squeezed the steering wheel and grimaced.

'No,' he said. 'That's just not true. We're doing our best, we've got some leads, we'll get there. And we know a lot when you come to think about it. We know the guy likes painting. We know he mixes in some kind of sex scene, maybe drugs too. We know he's into the bulls. And all that other stuff, the old stuff, maybe it's something, maybe it's not. It's like that sometimes. It doesn't just happen. Life's a mess, Maria. Cops just reflect that. You think you're way behind everything, that it will never come to an end. Then you turn a corner, half thinking, and suddenly you're there. Bingo.'

'Yes,' she said.

They were coming into her street now. In the closed optician's shop she could see a giant pair of neon spectacles flashing on and off in the night: red, green, blue and yellow. She thought of the system behind it: triggers, relays, power cables, the ions of the gas dancing around inside the tubes, everything jumping to attention every time the switch turned itself on and off. Just like us, she thought. Trigger, response, trigger, response.

Torrillo pulled the car in to the kerb and turned off the engine.

'You OK?' he said.

She nodded. 'I'll be fine. It's been a long day. That's all. And talking to Caterina Lucena was not a particularly cheering experience.'

'Welcome to police work. You want to hear nursery rhymes, you go work in a kindergarten.'

Maria smiled. 'Some of the nursery rhymes are pretty scary too, Bear. Think about it. Hansel and Gretel, Little Red Riding Hood . . . cannibalism, some pretty deep sexual allusions.'

'Yeah.' Bear grinned. 'I always liked those stories when I was a kid. The gruesomer the better.'

'Why?'

'Why? Simple. 'Cos when your dad's scared the living daylights out of you with one of those little horror stories it makes everything else – the normal world – so real. So safe. So comforting. Didn't you feel that? When you were a kid?'

Maria shook her head. 'I never felt that, Bear. You live with this stuff but it scares me. The world, the real world, still scares me.'

'Scares all of us sometimes, Maria. But you can't spend your whole life scared. It'll get us all in the end, for sure, but you don't live for that. You live for what happens before that. Otherwise, what's the point?'

'Life is about being safe.'

'Never walk out your front door and you'll be safe as hell till the day you die, Maria. Unless there's an earthquake. Or your kidneys start to go rotten. Safe as hell. You want that?'

She didn't answer. A picture came into her head. She couldn't have been more than four years old and on the TV was some nature show about the jungle. The picture was full of all the things she hated: insects and snakes and poisonous plants, a forest of things that wanted to bite and spike and kill you just because you walked in there, no other reason, just because that was how they *are*. And there, four years old, she had thought of the answer. Something she'd seen on another TV show: The Boy in the Bubble. You just wrapped yourself up tight in this big thick plastic

254

suit that sealed you off, hermetically and finally, from everything out there that was nasty, the suit with the airhose going to the outside world, and plenty of filters on it to keep the dirt out, and you just lived there, snug and tight and *safe*.

The Boy in the Bubble. The Woman in the Cocoon.

Pretty soon you'd be swimming in your own piss and shit, Maria. And there'd be no one there to clear it out. You know that really, don't you? You're not that dumb.

The foul little interior voice laughed away at the back of her head and she waited for the sound to go away. She wanted to be home, in Salamanca, safe, and untroubled and alone.

'Tell you what, Maria,' said Bear, and she wished, just for one moment, he wasn't so persistent, she wished he would just let her go. 'On the corner there, you see that bar. Let me buy you a beer. We can talk. It's still early now.'

'Early? Bear, it's nearly midnight.'

'For the city, believe me, it's early. They got one of their big parades on tonight. The biggest before the really big one at the weekend. When that happens you won't be able to move for bodies, but we got time. We can talk.'

'About what?'

'About anything you like. I talk, you listen. Vice versa if you like. It helps. At the end of the day. That's why cops drink, you know. To talk it out, let it all go. You got to do it otherwise you'd go crazy. Anyone who tells you we hang around the bars with the sole intention of getting shit-faced is a lying two-faced scoundrel asking for a punch in the mouth.'

Maria tried to smile. 'That's kind, Bear. But I think I'd fall asleep on you before I'd even heard a word. No offence meant. It's not you. It's me. I'm tired out and if I'm going to be back there first thing in the morning I need some sleep.'

'Sleep? Sign of a civilian. Medical science has proved conclusively that the most any of us need is two hours, maybe three hours, a night. No more. Everything else is a selfish luxury, Maria, and you know it.'

'In that case I intend to indulge myself in a little selfish luxury. But you go ahead and have your beer. I won't tell.'

She opened the car door, said good night, then walked across the road. Torrillo watched her fumble in her bag for her keys, put them in the door, then open it and go inside. A few moments later a light went on in the upstairs flat and he saw her staring out of the window, a wan, motionless silhouette.

'That,' said Torrillo to himself, 'is one sad and lonely woman. And God alone knows who's going to shake her out of it.'

He looked at his watch: eleven thirty. Then licked his lips. He knew the bar on the corner of old. It served good beer, all the usual Cruz Campo stuff but some foreign ones too. Torrillo closed his eyes and thought of a long, tall glass, iced so well it was opaque, with a big golden stump of cold Miller Genuine Draft in it, fresh from the bottle.

'One and one alone,' he said and reached for the door handle. 'Unless the mood takes me.'

He got out of the car then waited in the road as a crowd passed by: young kids in jeans, a priest, some choirboys carrying candles. There was the smell of incense and cheap cigarettes in the air, the first, far-off hints of that high, electric buzz that came from the really big ceremonies, the really big parades.

Torrillo let the group pass then fell in behind for twenty yards until he found the door to the bar. He stepped inside briskly, smiling with anticipation. Something tugged at his

256

mind. He tried to put a finger on it. When the glass arrived on the counter, looking as welcome as he expected, it finally clicked. In the party on the pavement, in among the white and the denim blue, there was a solitary red robe. A penitent's robe. *On its own.*

Torrillo shook his head and tried to clear it.

'Shit,' he said to himself, 'she's getting me thinking that way too.'

Then he downed the beer in a single gulp, threw two hundred-peseta coins on the bar, and walked back out into the street. It must have been the drink, thought Torrillo. It must have been too cold. Suddenly, he was shivering and he could feel the sweat sticking his huge white cotton shirt to his chest.

Maria rolled over in bed and willed herself to sleep. She was naked, under a single sheet. The window was partly open and a light, almost cool, breeze fell lazily through the gap. But still sleep would not come. When she closed her eyes, shapes and images started to roll around in the dark. They made her feel giddy. Her head whirled. There was a dull, persistent ache behind each temple. It was as if the fatigue itself was keeping her awake.

She pulled herself upright, put on the light, fumbled underneath the sheets, and found a thin, crumpled dressing gown. Then she got out of bed, went into the kitchen and drank a glass of water. It was close to midnight. At this rate she might be lucky to get five hours' sleep before she got up again. Maybe Bear was right. Maybe she didn't need to sleep so much. After a while, maybe you adapted and it didn't matter.

She went into the living room and sat down on the sofa. Was it only twenty-four hours since she had been in precisely the same position, thinking about Paolo, looking at herself and wondering: is this me, the same me? The longer she stayed in the city, the more distance there seemed to be between her old self, the university self, calm, cold, unreflective, and this new person, this fragile person open to damage, to being touched by the events around her. There was a bleak simplicity about her life: if you cared for no one, not even yourself, it was impossible to be hurt. If you erected enough walls, enough barriers, between yourself and the world, nothing could peek through the cracks. Great idea. Pity this was the city. There were no walls high enough, there was nowhere that someone could not pry. This was the city . . .

Maria found herself nearly sleeping, with her eyes open, bolt upright on the sofa. Dreaming of nothing in particular, a dull thud dimly hurting her brain. When she heard the sound it took her a moment to detect it, another moment to recognise it. Then, with a distinct physical lurch, she was back in her body again, back inside herself. And the phone was ringing.

She walked over, picked it up and said, 'Hello.'

A voice she almost recognised, a man's voice, young, but not juvenile, spoke the moment she answered. 'You still don't know yet, do you? I can't believe it. You *still* don't know.'

Maria tried to think, to get the conversation straight. The call from last night was slowly coming back to her.

'Don't know what? Who *are* you?'

The voice on the other end of the line laughed.

'Not that you should not have to ask,' he said and Maria suddenly felt cold.

'What do you want?' she asked.

'Some recognition. I want you to *recognise* me, Maria.'

It sounded wrong when he used her name.

'I'm putting the phone down,' she said, and she pulled

258

it away from her ear. Then held it there, listening, still listening, for what he would say next.

'Look in your bag,' he said, the voice now a tinny, thin sound coming out of the earpiece. 'Look at what you've lost. Then try to think where you've lost it. Then . . .'

She slammed the phone down and crossed her arms. She went over to the apartment door and looked on the chair. Her jacket and bag were on the floor beside it: another bad shot, Maria, she thought.

She stuck her hand inside the bag. Tissues, keys, a packet of sweets, a purse, some loose coins, the collected fluff of ages, a couple of tampons. It was impossible to count things, impossible to tick them off.

She picked up the bag, turned it upside down, emptied the entire contents on the floor then kneeled down beside the mess. One by one, she picked the items out, put them to one side, tried to kick start her throbbing brain into some kind of action. When she had sorted everything out, every last paper clip, every last widowed biro top, she sat back on her haunches, mouth open, gasping.

The green mask and the red velvet walls

It was a struggle to think straight, but when she tried hard enough, it happened. And then suddenly the world came into sharp, painful focus. Maria ticked off the points, one by one. She had lost her address book. It fell out, with the rest of the contents of the bag when she got scared at the brotherhood's office. It got picked up by the man in the red robe. The man who went on to kill Miguel Castaneda.

The phone was back on the hook five yards away on the table. She dashed over to it, grabbed the receiver and started to dial 911. Then she listened. Nothing. The line was dead, silent. She stabbed the buttons again. Again silence. Then, from somewhere down the line, a voice.

'You hung up, Maria. I didn't. You can't dial out if somebody else is on the line.'

She grasped for words. 'Who *are* you?'

'Irrelevant,' he said, instantly.

'Why are you doing this?'

'My business. Mainly.'

'You're *killing* people. Do you understand that? What it means?'

'Oh, yes,' he said. 'I understand. Very well.'

She stabbed at the phone buttons again.

'It's no good, Maria. You can't drop the line. Not while I'm on it. Don't you *know* that?'

'You need help,' she said. 'There are doctors who can help you. You're sick. The doctors can help. This isn't a police thing. You'll go to hospital. Not to jail.'

He laughed again and she was shocked by how ordinary, how *normal* he sounded. Too normal. Too controlled.

'I'm not going anywhere. Anywhere.'

'I can get help. I can help you. Let me do that. I'm not the police.'

'You can't help me, Maria,' he said.

'Why?' she said. 'Why not?'

'Because you're already dead,' he said in a flat, monotone voice.

She could picture what happened then, picture it from the spiky little electronic sounds coming down the phone. He put the handset down somewhere, maybe on a table, maybe on the shelf in a booth. She heard him place it there, heard the distinct clack of plastic meeting plastic. Then a door opened. There was sound: pop music, people talking, people drinking. A bar. He was phoning from a bar. From a phone that was separate from the drinking area itself. Maybe outside the toilets.

She could hear him walk away. Then there was just the

bar sound again. The drunken voices, the cheap music.

Maria drew herself together and screamed, screamed as loud as she could into the ivory-coloured receiver.

But even as she did, she wondered why. She knew no one could possibly hear her.

And then the street seemed to explode with people. One moment Torrillo was standing on the pavement, looking right and left, frantically scanning the crowd swarming on the street. The next he was in a seething flood of bodies and voices. The procession had come around the corner from the big broad shopping avenue in a big human tidal wave, then found itself channelled into the narrow, high-walled street, crushed together by its own momentum, like insects being crammed down a funnel. Far off, on the shoulders of people he couldn't see, he could make out the white doll-like face of a Virgin, cheap jewels glittering on her veil, bobbing up and down in the chequered darkness. The bearers were maybe fifty feet away but it was difficult to make out. Everything had changed. Everything now *swayed* in front of him, up and down, from side to side. The air was full of frantic, wild excitement and the electricity of hysteria.

He pushed people out of his way, swearing. They glared back at him. Someone raised his fists then dropped them in an instant when he saw Torrillo, huge and bull-like, trying to force his way through the crowd, searching frantically around him.

There were no red penitents. No red penitents he could see. Lots of people dressed in ordinary casual clothes. A bunch in black, faces hidden under cowls. The group of choirboys he had seen earlier, still holding candles. Now their faces looked eerie in the street lights, pale and drained and blank. He felt he was being engulfed by a blind, mind-

261

less animal, swamped as it bore down on him, drowning everything in his way.

There was a street lamp, cast iron, painted black. He threw himself towards it, let the metal deflect, if only briefly, the flow of bodies past him, then reached into his pocket. The crush was so bad now that it took him three good tries before he could get it out and look for the little red power light. It came on, a tiny beacon in the night, then Torrillo wondered what he was supposed to say. Something scared him? He had a bad feeling?

He stabbed the talk button, tried to make out what the radio operator was saying, screamed three times into the mike, then gave up. He looked at the emergency squawk button, thought better of it, then stuffed the radio back in his pocket. It wasn't going to help.

He looked across the road, up to the first-floor window. Face illuminated by the dusky yellow of the street lamps, Maria stood at the window, a terrified silhouette. Torrillo took in the picture in an instant. She had the phone in her hand. Her face was contorted, a mask of fear and agony. She was screaming, silently, pointlessly, into the darkness.

He took a deep breath, stepped out from the temporary protection of the street lamp, then plunged, fighting, roaring into the flood of bodies streaming down the street. It was like jumping into a river moving at the speed of an express train. He turned his face away from the flow, set his right shoulder against the crowd, then pushed with everything he had. The crush parted not one inch. He found himself carried along with them, felt his feet stumbling underneath him, then remembered some of the accidents, some of the incidents of the past. People falling, people being crushed underfoot. It happened like this, Torrillo thought. Just like this.

People were starting to yell at him now, first in anger,

then in fear as they began to feel the nervous tension in the mass of bodies, the sudden realisation that there was too much humanity here, that it was living on the edge of something that could, in an instant, turn deadly.

'Police!' Torrillo yelled. For a moment, he held up his right arm and then he felt himself lifted, carried along by the weight of bodies, feet clear of the ground. He rammed his arm back down into the mass, turned to roll with the momentum, found himself running to stay upright. He looked at the faces around him. They were scared now. They wanted to get away, to flee, but there was always something, some other slab of humanity in the way, blocking the path.

It was hard to tell where he was. Torrillo guessed he might be in the middle of the street by now. He might have covered fifteen feet since he plunged into the swarm. He looked to his right and the glowing fluorescent lights of the optician's shop swam past in a blurry fuzz of colour. He had to get out of the centre, get to the other side, stop being pushed along with the flow.

To his right, someone went down on the ground. A whole mass of heads behind him disappeared as they tripped over the fallen body. Torrillo reached into his pocket, felt for the radio, tried to recall the feel of the buttons, to remember which one was the emergency squawk. He felt what he thought was the right one, pressed it, hoped to God it would work.

From somewhere off to his left he heard the sound of breaking glass. Someone was smashing the shop windows, trying to escape the crush. The crowd was now nearing a uniform pace, a fast half march, half run. You kept to it, kept to it exactly, and you stayed upright. You fell behind, or tried to race in front, and you went down, taking a whole line of people behind with you. The whole thing was precise, like a deadly metronome, and he couldn't think of any way to break it, to break out enough to reach the other side, to, first, steady himself against the flow, then wait, wait long enough for it to subside, so that he could retrace his tracks back to the apartment, back to . . . what?

He was pushing now, pushing to the far side of the street, in any case, just because that seemed to be the right thing to do. The crush had slowed a little, it was easier to stay upright. It had been through the worst, probably, the wave had hit it as the crowd had funnelled into the narrow street, then the tremors had barrelled backwards and forwards through the mass of people, pushing them, shoving them, wherever it wanted.

From behind, now, he could hear the screaming, loud, and terrified and persistent. He did not want to turn around and look.

His feet hit the kerb, he stumbled, someone pushed from behind. It filled his mind, a vivid, colourful picture. He was falling, falling forwards, hands outstretched, falling flat on the ground, ready to be trampled by the screaming masses behind. But then some automatic pilot took over. His legs caught up with him. His head jerked upright, the breath came streaming into his lungs, hot and painful. He looked up, saw it and found, in the midst of the throng, that he could still think.

It was the kind of sign you still found outside old-fashioned ironmongers. A giant pair of scissors, maybe ten feet long, fashioned out of cast iron, black and ancient. The sign was set so that the blades were half open. On the side of the wall, two great circles marked the handles. They disappeared into the brickwork through fastening he couldn't see. Maybe a couple of screws. Maybe something stronger. Torrillo didn't give it a thought.

He was close in to the edge of the street now. He pushed

out his right hand in a momentary gap between the bodies and felt the wall scrape the skin of his knuckles. He edged his way in to the side. Now there was no one between the brickwork and him. Just the steady, insistent push of people from behind, the tramp of feet, from some way off the sound of crying.

He slowed a little, just enough so that the bodies behind were pushing him a little harder, just enough so that there was a small gap between him and the body in front. He could see it clearly now. The huge ornamental scissors were silhouetted in the street lights. They seemed bigger than he first thought and he felt grateful: something that size would have to be secured properly into the wall.

One chance, he said to himself, one chance, as the big shadow loomed overhead.

Then he jumped, hands high above him, reaching, reaching, reaching.

Torrillo gripped old, rusted metal in his fingers, gripped as hard as he could. He could feel his legs hitting heads and shoulders in the crowd below, heard them cursing him, tried to pull himself up as quick as he could to stop the catastrophe getting worse. The big iron sign moved slightly, with a tremor, on the wall as he struggled to get higher, there was the groan of ancient metal moving. His muscles ached. His arms seemed about to be ripped from his shoulders.

'Don't fall,' said Torrillo quietly to himself. 'Whatever you do, don't fall.'

His hands found the top of the lower circular handle. He jerked himself up higher, reached up and found the upper one. Now the pain was real. It shot down his arms, from the shoulder to the elbow, and maybe something, some sinew, some muscle, was damaged. Scrambling, he managed to get his feet onto the frame of the sign. It was still holding. It *would* hold.

The stream of people was still rushing beneath him. No one seemed to have fallen as a result of his efforts to get out of the crowd. He made himself secure, one great arm gripped around the ironwork, then tried to look around. The street looked like a battlefield as the fighting drew to a close. The great crush of the crowd was nearly past him. In a few seconds it would be safe to get down again. But, in the wake of the flood tide, bodies were strewn everywhere. Some moved, making low, soft sounds. Some were still. Far off, close to the street entrance, Torrillo could make out a small pocket of white motionless on the ground. The choirboys, he thought, and the enormity of what had happened began to hover around the edge of his mind.

Then he changed his position again, found a firmer footing, worked his way around to look back along the full length of the street. He was a good ten feet off the ground. The moon had come out from behind a cloud. It cast a chill silver light on the scene. Torrillo was reminded of some picture he had once looked at in a gallery when he was a kid. Maybe it was Goya. Whatever it was, it had given him nightmares for weeks. This was what it came to, it said. This was where you ended up.

He jerked his head further to the left and felt the tendons straining in his neck. Outside the door to Maria's apartment the street was clear now. Apart from a single, dark figure waiting outside.

Torrillo waited for a second, watched the neon lights play over the shape at the door, then gently let himself down to the ground.

From some way off came the sound of a siren. An ambulance, Torrillo thought. Maybe the emergency button worked. Even if it didn't, something this big, something of this *size*, would bring them running in any case.

The vehicle came gently around the corner, wary of the

bodies on the streets. Its headlights were the colour of milk. Torrillo followed them and there could be no doubt. The figure outside the apartment was wearing red, a dark-red penitent's costume. And it was trying to open the door.

Without thinking, the big man broke into a run.

'Think,' said Maria to herself. *'Think!'*

She put down the phone and stepped back from the window. Then she pulled the dressing gown more tightly around her and knotted the belt firmly at the waist. Suddenly, the street erupted in noise. She looked down and saw the crowd, half delirious, half terrified, pouring into the narrow road in their hundreds. They formed an entire mass of humanity, an impassable wall of flesh moving, without pause, along the width of the street.

This was something new. This was something he could not have expected. He was calling from a bar. The nearest was a good two hundred yards away, the one that Torrillo had talked about. If he'd been there, then he just might have made it across the street in time. But there were any number of little bars in the neighbourhood. If he'd been anywhere else, the sudden rush of people would have barred him from the apartment. If he was in it, there was no way he could stop. If he was behind it, he would have to wait for the street to clear before he could move.

Maria went into the kitchen, opened the pine drawer built into the sink unit and looked at what was in there. She picked up a medium-length cooking knife, ran a finger gently along the edge. It was sharp. Sharp enough.

She held the knife tightly in her right hand then went back into the living room. Maria thought about the layout of the apartment. There was no easy access front or back to the windows at first-floor level. No verandas, no overhanging ledges. He would need a ladder to get in that way. It was impossible from the front. She walked into the bedroom, looked at the back window then slammed it shut. Beyond the glass, the night was black and impenetrable. She tried to remember what was behind the apartment. A yard? Some small huts?

It didn't come. She dropped the knife, bent down to try the small chest of drawers by the bed. It was heavy. Straining, she managed to lift one end then lever the rest onto the bed. She rolled it over, drawers spilling clothes on the coverlet, rolled it again, then pushed it hard against the window. With some effort, she managed to tip it on end so that the length of the drawers sat upright against the window, leaning against the frame at the top.

It wouldn't stop him, she thought. But it would hinder him. And by that time she would be out of the front door.

She went back to the living room and looked out of the window. The crowd was still coming into the street in a frenzied crush. Now every emotion had gone except fear and a growing sense of panic. She could see people falling over in the mêlée, watched the shock waves of their bodies ripple through the rest of the heaving, shifting crowd.

For a crazy moment she wondered: could he have caused this? Is that *possible*?

But it didn't make any sense. Why call? It must have been as big a surprise to him as it was to any of them.

There were people screaming now, others trying to help them, and finding themselves swept away in the crush. She saw one man picked up by the crowd and dashed against the wall, falling senseless to the floor. The entire mass moved as one, shaking itself to pieces as it did so.

She picked up the phone, banged the buttons till she wanted to cry. Still she could hear the sounds of the bar at the other end: pop music, maybe a TV, the sound of voices. The same as before. And if that was the case, they couldn't be too close. The frenzy, the chaos on the street was loud, was overwhelming. Even half a street away they surely would have noticed.

She looked at the apartment door and felt her heart sink. The lock was a simple one flimsily screwed to the wood-work. Even she could probably kick it off if she wanted to.

'Downstairs,' she said. 'If I can stop him downstairs, he can't get in.'

She opened the apartment door and looked down the long staircase. It was pitch dark. She punched the light time switch on the wall, saw the single bulb catch fire, listened to the ticking of the timer in the switch housing. How long did it last? She tried to remember. You hit it downstairs when you came in, you walked up the stairs listening to the ticking, then just as you got the keys out, the light failed. When she first moved in, she just punched the top switch again and looked for the lock. Now she could do it by feel, by memory.

Maria pushed her fingernails deep into her palms. She could feel them digging in like spikes. She thought she might have drawn blood but it didn't matter. She had to check the front door. She had to secure it.

The kitchen knife held in front of her, she walked down the narrow, straight staircase, staring at the heavy wooden door at the end. Nothing moved there. There was nowhere he could hide. He was not in the apartment. If she could make sure the front door was locked, double locked from the inside, there was no way he could get in, not in a hurry. And once she'd fixed the front door, she was going back upstairs, back into the living room, waiting for the crowd to subside, and then screaming out of the window until the cops came. Given the mess in the street, that wasn't going to take long.

Maria got to the bottom of the stairs, heard the ticking

of the top switch slowing down from behind her, looked to one side, then punched the lower time switch. It started ticking like an overheated insect and she looked at the door.

This was a real lock, built into the wood, big and brass and solid. She tried to remember what she'd been told when she moved in. You turned the key twice from the outside to activate the deadlock. From the inside, you pushed over the small brass latch button and it locked into place. Once you did that, it was solid. She was safe.

She tucked the knife into her dressing gown pocket, reached up and shoved over the brass button. It moved half an inch to the right and clicked into some kind of socket. She took her fingers away, then watched, astonished, as it sprang back to its original position.

'Shit,' she said and then pushed it over again. Again she felt something hard and metallic grip the button on the inside, again she felt it let go, let the whole thing slip back to where it was before. She held the button in place and tried to open the lock with the door latch. It stayed blocked. Then she let the button go back to the original position, the position it wanted to be in, and tried the latch again. It moved, so easily you could open it with a little finger. She peered closely at the shiny metal around the button. It was covered with scratches. The kind of scratches you got from a metal screwdriver.

Automatically, Maria pushed the button back and held it there. She couldn't work out how this could be possible. The lock wasn't broken. It had been fixed to be like this. He'd planned to come in this way, planned to get in through the front door. Was planning to do so now.

She held it tightly in place with her right hand, felt for the pocket with her left, and pulled out the knife. And the thought hit her almost instantly. She couldn't stand like this for long. It just wasn't possible.

A noise came to her, from behind, a simple, familiar noise. The sound of a timer winding down, the ticks dying away, one by one until there was half a second, then a second, then two between each one.

The light went out and now she stood in perfect, complete darkness, feeling the cold sweat running down her forehead and stinging her eyes, feeling naked and unprotected under the flimsy night clothing.

When it came, it was a simple, practical decision, the kind of decision she might make in a supermarket or on a motorway. She could not see, not a single thing, and the darkness was now becoming disorienting. She could feel her balance slipping as she lost her bearings inside the vast black pit which had become her world. If she did not move soon, if she did not move *now*, she would never reach the light switch at all. And he would come in, through the door, the blinding light of the street behind him, ready to strike.

Maria wiped her forehead with the back of her left forearm, thought carefully about where the light switch was positioned in relation to the door, let go of the button and punched hard on the wall to her left. Her knuckles hit hard plaster and she could feel the tears of pain spring into her eyes. She stamped the wall again, and again. Still the switch eluded her and the more she tried, the more confused she became. Within moments she was on the floor, crying, trying to work out which way was left, which way was right, which way was up, which way was down. The world had become an ocean of blackness, devoid of size, as big as the cosmos, as tiny as an atom. She cowered in it, blind and panting, hunched on the floor making her eyes ache as she fought to distinguish a shape, a flicker of light in the sea of living, breathing darkness in front of her.

Briefly, yet it seemed as if it lasted for ever, she was aware of herself, of everything about her, the blood that coursed through her veins, roared in her ears, the breath in her lungs, the spittle in her mouth, everything about her was palpable and real, a small, extant piece in a complex whole.

Then she heard nothing but silence. Even past the door, the street seemed quiet. The world paused, held its breath.

Shrieking, as much from fury as from fear, she dropped the knife and began to hammer the wall with both hands, searching for the light, the light she thought might disperse the darkness for ever.

The switch smashed underneath her fist. A sudden, swift, blinding radiance filled the narrow hallway and then she heard the sound, so familiar, so frightening, the sound of a key in the lock, and the door opening slowly, steadily, behind her.

Maria turned round, looked up and saw the night obscured by redness.

33

'I knew this was a fucking lousy idea,' gasped Quemada. 'Tempting fate. You go outta the office, you take your radio. They wait till they put the beer in front of you. *Then* they call . . . If only we picked somewhere nearer the station.'

They were running now, a solid half-trot, jackets flapping around their waists, running down the darkened shopping arcade, aiming for the street at the end. From around the corner came the cacophony of an ambulance.

'Jesus,' grunted Velasco, out of breath. 'Will you quit moaning? How was I to know we'd be just round the corner when the call came in?'

The two men came to the end of the wide arcade, stopped, stood motionless, panting, hands on their waists, looking at the devastation in the street. Looking at the bodies, some still, some moving. The air was filled with an uncanny, quiet moaning.

'Shit,' said Quemada. 'Looks like a bomb went off. They say on the radio what it was? What happened?'

'Some sort of crowd panic. That's all.'

There was the sound of more ambulances now, from the opposite end of the street.

'I came bottom in first aid,' said Quemada. 'Let's leave it to the medics.'

'That'll look real good.'

'Well. Let's ask them what we can do. Situations like this, my feeling is you leave it to the experts.'

'Yeah . . .' said Velasco.

But he was thinking about something else.

'Say . . .' He pointed down the half-dark street, to the opposite side of the pavement. 'You see that?'

Quemada followed the line of his finger. A huge figure was running along the pavement, faster than seemed possible for his bulk, arms pumping, head rolling like a charging steer.

'You know . . .' muttered Velasco. 'Something . . .'

'That's Bear, for fuck's sake. *That's Torrillo.*'

'Yeah,' said Velasco. And automatically the two men began moving, resumed their ungainly jog across the street, watchful, wondering, sweat now standing out on their foreheads, the moisture clinging to their upper bodies.

As they ran Quemada reached inside his jacket, undid the holster, then pulled out a .38 police pistol. Without thinking, Velasco did the same, and they ran on, slowly, steadily, towards the pool of light that had now engulfed Torrillo.

'You hear that?' panted Quemada.

'Yeah . . .' said Velasco, and tightened his grip on the gun.

As they got closer, they could hear the sound of someone screaming.

Maria rolled, instinctively, rolled to the left on the hard, dusty floor of the hallway.

The green mask and the red velvet walls

She heard a whistling noise fly past her head, heard something bang into the woodwork and thought: the dart. The first dart missed. It was light now, the bright, harsh light of an unshaded electric bulb too powerful for the job.

'*No!*' she screamed. '*No!*'

274

She could feel his presence a few feet away, feel his confusion. When he had come through the door, when the light had suddenly burst on, she had had this momentary vision of him, tall, erect, but shapeless. It was as if there was no face beneath the cowl, no form beneath the fabric. The redness, amorphous and malevolent, was everything, a creature in itself. Then the dart had missed and she could sense, could almost measure, his confusion. He didn't step forward and try to harm her in some other way. He stayed a good six feet distant, and she saw him fumbling in the coat for something else. It came to her: he will not come close, he will not approach *until* he has wounded in some other way. There was a mechanism, a procedure, and he had to follow it.

Briefly, she was close to hysterical laughter. Until he found the next part of the process, the next step in her slaughter, she was safe, able to think about how to defend herself. The silver of the kitchen blade flashed on the dusty floor. She rolled again, turned 360 degrees across the dry, grey linoleum, turned face down again straight in front of the door, now only a stride away from him, the knife a few inches to her right. Her hand went out to grab it, fingers outstretched, and she wondered: would I really use it? Will this really defend me?

But she never got there. A foot came across her field of vision, kicked the blade away, she heard him laughing – *laughing?* – and suddenly her right shoulder blade exploded in pain, a sharp, stabbing agony that tore into the muscles of her back like cold fire.

She screamed, louder than ever, as loud as she thought possible, then pulled her left hand from underneath her, reached round behind her back, felt the sinews straining in her arm. The dart was there. She could feel the feather and the shaft, embedded deep into her flesh. She steeled herself for the pain, pulled hard on the hard metal shaft, then yanked it out of her back, roughly, from a side angle, making the wound complain more, making her head throb with the pain. The agony cut through her mind like a knife. There was a preternatural clarity to the sequence of events now. Every moment was lucid, apparent to her in its finest detail, every tiny action had a finite life to it, like frames in a film. She could see the grains of dust floating up from the floor as she rolled over again, onto her back. She could smell him now: sweat and shoe polish and the faint sour odour of urine. The sounds of the night, of her small, diminishing universe, came to her as individual stamps of identity, each carrying its own label: the far-off hammer of a klaxon beating against stone walls, the lilting moans of the dying and injured in the street, the rustle of the man's robe above her. The beating of wings, moths' wings, in the humid, cloying air.

This is what happens before you die, she thought. This swift magnification of the senses, this momentary focusing of the personality on the last, immediate elements of existence. She felt her life flickering like a candle in the breeze above her. Then she stopped moving, was flat on her back, eyes wide open, staring at the figure above her. He had pulled back the cowl now: an ordinary face, thirty, perhaps older; dark hair short and tight around the skull; dark, flashing eyes; a smooth, tanned complexion. He was grinning. In his right fist, clenched tightly upright, sleek and silver, was the sword, and he was stepping forward, slowly, deliberately.

'I don't know you,' Maria said quietly, her aching back against the ground, staring up at him, listening to the ticking slowing again, waiting, hoping. 'I don't *know* you.'

Another shape filled her view. Large and familiar, shouting, a voice she recognised, a voice that held hope. She saw the sword go up in the air, heard the ticking falling away to nothing.

The night paused, then plunged back into darkness, and she was moving again, rolling any way she could, right and left, trying to get out of the way of the mayhem above her, the shouts, the lights, the noise.

There were more voices, more screams. She yelled in agony as someone stepped on her, making the wound in her back jump like an electric shock, then stepped over her.

Footsteps racing up the stairs in the blackness, the sound of her apartment door slamming.

Some kind of peace.

Some kind of safety.

The light went on again, blinding her, making her cover her eyes with her hands. She tried to think about her body: the pain in her back. Was there something else? Was she hurt more than this?

There was nothing else. That, at least, seemed certain.

The voices. *Quemada? Velasco?* They were coming down the stairs again, yelling at each other, yelling obscenities that echoed off the narrow walls like the shouts of madmen.

She opened her eyes and looked at them. They held their guns limply by their sides and now they were rushing steadily down the stairs, something else on their minds.

In the doorway, fallen like a great beast, lay Torrillo. The sword stuck out from his jacket like a silver stump. His face was as pale as writing paper. His huge chest rose and fell in shallow movements.

She crawled over to him and put a hand to his face. It was cool and moist. Around the base of the weapon the blood coagulated, dark and sticky. She leaned over and whispered in his ear, 'Don't die, Bear. Don't die.'

And then she was sobbing, shoulders heaving, her body gripped by an involuntary animal spasm.

'I'll get the medic,' said Quemada, and he stepped over them into the street.

What seemed like an age later he returned with a thin young man in a white nylon jacket, a red cross on the front.

'I'm going to report you for this,' the medic said. 'I got work out there.'

'Yeah,' said Quemada, waving the pistol at him. 'You got work here too.'

'Put the fucking gun down,' yelled Velasco. 'Are you crazy, for chrissake?'

Quemada walked over to his partner and thrust his face in front of Velasco's nose, so close only a pencil-width separated them.

'It was the only way he would come. Understand? *Partner*? It was the only way he'd come. You know what it's like out there?'

Velasco pulled back, sniffed and stared blankly out of the door. Then he looked at Maria and said, 'You OK?'

She was lying by the side of Torrillo now, talking to him, whispering in his ear.

She looked OK, thought Velasco. He didn't want to ask more. He didn't want to *know* more. He didn't want to be here.

The medic bent down, looked at the weapon in the big man's chest.

'Jesus,' he said. 'What the fuck . . .'

'Just do something,' said Quemada. 'Pull it out. Whatever.'

'I pull this out, man, he's dead for sure.'

He took Torrillo's pulse, looked again at the wound. Then he got on his radio.

'You. The headcase with the gun,' said the medic. 'Go to my van. Ask them for the serious injury bag. The one

278

with the plasma in it. There's nobody else out there with this kind of injury tonight. It shouldn't be used.'

Quemada disappeared into the night.

Maria listened to his breathing. It was so shallow it seemed insufficient to support him, to push enough oxygen through that massive frame.

'He gonna live?' asked Velasco. 'He's a cop. Good guy. He gonna live?'

The medic looked at the wound, looked at the blood slowly seeping from it.

'Search me,' he said. 'Search me.'

Then he looked at her. Maria had passed out on the floor, rolled over onto her side. A small bloodstain was now spreading out from near her shoulder blade, making a dark circular patch on the fabric of the dressing gown.

'Shit,' said the medic, and he climbed over the great fallen form of Torrillo and felt for her pulse.

34

Buzzing ...

The rustle of a thousand tiny wings.

Buzzing ...

In front of her face they swarm and swim, a thick, live blanket of tiny bodies, red and yellow and black. She holds her breath till her lungs turn black with pain, till she feels they will burst. Still she refuses to breathe. They swarm so thickly, so thickly, that to do so would be to take them into your own body, to populate your lungs with that quick and stirring mass of thin and chitinous creatures.

Buzzing ...

Still louder, still darker, they begin to block out the light. She can feel their wings, their hard, shiny bodies on her skin, can feel them crawling over her face, their thin, spidery legs probing, tormenting. She wants to flail her arms, she wants to tear them off her body, but she knows this is impossible. The wasps, they are the universe, there is nothing more there now. The air itself has gone. The world is a thick and endlessly moving swarm of vividly coloured insects engulfing her. The light disappears, her lungs are bursting now. A pain, hard as steel, shoots up from her spine and stabs into the back of her head. No oxygen, no life. She opens her mouth and tries to scream, but as she does they fly in, they crawl inside her, tiny, dirty legs on her tongue, her teeth, the small dry bodies in her throat, then further, and further and further. She can feel them inside her, *crawling*. She can feel the tiny legs in her windpipe, her lungs, her stomach. They populate her, as readily as they would populate a dead thing, and Maria wonders, from somewhere within her that they have not yet reached: *Is this death? Is this dying?*

Then, from the very pit of her stomach, the nausea begins, a simple reflexive heaving that carries no intelligence, that ignores the fear the reasoning side of her mind now kindles: they will sting, as they are disturbed, as they are forced from her body, they will sting her, from the inside out, stab tiny needles of poison into the pulsing blood vessels of her tortured body, kill her with a thousand deadly needles.

She sits up and the heaving gets worse. There is a rush inside her, a dry, living rush, she opens her mouth wide and they leave, the swarm is pushed out into the dark, still buzzing, still angry.

She heaves again, and this time there is light from somewhere, a bright, yellow light, still somewhat hidden by the retreating mass of the swarm, the kind of light you get from a single bulb, too bright for the job. It gets brighter and brighter as the swarm retreats. There are shapes she can make out now, half familiar: she is in a room, the walls, the floor, everywhere is now pale, almost translucent, with a faint violet tint. The light bulb, livid yellow, swings above her, hanging from a twisted corded wire that falls from the ceiling. She looks at it: there is no join, the wire swings gently, from side to side, through the ceiling itself, like some cheap pendulum, attached to a pinion far, far above her.

She looks again and there is a table that was not there before. It is dark, grained wood, the pattern repeated in blocks on its surface, like one of those rendered computer graphics they used in the university: a simulacrum of something organic, a fiction which reduces reality to a mechanistic algorithm.

There is someone sitting at the table. Perhaps more than one person. She blinks, then looks again, and she is sitting at the table herself, still in her dressing gown. Her arms, now holding tightly to the chair in which she sits, are covered in blood. It stains her hands a deep scarlet and she wonders if it will ever come off. Across the table someone is smiling at her. She can feel the warmth there even before she lifts her head to see. She looks but she knows, before she sees his face. Luis is sitting there, the old Luis, the *healthy* Luis, before the cancer began to eat him. He sits, the familiar posture, shoulders a little hunched, thin collar bone visible at the suntanned neck. He wears a pale-brown cotton shirt with a button-down collar. She remembers washing it for him, remembers how he used to laugh when she ironed it, remembers his laughing words: 'We got jobs in a university so that we could *iron*?'

Luis looks at her and he *is* the old Luis. There is a light in his eyes that disappeared a good six months before the end. Maybe even before he knew he was ill. The body begins to die before the mind acknowledges the change: this must be true, she thought. How else could you cope?

He smiles again, and this time his mouth is opening. Maria watches, is forced to watch, though, inside, her head is bursting, screaming to get away, pleading for some respite.

Luis opens his mouth. His teeth, once so white, so perfect, are now blackened stumps, shiny in the bright yellow light. The odour of decay comes to her from across the room: sweet and sickly. It hangs in the air like a fetid cloud. And still his mouth opens wider, wider than any human mouth possibly could.

Maria tries to look away, but her head refuses to turn. The smell is becoming unbearable now. She feels herself breathing it in, feels the taste of it on her tongue, in her throat.

Inside his mouth now something moves, a dark thing, live and threatening. It grows, changes shape, comes out from his throat, swarms over his teeth. They crawl onto his lips, scarlet red, yellow and black, the wasps, the bloodied wasps, they swarm from his lungs, they begin to devour his face.

Her voice locks as it tries to scream. Now they are starting to sting. She can see his lips swelling with the poison; they become bloated, fleshy protuberances, livid and ugly. And still he smiles, while the buzzing gets louder and louder.

She can hear a thin keening sound. It is her own voice. Something escapes the spell that keeps her in check. This slender fact raises some spark within her. She looks at Luis and thinks: you are not real. She tries to say the words. They come but they do not sound right. The noise sounds like baby talk: *yu unot ril.* The buzzing fades a little, the creature across the table loses something of its focus. The ghastly, distended face becomes hazy, unreal. The light dims. It is now paler, more ethereal, and the figure across no longer resembles a human being.

I am looking at the Devil, thinks Maria. This is him and all his works. And I am not afraid, I am *not* afraid.

She leans over, tries to focus on the figure, finds it impossible. She breathes deeply. The air is close, hot, steamy, but it no longer tastes of putrefaction. The buzzing is almost gone. She could believe, she *does* believe, that it existed – *existed?* – only in her head.

'You are not real,' she says, and this time the words ring out. It is her voice, her own voice, unmistakable, unwavering.

She pulls her body back, sits upright, feels the pain stinging her in the shoulder, then wills her eyes to close. They do, the world becomes soft, blood red shot through with the pattern of veins, the room fills, for a moment, with the sound of a massive insect, the sound of giant wings. She feels their flapping, feels the air on her face. She does not breathe in. Then the sound is gone, the air is fresher, cooler.

She opens her eyes. Across the table sits Torrillo. He is wearing a white shirt. Red stains, dark and wet and shiny, mark the lower half of his body. The silver blade still protrudes from his abdomen. He is smiling, the old smile, the real smile. His teeth are real, though there is blood on them, and blood in his throat too. But this is the real Torrillo. Somehow, she *knows*.

'Bear . . .' she says. And then the words fly away from her, hang distant in the air somewhere out of reach.

He grins, the big familiar grin.

'He stung you, Maria? He stung you, huh?'

She nods.

'It hurt?'

She shakes her head. 'I . . . I don't know.'

'He sure got me.'

Torrillo puts his hand around the hilt of the sword, tries to pull it out of his body. He grins.

'Stuck me good, Maria.'

The green mask and the red velvet walls

The voice is thin, a little cracked. She tries to look behind his eyes. Somewhere there, somewhere he doesn't want her to see, flits the tiny, foreign shadow of fear.

'You saved me, Bear.'

'I did?' he says, eyes wide open. 'I did? That's good.'

'Can I . . . ?' She wonders whether she should ask this, whether she needs to. 'Can I save you?'

He thinks about this. 'I don't know, Maria. Like I said. He stuck me real good.'

'I want to. I *want* to.'

She can feel the tears starting to brim in her eyes now.

'Let me do something.'

He is still smiling. He is still thinking. 'You ever see that Woodstock movie, Maria?'

'*Woodstock*?'

'Sure. Cops are allowed to watch movies, you know. Cops are allowed to like music.'

'Yes. Years ago. I saw the Woodstock movie.'

'You remember that part where it starts to rain? Rain real bad?'

'I remember. I think I remember.'

'You remember, the guy on the stage, he's called something like Wavy Gravy or something, he's watching it all fall apart, he's feeling the people in the crowd getting pissed off with the thing, getting *angry*?'

'Yes.'

'So he says, "Maybe, just maybe, if we all started thinking about the rain, willing it to go away, it would." So they all start thinking. They all start shouting, "No rain, no rain, no rain ..." Thousands of them. Hundreds of thousands of them. "No rain, *no rain, NO RAIN*."'

'Did it work? I can't remember. Did it work?'

Bear laughs. A thick wet line of blood runs down his chin, stains the front of his shirt.

'You know the funny thing? I can't remember either. The rain stopped, for sure, but did it stop quickly? I don't know. I just don't know. They didn't put that in the movie.'

'This isn't a movie, Bear.'

'No, Maria. It isn't.'

'So?'

'So, maybe what we need is that kind of faith. I don't know. I *do* know that you're the one who can supply it. It can't come from me. It can't come from the Captain or any of us cops. It's got to come from you. That's why you're here. Don't ask me how I know. I can't answer. I just *do*.'

'Why? Why me?'

He puffs out his cheeks, looks a little like Dizzy Gillespie, blows out a big puff of breath. He looks paler, she thinks, he looks tired. His face, his body, is becoming fainter, disappearing like the grin of the Cheshire Cat.

'If I knew it all, Maria, I'd tell you,' he says.

Then he folds his arms in front of him, one resting lightly on the sword embedded in his body, closes his eyes and goes to sleep, fading, fading, fading.

'Bear?'

No sound.

Buzzing . . .

Loud this time. A pain, deep and sharp, stabs her arm.

Buzzing . . .

She screams, the nausea comes back, but this time it is real.

A harsh liquid, acid and vile, fills her throat, the bile rises inside her, she throws up, feels the hot, scorching vomit spit violently up from her, gags on the last, bitty remains in the mouth, sniffs noisily, feels the bitter taste behind her eyes.

Someone is holding her. A voice makes comforting noises. The light is glaring. The night is full of sound: sirens and shouts, crying and the clatter of gurneys on stone.

She opens her eyes. Close above her, one arm around her shoulder, stands a medic. In his free hand he holds a hypodermic. His face swims into view: neutral, watching, impassive.

He speaks and the words are out of synch with his lips.

'You'll be OK,' he says. 'The wound's not so bad.'

She rolls over onto her side, feels the pain in her back shouting at her.

'Bear?' she asks, quietly. But the body has gone and outside the night is alive with activity.

'Bear?' she says again.

Then the darkness comes on her again, falls like a heavy, leaded curtain, takes her into unconsciousness in spite of herself.

'*No rain . . .*' whispers Maria, and then the big chemical barn door of the drug slams her into sleep.

35

In the hard hospital bed, Maria awoke. The aftermath of the medication clung to her head like a metal circlet, pressing, pressing, pressing. She sat upright, supporting herself on her hands. She wore a white hospital shift. In the centre of her back was something padded. A dressing. The wound throbbed, a dull, distant feeling, like a bruise. She felt the wad of bandage with her hand. There was a lump, the size of a small egg, covering the hurt. When she pressed it, the pain scarcely changed.

'You'll live,' said Menéndez. He was seated in the corner of the small room, in the shadow, just beyond the bright yellow trapezoid cast by the big long window beside the bed. She blinked, trying to focus on him. Silence seemed to hang like a cold cloud around his form. It was hard to concentrate. She wondered how long she had slept. Outside, the street was silent. This was strange. Normally the streets would have been alive with traffic and sound, in Semana Santa even more.

'It is so quiet . . .'

Menéndez leaned forward, put his face in his hands, rubbed his eyes. She could see him more clearly now. He looked exhausted, ill.

'The city is in mourning. Today the events have been called off. As a mark of respect. People stay at home, I guess.'

'The crowd? Last night . . . I only half saw what was happening.'

'There should have been some better form of control. There were too many people, they came round the corner too quickly, they panicked. It's not the first time. Football, the bullring ... public events, these kind of things happen. They shouldn't, but ...'

She waited for him to go on.

'There were nine people killed. Crushed to death. A lot more injured, though few of them serious, thank God. Today, everyone stays home. They go to the corrida, it's over, except for a few parties. This year ... I guess the parties won't go on for long.'

'Bear?'

Menéndez's face moved back into shadow. She could read it no more.

'He's here. Intensive care.'

'Can I see him?'

'I can't answer that, Maria. You need to talk to the doctors.'

The events of the night were still blurry to her. They swam around her mind.

'He saved me. Didn't he? Without him, I would have been dead.'

'Yes,' said Menéndez. 'I think so.'

'Will he be OK?'

He paused before answering. 'I don't know. The doctors don't know. He's in intensive care. Unconscious. They say the wound is very bad. He lost a lot of blood. Even if he does live ...'

'Yes?'

'If he does live, maybe there will be some paralysis. They just don't know.'

Maria closed her eyes, willed herself not to cry, won the battle.

'He is a good man,' she said. 'A *good* man. You can feel

289

that about him. It's like sitting next to a fire, you can feel the warmth.'

'I know,' said Menéndez. 'He doesn't like me. I know that. Few of them do. They think I'm too *ambitious*.'

He rolled the word around his tongue, as if it tasted bad. 'Maria?'

She was staring at nothing at all.

'Yes?'

'You haven't asked about yourself. You haven't asked what happened to you.'

'No,' she said and thought to herself: I don't care, I no longer care.

'It hurts a little. Like a bruise. It can't be much.'

'Maria. He threw the dart at you.'

'I remember,' she said curtly. 'I remember that.'

'The doctors say it was that much' – he held up his hand in the light from the window, the finger and thumb nearly closed together, casting a shadow like a light show on the whitewashed wall – '*that* much from piercing your lung. You were lucky. Really lucky.'

She thought about the wound and it ached on cue, as if in recognition.

'But it didn't. It didn't harm anything.'

'No,' he said, and tried to understand her lack of self concern. 'No. They say it went through the muscle, stopped there. Maybe this evening you can go home. You have to spend the day here. You should rest.'

'I want to help.'

'If you rest, you will be helping.'

'No, I won't. That's a patronising thing to say. I'll be lying here on my back while you keep stumbling around in the dark looking for the person who keeps doing this.'

He listened to the steel in her voice and was grateful their opportunities for argument were likely to be few.

'You saw him last night? Quemada and Velasco thought he had his hood down when they came in but it was difficult to see. They were pretty sure it was none of the people we've been talking to. Someone else.'

'I saw him. And it *was* him this time. No disguise. Maybe he thought I would be so easy. And no. He wasn't someone I knew.'

'If I send in a photo-fit officer, can you work with him on a description? They have some pro formas, tools they can work with to help you.'

She nodded. 'When?'

'I'll call in a few minutes, send someone round.'

She tried to make sense of the sequence of events, tried to pull more out of her memory. It didn't work yet. Maybe there was nothing more to retrieve.

'I don't understand. Quemada, Velasco. They were there? Why is he still free?'

'It was dark, Maria. You were wounded. Torrillo was wounded. The man ran up the stairs, seems to have got out of the back somehow. He knew what he was doing. They were torn – did they chase him, did they help you? In the end they did a little of one, a lot of the other.'

'They should have stopped him.'

'Would you, in the circumstances? They're cops but they're human too.'

'It was the best chance we've had. Maybe the best chance we'll ever have.'

'Maybe. I don't know. *You* don't know.'

There was a side to his voice now, a harshness that came too easily. She was testing his sympathy, testing his politeness.

'He picked up my address book. When we were in Castaneda's office. When I dropped my bag. He picked it up. He phoned me the night before. Just checking. I thought

291

he was just a stray caller. The type who like to phone women.'

'I wondered ...'

'He had a key. He had a *key!* How could that be?'

'I don't know. I've got men making inquiries around the area. Maybe they'll find something. Somehow we'll find something. What I don't understand is ... Why try to kill you?'

She tried to remember his face, tried to recall his expression.

'Is it all just random?' asked Menéndez. 'He sees an opportunity, he finds an address book, he takes it. Are we just going off on a tangent with the Alvarez stuff?'

'You found nothing?'

'Nothing. No records in Melilla. Nothing but some old criminal stuff on Alvarez himself.'

'Criminal?'

Menéndez said, 'In the sense that it warranted prosecution. Alvarez had a list of complaints an arm long about sexual relations with under-age girls. Rape. Some of them were pregnant. None came to court. He was too well connected for that.'

'He *liked* young girls?'

'Seems so.'

'Before Caterina Lucena? Or after?'

'These complaints all date from the forties on and go on for nearly twenty years, and that's just the ones we know about. After, I guess. Maybe Caterina ...'

His voice drifted away into nothingness. It seemed a terrible thing to say.

'Maybe she gave him the *taste?*' she asked.

'Maybe.'

Maria tried to make sense of what she was hearing. It held some significance, but she could not see what it was.

'Have you traced any of the girls who complained? The ones who were pregnant?'

'Not yet. We're working on it.'

'And he never came to court?'

'Every case was blocked, though looking at the records now it would have been easy to get a prosecution on them. There was some complicity in some cases, money changing hands, that kind of thing, but that didn't change the offence. What tripped up Alvarez in the end was something much simpler. He was treasurer of the brotherhood, he embezzled from them.'

'A lot of money?'

'Probably around two million pesetas as far as we can see. Maybe more.'

'A lot of money.'

'Yes. And again, he wasn't prosecuted, though it seems to have led to his political downfall. He was out of the council after that, out of the brotherhood. Finished, socially and politically.'

'And they made him pay it back? The money? They must have done.'

'You'd think so.'

'But does it say that? Does it say in the record?'

'No. But in cases like that it wouldn't. If it's a gentleman's agreement, you keep what's on paper to a minimum. Making some formal, written agreement to repay the money would be tantamount to admitting taking it, so maybe it was done privately.'

'The brotherhood's records . . .'

'The brotherhood's records would show, yes. I guess so. Except that the key ones are missing. Maybe, and we are guessing here, *maybe* they were taken when Castaneda was killed. I anticipated you a little there. I *am* a policeman.'

'So there could be a motive for some of the killings. Not just revenge, maybe money too.'

'There could be. But where does that leave a motive for killing you?'

She thought about it. There was an answer. 'You remember what Bear said. What if some of the killings had a motive and some of them were random? Perhaps the point of the random killings is that they *are* random. By making them random he hopes we'll think they are *all* random. That there is no picture behind it all, no framework, no logic, no structure.'

Menéndez looked at his watch. 'Is he that clever? Do you really think so?'

'Yes,' she said, straight away. 'He's that clever. Also, like Bear said, he likes it. He likes killing people. I could see that. Last night. He took pleasure from it. Maybe it's the only thing he does take pleasure from.'

'Nice man,' said Menéndez. 'I can't wait to put him in a cell.'

She remembered his words from the night before: that was the last place he thought he was going.

'Maria. I am late. I have much to do. You must excuse me. I will send an artist to see you soon. You must rest. You must stay in bed. When the doctors have seen you, discharged you, call the station. I will send round a female officer. She can pick up some clothes from your apartment. If you like you can stay there. I will put a guard there twenty-four hours. If not we'll find somewhere else for you. Think about it. You don't need to decide now. In the meantime, please, *please*, rest. I will send someone in with something to drink, some food if you like.'

Just the word made her feel ravenous. Her stomach felt empty and hollow.

'Food. Yes. That would be good.'

He shambled out of the door looking like a man who had not slept in days. Two minutes later, a nun appeared holding a tray: coffee, orange juice, some pastries. She ate and drank greedily, feeling the strength return, feeling something else too, a certainty that events were moving, in one way or another. That there would be some conclusion. And that she would be part of it.

The nurse came back to collect the tray. She looked no more than twenty, plain-faced, slim, quiescent. Maria could not, for a moment, understand what would lead someone to that kind of life, at any age.

'I want to be released,' she said. 'I want to go home.'

'You need to see a doctor first,' said the nun, smiling. A badge on her shoulder said 'Sister Alicia'. 'The rules are that only a doctor can sign your release form. This afternoon, I think. That will not be a problem. Why don't you rest until then?'

'I will,' she said, then added, 'There are two friends of mine in this hospital. Before I go, I would like to visit them. Is that possible?'

'The policeman? The one who came in with you?'

'Yes.'

She shook her head. 'He is in intensive care. He is very sick. I will ask. Perhaps the doctor will let you see him from outside the room. But he is unconscious. He will not know you are there.'

'No. But I would like to see him all the same.'

'I will ask for you. And your other friend?'

'Caterina Lucena.'

'Ah, Doña Caterina.'

Maria could not read the expression in her face. She guarded it too well.

'She is still here?'

'Yes,' she said. 'She is still here. She makes a little progress, then sometimes she falls back a little.'

'I may see her?'

'I will ask. I will certainly ask.'

'Thank you.'

Twenty minutes later there was a knock at the door and Sister Alicia showed in a thin young man in a denim suit. He carried a notebook computer and introduced himself as the police artist. They spent half an hour looking at faces on the computer screen: she flicked through noses and eyes and foreheads, adjusted hairstyles, changed the shapes of eyebrows and ears, the jut of a cheekbone, the prominence of the chin. In the end, she thought it was a pretty good likeness. He printed out a draft copy on a small battery printer. They looked at it in more detail. He sketched in some additions with a pencil. It got better. Then they went back to the computer, entered the changes, printed out another draft. This happened three more times: draft print-out, pencil revisions, changes on the screen. In the end, she thought, they had him. This *was* the man.

'Will you print out two copies?' asked Maria.

'Two?' he said, surprised.

'I'd like one. To look at. To think about.'

'Sure.' He nodded.

When he was gone, she looked at the face again. Tried to imagine it with a thin moustache, tanned by months of hard sun. Then she put it on the bedside table and went to sleep.

36

Menéndez looked at the file Quemada had passed him and grimaced. He could tolerate poor police work. He *had* to tolerate poor police work. People made mistakes. People overlooked things. But this was different. This was just plain sloppy. Someone should have picked up on it earlier. Someone straight away should have seen the signs. He'd been away when Romero was found, but there were others in the department who ought to have known.

The body of Luis Romero was found by a gatekeeper in the Alfabia park at six in the morning on 11 January. The dead man was in the driver's seat of his gold Mercedes saloon. Both wrists were cut. A hosepipe led from the exhaust into the car through the front passenger window. The car had been left idling all night until it ran out of petrol. The autopsy had measured the level of carbon monoxide in Romero's blood. It was almost non-existent. The cause of death was loss of blood due to the cuts on the wrists. No conclusions were drawn from these two facts. The death was marked down as suicide and the case was closed.

Menéndez tried to understand the premise of the suicide conclusion. The investigating officer, a rank junior, believed that Romero had intended to kill himself in a way which could not be reversed. Sometimes, most times, suicide attempts were not serious efforts to die. People left loopholes – taking just enough pills to be ill but not enough to kill them. Sometimes they went the opposite way. They wanted to make some kind of statement to the world that they were *not* attention-seekers. And they did it by killing themselves in a way that brooked no escape. Jump off the top of the cathedral belltower and you pretty much make sure you're dead. This, so it was supposed, was what Romero was doing. He fixed the hosepipe to the exhaust, then climbed into the car, put the hose through the window, wound up the window and sat in the driver's seat, breathing in the fumes, while he cut his wrists.

Quemada read the sour look on Menéndez's face and said: 'It stinks. You know, I read that autopsy and, OK, it was done by two different guys, one did the body, the other did the blood analysis, but you'd think they'd be talking to each other. You'd think they'd get together and put the poor cop straight.'

Menéndez thrust his arms out in front of him, wrists uppermost. 'If you wanted to cut your wrists, how would you do it?'

Quemada wished Velasco hadn't taken time out to look at some more records. He hated it when Menéndez wanted to bounce around ideas. That was what Bear was for. He didn't like trying to step into those big shoes.

'I'm not so good at this sort of thing, sir. It's not me.'

'Start. Think about it. Think about how you're going to do it.'

Quemada looked at Menéndez's outstretched arms.

'You need room. You need space. It's crazy. He goes back, puts the hose on the exhaust, then climbs back into the car and sits in the driver's seat. Makes no sense. You seen the wheel on those Mercedes? Like a truck. It'd get in the way. You'd sit in the passenger seat for sure. Not the driver's.'

Menéndez dropped his arms onto the desk. 'He could

have cut his wrists then got over into the driving seat. That's where he normally sat. He might be more comfortable there.'

'Yeah, he could. There was time. Or there should have been time if he really died in the car. The wrist wounds weren't that deep. The coroner's guy I spoke to said it would take maybe an hour if you got cut like that. But the odds got to be, he didn't die in the car. There's not enough blood there. And if he spent an hour, with those fumes pumping in from the engine, he'd have been dead of carbon monoxide, not of blood loss. Which he isn't. In fact there's hardly any carbon monoxide in his blood. Whatever happened, he was not alive for long in the car while the pipe was through the window.'

'Meaning?'

'Meaning either he cut his wrists outside the car, bled a lot some place else, put the pipe on the exhaust, then climbed in the car, then died. Which even for a university professor seems a somewhat complex way to go about things. Alternatively, somebody, let's say, *helped* him. Somebody cut his wrists for him, put him in the car when he was dead or nearly dead, then put the pipe on the exhaust. My guess is the latter, there I got to be honest.'

'And this is all the evidence we have?'

Quemada nodded. 'Everything. The car got looked at in some kind of perfunctory manner. You got the photos there. Don't tell us much we don't already know. These guys who did the job, they just assumed it was a suicide from the outset. Stamped the file straight away.'

'Even though his wife said it was impossible. Said he was incapable of killing himself.'

'Excuse me if I sound like I'm talking down to you on this one, Lieutenant, but I done a lot of suicides myself. They *always* say that. It's automatic. It's their way of trying to take the blame off of themselves. Most of these guys, they kill themselves because of some trouble at home. Maybe she's sleeping around, maybe there's money problems. A woman don't want to admit that. When they say, "He didn't do it", what they mean is, he did but I don't want to admit it. Believe me, it's not unusual.'

Menéndez shuffled through the file. It was thin, depressingly thin. There was scarcely anything on Romero's background, his job, his family life.

'Do we know much more about Romero than this? Who he was? There must be something on the death certificate.'

Quemada reached over and picked up the single-sheet biog. 'Pretty flimsy, huh? I can't believe they just left it at that. Thing is, Lieutenant, we don't know much about Romero. I looked at the death certificate. It was an issue job. You know, the one they put out when they don't have a birth certificate for the guy? We talked to his wife. She said he never had one. It gave him some trouble when he wanted to get a passport. Same thing happened to a lot of people born during the war. A lot of the paperwork just isn't there.'

'Have we asked his wife about his family?'

'I sent some boys back there yesterday, talk to her some more. They didn't come back with much. Seems Romero said he was an orphan, got brought up in some home here in the city. No relatives she could tell us about. Seems he didn't like talking too much about his childhood. It was just an area he'd rather avoid. Interesting, huh? You thinking what I'm thinking?'

'That there could be a link with Caterina Lucena? The city's got lots of orphans, particularly of that age. It's a long shot.'

'Yeah. And I don't know how we could prove it. Maybe

the guys in Melilla will get back to us with something.'

'What about his work? You talked to people at the university.'

'Yeah. The guys went there after they spoke to his wife. Funny thing is, you know she painted that picture of him, kind of like a playboy figure? Screwing around, not minding much what he was screwing? Well, if he did, he did it quietly. The people at the university, they seemed to think he was a pretty ordinary guy. Hard-working, pretty straight, quiet. "Kept himself to himself" – you know the quote. They didn't see him as the playboy type so maybe he just did it after hours. I got some people looking into that. Nothing so far.'

'Did they talk about his marriage? His colleagues?'

'They said . . . maybe it wasn't so good. Seems she never showed up at the university. Never went to any of these things they put on, you know, the art shows, the social evenings, Jesus, those college people got a party a night you want to go to one. Some nice women around too, not that I found anyone who thought old Luis was chasing them much. Couldn't have blamed him. Seems most people thought his old woman was a seriously cold fish. Not liked. Not liked at all.'

Menéndez looked at his watch. It was two in the afternoon and he felt as if everything around him was dragging, was falling into a pile of sludge. The city was half dead under the shock of the previous night's calamities. Torrillo hung between life and death. They seemed no closer to the killer, no nearer to seeing a glimpse of the identity behind the cowl.

'The papers, they're printing the Photofit this afternoon?'

'Yeah. It went out on the lunchtime news too. We had some calls already. They're following them up. He looks like a lot of people, though. He really does. This Photofit

301

stuff can be nice if you got something definite, something outstanding, like a tattoo or something. Or if you got somebody in the frame already. But when everything's cold ... I dunno.'

'I want every call followed up. Properly.'

'Sure,' said Quemada. 'I'll see to it. You mind my asking – any news about Torrillo? The guys will ask, when I come out of the office, they're sure to ask.'

Menéndez's face was expressionless. 'It's just the same,' he said. 'He's unconscious. He's lost a lot of blood. If he survives, there may be some long-term damage. It's too early to say.'

Quemada folded his arms tight and grimaced. 'Jesus. You think I had that guy an arm's length away last night and he got away. I can't believe it. Things like that don't happen to me.'

Menéndez closed the file in front of him. 'Don't think about it. It could have been any of us. You had a lot to cope with. The crowd outside. Torrillo, the woman. No one could expect you to handle all that and make an arrest too. You did as well as any of us could.'

'Yeah,' said Quemada, a note of bitterness in his voice. 'Trouble is I keep remember him climbing up those stairs, I keep remembering the sound of his steps, and I think if only, if only I'd just taken him then. Instead of waiting.'

'You can't live on "if onlys ..."'

'No. I understand that. But you know one thing? When we got to the top of the stairs, when we saw he'd climbed out the back window, got down into the yard somehow, I did fire. I did see his back and I shot at him. And I tell you something, Lieutenant, I may be a second-rate cop but I'm a first-rate shot. I could have sworn I hit him. You hear that sound. Like a groan. A thud somewhere. That's what it sounds like when you shoot someone. You never forget it. Well, I heard that then. I swear. And I went back there this morning. I looked in the yard. Nothing. Some garbage kicked over. Nothing. No blood. No sign. That I do *not* understand.'

On the way out Quemada stopped at the door. 'Lieutenant?'

Menéndez looked up from the desk.

'There was one more thing that was bugging me. About Romero's death.'

'What's that?'

'We're working on the assumption that he was killed. Right? We think someone killed him, then tried to make it look like a suicide?'

'That's got to be the assumption, yes.'

'Well, what bugs me is – how do you cut someone's wrists like that? Both of them. How do you actually *do* it? Romero was not a small man. He isn't going to just let you get on with it. There's no trace of drugs in his blood like there was with the Angel Brothers. So he wasn't doped or anything. There's no marks on his body to suggest he was tied up. So how could he do it?'

Menéndez looked at Quemada. Maybe Torrillo's absence could be accommodated after all.

'I don't know. It would be very difficult.'

'Unless . . .'

'Unless what?'

'Unless there were two of you. That would make it easier. Come to think of it, that would make the Angel Brothers a lot easier too.'

Menéndez stared at Quemada, a little stunned.

'That's a very interesting idea, detective,' he said. 'Let's think about it for a while.'

37

'This is a wonderful job. This is a *truly* fucking wonderful job,' said Quemada.

They were cruising the barrio in an unmarked grey Opel that smelled of stale cigarettes and sweat. Outside, the city had a queer atmosphere: silence underlined by tension. People weren't going to work. It was a traditional holiday. But they weren't going out to play either. They just mooched in bars or sat outside their houses in the barrio, silent, miserable, on wicker chairs. Even the kids weren't kicking footballs around.

Quemada stared into the street and said, 'Jesus. I hate it like this. It's better when they're all rolling drunk and fighting. At least you know what's going on.'

Velasco flicked a cigarette out of the window, out into the hot, dusty air of the afternoon. 'Give it time. Give it a day. Come the bullfight tomorrow, they'll be back to normal. They won't remember a thing. Meantime, *meantime . . .*'

'Yeah. Meantime,' said Quemada. 'Meantime maybe the Captain ought to be coming up with something. You know I don't like saying this but it's true. Menéndez is running this one. Really, he is. The old man's just sitting back and I don't understand why.'

'He's done it before,' said Velasco. 'I've seen it a dozen times. Lets us stay in the dark then comes through with something in the end. Maybe he's just letting Menéndez hang himself before he comes in. No secret the creep's after his seat.'

'Fuck these little games. We want something *now*. We got Bear in the hospital for Christ's sake. It's not just the scum getting hurt out there.'

'No,' said Velasco.

'You think he'll come through? Sure as hell I don't think Menéndez will. The guy's all flash, no beef, you ask me.'

'Yeah,' said Velasco. 'You bet he'll come through. Don't he always?'

'Yeah. I guess so,' said Quemada. 'You ask me, I still think this is a truly fucking wonderful job.'

Then he looked through the mess of papers on his lap and tried to think about the next name on the list.

They had visited the last known addresses of three of the complainants who had filed rape allegations against Alvarez. They were ticking off the pregnant ones first. That seemed the most obvious bet. They were not making progress. The first address was a tiny two-up, two-down hovel close to the river. It was boarded up and derelict, the roof missing, the windows black holes like rotten stumps of teeth. A whole line of houses in the street had been condemned by some urban improvement scheme, then left to moulder while the city hall found enough money to go ahead with the work. That was a good ten years ago, or so they were told by the nearest resident they could find. Everyone got moved out to one of the tower blocks in the suburbs. Quemada made some notes, shrugged his shoulders and notched up another task to pass on to the growing case team back at the station. You could waste days, weeks even, trying to track down anyone who'd gone out into the big arid flatlands of the tower blocks.

Then they drove over to the other side of the barrio and knocked on the door of the second address. There was no reply, so they knocked up a neighbour, flashed their cards, used the name they had in their records. No recognition. From what they heard, it sounded like the family now in residence had no connection with the one there twenty years ago. Another trail winding off into nowhere. But at least that didn't happen with the third name. An old woman with whiskers, dressed in a shabby red floral dress and carpet slippers that looked like they came out of the ark, told them straight: she was dead, killed in a car accident a good five years before. And the kid had been stillborn.

Velasco checked out the details of the current name again. Magdalena Bartolomé had, with the aid of her mother, filed a complaint of repeated rape against Alvarez in June 1960. She was thirteen at the time. According to the records, Alvarez had been a regular visitor to her house and, when left alone with her, had forced her into sex. The girl was pregnant. According to the case notes, scribbled in some spidery ancient hand by a detective long gone from the force, Alvarez had vigorously denied the accusations. He said he had visited the Bartolomé house regularly but out of charity. Though he was no longer formally attached to the brotherhood, he still helped by handing out allowances to poor families who applied for them. Nothing had happened when he went to the house, the mother had never left them alone, and he was innocent of the charge. The detective asked around the barrio about the girl. There was no evidence to suggest she was involved in a sexual relationship with anyone else. There was no evidence to the contrary either. The detective described the girl as surly, unhelpful and untrustworthy, and totally under the spell of her mother who seemed to be instrumental in filing the complaint. Recommendation: *no action on the grounds of insufficient evidence.*

'What you think?' asked Quemada, slowing the car to a crawl as they turned off the inner ring road and back into the barrio.

'Sounds like the mother was charging him for his pleasure. When he quit paying, she tried to get her own back.'

'Yeah. I mean. They're saying there he screwed her – how many times? – ten, twelve?'

'Something like that.'

'And they wait that long before complaining?'

'Mother says she never knew.'

'Sure. Man comes along wanting to give you money. You leave him in the house, alone with your thirteen-year-old daughter for an hour or two. What did she think they were going to do?'

'You can see why it didn't come to court.'

Quemada stared at his partner. 'Like hell I can. They should have nailed Alvarez for under-age sex *and* the mother for prostitution.'

'Great. Alvarez and the mother go to jail and the girl goes to the poorhouse. There's justice for you.'

'Not talking justice. I'm talking the law. Someone else wants to make those decisions, some politician, some judge, fine. Let them do it. It's not our job. You break the law, we charge you. Beginning. End. Not our job to work out the consequences. Let some other sucker do it.'

He looked at the street sign. They were nearly there. The little square blue and white house numbers counted down. Quemada parked the car in a gap between a bread van and a rusting Seat sitting on its axles. The street smelled badly of rank drains and cat piss. It comprised a long, low line of dirty white terraced houses, two storeys mainly with the occasional, probably illegal, third floor added. There was the odd balcony, a few flowers, a striped sunshade. The pavements were strewn with rubbish that had been gutted from black refuse bags by the feral cats that now lay still but attentive in every shaded corner of the street.

'Nice neighbourhood,' said Velasco.

'Consequences,' muttered Quemada.

'You still on about that?'

Quemada sat rigid in the car, refusing to get out until the conversation had been closed.

'Yeah. I'm still on about that. Think about it. Think about the woman for once. We're going in there, asking about how her mother was hiring her out for sex more than thirty years ago, asking what she remembers, how she feels. What if her old man's around? What do we do then?'

'We ask him to leave. That's one of the nice things about being a cop. You get to tell people what to do.'

'And what then? What if he comes back? Beats it out of her? What if we start something, it ends in a divorce, her marriage goes out the window?'

'You got too active an imagination. What if . . . what if . . . What the fuck?'

'Maybe it bothers me more than it does you.'

'Yeah,' said Velasco. 'I always did have you marked down as the sensitive type. You know what bothers me? Bear. Bear and those other people getting killed like that. The ice queen. We cause a little marital discord on the way to stopping that, I guess I can live with it. Besides . . .'

Velasco looked at the house two doors along where they were headed and tried to cut some kind of mental pathway through the mucus that was now beginning to clog up the inside of his head.

'Besides, somehow I don't think that kind of eventuality is something we're going to encounter hereabouts. You know this kind of neighbourhood. You got someone who's a cat burglar here, they're upwardly mobile. Just relax about

308

it. My guess is, anyone who lives here, the state of their marriage is the last thing they got to worry about.'

They got out of the car and walked to the house, trying to ignore the smell of bad drains and cooking that hung on the air. Then Velasco placed his thumb on the doorbell, pushed hard and listened for a ring. No sound. He put his ear to the door, pressed again, again heard nothing except the far-off chatter of a TV set and what sounded like a child wailing. He balled up a fist, drew back his arm and started to hammer on the door.

38

Over on the far side of the city, Maria Gutierrez awoke with a start, her head filled with the after-images of unpleasant dreams. Somewhere a headless dove had fallen to earth, blood streaming from its open neck. Somewhere a blade had flashed silver in the moonlight, a metallic streak across a starry black sky. She lay back on the pillow, closed her eyes, tried to recapture the pictures.

They no longer frightened her. They had something to say. But nothing remained, nothing except the blur of phantasmal colours, streaked across the darkness of her inner vision.

She opened her eyes again, sat upright, then swung her legs over the side of the bed. The iron frame creaked as she moved, she could smell that unmistakable hospital odour: fresh sheets, antiseptic, the sharp, chilling aroma of medical chemistry.

On an upright wooden chair opposite the bed, neatly folded, was a pile of her clothes. Menéndez must have asked for them to be sent while she slept. Someone would have crept quietly into the room, some nun, moving silently like a grey ghost. Maria wondered at her vulnerability then tried to push the thought out of her head.

She rang the bell and the same sister came, in the same quiet, unemotional way. She was followed by a doctor, young, with a matter-of-fact manner. He made her turn over, undid the shift, pulled off the dressing with a quick, efficient hand. The nun rubbed some cream gently into the wound, covered it with a simple, light plaster then tied the drawstrings of the gown again. Maria turned over. There was nothing in the doctor's face. He signed a piece of paper, told her she could leave at the end of the afternoon, prescribed some antiseptic cream to rub into the wound, and advised her to rest.

'Why can't I leave now?' she asked.

'Because I don't want you to,' he replied. 'Physically there is no reason. But you may still be suffering from shock so I just want you to stay a little longer. Besides, we must pick a time. The police want to take you themselves. They want to know where you want to go. Whether you want them to arrange something or go back to your own apartment.'

'The apartment,' she said. 'You can tell them that now.'

He nodded. 'I will. If you change your mind . . .'

'I won't change my mind.'

'No,' he said, and there was the trace of a smile on his face. 'I imagine you won't. All the same. I would like you to rest for a few hours. *Here* . . .'

'I can wear my own clothes?'

'Of course. The sister will show you to the bathroom if you wish. She can help you there if you need some assistance.'

'Thank you.'

'It's nothing. Now, if you will excuse me. We have a busy hospital at the moment, as I am sure you will understand.'

'Doctor?'

'Yes?'

'I asked if I could see the Sergeant. The man who came in with me. And someone else too. A patient in the geriatric wing.'

'Yes. I know. There is no problem with the woman. We asked her and she is content to see you.'

'Is she well?'

He made a rolling gesture with his hand. 'At that age it is difficult to tell. Each day is different. It is not a good condition to contract for someone of her age. She is fine at the moment. But I don't see her leaving the hospital. At least for a few weeks.'

'And the Sergeant?'

She did not like the expression on his face. It was the kind she had seen doctors use before. It had that medical arrogance she had come to know well: the one which said that it was kinder to tell the lie than to reveal the truth.

'Sergeant Torrillo is stable. I can say no more. He has a long way to go. He is unconscious, on life support. You may see him from outside the intensive care room but that's all.'

'You understand why I want to see him?'

'I read the papers. Yes. I understand.'

'Will he live? Please. Don't try to *spare* me. It is not necessary.'

'No?'

'I can take the truth.'

'The truth . . . the truth is that Sergeant Torrillo is on a life-support system. It is that which keeps him alive. We can keep him alive in this condition for some time. Perhaps even years. But of course that would not be *alive* in the sense that we know it and it would be for his family, or the courts, or the medical insurance people, or all three, to decide when it should be switched off.'

Maria shut her eyes for a moment and tried to quell the anger rising within her. The thought of Torrillo, so strong, so full of life, reduced to such a condition infuriated her.

'You asked me for the truth,' said the doctor.

'I am grateful you gave it. Is there no chance that he may improve?'

The doctor made a half-smile. 'Of course there is a chance. What there is not is a probability. He was very severely injured. He lost such a large amount of blood that it may be impossible for him to recover the functions which the life-support system now performs for him. It is possible but it is not likely. All we can do is wait and see.'

Ten minutes later, after she had showered, made herself feel more human, she looked at herself in the mirror. The clothes the police had picked were old ones. They looked baggy on her now. She had lost weight. Just in the few days she had been in the city, the pounds had fallen off her. She had changed, was changing. Her face looked older too. There were lines, a dryness to the skin she had not seen before. She combed her hair looking for grey streaks. There were none, but they would come. She was sure they would come.

Then she left the room, asked directions, walked along a corridor lit by bright fluorescent lights, past bed after bed, past the rows of silent, pained faces, took a lift to the second floor, asked directions again, and walked through a set of folding doors.

Torrillo was behind a glass wall that went almost from the floor to the ceiling. She could hardly recognise him. His body was covered in pipes and tubes and skeletal metal frames of medical equipment. She was reminded of an engraving she had seen once, from an early edition of *Gulliver's Travels*: the hero, unconscious on a beach, being tied by tiny men who crawled over his huge body, pulling ropes, erecting wooden scaffolding, using blocks and tackles and pinions to entrap, to enslave the giant.

There was a shallow movement from his chest. A hint of a breath. Behind his body electronic meters chattered and whirred, painted green phosphor blips on circular screens threw up digital numbers on LCD panels, a mass of wires and clips and gadgetry. Pumps and ventilators rose and fell with a mechanical rhythm that tried to look organic. Was this all that kept him alive? *All?*

'No rain,' said Maria, so close now that her breath briefly clouded the glass with the words. 'No rain, Bear. Please. *No rain.*'

39

Quemada scraped a horny hand across his sweating bald patch, gazed across the room and sighed. The place looked like the inside of a trashcan. Clothes, some clean, some dirty, littered the floor. In the corner, silent, eyes tightly set on some unseen point on the carpet, sat a teenage girl: olive skin, dark eyes, faint prettiness, puppy fat sagging around her jowls. A baby, no more than six months old, with dark curly hair around a face that looked like it had not been washed in days, played in the mess. Quemada registered the smell of used nappies and stale piss. The girl – the mother, surely – didn't seem to care. The walls of the room carried a motley collection of religious icons: a few crucifixes, cheap images of Jesus and the Virgin Mary. Alongside hung more modern idols: pop stars Quemada recognised only by their features, familiar from the weekend magazines. They grinned with perfect white teeth and wore the clothes he'd seen in American baseball on the TV.

Quemada looked at the baby, and said, 'Sometimes, they're doomed from birth.'

Velasco scratched his nose with a long, thin forefinger then said to the girl, in a voice without warmth, 'You the mother?'

She took her eyes off the carpet for a few seconds and nodded.

'You can get help with the kid, you know,' Quemada

said. 'From the social. They'll do things for you, show you how to do things.'

Her face turned into a sneer, the kind of teenage sneer – insolence and stupidity all mixed up into some bilious cocktail – that cops the world over had come to hate.

'The social? They come here. All the time. You know what Maggi tells them? She says, "Fuck off, we look after our own."'

'Well, I guess if that's correct they won't want to come back, will they? *If* that's correct and looking at the kid I somehow wonder.'

'He's OK,' she said, that sneer on her face again. 'We wash him, we feed him. He's just between changes, that's all.'

Quemada sniffed the air and said, 'Long between, smells like.'

The girl stared at the carpet again.

'You on your own?'

In a small voice, the girl said, 'Yes.'

'And this Maggi. She's what? Sister?'

'She's my mamma.'

'Jesus,' said Velasco. 'My kids call me by my name, they'd get a good hiding. I ask: what's the world coming to?'

'I always call her Maggi. Everybody calls her Maggi.'

'How old are you?'

The eyes bored a hole in the carpet. 'Sixteen.'

'Starting a little young, aren't we?'

The girl said nothing.

'So where is *Maggi*?'

'Out working.'

'Exactly what kind of work is that?'

'She works in a bar.'

'Any particular side of the counter?'

The girl's eyes blazed at them.

'Ask her that yourself. She could tear your face apart.'

'Nice family,' said Quemada. 'When you expecting her back?'

'Soon. She should have been back already. Sometimes she works late.'

'I'll bet she does,' said Velasco. 'We'll wait.'

The two cops threw some clothes off a sofa onto the floor and sat down. The coverlet felt damp.

'You gonna offer us a coffee?' asked Quemada.

'Fuck off,' she replied, to no one in particular.

'I take it that's a reply in the negative. You ever heard of Antonio Alvarez?'

They watched her face for some sign of recognition. There was none. She shook her head.

'Maybe some friend of your mamma's?'

'Maggi's got lots of friends.'

'I bet she has,' said Quemada. 'Working in a bar like that. It's sort of a congenial environment. I just *bet* she has.'

Velasco turned and muttered to him. 'We could be here for hours. This kid knows nothing. We could be here hours, the woman shows up, she knows nothing too.'

'Yeah,' said Quemada. 'Tell you what. We give it thirty minutes. She's not back by then, we'll try somewhere else.'

Velasco looked at him. 'You think there might be something here? It's worth it?'

'I think it's better sitting on a sofa, even this stinking dirty sofa, for half an hour instead of sweating to death in that car like we do most days. Take a break, man. Relax.'

'Huh,' Velasco grunted then leaned back into the sofa, reached into his pocket, pulled out a packet of cigarettes and lit one.

The girl looked at him, hoping.

'Too young,' he said. 'Too young for lots of things.'

They watched the smoke dance through the sluggish hot

317

air, watched the flies buzz pointlessly around the curling plume. Just as Velasco was stubbing it out in a brimming ashtray set on the floor, they heard a noise at the front door.

'She's back,' said the girl and Quemada wondered, for a moment, if he'd seen terror or one of its relatives flash briefly across her face.

Maggi Bartolomé was a big-boned, blowsy woman somewhere in her mid-forties. Her face was overlaid with make-up and her hair was tied back severely in a bun. She wore a fairly typical whore's uniform: a tight red shiny skirt, cut short above the knee, yellow blouse with a deep cleavage exposing full, tanned breasts and a gold chain around a neck that was starting to show signs of age. She took one look at them, then swore. Quemada smiled: he'd worked the vice squad beat two years previously and he knew the crowd.

'Maggi,' he said. 'And I never knew your real name.'

She peered at him myopically, grimaced, opened a drawer then pulled out a pair of cheap tortoiseshell spectacles and put them on. The glasses changed her appearance entirely. She turned into a headmistress all dressed up and painted for a risqué part in the annual school show.

'I know you?'

'Guess I shouldn't be offended. You must run into a lot of cops in your line of business.'

'Too many,' she said and peered at him again. 'I *don't* remember you.'

'Three, maybe four years ago, we cautioned you. Hustling for business outside the cathedral. Personally, I don't mind you hustling but maybe it's best if you do it some ways away from God, you understand. God and the tourists, though you listen to the city council and you start to think maybe they're the same thing.'

'You *cautioned* me?'

'Yeah. Then you walked on your way.'

'You didn't expect no favours? You cautioned me, then you just let me go?'

'Yeah.'

'I should've remembered that. Usually I have to wind up doing something with your little pricks before I get to go away. You just let me go without nothing and I don't remember it. Funny. Guess I must be getting old.'

Quemada smiled, a smile that said 'guess so', and stayed silent.

'You want to state your business and fuck off out of here? You got no reason to hassle us.'

'We don't want to hassle you, Maggi. Really we don't. We just want some information on one of your customers. One of your *old* customers.'

'Really. I don't even know their names. You realise that. You know what sort of hooker I am. *I don't even know their names.*'

'You knew this one's name,' said Velasco. 'His name was Antonio Alvarez.'

She looked at them as if they had come from another planet, her eyes big white circles staring through the glasses.

'Shit,' she said, then walked to the sideboard, pulled out a bottle of cheap brandy, and filled a long tumbler with the oily brown fluid. 'I never thought I'd hear that name again. I never wanted to.'

'It's important,' said Quemada. 'This is nothing to do with you, with your business. We don't want to lay anything at your door. We just want you to tell us everything you know about old Antonio. And then we go. No problems.'

'That a promise?'

'We're chasing bigger fish than regular whores, Maggi. *Much* bigger fish.'

'Dead fish. You know he's dead. You know that, don't you?'

Velasco nodded. 'We know that. We're not dumb. We still want to ask some questions.'

The woman took a big gulp of the brandy, then wiped her mouth with the back of her hand. A big labourer's habit, thought Quemada.

'You.' She looked at the girl. 'Take the baby. Go upstairs. Change her; she stinks. Change her like I showed you how. You should know how to do it by now. You stay up there, you don't come down till I tell you. Turn on the radio. I want to *hear* the radio, I don't want you listening through the floor. You understand?'

The girl nodded briskly. She scooped up the child roughly from the floor, went into the kitchen, reappeared carrying a can of beer, then left the room. They heard the thud of footsteps, hard and deliberate on the stairs, then through the floor above. The sound of cheap pop music played through a tinny radio began to boom above them.

'Little cow always wants to play it when I want some peace and quiet. She can play it when I *do* want it for a change.'

Quemada looked around the floor then it struck him, the thing that had been bothering him. There were no toys. Not a rag doll, not a cloth book. Nothing.

He watched Maggi Bartolomé pull a cigarette out of the packet with a long, artificial, shiny pink fingernail, watched her light it, then suck through cracked, painted lips and said to himself again, 'Sometimes they are just plain doomed from birth.'

40

She had no idea how long she had watched Torrillo, watched the great chest rise and fall in shallow breaths, the lights flash and wink at her without meaning. Here, in the hospital, time seemed to be frozen. Nothing moved, nothing changed. The slow, relentless fading of the world into emptiness was imperceptible, a tiny feeble beating beneath a flat, evanescent normality. Yet for all the world's efforts, the beating was there, primal in its cruelty, ticking off the seconds, the days, the hours, in a fog of antiseptic, white tiles and the metronomic clicking of heels on polished stone floors.

Maria stood up and tried to quell the sudden sense of giddiness. She was soaked in sweat. The clothes stuck uncomfortably to her skin like a new, ill-fitting layer to her body, a sticky chrysalis only half shed.

Ch-ch-ch-ch-changes, sang a voice somewhere back in her head and, for the second time in a few days, she found herself looking back at the old Maria – the young Maria – fifteen years or more distant, and wondering to herself: was that me? Was that *really* me? And if it was, what happened in the distance between us? What is happening in the distance between the me-now and the me-to-come? What *is* the me-to-come? What will she look like? What will – what *is* – shaping her?

She wiped the palms of her hands on her top, tried to breathe deeply and slowly. This sweat, this giddiness, it was not just the heat, not just the hospital. The wound was almost forgotten now. It nagged her no more than a mosquito bite. She was afraid. Afraid to go on. To confront Caterina Lucena. To confront what lurked behind that ancient, grey face.

Maria wiped her hands again, closed her eyes and tried to focus herself. There were shapes, red and black and violet, swimming in the dark. Then she took one final look at Torrillo, and walked out into the corridor.

The clock said 3 pm. Soon she would be able to leave. Soon the police guard would come, would drive her home, let her think. But before then, she had to see, had to speak with the old woman. She felt for the piece of paper in her pocket, felt it fall under her fingers, then searched the signs for the way to the geriatric ward, found it and walked down the long, echoing corridors at a steady pace.

It hung in the air, like static waiting for the coming of the storm, a deep, basal certainty: she would never see Bear alive again.

41

Maggi Bartolomé sucked at the cigarette until the end glowed red and fiery, then she poured herself another brandy.

'You guys mind if I get out of this shit?' she said.

Quemada raised an eyebrow. 'Now you're not gonna do anything stupid like trying to run away? It's real hot out there and we could all save ourselves the exercise.'

'I'm not going to run away,' she said. 'I have to look like this to earn a living. Doesn't mean I have to wear it in my own home.'

'OK,' said Quemada. 'But don't be long. The Captain hates paying overtime.'

'You cops hate paying for anything,' she said, then walked upstairs. They heard the radio turn down for a moment, the sound of low voices, movement. A shower came on somewhere. They waited. Then she came back down again wearing cheap jeans, a nylon top and no make-up. She looked like someone completely different: older, sure, thought Quemada, but not worse. In another life . . . what? He wondered for a moment then mentally kicked himself: you don't get another life.

She picked up the drink, stubbed out the cigarette, lit another straight away.

'Why me?' she said. 'Of all people. Why me?'

'You laid a complaint. In 1960. You said he raped you, repeatedly. We'd like to know more.'

'That was over thirty years ago. The bastard's dead. You want to know *more*?'

'I thought I just said that.'

'Mind telling me why?'

'We don't mind, Maggi,' said Quemada, working on the basis that you give a little, you get a little. 'You been reading about these murders in the city?'

'You mean those arty guys and stuff? One of you cops got hit too?'

'Right.'

'So what's Antonio got to do with it?'

'We don't know. Maybe nothing. Maybe something. Thing is, there's kind of a connection between him and some of the people who got killed. You heard of La Soledad?'

'Just the stories. You know. Everyone heard the stories.'

'He never mentioned it.'

'Never. You think we *talked*?'

'So what did you do, Maggi?' Quemada asked.

'You want the details? This something for the cops' Christmas party, right?'

'No. This is serious. Really serious. We know what you said happened when you laid those complaints. We need to know what *really* happened. Who else he was messing with. That kind of thing.'

She stubbed out the cigarette, walked to the stairwell then yelled upstairs for the girl to turn the radio up. Some pop song got louder.

'We just pass it on, you know. My mother to me. Me to her. You get knocked up with some kid, your life just goes to shit. Like it's automatic.'

She gazed at nothing in particular.

'If it hadn't been for Antonio I wouldn't have started this "career". That's true. Really. That, at least, began with me, you see. My mother, she just cleaned hotels, cleaned people's houses, that kind of stuff. My father was gone. Maybe dead. Maybe not. She never really let on.'

'Your mother's dead now?'

She nodded. 'Ten, fifteen years ago. Don't ask me exactly. I never spoke to her much once I realised.'

'Realised what?'

Maggi Bartolomé poured herself another drink and said, 'Realised she was pimping me for Antonio.'

Quemada stopped making notes and looked at her. She was leaning well back in the scruffy armchair now and there was something liquid about her eyes. He shook his head and said, 'Your own mother was a cleaner, an honest woman, then she started pimping you?'

'That's right.'

'But why?'

She laughed and Quemada tried to stifle the thought that it was quite a pleasant sound. 'He could do that kind of thing. He could charm the birds out of the trees if he wanted something. That was how he *was*. He played the tune, the world danced. And he had something else nobody else had.'

Velasco said, 'Let me guess. Money.'

She nodded. 'Money. Lots and lots and lots of money. God knows where he got it from. They said he took some of it from some charity he was involved in but there was more money than that. He must have been putting it away for years. Me, I think he was a gangster. He *controlled* people. All over. Everywhere. He could pay for anything he wanted and he did it in this really clever way. So that you didn't know you were being bought and sold. That was the smart thing. You didn't know until it was too late.'

'You mean your mother didn't know?'

She pushed the drink over to the other side of the table and stared at them. 'Don't let me have any more of this crap, will you? I start on it this time of day, I can't move

325

by eight and I got work to do this evening. No one pays good money for a drunk whore.'

Quemada got up, picked up the glass then poured the drink back into the bottle.

'That's nice,' she said. 'Some self-righteous shits would have poured it down the sink. You're *economical*. That's nice.'

'I just don't like the idea of making you work harder to buy more, that's all,' Quemada replied. 'Seems you work pretty hard as it is.'

'Yeah,' she said. 'But I don't clean houses. Like my mother did. She cleaned. She got on her hands and knees and she cleaned and polished and did whatever they told her. Then came home with enough money to buy a loaf and a few vegetables. If we were lucky. I get a little more than that. Not a lot. But enough so's you'd notice. And when I get down on my hands and knees I don't have to stay there too long.'

Quemada said, 'She cleaned for him. That's how it began.'

'Yeah. She cleaned for him. Twice, maybe three times a week. She'd been doing this for a year. Then, one day, she took me with her. Just to help a little. I was eleven, twelve maybe. I can't remember.'

'And you saw him?'

'No. I never did. He saw *me*. Little girl, some cheap little school uniform my mother had made herself. I was quite pretty then, too. You might find it hard to believe but I was.'

'I don't find it hard to believe, Maggi, really I don't,' said Quemada.

'Wow. A cop who's a gentleman. Is this for real?'

'It's for real,' he replied. 'How soon did it start?'

'Two. Maybe three weeks. Slowly at first. That was the way he worked. First of all my mother said, "You got to come round the Alvarez house with me, the señor likes having you around." So I'd go and while my mamma did the cleaning he'd show me things. Show me a record player, some paintings, rooms that had this good furniture in. Things I'd never seen before. It was like magic. Like being some place you'd only dreamed about before. I was a kid. I liked it. Who wouldn't?'

'And nothing happened at first?'

'Nothing. Nothing at all. He was just this old guy. He looked a little ill sometimes. There was a smell about him, a kind of old smell, like bad breath but worse somehow. I didn't like that and sometimes he used to get close so I really didn't like it at all. But my mamma always said to me, "He's a good man, you should do as he says." And I was just a little girl then. I *did* do what he told me even when it seemed wrong, even when it *hurt*. That's what you were supposed to do. Wasn't it?'

'Did you know he was giving her money?'

'I knew we *had* more money. More food, better clothes. I knew that and I knew in some way it had something to do with me. That my cooperation, my doing like I was told, sort of guaranteed that the money would keep coming. I didn't put it all together until later, of course. You don't. It doesn't work that way. One day he's showing me his record player, playing these songs from Disney movies I'd only heard of, and I'm listening there with my mouth open. The next he's saying, listen to some more, sit on my lap, listen to some more. The next, he's saying, touch this, it will be nice, touch it, we will all be happy, you, your mamma, me, we will all be happy together. So I touch it, this *thing* I didn't even really know existed. Then one thing leads to another. Next thing I know he's coming to the house here, I'm seeing him where he lives, when he likes, doing *what* he likes, things I don't understand. Things that

327

hurt me. And when I say to my mamma I don't like it, mamma it *hurts*, it gives me pain, she's saying, think of the food, think of the clothes, think of the little holiday we're going to have in El Puerto, the first holiday we've *ever* had.

'You know something? By the time I was thirteen I knew how to do things to men most wives out there still don't know, most of them will *die* without knowing. And that was him. That was all him. I hated it. Every moment of it. I hate it still. Sex, it's something I do with my body that gets me money, like the way a butcher cuts up a carcass of meat. To think that someone gets pleasure out of it, that kills me. It really does. And I tell you something else. I go out there at night, the number of times a man wants to fuck me, just plain fuck me, I count on one hand. What they want to do, you got to imagine. But there's never anything, not one thing, that Antonio didn't do before. That was him. What we were to him was something *unspoiled*, something he could mess with, ruin. That was his kick. He didn't use whores. He made his own. Then, after a while, when he thought they'd got spoiled themselves he just forgot about them. You were out on your own with just a little money to keep you quiet.'

Velasco rapped his pencil on his notebook then said, 'So why didn't you keep quiet?'

'I would have done. I didn't know what was happening really. I didn't *know*. It was her. She was getting the money. She wanted the money. For ever. So she made me tell lies. About my periods. And then they weren't lies at all. They were for real. Antonio tried to be careful, he used condoms when he remembered, he didn't want the hassle of girls getting pregnant. But he was getting old then. He didn't always remember. Also, I think, he didn't always want to remember. He just wanted to do what he wanted. When I used to go in there I'd no idea *what* he wanted. Sometimes

328

it might be something that could make you pregnant. Sometimes not. You couldn't guess. So she made me lie about my period, so it got more likely I would get pregnant. And I did. Surprise, surprise. Thirteen years old with one of Antonio's little bastards inside of me. I wasn't the first. I guess you know that.'

Quemada scanned through his earlier notes. 'We looked at the case files. Most of them are still there. Why didn't he wind up in court?'

'Something happened. Some money. With my mother. I never saw any of it. Except for one thing.'

'What?' asked Velasco.

'They put me on a coach to Cadiz, said I was going on holiday. I got there, someone gave me something to drink, I passed out. When I woke up I was bleeding. Down there. They'd got rid of the baby. Never said anything to me about what they were going to do. I wouldn't have understood in any case. To be honest, I don't think I really knew I had a baby there. I was so young. So young.'

'Did you see him after that?'

'No. Once or twice in the street. I never let on, of course, and to be honest I don't think he would have recognised me. The way he treated us was, I don't know how to put it. When we were there, when he was doing what he wanted with us, there was nothing else in his life. In a way I think he genuinely loved you. He tried not to hurt you, he tried to be kind. But once you were out, once he'd decided there was nothing left to spoil, you just didn't exist.'

'Does he have any relatives left in the city?'

'You mean *legal* relatives? No. Not that I know of. He had a wife. He talked of her sometimes, talked of her like she was an old, dead person, not part of his life. But they never had kids or brothers and sisters as far as I know. He never talked about any anyway. He used to say I was his family. I guess he used to say that to everyone. He had a whole line, you know. You know that?'

Quemada nodded. 'There's a whole string of complaints in the book. We don't understand how none of them ever came to court.'

'Yeah. A whole line.'

'Did you know any of the others?'

She lit another cigarette. 'Jesus. It's such a long time ago. I can't remember. I mean we didn't go around comparing notes. It wasn't the kind of thing you wanted to talk about.'

'Did he always finish one relationship before he started another? Was it consecutive like that?'

'"Relationship." That's a nice way of putting it. No. I think he kept a number of girls on the go at the same time. He even had our pictures in the house. In his study. Pictures of girls, young girls, portraits, you know, like school portraits. Sometimes they'd be there one week and the next they'd be gone. I guess that happened to mine too. I liked my picture. It was the best anyone had ever taken of me. He could have given it to me. I would have liked it.'

'You heard of the bullfighter? Jaime Mateo?'

'Sure. Antonio, he was the father. Everyone says that in the barrio. Everyone. Don't ask me who the mother was supposed to be. We didn't keep track of those things. We didn't like to ask. So what? It was so long ago.'

Quemada scratched his chin with the top of the pencil. He looked lost. 'Maybe. But it's still jerking someone's chain.'

'Beats me who. Now you got anything else to ask or do I get some sleep before I go back "on duty"? You know the old joke: I been on my back all day.'

Quemada closed the notebook and put it in his pocket.

'Why you bother with this, Maggi? You're intelligent enough. You could get a job.'

'What? Cleaning floors? You don't get it, do you? Cops never get it. This *is* my job. It's what I choose to do.'

'Hell of a thing to choose,' said Quemada. '*Hell* of a thing.'

'And what you do is so much better I guess? Hassling the likes of me? Pulling in drunks? That's a real public service? Least I send them home happy, most of the time anyway.'

She reached for another cigarette and Quemada watched as the mask went back up, hard and coarse and impenetrable.

'You send yourself home happy, Maggi? How about that?' he said.

'I gave up on that a long time ago. You got some old guy sticking his thing in places you thought had other functions every time he feels like it, just around the time you ought to be thinking about going to school and learning how to write, you soon give up on that.'

'Yeah,' said Quemada. 'I can appreciate that.'

'Can you?' she answered and Quemada didn't want to look in her eyes. 'Can you really?'

'No,' he said flatly. 'I can't. But it seems a shame to let him fuck your life up twice over. And maybe not just yours. What about . . .' He jerked his thumb upstairs. 'She out there making it too?'

She laughed. 'My daughter, detective, works in a supermarket. Or should I say *worked*. She got knocked up by some kid who used to stack the shelves. Now she sits moping at home listening to junk music and waiting for me to come back with the spending money. There's justice for you. You may not like the idea, but I'm the respectable one in this family.'

Quemada let out a little laugh too then, and it caught him by surprise.

'Let's get out of here,' said Velasco, looking uncomfortable. 'We still got loads of names on the list.'

'Can I see that?'

'Sure,' said Velasco and handed her the sheet of paper. She ran down the names one by one, never stopping.

'You know any of them?' asked Velasco.

'Some of the names sound familiar. Barrio families. We were all barrio families. All . . .'

Her voice drifted off into nothing. The two cops watched and waited for her to come back.

'You're thinking, Maggi,' said Quemada when the wait got too long for him.

'It happens from time to time. Full moon, leap years. Sometimes I get to think and walk at the same time too even.'

'This a private thought or do we come in on it?'

She looked at them and, for a moment, the mask dropped again.

'What I just told you, that was wrong. We weren't all from the barrio. There was someone else. A picture. The girl was older, a little older than the rest of us. I never saw her. I just saw the picture. Sometimes he'd talk about her and it was different, the way he talked. He was screwing her, for sure, else why else would he put the picture there along with all his other *trophies*. But it was different somehow. I sort of got the impression that she was special. Her picture had been there before ours ever got on the wall. And it was going to stay there long after ours came down. And she *didn't* come from the barrio. I remember he said that. Maybe she even lived outside town for a while. El Puerto, Cadiz, somewhere on the coast. Shit, I can't remember. My mind isn't what it was.'

'Not one of these names? On the list?' asked Velasco.

'No. *Definitely*. This kid came from somewhere else.'

Quemada pulled out a card from his pocket and gave it to her. 'You remember the name, you give me a call. It might be important. This guy, he's dangerous. He's killing people and we don't know why except maybe it's got something to do with Alvarez. Anything you can tell us, *anything*, might help.'

She looked at the card. 'Quemada, C. What does the C stand for?'

'Carlos. Most people just call me Quemada.'

'You don't look like a Carlos. Maybe that's why.'

'Pardon me but I have to say you don't look much like a Magdalena neither.'

'You don't read the Bible, Carlos, do you? I'm just following the calling.'

'Yeah,' he grunted. 'Well, you got the card. You phone me you think of something. We're going.'

Velasco walked out the front door leaving the two of them in the room.

'Hey,' Quemada said. 'Mind if I suggest something?'

Her eyebrows made wide inverted vees on her forehead. 'I guess that kind of depends.'

'No. What I meant was this. You should go a little less heavy on the make-up. A woman don't need that stuff, a good-looking woman. It makes them look hard, makes them look old. Use a little but use it lightly. I used to tell my ex-wife that but she still went out looking like something out of the chorus in the shows. Like talking to a brick wall. Men look at faces, they want to see the face, not something that looks like someone's painting a new bathroom.'

'Thanks for the advice,' she said. 'When I start meeting men who look at my face maybe I'll think about taking it. Right now . . .'

She held open the door; Quemada grunted and walked out into the bright sunlight. The day was as hot as when they went in. There was humidity in the air and off in the distance the ominous low gatherings of storm clouds far away on the plain.

'You like it, don't you?' said Velasco as they walked back to the car. 'You actually like talking to these women, these *whores?*'

'Seemed to me there might be quite a nice woman in there trying to get out.'

'Sure. Doing ten tricks a night. Real nice.'

Quemada stopped in the street. Velasco came to a halt and watched him.

'You tell me something?' asked Quemada. 'Ordinarily I wouldn't ask this but this isn't ordinary, is it?'

'Ask away.'

'You been on vice too. When you stop the girls, when you caution them, you ever *accept* something? You know. A little *propina?*'

Velasco went bright red and looked as if he was going to explode. 'You're suggesting, you're *seriously* suggesting . . .'

'No,' Quemada corrected. 'I'm *asking*. Not *suggesting*. *Asking.*'

'What kind of a fucking question is that? *What kind . . .*'

Quemada turned his back then started walking again, stuck the key in the car door and climbed inside. When Velasco was strapped into the passenger seat, he turned to him and said, 'Yeah, you know, I didn't enjoy it either.'

Then he turned the key and drove off at a steady thirty kilometres an hour.

42

She looked older. Her face, dappled by the rippling shadows of a eucalyptus tree outside the high casement window of the private room, looked much older. Caterina Lucena lay back on the pillow, eyes closed. Wrinkles puckered the line of the mouth. The skin, relaxed in sleep, drew back from the jawline, making the skull become visible, real beneath the flesh.

Maria walked in quietly, sat down on a plain green metal chair by the bed, and thought: she is dying. Slowly, in front of me, she is dying.

And then wondered: was her story, the story of La Soledad, some part of the process, some stage in her release?

She was in a different room now, moved for those inexplicable reasons which seem so important to the bureaucracy of a hospital. Yet the room where they had first spoken about the war, about La Soledad, was still imprinted on her mind. She could remember how it looked, its smell, its character, the way the heat hung in the air, the light came dazzling through the window. This was a moment in time which would live with her, which held some extra, unwanted importance. She looked at the frail body on the bed, watched the sheets rise almost imperceptibly with each dimly laboured breath, and wondered if the time for revelations was past. If Caterina Lucena had one tale to tell, one song to sing. And having sung it would feel the need to live no more.

Maria closed her eyes and let her head fall backwards, resting. From outside came the faint, distant chorus of birdsong and the low, complaining rumble of traffic. Elsewhere in the hospital gurneys travelled corridors on squeaking wheels, doctors and nurses spoke slowly in low, conspiratorial voices, there was the clatter of dishes, the tired shallow sighing of the infirm. She thought back to the hospice, the painting by Valdés Leal, the peace, the *apparent* peace, they had witnessed there. A pair of artists murdered in an artistic fashion. An unexplained attack. The killing of an official of one of the brotherhoods, and such a strange, such a sinister one too. Her own close brush with death. The city reached out to her in a hydra's head of events, ideas and notions, unsorted, without priority, without logic, each fighting for its own space in her confused anxious mind.

And no device, no ready Occam's Razor, was at hand to cut through this sea of material, cut through to the quick, to the bone.

Occam's Razor, Maria thought, and for a moment it brought back the hazy, distant pleasures of philosophy classes, long ago, a lifetime ago, in a quiet city of spires, when the world existed primarily as a topic of learned debate: life, *discuss*. For a brief moment an image floated above her, an image of a blade, silver sharp, scything through the night, sorting myth from fact, deceit from truth, what is necessary from what is spurious. It shone, a metallic beacon lighting the darkness, then disappeared, leaving an after-image in its wake. Maria held her eyes tight shut, hoping for it to return, but there was nothing.

She opened her eyes and felt Caterina Lucena's cold, aloof stare wash over her.

The old woman lay still on the bed. She now seemed to be too weak to move. There was little life left in her, except

for the eyes. They now watched Maria, grey and icy, something like amusement lurking behind them. The mouth
opened, gave a small, unreadable smile, then closed in on
itself again.

'Did you find him?' she asked, her voice the rustle of dry
leaves across parched earth on an early autumn day.

'Find who?' replied Maria, trying, with little success, to
disguise the harshness in her voice.

'My boy. My son?'

'No,' she said. 'Not yet.'

Caterina gave a little cough. Perhaps she was trying to
laugh, thought Maria.

'Not yet . . . Such a fine police force.'

Maria reached into her pocket and pulled out the police
print-out from the computer. She had sketched in the
moustache, as best as she could remember from the old
woman's description. And added in a few lines to the face
too. It made the face more human, somehow. She could
see the attraction there, the crude film star looks, could
imagine how this man might appeal to a young, inexperi-
enced girl.

She thrust the portrait in front of Caterina Lucena.

'Do you recognise this man?'

The old woman screwed up her eyes and stared at the
print-out. She went silent, her lips drew tight together,
making the pucker lines of age stand out as deep, unsightly
wrinkles on her face.

'You *know* this man,' said Maria, and it was a statement,
not a question.

Caterina Lucena breathed in deeply through her nose,
the grey eyes stared at the ceiling.

'You play jokes with me. This is your idea of amusement.
To play jokes on an old woman.'

'This is no joke, Caterina. People are dying because of

337

this man. Last night, this man, *this man* tried to kill me. He has as good as killed a police officer. A good man. He will kill again.'

'This, *this* . . .'

The old woman's breath came in gasps. Maria watched her strain and the cruelty of her own thought processes astonished her: do not die before I know, she thought, *do not die beforehand*.

'This man,' said Caterina Lucena, 'this man kills no one. This man is Antonio Alvarez. He is dead, long dead.'

Maria smiled. 'I know,' she said. 'I did play a joke.'

She took the paper, pulled an eraser out of her bag, rubbed out the moustache, the extra lines.

'This is the man. This is the man who is doing these things. Who is he? You know. You can help us stop the killing. *Who is he?*'

There was something about her voice now. It was too loud, too shrill. Something had been pushed too far, it was over the edge, and Caterina Lucena had retreated, returned to her own private hell, to brood, to gloat, to contemplate. A figure bustled around Maria. She had not heard the door open. Grey and white, the smell of soap and antiseptic. A nurse's face appeared in front of her.

'You have to leave,' said the voice, a strong, insistent female voice. 'You have to leave. She is an old woman. She cannot be upset like this.'

Maria felt the fury burn through her. 'Upset? This woman is ice. Nothing *upsets* her.'

She broke away from the nurse's grip and leaned over the old woman, now lying on the bed, eyes closed, face a leathery, wrinkled death mask.

'People are dying, Caterina. *Dying*. Because of what happened at La Soledad. And you won't help us stop them.'

The nurse held her, arm twisted behind her back, pressing

painfully on the wound. She was starting to shout for help. Outside the room came the sound of hurried footsteps. It was no good. Maria relaxed, came back from the bed, held out her hands, said, 'No. It's fine. I'll go.'

She was almost through the door when the old woman spoke, the last words Maria would ever hear her say.

'He loved me,' she said, voice cracked, dry and brittle. 'That is why he died as he did. The cancer. The pain. It was a *judgement*. On him. On me.'

Maria turned and walked down the corridor, down the stairs, through the swing doors and out into the bright sunlight of another perfect day.

43

'Nothing,' said Rodríguez. 'Nothing links any of this together. It doesn't make sense.'

Menéndez looked at the Captain's face and wondered how much longer he could keep the job going. There were lines of fatigue on his face. They showed through in his impatience, his unwillingness to listen. He was weary and it was starting to show.

'Nothing. No link to the Alvarez story. No students at the university who come anywhere near the profile. Nothing except the circumstantial stuff – he knew Mateo, he seems to have known the dating agency . . .'

In front of him, on the desk, Rodríguez had the morning papers. They were plastered with the story. It seemed to grow bigger, more sensational by the hour.

'Where are Velasco and Quemada?' Rodríguez asked. 'I think you're in a dead end trying to chase this history thing. This is just some crazy. Some psychopath. We should stop wasting our resources on this research *now* and just throw a wider net on what we already have.'

'I think,' said Menéndez, 'that maybe we should cover both ends. We're somewhere with this investigation. It may be a dead end. Maybe not. But I agree. We can't simply close our eyes to the possibility of just a random psychopath.'

'Good. You read this stuff?'

Rodríguez pushed the newspapers across the desk.

'*I* carry the can with these people, Lieutenant. Not you.

They don't see something happening soon they're going to be baying for my blood. You run your show with what you've got – Velasco, Quemada – and that's it for the moment. I'm putting this out as a major surveillance piece right through the uniformed branch and taking personal charge of it. We're going to have them checking IDs right, left and centre, random road blocks, whatever else I damn well think of. While we're at it we can take a look at some of those gay clubs too. You can tell everyone out there they'll be on permanent overtime until this show's over.'

'Sir,' said Menéndez, and felt both belittled and somewhat grateful at the same time.

The door opened and Maria walked in. She was wearing the same drab clothes she had found in the hospital. Menéndez looked at her and thought she looked just a touch deranged.

'I thought you were going home.'

'I changed my mind,' she said.

'We sent an officer to look after you.'

'She's waiting outside. Thanks. I don't know what she might do to our man but she scares the living daylights out of me.'

Rodríguez had assigned her protection to one of the uniformed women in the force, a 200-pound amazon by the name of Michaela Costas. She wore a uniform that was one size too small in order to emphasise the extent of her biceps. Maria had never seen a gun belt shine so much. It looked like a mirror. It took all the persuasion she possessed to steer Costas away from taking her home into driving her to the station instead.

'You should go home and rest,' said Rodríguez. She looked at him and noticed some change. The politeness had gone. He looked jumpy, nervous, and this depressed her:

341

like the rest, she looked to him for something from outside, some kind of inspiration. 'We've got precious little here. There's nothing for your report. From now on this just turns into a major security exercise. We clamp down the city until this bastard comes out of hiding.'

'I've been resting all day,' she said. 'I'm sick of resting. This thing keeps hammering around my head like a pinball machine. I can't turn it on and off like that. You know my brief – to follow everything through. Besides . . .'

'Besides what?' asked Menéndez.

'I talked to Caterina Lucena again.'

'She say anything?'

'I drew a moustache on the computer picture. A few lines on the face. She thought it was Alvarez.'

Menéndez thought Rodríguez was about to explode. 'Be realistic, *Professor*. She's an old woman. They get fuzzy thoughts in their heads at that age. You've had a hard time. A stressful time. Go home and leave this to us.'

'That's wrong,' said Maria. 'You haven't met Caterina Lucena. I have. She has thoughts and she has no thoughts. But I don't believe she has fuzzy thoughts. So what does it mean?'

'That the killer has an incredibly strong facial resemblance to Alvarez,' said Menéndez. 'So presumably he's related.'

'Come on,' said Rodríguez. 'How often do you get some kind of resemblance that strong? How often? The old bird's just short of a few cells. That's all.'

'It happens,' said Maria. 'Not often, but it happens. It happens more often in families where there is interbreeding than in those with very separate gene lines. Think of it. You've been to some of these very isolated rural areas, places where the gene pool's quite restricted. Don't you notice how much some people in the same family can look alike, even two generations apart?'

342

Rodríguez's eyes were closed. He looked as if he were in pain.

'Fine. So you're saying it might not just be his son, it could be his *grandson*? Does this make sense?'

'It's possible,' Menéndez said.

'Possible. Everything's possible, but we can't go chasing *everything*. Say it is a grandson. The only way you' – she noticed how Menéndez reacted to the use of the word 'you' – 'can trace him is through the parents. How else could you do it?'

Menéndez shrugged his shoulders. 'I don't see. We've got a list of girls who complained. We're working on them now. God knows how many never complained, just got paid off, sent down the abortionist, whatever.'

Rodríguez shook his head. They could feel him being drawn into the idea, in spite of himself. 'The women on the list you've seen so far. They tell you anything?'

'Nothing much. It was a long time ago for these girls. Not something many of them want to remember.'

'Could Romero be part of the link?' Maria asked. 'Somehow he seems to be.'

Menéndez shook his head. 'We traced his family, eventually. The records just aren't there. There is nothing to say he has any connection with the Alvarez line at all. If there's a connection there – and I still think some of these are random and some are not – then it's through something he found, something he saw at the university.'

Occam's Razor, thought Maria. Pare it down. *Occam's Razor.*

'You said Alvarez stole money from the brotherhood.'

'Yes,' said Menéndez. 'A *lot*. Two million pesetas or more.'

'What happened to it?'

'Spent it most likely. The way he used it on these girls

343

he had a lot to throw around. They make it sound like he was seriously rich. They're girls from the barrio of course, so maybe their definition of rich is different to ours. But it sounds like he had a lot of money and he knew how to use it.'

Rodríguez watched them throwing the idea around, hands flat on the desk, not writing, not taking notes. Then he looked at the papers again and closed his eyes.

Maria tried to separate the strands, tried to think them through. 'We don't know of a reason, a motive, for this. We don't know of any reason for revenge. Alvarez is dead. Would anyone seriously try to take revenge on people who knew him, people who had some link to him?'

'Crazy people do,' said Rodríguez. 'They'd do it for any reason they feel.'

'But this man is *not* crazy. Can't you feel that? There's some kind of logic, some relentless logic there. Even when he's random, it has a purpose. Trying to kill me. That *had a purpose.*'

'To convince us he was crazy,' said Menéndez flatly.

'In which case he must have a real motive. A sensible motive,' she said.

'Money,' said Menéndez. 'Who collected the money when old Antonio died? Not his wife. She predeceased him. No kids. No relatives. Sure, he handed out money to his bastards in the barrio and it may have seemed a lot to them, but it was nothing compared with what went missing. Where did the rest go? *Who got the money?*'

'Do you keep records of that sort of thing?' Maria asked.

'If they do it legally, we do,' Rodríguez replied, and the Lieutenant was glad, was gratified to hear him being caught by the thread. 'Under the bed stuff is harder to trace and wouldn't you think this kind of thing *would* be under the bed? What's the point in stealing the money then letting everyone know you've got it, the taxman included, when you die?'

'You'd be surprised,' said Menéndez. 'Every crook I ever knew made a will. Let's check the registry. Let's see what's there.'

Menéndez made a note with his pen.

'These things take time. You won't get it tonight,' said Rodríguez. 'Remember what I said. You've got the resources you've got. No more. And if anything does come up, I want to hear about it. Straight away.'

Maria felt like talking, felt she could talk for ever. 'If it was for money, then some of the people involved, the ones that weren't random, they must have stood between him and the money. They must have been blocking him somehow.'

'How?' asked Rodríguez.

'If the money was in the legal realm, other relatives might have had a claim. If it was illegal, people who knew about it could have used that knowledge. Blackmail. Whatever. The Angel Brothers knew a lot of criminals. They could have found out. Castaneda, too, he had the records, he could have known.'

'And Romero?'

'I don't know. I just don't know.'

Menéndez screwed up his face and reached in his head for something. 'One of these women, the women who made the complaints against Alvarez, she said she thought he had a special kind of girl. Someone he felt special towards. No name, nothing much to track her by. But she thought there was something different there.'

'Why not go back? See if she can remember any more,' said Maria. 'This money idea. It makes sense. More sense than anything else.'

'None of this makes sense,' said Rodríguez, and there

was colour in his cheeks now. 'The whole thing is shot through with illogicality, unpredictability. I've let you pursue this too far already and we'll all be lucky if we come out of this with our reputations intact. This time next week you and I may both be facing an internal inquiry, Menéndez. Better get used to the idea. Best thing we can hope is that this lunatic, this crazy, pops off in front of one of the uniform teams some time soon and we can crow about it all to the papers.'

Menéndez nodded. He'd been thinking much the same himself. This was meant to be the case that got him the Captain's chair. Instead it could see them both set back in their careers. Maybe for good.

'You sit here talking like this,' said Rodríguez. 'The truth is you've been chasing through the history books for four days now and you've got nothing. Just make your report notes nice and clean and tidy from now on.'

'That's not the case,' said Maria. 'We do know something. Maybe we don't recognise it. Maybe . . .'

And the thought came quick and unheralded. It made her shiver in the warm little room.

'Maria?' asked Menéndez.

'I thought,' she said. 'I just thought, maybe we know something but don't recognise it. And the reason he wanted me dead was because he knew that. He wanted me dead *before* I recognised it.'

'Oh, Jesus,' said Rodríguez, and the force with which he spoke took them both aback. 'This is not an academic exercise, Professor. People are getting killed and this whole exercise is getting out of hand. I am telling you now, as Captain of this division, as someone who has spent more time on those streets than *anyone* in this city, what we have here is a crazy. An unpredictable, psychopathic crazy. We get lucky, we flood the streets hard now, we got a good chance of catching him. If we don't, chances are that once the cycle's over, once Semana Santa is over, he goes back to his day job in any case. You can play your little game until the whistle blows, but it's going to be blowing damn soon. And I'll be blowing it.'

Menéndez stared at the old man and kept his peace.

'Maybe it will be over even if you don't find him. Until next year,' said Maria, and instantly regretted it.

The atmosphere was cut when Velasco hammered on the door, then walked in without waiting to be asked. They all turned to look at him.

'Two calls,' he said to Menéndez. 'We got two calls while you were in here.'

'Yes?'

'Someone in Melilla rang, said they managed to trace the couple. They were both long gone from there but someone remembered them. And yeah, they remembered the kid.'

'The child,' said Maria. 'There *was* a child.'

'Yeah. We got that much right. But not a lot more. There was a child, see, but it was a girl. Not a boy. A girl. A little girl, weird, quiet kid, dyed her hair when she was only six or so, never talked to no one, the sergeant said. No one knew her. No one liked her.'

'They say what happened to her?'

'No. She left for the mainland when the couple did. No one knows where.'

'They give you a name?'

'Yeah,' said Velasco. 'I was coming to that. But there was another call too. Quemada's friend. This Maggi woman. One of Alvarez's lays? She called from some bar somewhere. Sounded a really *nice* sort of place. Said she remembered the name. The name of that girl Alvarez liked kind of special. You know what? Same name. The guy in Melilla, the whore in the bar, they give me the same name. The *same* fucking name.'

Menéndez stared at him. 'Yes?'

'Teresa. Said she was called Teresa. Nothing more.'

Menéndez shut his eyes and felt his fists clenching automatically. Maria could see the tension inside him.

'Teresa,' said the Lieutenant. 'There is one Teresa here, one in the loop.'

'You mean the kid wasn't Romero, it was Romero's wife?' asked Velasco at the door.

'It makes sense.'

'And you mean . . .' Velasco was adding it all up, like a bill, in his head. 'Jesus. He was screwing his own daughter. The picture on the wall *was his own daughter.*'

Maria wondered. Did it click just like that? Like a piece in a puzzle? A circle joined with some awful, terrible symmetry. She walked out of the station, down the stairs, into the parking lot, into the car, her head whirling, oblivious of everything around her. The dam seemed about to burst.

Back in the office, Rodríguez looked at the papers again, swore quietly to himself, then phoned his opposite number in the uniformed branch. There were procedures for this kind of thing, plans going back years that involved street searches, road blocks, random ID checks, a host of very public policing procedures that would make this Semana Santa one no one was going to forget.

'As if it isn't already,' said Rodríguez quietly to himself. Fifteen minutes later, a convoy of police trucks, sirens flashing, klaxons blaring, pushed their way through the crowds and into the plaza. Everything Rodríguez could lay his hands on was going out there and pretty soon there'd be scarcely a soul in the city who wasn't aware of it.

44

The mourning was over, the city was coming back to life. They sped past crowds, quiet crowds, repopulating the streets. The great plateresque candelabra shone in the incense-filled gloom of the parish churches. Vast, hulking silver ceremonial hearses toured the streets. Tomorrow was the last day: the final service, then the feria which marked the conclusion of the week, and with that the great corrida that served as the final act. Maria closed her eyes and willed it to be over, willed for an ending that spilled no more blood.

In the car Quemada and Velasco checked their weapons: fat chunks of grey metal that smelled of mineral oil. The atmosphere in the vehicle was hot and close and rancid, even with the windows half open. They were sweating, they were nervous, with excitement, with a little fear.

Quemada took a corner too fast and the tyres sang across the cobbled street. She could see heads turning in the crowd, she could hear voices being raised. Then they were out of the barrio, into the broad avenues of Carmona, driving underneath a canopy of palms, waving lazily in the hot, black evening air, driving past angular cast-iron street lamps throwing pools of yellow into the night. Menéndez sat silent in the back of the car, alone.

'He's not there,' she said. 'He's not at the house.'

'How do you know?' asked Velasco, still fiddling with the weapon.

349

'I know,' she answered. 'I know.'

He shook the gun. The barrel fell upwards, locked in place, with a flat, metallic slap. 'All the same,' Velasco said. 'Precautions. This guy don't like cops too much.'

'This guy,' said Quemada, slowly turning the wheel to take another bend, 'this guy don't like anyone.'

And Maria said to herself: they don't understand. He's not there. He's not there because it *is not his place*.

Quemada slowed the car down, turned into the drive. The gates were closed. Velasco got out of the car, opened them, then followed as the car drove past and parked outside the front door. It was just past midnight and in a downstairs room a light burned feebly. The air was thick with the scent of oleander blossom, sweetly cloying on the breeze. Menéndez stepped up to the front door and rang the bell. She watched Velasco fumble for the weapon, hold it gingerly underneath his jacket. Quemada stood stock still, hands in his trouser pockets. He looked at her and whispered, 'You're right. He's not here. But all the same, I'm glad we came.'

There was a sound from behind the door, a light came on, the clatter of a key in the lock. It swung open and Teresa Romero was there. She wore light slacks, a light top. Her hair looked grey. There was a fine gold chain around her neck which glittered, sharp and shining, under the lamplight.

'Are you alone?' Menéndez asked.

She looked at them, at Maria in particular.

'This is the woman?' she said. 'The woman in the paper, who was attacked.'

'Yes,' said Menéndez.

Teresa Romero sighed and said, 'Yes. I'm alone.'

'We must talk,' said Menéndez. 'Now.'

'If you must,' she replied, turned her back on them and walked into the big, open living room. They followed,

350

Velasco still clutching his gun like a totem against the dark.

'Brandy?' she said when they were seated in the soft leather armchairs. 'No? Well, I will.'

She poured herself a long, viscous glass of spirit, then sat back in the chair. She looked, thought Maria, like a woman close to the edge. The face, drawn and lined, framed by dyed blonde hair cut too young for her, had an angular kind of faded beauty. No family resemblance to Caterina Lucena there. Or, as far as she could tell, to Alvarez either. But there was pain, still there was pain.

'You know why we are here?' said Menéndez.

'Do I?' she asked, clinging to the glass. There was almost a look of amusement in her face.

'We believe these killings, including the death of your husband, are connected in some way with a dead councillor in the city, Antonio Alvarez. Do you know the name?'

She nodded. 'I know the name.'

'Did you have a sexual relationship with him?' asked Menéndez.

'How politely you put it. You make it sound like a flirtation.'

'This is not prurience,' said Maria. 'We are not here out of curiosity. People are being killed. *I* was almost killed.'

There was grief in Teresa Romero's face. The façade of strength was paper thin.

'*They* will not understand,' she said to Maria. 'They never do. I was *given* to Antonio Alvarez. I was a *gift*. My parents arranged all this. When I was thirteen. They introduced me to him. They told me to do what he said. And they were not people you could disobey. Not at that age, not when you depended on them for everything.'

'Your *parents?*' asked Menéndez.

She stared at them, uncomprehending. 'Yes. Why do you say it like that?'

'The way we heard it . . .' began Quemada, and Menéndez talked him down.

'We had information that you were brought up by guardians. In Melilla. And came here later.'

She shook her head. 'Your information is wrong. Again. Where do you get your ideas from? My parents came from the city. My mother still lives here. In Carmona. They worked for the city. Always.'

Menéndez blinked and looked lost for a moment. Something had thrown him.

'Why did your parents do what they did?' asked Maria. 'Was it for money? What could make them do such a thing?'

Teresa Romero stared at her. 'At the time I thought it was money. That was part of it certainly. Antonio was a strong man, a powerful man. He had *power* over people, particularly anyone who had something to do with the city, like my parents did. Does that make sense? No. You never met him. He could make you do things, things you didn't want to do. Without overt threats, without any visible *unpleasantness*. He had a kind of charm, a sinister charm, and you just went along with it, without thinking.'

'You had a child,' said Menéndez.

She gulped at her drink. 'When I was fifteen, when I began to understand what he was doing to me, I realised I was pregnant. I tried to hide it. You can do this for a while, then it becomes impossible. When they realised, when my parents understood, they told him. They said I had to go to see him. To talk to him about it.'

Maria said, 'You mean it was his decision. He decided what would happen?'

'Everything was Antonio's decision. Everything. He *controlled* everything.'

'And he said what?'

She closed her eyes. Her skin was so pale it looked trans-

352

lucent. 'I thought he would send me to the abortionists. He had done that before. With other girls. My mother. She had told me. She had said it would hurt, it would rip me apart. But that was not what happened. He said I was special. Special to him. He sent me to some clinic in Cadiz. I stayed there until the child was born. The birth was messy. They did something to me. I could not have children again. I was there two, perhaps three months recuperating afterwards.'

'And the child?' Maria asked.

Her face flared in fury. 'The child? The child was Antonio's child! *His*. Do you understand? He did not belong to me. I was just the *thing* that brought him into the world. They took him. As soon as he was fit to be taken, they took him. And you know what they said to me?'

She stared at them, something crazy in her eyes. 'They said they were doing me a favour. They wanted me to be grateful to them, grateful to Antonio, for saving me from this. From this stigma of being fifteen and with a baby.'

'What happened to the child?'

'I don't know. I *didn't* know. When I came back to the city, Antonio waited a few months. Then they told me to go and see him. You know what he wanted? To go back to the old ways. He wanted me to have sex with him again. The child, he never mentioned the child. It was as if it had never happened. I was just meant to go back to doing what I did before. Whatever he wanted.'

'What did you do?'

'I spat in his face and I said, I remember saying this still, "If you touch me, I will kill you." He looked at me like I was insane. I thought he might have me killed. He could do that. He *had* done it. He was a gangster, you know. For all that pose, all that pretence, he was a gangster. The money he had, he stole it, then used it to make more gangster money. Everything then, the police, the politicians, the people around him, he controlled them all through his money. Why do you think he got away with all this?'

'Did he accept this?' said Maria.

'Accept? Antonio accepted nothing he did not want. He held me. He said he loved me. He said I was special. Then, when I said nothing, when I did nothing, he let me go. I *died* for him then. I disappeared from his sight. When I returned home, my mother and father looked like death. They drove me round to some little apartment they said he'd paid for. They sent a maid around each day. I was left there, left on my own, paid for, like a grocery bill, left to exist. Eventually I got a job as a secretary at the university. I left the apartment. I found somewhere of my own. I did not want his money. I met Luis at the university. The rest you know. It was not a happy marriage. I don't blame Luis for that.'

She put the glass back on the table and left it there, waiting for them to go on.

Maria asked, 'You were contacted. Recently. By someone who was connected with all this.'

Teresa Romero spread her long, thin fingers across the top of the glass table, stared at them, and said, 'Six months or so ago I got a call, here at home. Someone asking for Luis. When he realised it was me, he started talking, started asking for me to meet with him.'

'Who did you think he was?' asked Maria.

She stared out of the window, refusing to look at them.

'I thought . . . I thought that possibly it was someone I might get to know. Luis had ignored me. Behaved as if I did not exist for years. Someone, someone young, rings me. Sounds nice, sounds flattering on the phone. Says he has seen me in the street, not dared to speak. And that he wanted to meet me. *Needed* to meet me.'

She looked at Maria, frankly. 'You are a woman. What would you think?'

Maria felt something grow cold and hard in her stomach. 'I would think that he wanted to start an affair.'

'Yes,' said Teresa Romero. She picked up the bottle and poured another long glass of spirit.

'I bought a new dress. I went to the hairdresser. I made myself look as attractive as I could. I had not done these things for years. To make myself attractive for a man. And then I went. To the park. We sat, at one of the open-air tables, drinking coffee, talking. And I could sense his interest, sense that he wanted me in some way. That there was something I could provide for him. And I . . . myself. Are you shocked?'

'No,' she said.

'He looked at me and . . . it was odd. I think he wanted to say yes. He wanted to come home with me. Then. That very day. He *found me attractive*. And he had to say it. Before we left. He had to say this nonsense, this crazy nonsense. That he was my son.'

She faltered, looking for the reason to go on. 'I just went blank. It was like a bad joke. All that time, all that effort I had spent preparing myself. *Offering* myself. And the reason he wanted to see me was to tell me that. And still he wanted to go through with it, still he wanted to go to bed with me.'

Maria watched her struggling with the story, trying to turn it into something that made sense.

'What was he like?' she asked.

'Like? He was like Antonio. To look at. And in some other ways too. There was something driving him. Something he couldn't help. When he said this, I couldn't think. I couldn't say anything for a while. He wanted to order a taxi. Then. To come home with me. And I said no. This was wrong. This was something that could not happen.'

355

Menéndez pulled a piece of paper out of his notes and passed it to her.

'Is that him?'

She nodded. 'Yes. I saw the picture on TV. I would have called you. In the end. It's just . . . it's just not that easy.'

Maria said, 'How did he find you? After all these years?'

'Luis. Our marriage went a little crazy ten years or so ago. He got sick of me, I guess, and just went off and did what he liked. He was a very *determined* man. When he wanted something he just kept on and on until he got it. He started this study project, on the city during the war? At night he'd come home and all he could talk about was what he was starting to dig up about the Falange, about what had happened at some camp near here. Things that had been hushed up, even though a lot of people knew they had happened. I wanted to tell him to drop it. To just let it lie. But Luis just couldn't do it. The more you tried to discourage him, the more he kept on. One day he came back and he was really excited. He said he'd found someone, a family who did things, ran errands, looked after business, for some crime figure in the city. They didn't want to know him but the family, they had some sons, one of them kept him talking. Talking and talking. And he knew a lot about the war, knew connections, links to things that Luis was looking at. Over the next few weeks they spent a lot of time talking, swapping different pieces of the same puzzle, putting things together. He was *so* excited. He talked about nothing else.'

'And this "son"? This was the man who rang you?'

'Yes.'

'And when you met him . . .'

She folded her hands, thin, bird-like hands, on her lap and said, 'And when I met him . . . I couldn't believe it. Any of it. He was Antonio's son, for sure. You could see it, just looking at him. But mine? I told myself there would be something there, some feeling, something I would *recognise*. And there was nothing. No feeling. Nothing. He sat there, calling me mother in this flat little working-class voice, telling me how he loved me, how much he missed me, how important to him I was. This, this *man*, he was a grown man, and he was behaving like a child. Behaving as if we could just take this all up from nothing, pretend it had never happened. I looked at him and all I saw was this picture, this *replica* of Antonio telling me how much he loved me, how he would now be part of my life. Always. No questions, no *request*. It was like his father. He arrived, he demanded something, he expected me to give it to him, just like that. There was money, he said, money he could put his hands on. We could live on it. I could leave Luis. We would be together always. All this, out of the blue, poured out at me, in the café in the park, and I sat there thinking, I am going mad, I will leave this place, I will never see him again.'

'You told him that?'

'I said, if it was true he was my child, *if* it was true, then I was sorry I had not had the opportunity to be his mother in the right way, as a mother should. But that was not my choice. Or his. What we had been deprived of was something we couldn't replace, something we couldn't pull back out of the last thirty years. It had never existed. We couldn't recreate it. I told him to go home, to forget the past, to live his own life, not one that might have been.'

Menéndez grimaced. 'You let him down gently?'

'As gently as I could. Until he started screaming at me. He was Antonio's son. You could see that. Antonio had this demon in him, it drove him, but it came out in the sex, it came out in the way he saw women, saw girls, as something to be used, a kind of physical instrument for whatever he felt like doing. This man, his son, he had the demon too but it was different. Antonio revolted me. This man scared me.'

'Did he threaten you?'

'Not directly. When he got mad he said he would destroy Luis. Destroy our life together. I thought – I *hoped* – this was just something he said in the heat of the moment. He felt rejected. I couldn't blame him. But I couldn't make myself feel, make my heart feel, something that wasn't there. I don't know anything about being a mother but I knew then, when we talked, that it was not just a biological thing. You couldn't create it out of nothing.'

'Did he contact you again?'

'Three months and there was nothing. Then one night, when Luis was out somewhere, God knows where, there was this call from some gay dating agency. Asking after him. Luis? I couldn't believe it. It just wasn't true. This was part of his game, part of how he said he would destroy our lives. He phoned afterwards, said he would start spreading rumours, start leading Luis into situations that could harm his reputation. They were still meeting, you see. They were still talking about the work Luis was doing and he was taking him to see people, to talk to people about the war.

'I told him to go away. I told him the same thing I told him before. It was not possible. Just not possible. A week later . . . a week later he phoned again and said that what happened, what had just happened and what would happen, was my fault. It was all my fault. It was the night they found Luis in the car. He killed Luis to spite me.'

She was silent for a moment until Menéndez prompted her. 'We need to know his name. Has he spoken to you since?'

'That is the last time I spoke to him. He called himself Antonio. He said he lived in El Viejo. That's all I know.'

'But Luis must have kept some record?'

'When he died, I went to the university. Everything had gone. Stolen. There had been some kind of break-in. There was nothing there of the project he'd been working on.'

Maria tried to catch her eyes, to look into them fully, but it was impossible. 'Teresa. He tried to kill me. He has killed other people. The Angel Brothers. Señor Castaneda. Why would he do that?'

'I have no idea.'

'Was it for the money? Did he talk a lot about the money?'

'He said there was money. A lot of money. The other people . . . I don't know. Luis had met them. He had met the Angels, he mentioned it, but I think that was some social event. With that bullfighter. Mateo? They seemed to move in the same circles. But why . . .'

She thought for a moment and said, 'What was driving him, it was not money. What was driving him was something else. He wanted *legitimacy*. He wanted some kind of normality. A family, or as much of one as he could find. And I could not give that to him. It was impossible. So I never told you. When Luis died, I never told you. When these other killings happened, I never told you. I waited for you to find out. I *prayed* for you to find out. But I could not tell you myself.'

'Why?' asked Menéndez.

Teresa Romero looked at him astonished. 'Why? Only a man could ask that question. Because of my guilt. Why else?'

359

45

'Nice woman,' said Velasco as he wheeled the car back into the centre of the city. 'Kid comes along after thirty years, says, "Hello, Momma, I'm your long-lost son", she tells him to fuck off. Nice woman.'

Maria fought to stop herself screaming at him.

'She was right,' she said, finally. 'You wouldn't understand.'

'Yeah,' Velasco replied. 'She was right. All this, all this fucking hassle, starts 'cos she can't cut it. Can't bring herself to speak with him. Sure. You can't expect her to say fine, move in with me, what you like to eat? But she didn't need to turn him off like that. No need.'

'That's bullshit,' said Quemada quietly. 'Crazy for the woman to blame herself. This kid, fine, so he doesn't like it when she doesn't want to know him. Doesn't mean he has to go round killing people. He must have been half crazy already. Just waiting for a trigger. In any case . . .'

His voice drifted off.

'In any case what?' asked Maria.

'How'd she know he was telling the truth? What proof did he have, except that he looked like his father? Maybe he was her son, maybe he wasn't. No way of knowing.'

'I think,' said Maria, 'I think that was what she was trying to tell us. That she did know. And he wasn't.'

'How could she know that?' asked Velasco unpleasantly. 'How could *you* know that?'

Maria sighed and wondered if there were the words that could bring it home to the man.

'You're a jerk sometimes. You know that? Partner?' Quemada looked genuinely angry. 'Women sometimes just get to know this stuff.'

'You believe that?'

''Course I fucking believe that. Like I told you before. They're *different*. Which makes the guy doubly crazy to think he can pursue it.'

The car cruised down empty streets, under pallid lighting, the sound of its tyres bouncing off the walls as it went.

'Someone has to know,' said Menéndez. 'Someone. In the barrio. If Alvarez was using a family, to bring up kids, they surely would have known.'

'Yeah,' replied Quemada. 'But would they tell us? They're so close these people. Like gypsies. The last people they're going to tell is us.'

'Then the university. She said she had looked there, the papers were gone. Maybe they were, maybe they weren't. We need to check.'

'We did,' said Velasco. 'They'd stockpiled what stuff of his there was in some storage place. All in cardboard boxes. Some of the day guys went through it. Nothing.'

'Then let's look again,' said Menéndez.

Quemada pulled a mobile phone out of his pocket, dialled straight in to the office and got someone on the night team.

'Yeah,' he said into the phone. 'I know tomorrow' – he looked at his watch – '*today* is Sunday. I *know* it's the feria. But there's got to be a guard there or something. Get him out of bed. Go through wherever they're keeping Romero's stuff, every last piece of paper. We want anything that has notes about the war, in particular people he was interviewing for it. Look for a diary, an address book. Make a note of any names you can find. Any. No. *Now*.'

He punched a button on the phone then put it back in his pocket.

'It's not much,' he said. 'Why are we still messing around like this? This guy, he was brought up in the city. He *lives* here. Alvarez must have paid someone for this. Why's it all so elusive?'

'Like she said,' Maria replied, 'he was a gangster. He had the city bought. He had the police bought.'

'He left no footprints,' said Rodríguez.

Maria thought about it, then said, 'Except for his children.'

46

Somewhere over the other side of town the man they knew as Antonio was sitting in his apartment, red in the face, speaking slowly, deliberately, down the phone. The cords of his neck stood out as if they had been carved from wood. He sat, rigid, over a plain kitchen table with a dirty dinner plate and a clean set of knives on it. All of the windows of the apartment were open. Moths, flies and mosquitoes circled the single light bulb above him in a slow-moving, diaphanous stream. He did not see them. Rhythmically, to a steady, deliberate metre, he clenched and unclenched his one free hand, watching the muscles flex then relax, feeling the power in his arm, feeling its strength, its naked capacity for force.

As he listened to the voice on the phone, whining, wheedling, he turned to look at the one item of decoration in the room. On the wall, next to the plain zinc washing range, pinned to the slowly crumbling off-white plaster of the wall, was a poster, ten feet by six. A poster he had bought in the city: *Two Knights of Calatrava*, by Juan de Valdés Leal.

Antonio's voice was not loud. There were others in this warren of cheap little apartments who could hear through the thin, paper-like walls. He knew they tried to listen. He could feel them intruding, feel the weak auras of their small little lives brush lightly against his own hard, impregnable exterior from time to time. Recently he had thought about killing one of them. Thought about teaching them a lesson.

That they belonged to a different order. That they had to learn their place in order to survive.

But killing one of them would draw attention to him. The police, the stupid police, now treated everyone as equals. They lacked the discretion, the ability to see life as something real, full of orders, of priorities, in the way they had when his father was alive. To kill one of the bugs, to extinguish even such a tiny little flame, would be to invite them into his neighbourhood. Possibly, if they were lucky, into his life. He did not wish this. Life was too enjoyable to think about someone, anyone, interfering with it. And there was the other thing too. He didn't like to do things too often that he hadn't been told. Sometimes the old man got mad. Sometimes the old man threatened him. And he could be scary.

The voice on the other end of the phone was still whining. It sounded like a wasp in a jar and Antonio found that he could no longer understand the words. They blurred into one another, a constant buzz, a constant drone, without syllables, without meaning. A memory came back to him, from years before. His father, on a rare visit, just after the time Antonio learned he *was* his father, watching a wasp on a windowsill, watching how it unsettled the others in the room, how they followed it nervously, from the corner of their eye, making sure that it came no closer, that it did not threaten them. His father had waited, for several minutes, letting the tiny creature encroach upon the conversation, letting them become more and more unsettled by it. Then, without a word, he had risen from the old armchair, the one with the thick black horsehair stuffing that leaked constantly from the seat, had walked to the window and, in one swift gesture, crushed the insect between thumb and forefinger, pierced its chitinous shell with a crunching sound, then let the tiny body fall to the floor. Antonio could recall his shock, could recall scanning his father's face for some sign of pain, for surely it had stung him. But there was nothing there. Pain was as absent from his father's face as emotion.

The next day, when his father had gone and the old house was empty, Antonio had searched every room, checked every window, until he found it. He had crushed the wasp with his thumb and forefinger, as his father had done, then tried to hold back the tears of pain. It was impossible. His face went scarlet with the agony, he watched his hand swell up to half its size again. He sat in the kitchen, holding his hand in a bowl of water until it went down to its normal size, willing the redness to go away. When it was close to normal again, he went back and looked around the house to find the next insect. And he did this until he could hold in the tears, until his body gathered enough immunity to the poison to keep the swelling down to a small, local redness.

He was seven years old.

The voice still buzzed and Antonio wondered how much longer he could take it. Where was the strength? Where was the determination? A half-brother, he said to himself. A real brother would not squeal like this.

Then the voice changed character, became real again, and the only buzzing in the room was from the crowd of insects circling the light above him.

'Antonio,' it said. 'It must stop. This *cannot* go on. They will discover us. They may have discovered us already!'

He could feel the anger bubbling inside him, mastered it, controlled it, channelled it into his intellect. Lately he had understood, had mastered this control of himself, and he knew that through it he continued to grow stronger.

'Brother, you sound like a woman. Or a coward. You sound like Romero,' and his voice changed pitch, became falsetto, for a moment, loud and shrill, '"*Please, please, please, I will give you anything, anything, but do not harm me, DO NOT CUT ME!*" Is this the way for someone of our blood to talk?'

'Antonio. I beg you. Stop this. We have gone as far as we can. I do not want to go to jail.'

His eyes were hard with rage. 'You *beg* me? My brother *begs?*'

The line was silent.

'My brother does not beg,' said the man at the table. 'You cannot be my brother.'

He put the phone back on the receiver and looked at the poster on the wall. He was smiling. He reached forward and picked up one of the knives, a big, long Sabatier. He rubbed his thumb gently along the blade. A thin line of blood flowed red through the skin.

47

The policewoman sat in one of the leather armchairs, almost flowing over the side. Her hair was tied back in a tight, severe bun that shone in the artificial light. Her face was flat and broad, the tan deep and leathery. She smiled, showing good strong, white teeth, held out a hand that looked like a paddle and said, 'You know, I don't think I really introduced myself properly at the hospital. No problem. Those places give me the creeps. My name's Michaela but everyone calls me Mike.'

Maria took the hand. It was dry and strong and muscular and pumped her up and down.

'What do you like to be called?'

'Mike's fine. Do you mind if I smoke?'

Maria shook her head. 'I'd rather you didn't. Sorry. But it smells.'

'Yeah.' The policewoman grinned. 'I guess it does. I ought to cut down a little anyway. Trouble is, I give up altogether and my weight goes through the roof. End up looking like a sumo wrestler.'

She looked Maria up and down.

'Guess that's not a problem for you.'

'Not really,' Maria replied.

'You diet to stay like that?'

'Not really. It's just how I am.'

'Yeah? Lucky you, I guess. The guys at the station they say I use a new kind of diet. The beer and bacon diet. They should talk.'

Maria smiled and said, 'Is there just you here?'

'Someone making periodic checks in the street too. From time to time. Personally I don't think you've got anything to worry about. We had the crime prevention people look the place over and they've done a few things. Look. I'll show you.'

She led the way into the back bedroom. The window was now closed. There were some new metal fastenings around the frame.

'Some kind of window deadlock. The keys are in the kitchen drawer. You lock them, no one comes in without taking out the entire window frame. They put them on here and a few of the other windows too, though if you ask me this is the only one where there's any reasonable outside access. The rest he'd need to be Spiderman to get in.'

'He had a key.'

'Yeah. So I gather. We changed all the locks. Put better ones on. I'll give you the keys when you want them. He won't be coming in that way. Hell, he won't be coming at all.'

'You don't think so?'

'He'd have to be stupid, wouldn't he? Why would he?'

And Maria thought to herself: I don't know why he came in the first place.

'In any case, I'm here all night. I'll stay in the living room. He walks up those stairs and I'm ready to greet him. Don't worry. It's fine.'

Maria got a glass of mineral water and sat down on the sofa. She was astonished to find she did not feel tired.

'You still got the adrenaline pumping?' the policewoman asked.

'I suppose that's it.'

'Happens to me. I get involved in something, it's hours before I can sleep. Real pain. Take it from me, the last thing you do, what you must *not* do, is drink coffee. You do that, you'll not sleep till Monday.'

Outside there was the distant sound of a band, shouting, the noise of a far-off crowd.

'Party time again out there,' said the policewoman. 'They pack it in for a day, wave everybody goodbye, then it's back out on the street. Can't blame them I guess. One week of the year when they can all go crazy. After tomorrow, after the service and they all go to the bulls, get drunk, then sleep it off, it's back to work. Back to normality. Thank Christ. This is the worst time of the year to be a cop in this city. They let you have leave over Semana Santa you wouldn't see me for dust.'

'You mean it's always bad?'

She laughed, her shoulders shook with the movement. 'Not *this* bad. No. This year we really broke all records. Killings. Street accidents. I been to quieter riots. Take my word. The Captain he's got people everywhere looking for this guy. I never known anything like it. Apart from me, Menéndez and those two other guys, there's scarcely a cop left to do anything else.'

Maria finished the glass of water. 'I think I'll try to sleep. See what happens.'

The policewoman looked at her, scrutinised her, then said, 'The Lieutenant called. While Quemada was bringing you back here. Said to pass on the message. The old woman? Caterina Lucena? The hospital called to say she died just before midnight.'

Maria tried to judge her feelings. There was nothing, no emotion there. 'Did she say anything? To the nurses?'

She shook her head. 'Nothing. You think she might?'

'I think . . . I think she could have told us more than she did. If she'd wanted.'

'I asked the Lieutenant about Bear, too.'

369

'And?'

'They said no change. Still in intensive care. Don't you love hospitals? So forthcoming with stuff. "No change." What the hell does that mean?'

'It means we wait, I suppose.'

'Waiting. What a way to spend your time. I love Bear. Like a brother, let me say that before you get the wrong idea. The police is full of shitty men but he just doesn't fall in with that crap. He's like a knight. God, that's a crazy thing to say, but you know what I mean?'

Maria nodded.

'There's just something fine hangs around him the way it doesn't hang around most men. I don't have much time for men. Maybe you guessed that. Jesus, that guy. And in the end . . .'

'In the end . . .'

'In the end we're all dead. Didn't somebody say that? In the end we're all dead.'

'Somebody,' said Maria then went into the bedroom. She slipped off her clothes, put on a short cotton slip, climbed beneath the cover. Outside, a few doors away, came the sound of loud rock music and laughter. She closed her eyes and the world drifted away from her. The next thing she knew was the ringing of the phone by the bed, sharp and insistent. It stopped. She heard the policewoman's voice, harsh and excited, from the living room.

The door opened and she walked in, a broad grin on her face.

'That was the Lieutenant. They got a name. They got a *big* break. He wants me to take you in as soon as we can.'

Maria tumbled out of the bed and looked at the clock on the side table. It read seven in the morning. She had slept a mere four hours and scarcely noticed it.

48

Jaime Mateo sat in the interview room and shook. He was faced, across the scuffed green metallic table, by Menéndez, Quemada, Velasco and Maria. She didn't know who looked worse. The detectives or Mateo. It didn't look as if any of them had slept that night. The room was filled with the musky smell of sweat, stale breath and cigarette smoke. She would have opened a window but the only one in the room, a three-foot-square opening high on the wall, was firmly and very visibly barred.

Menéndez flipped on the black plastic tape recorder he used for formal interviews, gave the tape a spoken caption, then said to the bullfighter, 'Señor Mateo. You are making this statement of your own accord and at your own request. That is correct?'

'Yes,' answered Mateo, then pulled hard on his cigarette. 'I . . .'

'Señor Mateo phoned the station early this morning,' Menéndez said into the mike. 'He told us he had information relevant to the murders of the Angel Brothers and the person being sought for them.'

Menéndez picked up the Photofit picture from the desk.

'Do you know this man?'

Mateo nodded.

'What is his name?'

'Antonio Mateo.'

'He's your *brother*?' asked Quemada.

The remark drew a pained expression on Mateo's face. 'That makes it sound different to the way it was.'

'How?'

'He was my *half*-brother. He lived with us for a while. He was not . . .' The words seemed to escape him. 'He was not my brother in the sense you mean.'

'Where is he now?' asked Menéndez.

'I don't know. He rang me. Last night. I don't know from where. He moves around a lot. Rents apartments, moves on after a couple of weeks. I don't know where he called from. He didn't say.'

'Where was the last place you *did* know he was living?' asked Quemada. 'I mean brother, half-brother, you must have had some address for him some time.'

'Calle Leon. In the barrio. Number thirteen. But that was months ago. The way he kept in touch, he phoned me. I didn't phone him.'

'And last night. What did he say?'

'He's crazy. He's just gone crazy these last few months. He calls me, he rants and raves. I don't know what the fuck he's talking about. Last night, he starts threatening me. Threatening *me*? Stupid little fuck.'

Quemada stubbed out a cigarette and said, 'You scared? You scared of your brother?'

Mateo glared back at him over the table. 'He is *crazy*. You hear what I say? The man is deranged. You look at the things he's done. You know he's crazy. I want some protection. That's all. I want you to catch him, lock him away. You want to know: am I scared? No. Just concerned.'

'So here you are. How many hours is it before you go in the ring? Six? Eight? Here you are telling us how concerned you are, just before you go into the biggest fight you got all year?'

'Concerned. Scared. Does it matter? Is this important?'

Quemada shrugged. 'Maybe. Maybe not.'

Menéndez picked up the Photofit and held it up to him. 'Why didn't you contact us earlier? You saw the picture. We interviewed you ourselves. Why did you wait?'

'I wasn't sure. How could you be sure? I mean. The picture. Could be anyone.'

'Couldn't be you,' said Quemada. 'Couldn't be the Pope. Michael Jackson.'

'*I wasn't sure.* OK?'

'But after last night, after he threatened you, suddenly you were sure.'

'Yes.'

'Did he confess? Did he say, "Hey, brother, you know that guy they been looking for in all the papers, it's me. Really. No. I ain't joking. It's me! *Surprise!*"'

'Not in as many words.'

'So how'd you know it was him? He talk about these killings before?'

'He sort of referred to them.'

'"Sort of referred." This guy's a scream. Goes around killing by inference. Quite something. So what he do, your brother? Professor of philosophy or something?'

'I don't know.'

'You *don't know*?'

Mateo winced then reached for the cigarette packet again. 'He's a crook. A petty crook. OK?'

'What kind of crook? Stealing?'

'Sometimes.'

'Drugs?'

'I wouldn't know.'

'Wouldn't you? My guess is, the reason your brother used to ring you was to sell you some dope. That right?'

Mateo's head hung down on his chest. 'No.'

'Really. He get in trouble with the law?'

'A couple of times. Nothing serious.'

'Here? In the city?'

'I think so.'

Menéndez scribbled down the name on a sheet of paper, went to the door and shouted for someone to take it.

'Maybe we got a file on him. If what you're saying is true.'

'What do you want us to do, Señor Mateo?' asked Menéndez. 'What, in all seriousness, do you expect us to do?'

'I want you to protect me. While I'm here. I fight this afternoon, I *have* to fight, you understand. After that I'll leave. Fly abroad for some time. Till this blows over.'

' "Blows over",' repeated Quemada. 'I like that. Makes it sound like an outbreak of the flu.'

'Do I get protection?'

Quemada grinned and said, 'Way I see it, *sir*, is, you come to us, you say the brother we're looking for, the brother who sells you dope, he's fallen out with you. For some reason you don't want to tell us. And you want us to divert precious *manpower*, on the busiest day we have this year, to look after you. My advice is, you got money, go get yourself some bodyguards or something. Can't see there's much here that justifies that kind of resource commitment. You might not have noticed it, *sir*, but we got 99.9 per cent of the police force out there hassling every innocent citizen we can find on the street looking for this guy. This guy, you don't know where he is. It make sense to you we should take them off looking for him and put them looking after you instead? 'Course, your memory improves, things could always change.'

'I don't *know* any more.'

'Then in that case,' said Menéndez, 'we all wish you a good day in the ring.'

Mateo picked up his cigarettes and lighter, then stuffed them into his jacket pocket.

'I don't believe this. I really don't. If that lunatic gets within a mile of me, I'll make sure you bastards pay.'

'Sure you will,' replied Quemada. 'Before you go, though, I wonder if you could tell us one thing. Luis Romero? You remember old Luis? The guy we found dead in his car? Seems he cut his own wrists? Or maybe not.'

'I told you before. I may have met him. I didn't know him. What more can I say?'

'Don't suppose you remember where you were the night he died?'

'Do you remember where you were months ago? Give me the date. I'll look in my diary. See if there's something there.'

'See, sir, the trouble is, you would have us believe your brother did this to poor old Luis. All on his own. But that just isn't the case. He couldn't have done it by himself. Come to think of it, I still don't think he could have killed the Angels by himself, either. There was dope in their blood, true, but even so. I think someone *helped* him. In those two cases anyway. Someone fit. Someone strong. Someone the people already knew so they didn't guess young Antonio was about to get his gear out.'

Mateo looked deathly pale. He said nothing.

'Now maybe that someone, he thought there *was* a reason for those early killings. He understood what was going on. Then, when Antonio got, like you say, a little crazy, when he started killing people just for *fun*, maybe his little help-mate cried foul. Said no way, I want no part of this. Which is not the kind of thing Antonio might want to hear. Might make him mad, you know. *Really* mad. You get my drift?'

'You're just making all this up,' said Mateo eventually. 'You're just sitting there guessing. He's out there, sitting, thinking what he's going to do next, and you're just frigging around in here like it doesn't matter.'

'Are we?' asked Menéndez.

'That,' said Mateo, standing up, 'that is it. I have had enough. I tried to help you people, you're obviously too stupid to understand it. I got to prepare for the fight.'

A plain-clothes cop opened the door, walked in and threw a manila folder onto the desk in front of Quemada. On the cover, in a little plastic typed pocket, was the name 'Antonio Mateo'. He picked up the folder, weighed it in one hand and gave a little wave of his hand: so-so.

'Have a nice time with the bulls,' said Quemada and opened the file as Mateo walked out of the open door.

49

'What a day,' said Quemada. 'What a wonderful fucking day for it. And that bastard Velasco calls in sick too. Wonderful.'

The heat felt like a vast moist glove that wiped their faces the moment they stepped out of the building. The humidity, even at a little past eight in the morning, was enervating. On the horizon, dimly threatening, stood a puffy line of nascent storm clouds, tops starting to mushroom up into anvils, their bases faintly blackening. The air was charged with static and atmospheric pressure. The weather felt as if it was straining, straining to break, to burst, in order to return to normality.

In the closed courtyard of the station, a dozen or so squad cars backed up nose to tail in rows, pouring hot choking fumes into the thin bright air. Waves of overheated air rippled above their hoods.

Quemada looked at them and grimaced. 'Chances of getting seriously about anywhere until three, four this afternoon, chances are nil. We're blocked.'

'You mean we can't use a car?' asked Maria.

'Same every year. First eight hours of the day this is strictly a foot operation. No choice. You got most of the city, most of a million or so people, out there. Spend the morning crying for their sins, the afternoon trying to work up a few more for next year. Bad enough on an ordinary year. Show the Captain's putting on out there is *far* from ordinary, I can tell you. The Pope turns up on a day outing out there he won't get nowhere without his ID, that's for sure.'

Menéndez surveyed the log jam in the yard. 'We got Jaime Mateo being followed on foot?'

'Yeah. I found some rookie mug from vice who looked like he'd been left behind in the rush, roped him in for the job. Mateo's apartment's not too far and in any case it sounded like he was going straight to the ring. It shouldn't be too difficult if he keeps close to him.'

'And the addresses? The ones we got for his brother from the files? Who's doing that?'

'I stole four of the day guys for the job. We got a couple of guys on the mother too. Just in case. Captain hears about this, he's gonna scalp you, Lieutenant. You know that, don't you?'

Menéndez ignored the question.

'Do you think he's genuinely in danger? The brother?' asked Maria.

'What do you think?' replied Menéndez.

'I think he's a bad liar. That he's scared of something but he doesn't really want to tell us what.'

'I can buy that,' said Quemada. 'What gets me is all those people out there thinking he's a saint. If they'd seen him squirming like we did back then . . . what would they think then?'

'That he was still a saint,' said Menéndez. 'It's not who he is that counts. It's what he does. For them anyway.'

'What did he do?' asked Maria.

'Maybe something. Maybe nothing. He *thinks* he's in danger, so maybe he is. He also thinks he's pretty much safe once the fight is over. Otherwise he'd be gone by now, otherwise . . .' Menéndez's words drifted away. His eyes were on the far gate and movement among the cars. It looked like the traffic sergeant had abandoned all idea of getting the vehicles out into the square. Engines were being cut, even on a couple of motorcycles next to the gatehouse. Uniformed cops clambered out of their seats, thrust big hands deep into their pockets and swore half-heartedly.

'They're going nowhere. We could wait for ever for this to clear. Go tell them, Quemada, we'll go out now. I planned a little sightseeing on the way. Log out with the gate.'

Quemada nodded then scuttled slowly through the crowd, his bald head bobbing among the dark police caps.

'When Quemada asked him about Romero,' said Maria, 'what was that about?'

Menéndez spoke without looking at her. His mind seemed to be somewhere else. 'I thought maybe he might have been involved. I still don't understand how one man can get another to cut his own wrists. It's not possible. *How?* And the Angel Brothers. It's all fine for the Captain to say they had some drugs in their blood. When didn't they? It still seems a hell of a lot for one person to do. To try to kill two men of that size. Of that background. You'd need a lot of confidence. Or you'd need some help.'

He looked over to the gate. Quemada was in deep, animated discussion with the duty sergeant who was busy scribbling in the log.

Menéndez took her gently by the elbow, then pulled her into the lee of the main doorway, out of the stream of bodies mingling in the courtyard. She looked at him, astonished. His face was taut and alert. He touched her on the arm, almost tenderly, and, only briefly, the mask fell from his face. There was concern there. Perhaps even fear.

'That paper we saw in Castaneda's office,' he said in a low voice. 'Do you remember the names?'

She shook her head. 'I just glanced at it. They were just book-keeping entries. Records of annual accounts. Weren't they?'

'Something like that,' said Menéndez. 'I took them home. A little light reading.'

She was astonished. 'You're not supposed to do that. There are rules.'

'Oh, yes,' said Menéndez with a dry laugh. 'There are rules about lots of things.'

The idea, the thought, that someone as rigid as Menéndez would do something like that she found deeply disturbing.

'Did you find something? In the books?'

He thought for a moment then said, 'I don't know. Genuinely, Maria, I do not know. There are entries that don't make sense, at least not without some other pieces of information, and I'm not sure I can get them.'

He looked over to the gate, across the crowd. The bald head was bobbing back towards them again. She felt his grip on her arm tighten until it began to feel half painful. He bent down and stared intently into her face.

'Maria. What happens today, whatever happens, you got to remember to trust me, please. I may be wrong, I *hope* I'm wrong, but I don't think this is over. I don't think it's over when the processions finish, when the bullfight's finished. I don't think it's over until it's *ended*. Until that happens, it's important we stay together. It's important you trust me.'

She watched Quemada bob towards them, watched how Menéndez monitored his progress. He was pushing hard through the crowd and did not realise they had moved. He couldn't see them and he looked worried.

'OK,' she said without feeling, and at that he pulled hard on her arm, pulled her into the body of the crowd, waved to Quemada, and they were walking, pushing their way to the gate.

*   *   *

'Good luck,' said the sergeant on the gate. 'You're going to need it.'

Then he threw back the big black iron bolt, rolled the gate to the left, and, for a few moments, opened up the yard to the outside world.

'Stay together,' yelled Menéndez. 'Follow me. I got somewhere we can watch.'

Maria had seen the square more times than she could remember but she didn't recognise an inch of it. At eye level there was nothing to see but people, a vast ocean of bodies moving, swaying, as if to a swell, spreading out in every direction, so tightly packed together that it seemed impossible anyone, any single person, could be directing the proceedings.

The gate slammed shut behind them and immediately she felt the press of bodies crush her back against the wood. The breath was squeezed from her chest in a single pained gasp and, for a second, she thought she would faint. Then Quemada stepped in front of her, turned his back to the crowd, took as much of the pressure as he could. Menéndez, back to them, facing the gate too, took her by the arm, and shouted, 'Hold on to me.'

And they began to fight their way along the perimeter of the square.

Within a matter of seconds, Maria had lost all sense of direction. She thought they had headed west from the station, out towards the river. But from what she could see of the buildings, the cathedral tower flashing briefly between the heads and shoulders above her, she was wrong. They seemed to be going the other way.

From the crowd came a cacophony of sound. The vast field of humanity seemed to speak a language of its own, one of cries and whimpers and low, fleeting groans. It behaved like a single creature, with a single, monomaniac

381

mind. What individuality lay in the body of the beast was temporarily submerged. The people had fused into a unified entity that lived a fleeting existence of its own. And in its fusion lay comfort, lay safety.

The noise grew louder. She could see bands of colour in the bodies beyond her. White, with ecclesiastical gold, the pointed hats of the penitents, black, saffron and scarlet, a forest of vivid peaks that jerked and twitched like something out of a puppet show. The wall behind her, biting into her back, became more uneven, more uncomfortable. Still Menéndez dragged her by the arm, elbowing a path at the very edge of the crowd, ignoring those who turned and stared at their intrusion.

She wondered where it would end. What it was for. Everything was too indistinct, too noisy and close, to make sense. It was like sitting at the very front of a cinema, a foot away from the screen. The sound, the colours became everything. There was no way to distinguish them from the components of the event.

Menéndez stopped in front of her, leaned his hand against a narrow wooden door and motioned for her to stand beneath him. Quemada joined them from behind. There was a key in Menéndez's hand. He pushed it into the brass lock and said, 'When I count three, we go in . . . one, two, *three.*'

The door flew open and she felt the pressure of the crowd force her into the blackness behind it, like a cork being pushed out of a bottle. Quemada followed her, then Menéndez. He jammed the door shut with his shoulder and they stood, panting in the dark. Menéndez clicked a light switch and they found themselves standing in a modest entrance hall for what appeared to be a small apartment block, converted from an older tenement building. Cheap little doorbells were screwed to the downstairs doors, weak lights illuminating the name cards. A worn red carpet covered the floor and a narrow set of stairs that led off from the rear half of the hallway. Menéndez turned on another switch and a light came on upstairs. They followed him, padding up the threadbare carpet, and, on the first floor, a wide open corridor with several doors leading off it, each again with a doorbell. Menéndez turned back, towards the street side of the building, walked to the last door, put a key in it and threw open the door. He was smiling, almost bashfully.

'Excuse the mess,' he said. 'You know how bachelors live.'

Maria and Quemada walked into the room. It was painted plain white, with a pine table, pine sideboard and pine shelving on the walls. At the front, a good ten feet deep, were casement windows that gave out onto the square. Three cheap canvas chairs were already lined up a few feet away from the glass, turned towards the street.

'Take a seat,' he said. 'I'll make some coffee.'

Quemada sat down first, followed by Maria. They watched him disappear into the kitchen.

'You know,' said Quemada in a quiet voice, 'I never knew he lived here, so close to the station.'

He thought about it. 'Matter of fact, I never knew he lived *anywhere* at all.'

Maria could feel her senses returning, her hearing going back to normal. She looked out of the window. The crowd was more comprehensible from this distance. The frightening closeness of its presence was kept in check. She could look at it, study it, and remain disinterested.

'Where did you think he lived?'

'General theory is ... in some coffin in a graveyard somewhere.'

He registered the disquiet in her face.

383

'It was a joke. Menéndez, you know, he's not the most popular of people around the station. Too quiet. Too aloof. Too *ambitious*. He got his sights on the Captain's job, fair enough, but he lets you know it a little too often.'

'I know what you mean.'

'Yeah. And this is where he lives. Look at the place. No decorations. No colour. Nothing. This guy got *nothing* in his life. No woman. No kids. No life. Nothing but the police. Why else would he live so close to the job?'

'But he's a good cop. You trust him.'

'He's a good cop. Yeah. Trust him? Personally I'd trust someone like that as far as I could spit.'

There was a sound behind them, half drowned out by the clamour from the window. Menéndez was putting a cafetiere on the table, watching them with an expression she could not decipher.

Quemada looked at the browny black fluid swirling in the glass tube and said, 'Mind if I have a beer?'

'Yes,' said Menéndez. 'I mind. We got a busy day ahead of us. Beer makes you sleepy.'

'Keeps me awake,' said Quemada. 'Honest.'

'I don't *have* beer.'

'You don't *have* beer? Guess it's coffee then. What you want us to do?'

'You watch at the window. See what's going on. You see. Over there?'

He pointed to the far side of the square where a huge gold and silver platform, a still figure held in its centre by a surrounding frame, was rocking slowly from side to side, making a stumbling ingress into the square.

'That's where the brotherhood will come in. They'll be following the line of the priests and choirboys. It's their church, their Virgin.'

'Yeah,' said Quemada. 'I knew that.'

'Good,' said Menéndez and passed them each a coffee mug.

'So what do you want us to do?'

'Watch them. Look out for anything unusual. I got some phone calls to make in the other room. Keep an eye on the people in red. Maybe our man is there, maybe he isn't. Keep an eye on the square too.'

'Jesus, Lieutenant, even if our man pulls out a machine gun and goes wild out there the guys in uniform are going to get to him before we do. It's hopeless. Can't we go in the crowd?'

'Anywhere in particular?' said Maria. 'There's got to be fifty thousand people or so down there. You can't *choose* to be anywhere.'

'Exactly,' said Menéndez. 'And besides, he isn't going to do anything like that. Want my opinion, he isn't going to do anything at all. Not there. He might not even be there. This isn't . . .'

Menéndez checked himself. They both saw it.

'Isn't what, Lieutenant?' asked Quemada. 'I think you're beginning to lose me a little here.'

'It isn't what it seems,' said Menéndez. 'Now, will you do as I asked? Like I said, I got some calls to make. Here.' He threw a pair of binoculars across to Quemada. They were narrow pocket Pentaxes.

'These are fancy glasses, Lieutenant. The kind you use for birdwatching?'

'You're picking up all my secrets today, detective. My, aren't you going to be popular in the canteen once this is over and done with?'

'You're the boss,' grunted Quemada and tried the glasses on for size. 'You get to look through these things without squinting?'

But Menéndez was gone.

'You try them,' said Quemada. 'They look like a ladies' size to me.'

Maria's fingers slipped round the matt gunmetal of the binoculars, felt easily for the focusing ring, then she pulled them up to her face. It took a moment or two to get the focus right, then the scene shot into close-up with a sudden, startling clarity. She scanned the faces in the crowd: the bare faces of the priests fixed in some sad rapture, the agony of the platform carriers struggling underneath the burden, struggling a little more than might really be necessary. And behind, in white and red and black, the masked penitents, hoods swaying in the hot breeze. She swept the glasses across the hordes of red faces and from somewhere came a noise: the distant rumble of thunder. It was if she was looking at some vast, living panoramic painting, a canvas that moved and lived and breathed in front of her as a single living mass.

'You see anything?' asked Quemada, and his voice made her jump. Something about the scene, its gripping primeval antiquity, had almost engulfed her, made her part of the canvas, not its observer.

Slowly, she shook her head. 'Nothing. Just people.'

'A *lot* of people,' said Quemada. '*Too* many people.'

The red robes of the penitents now formed a long, broad stream behind the platform as it entered the square, a defined scarlet shape that cut through the multicoloured mass of the crowd.

Menéndez is wrong, she thought. Somewhere, somewhere in the crowd, is the man who tried to kill me. He may not be wearing the red robes, but he is there, somewhere. And he is not finished. Not yet. The certainty hung in her gut like cold, undigested food.

'You look like someone just stepped on your grave,' said Quemada, unsmiling.

'I do?'

'Yeah. You went all pale. You OK?'

'I need some water,' she said. 'I'll get it.'

The kitchen was tiny and spotless, not a knife or plate anywhere. She looked in a cupboard, found a glass, pulled a bottle of Lanjarón out of the refrigerator and poured some water. It fizzed in the glass with a sudden energy and felt hard to her palate. From the bedroom next door she could hear Menéndez talking in low, persistent tones, she could almost make out the words. He stopped speaking, she gulped down the water so quickly it made her feel uncomfortable, and stood in the kitchen. He came through the door, eyes glinting avidly.

'You were listening?' he asked in a quiet, firm voice.

'I . . . I wanted some water. I felt faint.'

'You were *listening*?'

'No.'

He looked unconvinced.

'Go back to Quemada. Tell him when they go into the church we move. On to the bullring. I want everyone in position by the start of the first fight.'

Maria nodded and walked out of the room. Quemada was sitting rapt by the window, his face a foot from the glass. He glanced at her when she sat down.

'You missed it.'

'What?' she said shakily.

'The Virgin coming past. They all came past, past the bishop or whoever the big guy is up there on the cathedral steps. Jesus, when I was a kid I used to take part in all that stuff. Now I couldn't remember how to say a Hail Mary.'

'What happens now?'

'What always happens with this religious stuff. Lots more of the same. All the little parochial churches get their Virgins into the square, work their way to the front, pay homage

387

to the cathedral, then work their way home. It takes hours but I guess they like it that way.'

'When does the service begin?'

'When the last Virgin has gone past. The people with it stick with the procession. The others either go into the cathedral or head off straight for something to eat and then the ring. It's a habit.'

'You mean a tradition?'

'Same thing really, isn't it?'

She watched the red flood disappearing out of the far corner of the square, the golden head of the Virgin bobbing down a narrow alley into the barrio.

'When the service begins, we go. He wants us to go to the ring.'

'Yeah,' said Quemada. 'You think he'll be off the phone by then? I never knew someone who loved the phone so much.'

'I'm off the phone already,' said Menéndez in a voice that made Maria jump. Here, on his own territory, he moved so quietly, with such certainty.

'Only joking, Lieutenant,' said Quemada, a simple grin on his face. 'Mind if we pick up a sandwich on the way? I got a feeling this is going to be a long day.'

50

The ring was only half a mile away but it took them over an hour to get there. The streets *swam* with people. There was no other way to describe it. If they found themselves in a stream going in the right direction, they were picked up, they floated along with the mass. Until the next street intersection, where they could only hope to go with the right flow. Once, with no choice, they found themselves swept, almost off their feet, into a bar full of singing drunks, glasses high in the air, faces red with the booze. They poured through the door, clung to the cigarette machine next to the entrance, waited for the pressure to lessen for a moment outside, then launched themselves back into the street. The centre of the city had become pure anarchy. There was no possible way of controlling events. And in the crowd that surged around them the mood had changed. Something cathartic had occurred in the square. The mourning, the grief had been purged, to be replaced by an urgent, almost manic, joy. Hysteria hung around the streets, mingling with the sweaty presence of the coming storm, humid, dense and enervating.

After twenty minutes, the throng became less confusing, gained more direction. They were approaching the ring now, through narrow streets of medieval terraces that towered over them. Roses, geraniums and lilies decorated battered iron balconies, faces peered from behind curtains. Iron grilles barred the doorways into the old mansions, kept them inviolate from the crowd. The stream of bodies in the street surged past quiet, shaded courtyards, cool, watery fountains in their centre, deserted on this, the city's greatest day.

And then, with a sudden last push, they left the narrow alleys of the barrio behind and were thrown into the hot, baking sunlight, and the small public park outside the entrance to the ring, a distant circle of white surrounded by the massing crowd. The park swarmed with people now, buying food from the vendors, drinking from the necks of wine bottles passed around from stranger to stranger without a thought. Already the queues were starting to form outside the gates, *sol* and *sombra*, sun and shade, those with little money, those with enough to keep them out of the scorching afternoon heat. A band played somewhere, its tinny, metallic tune fighting a losing battle with the low roar and guttural chatter of the crowd.

So many people, thought Maria, so little identity. It was as if a single, many-celled beast had assembled for the ritual, and the presence among it of the police, of *authority*, was no more than the buzzing of a fly around the body of the bull itself.

Menéndez pushed through one of the queues for the gate and they followed him, wading through the swarm of bodies in his wake. Above them loomed the circular walls of the ring, painted white, bright, blinding white, with carved stone curlicues over the gates and the circumference of the upper plasterwork. There was a smaller, quieter entrance, the words 'Administration' over it and a little group of hangers-on arguing with the officials at the door: free tickets, press passes, favours for an old friend. Menéndez barged his way through, showed his ID. The doorman, a small, thin man of late middle age, dressed in the best suit he could afford, threadbare blue barathea, looked at the picture on the card, looked at them, then nodded them through. They passed through the door and, in a moment, they went from tortured heat and crowds into blackness, cold and slightly damp.

'Wait,' said Menéndez. And they did, as their eyes strained painfully, trying to adapt to the sudden absence of light. After half a minute, when the dim light bulbs of the corridors had done what they could to illuminate the hidden, secret interior of the ring, he motioned them to follow. They walked to the right, along a narrow, dank corridor no more than six feet wide. Then Menéndez came to a junction. A wide arcade, open to the street and the ring, ran at right angles in front of them. To the right, hands fast on the tall, iron gate, the crowds waited to be allowed into the stadium. To the left, the ring stood golden yellow in the sun, a handful of attendants carefully raking the sand to a fine, even finish.

'One more corridor,' said Menéndez and stepped briskly across the arcade, into another dank artery built beneath the seats of the ring. They followed, crossed a second arcade, walked halfway along the next corridor, then turned into a door marked 'Police'.

Menéndez opened the door and they walked in. Rodríguez sat at a simple, ancient wooden desk, riffling through a pile of papers. With him were three uniformed men in blue, standing bored to one side of the room, smoking.

Rodríguez looked up from the papers, smiled coolly for a moment, then motioned for them to sit down.

'He's here,' the Captain said. 'I can feel it. He's here. And the manpower I've got inside these walls there is no way he gets out again.'

He looked at his watch. The corrida was due to begin in an hour, with Mateo the first to fight.

'We have men in the crowd,' said Rodríguez. 'We have

people with binoculars on the roof. He cannot escape.'

'Why are you so sure?' asked Menéndez. 'You *know* he's here.'

Rodríguez nodded and she could sense something new in Menéndez now: an impatience with the Captain, an impatience that would never have been so palpable with Bear around, bathing the old man in his loyalty, his vast well of affection. She could feel Menéndez struggling to hold back from saying what he really thought. That maybe the old man was tired and spent and, ultimately, out of his depth.

'Like I told you,' said Rodríguez, and the way he kept shaking his head, with more force than she had ever seen, made her think he realised the change too. 'Like I *keep* telling you. He's a crazy. A crazy that got started by this history stuff, maybe, but a crazy all the same. Once we got him, that's it. Over and done with. An hour ago we found where he was living. It wasn't that hard. Antonio is a dope dealer. That's what he does. We traced him through some contacts in the drugs people. He had an apartment in the barrio. We found the weapons. The robe. It's enough to get a conviction, even if we find nothing else. And I'm pulling in that shit of a bullfighter too. You see the headlines we're going to get there?'

'But how do you know he's here?' asked Maria.

'On the wall. He had one of those poster calendars. From a beer company. It was written in for today. The time. The place. He's here.'

Menéndez blinked, looked briefly at her, then said, 'He *wrote* this on the wall.'

'Like I said,' Rodríguez muttered. 'He's a crazy. Are you questioning this too, Lieutenant?'

'No, sir,' said Menéndez. 'What do you want us to do?'

Rodríguez passed over three sets of army binoculars.

'Take these. There's an observation box. Behind the shade

seats. You know it? Good. You'll get a good view. I want the three of you in there. We have a discrete radio frequency for everyone in the ring. It's going to be hard, I know, but I want you to scan the crowd. Face by face. You've seen him, Maria. You know what he looks like. When you find him, you get on the radio. Start with the first row of the sun seats then work right to left, up and down. I got other people doing the same working the other way. If you don't see him from this platform, we'll swap you around to the one on the other side some time during the intervals between fights. We've got time. The ring is sold out. Once they close the doors, no one gets out until they're opened again, and they won't open until I say so.'

'Good planning,' said Menéndez.

Rodríguez smiled over the desk. 'Thank you, Lieutenant. Now shall we begin?'

Menéndez nodded and the three of them walked out of the room.

'You understand the layout of the ring?' asked Menéndez as they ducked underneath some low beams in a barely lit bend of yet another narrow corridor.

Maria was following him. Quemada was last, some feet behind.

'No. I'm lost,' she said. 'And also I hate this. I hate these narrow spaces.'

Menéndez rounded the corner, opened a door that she could hardly see in the dark, and light poured painfully on their faces. There was a stepladder on the far side of a narrow alley leading to the ring. He motioned to her to go first. They climbed up a good twenty feet then clambered onto a flat wooden platform, fronted by a low iron guardrail. Five cheap metal seats stood up at the back of the observation deck.

Maria walked to the front and looked over. The breath disappeared from her lungs. They were at the very top of the ring, underneath the rim of the shallow roof. Beneath, the spectators' seats ran out in concentric circles, band after band of them, half in sun, half, the half beneath her, in afternoon shade. The ring itself, a golden ellipse of sand, seemed tiny in the vast enclosing bulk of the stadium.

'I didn't realise we were so high,' she said, still half in shock.

Menéndez watched Quemada climb onto the deck, pull out a chair and collapse on it, then he came to the front of the platform and leaned over the edge with her.

'No. I didn't the first time either. You see the ring from the outside and all you see are the walls. You see it from the inside, as a spectator, and all you see is the bullfight. This is a huge building. You've got, underneath the seats here, a hell of a lot of space. Some of it just empty, some of it used for storage. Then there's the dressing rooms, the area where they keep the animals. Administration offices. And you get to them, almost all of them, along corridors, the little ones like we used today. This building's almost two hundred years old. It was built in parts, they'd finish one bit, then tack on another. We've got police IDs, we can go anywhere we want, but you *don't* wander off without knowing where you're going. It's a maze down there.'

'Like the Minotaur's labyrinth?' she asked quietly.

Menéndez smiled. 'Yes. If you like. Like the labyrinth. When I was a kid I was a ring junkie. I used to hang around, help clear up the mess, do anything to get some free tickets, to be near it all. I know maybe half of my way around all those places you just saw. And still I take it easy. So don't wander off. Whatever happens. Stay in the public parts, the well-lit parts, and then you've got no problems.'

She looked at the stadium. People were starting to filter

in now, men in black suits, women in colourful fiesta costumes, with high mantillas, all distant, like gaily painted ants. On the horizon, the clouds were starting to bunch together, roll upon roll of cumulus with lowering dark stains underneath.

'How big is it?'

'The capacity is maybe 75,000 people and it *will* be at capacity today.'

'And I'm supposed to pick one person out of the crowd.'

Menéndez shrugged. 'Lot easier than you might think. You do it methodically, scan one row, scan the next. Ninety-eight per cent you'll be able to reject straight away. Then you concentrate on the rest. Put that way you're only looking at fifteen hundred people or so. It's not so many.'

'And if he's disguised?'

Menéndez looked at her and she almost had to pinch herself, had to think twice: what was this look? Was it really something akin to admiration?

'If he's disguised . . . then I guess we're wasting our time. But we got our orders.'

'Yeah,' said Quemada. 'And a cop *always* obeys his orders. So we might as well get started.'

He picked up a pair of the binoculars, put them to his face and started to adjust the focus wheel. Across from them the top few rows of the stadium were beginning to fill up. She picked up one of the spare pairs of glasses and started to scan the faces: ordinary people, a little bored, more than a little tired, looking for some spectacle to end the week. They sat quietly, waiting. No one looked familiar, they were just a mass of unknown faces. She put the binoculars down.

'This is not going to be easy,' Maria said, playing with the focus ring.

'Tell me what is,' Quemada grunted. 'In Semana Santa

nothing's easy. But next week . . . next week we get to relax a little.'

He laughed, took the glasses away from his face and pointed across the ring. 'See that guy? The one in the second row down from the upper gate, three seats along? I *know* him. Runs the grocer's store near my sister's. And that is *not* his wife with him, that's for sure. These guys kill me.'

Menéndez looked at his watch. 'Fifteen minutes,' he said. 'Fifteen minutes and the first fight should begin. Let's make the most of it.'

'OK,' said Maria and turned the glasses back on the growing crowd.

51

Two floors below and four hundred yards to the west, in a small well-lit dressing room with an illuminated mirror of the kind normally found in theatres, Jaime Mateo looked at his watch too, saw the minutes ticking by, and felt the fear cold and hard in his belly. He was wearing a silver suit of lights that clung tightly to his body, tight white socks that gripped his ankles firmly, and trim black shoes. The small velvet matador's hat lay on the dressing table in front of him. He put it on last, before he went out of the gate, and always, *always*, he threw it away before the kill. The corrida was a public ritual, but within it lay a private ritual too. Things that he had always done before, habits that kept him alive. No sex the night before, no drinking, no dope. The watch, the old, cheap Timex he'd had since he was a teenager ripping off handbags from tourists, was strapped to his wrist, as it always was, although the mechanism had long since given up the ghost and the minute hand flapped uselessly half attached to the pivot. And the cap, always worn when he walked into the ring – though many modern matadors now began the contest bareheaded – and always discarded before the final kill.

Mateo ran through the minutiae of his own private ritual, checked each detail, satisfied himself it was complete. And still he sweated. He looked in the mirror, saw the crudeness of the make-up he had applied to his face. This was what they wanted: the boy wonder, the young, handsome hero.

The face beneath the mask . . . they had not paid for this. They must not see it. He looked harder into the mirror, wondered if the mask was good enough. Wondered how long it could be maintained. How many fights, how many years before the deception became impossible to hide?

The night before, the long night after the phone call, when he had briefly managed to sleep, he had dreamed of the ring, of the fight to come, a strange, disturbing dream. He had dreamed that the fight, the *real* fight, was not with the bull but with the crowd itself, with the people. The animal was a proxy opponent. What he fought, with knives and swords and anything else that might maim and wound and kill, was the single, unified, primitive slew of humanity that had come to watch him, to challenge him, to test his humanity, to test his will to survive. And he dreamed that when he had slain the bull, when its carcass lay defeated, bleeding red gore onto the yellow sand of the ring, they had risen from their seats, applauding, clapping and shouting wildly, their faces split wide open with great, tombstone-toothed grins, and they had come for him. They had left the rows and rows of benches – now rows and rows of *graves* in his fevered dream imagination – they had walked slowly, deliberately down the aisles, climbed over the walls, the barriers that separated the ring from the audience, come to him, grinning all the time, with pleasure, with ecstasy and an overpowering sense – *smell, was there a smell too?* – of victory.

He had waited as they surrounded him, covered his ears to try, in vain, to block out their deafening sound, the roar of their joy. And he had watched as they struggled, no, *fought*, to pick the weapons from the ground, to pluck the sword from the bull, to hold the bloodied silver to the sun. He had watched a woman, in a fine white lace dress, a matron with delicate aristocratic features, watched her lick the blood from the sword, caress her tongue with the sharp metal blade, half cutting through the flesh, laughing, tears in her eyes, *laughing* at the pain.

And then they had turned on him. They had cut him to pieces, he had seen the parts, the limbs, the organs of his body, bleeding freely, on the ground *in pieces*. They had cut him and the last memory he had, the last thing he could recall before he woke, was the final sound, the final feeling. The sound of their eating, jaws chomping, lips smacking, faces smeared in red. The sensation of their teeth biting into his flesh, hard sharp ivory ripping into muscle and fat, clamping upon the bone.

Mateo opened his eyes and stared at himself in the mirror, stared hard into the reflection, silently screamed at himself for something like control. When he had stopped shaking, when he had convinced himself that it would be a bad idea, a *very* bad idea, for him to reach into his suitcase and take out the little silver container with white powder inside it, he stood up, turned round and looked at the back wall of the dressing room.

It was always the same. In Madrid or Seville, Barcelona or Cadiz. In each dressing room, nailed to the wall, was a simple crucifix. In this city, *only* in this city, did he find something else. Next to the tortured tiny figure on the cross hung a small Murillo portrait of the Virgin, a pale white face with fearless, piercing eyes, eyes that could look at all the pain and dread and misery in the world and still stare back undaunted.

He looked into her face and felt he could lose himself there. There was a promised universe in her expression, a universe that spoke of peace and tranquillity and escape. Not knowing what he was doing, Mateo closed his eyes, put his hands together and tried to pray, pray for one thing: *Let me live! Let me live and I will make amends ...*

When he opened his eyes, the face still looked at him with the same distanced scepticism. He turned away from the wall and flicked a hand over the jacket. Then he reached down into the case, picked out the little silver casket, poured some of the white powder onto the lid and sniffed it through a small metal tube. There was a sudden rush inside his head, a rush that was once pure pleasure and was now merely a release from pain. He sniffed again and tears began to stream down his face. He went to the table, picked up a tissue, and dried them. Then he sat down and waited. Until it was time, until he felt better, felt more capable. From outside, beyond the walls of the little dressing room, came the gentle, persistent murmur of the crowd, the discordant metal melodies of a small brass band.

He was El Guapo. He had killed bulls the length of Spain, with scarcely an injury. He had honours in the ring to match the very best, to match El Cordobes and maybe even Manolito himself.

Jaime Mateo walked to the dressing room door, walked down the long, narrow, darkened corridor towards the circle of light at the end, walked out into the light. The crowd erupted. They stood and shouted and waved, women threw flowers, handkerchiefs, garters over the wall, there was a cheering, a long, single deafening roar that echoed around the ring, from *sol* to *sombra* and back again. To his right and to his left the attendants, the minor players in the drama, fell back to the edge of the ring to acknowledge his presence. He could smell the horses, the strong aroma of dung cut through the hot and thundery afternoon air. This was his moment, the reason he existed, the focal point of his life.

Unseen to him the TV cameras pounced and, knowing they would, he smiled, the big, broad smile that would make the nightly programme schedules, be plastered over the papers the next day. The smile of victory and confidence. The smile of mastery over the primitive, enclosed world of the ring.

High above him, above the ecstatic, heaving crowds, the TV commentators began to ad-lib on their scripts, began to interpret, to explain the ritual. They were well briefed. Not one of them failed to mention that, for the first time anyone could remember, El Guapo had changed the habit of a lifetime and walked into the ring bareheaded.

52

Quemada shifted the glasses onto his knees, rubbed his eyes with the backs of both hands, and said, 'This is one long way to go about making steak.'

Down below, in the ring, the contest was nearing its end. The *banderilleros* and picadors had finished their work and Mateo was gently playing the animal towards its death. Even from the heights of the stand, and without the glasses, they could see the ribbons in the beast's back, and the line of blood marking its body and its muzzle.

'Every year I seem to get duty here and every year it's the same. What do these people see in it? Beats me.'

Maria took a pause from scanning the crowd and ticked off another row in her notebook.

'Nothing, huh?' asked Quemada.

She shook her head. 'There are men out there who look vaguely like him. I looked at a few quite closely. But they weren't him.'

'You're sure?' asked Menéndez. 'It might be worth keeping them behind afterwards just to talk to them?'

'I made a note of their seat numbers if you want to. But I'm not convinced.'

Quemada grunted as if to say: what do you expect?

'Have they seen anything from the other platform?' she asked.

'Nothing,' Menéndez replied. 'Nothing to write home about. It's a very quiet corrida. Normally we've picked up a few drunks, a few fights by this stage. But we don't even have that. More cops here than ever before and all we've got to do is watch the ring.'

'If that turns you on,' muttered Quemada.

'When he's finished, when there's a break, we'll get down and switch places with the platform on the other side.'

'If you think it's gonna work,' said Quemada. 'You been checking the weather? Personally I doubt we're gonna see this whole thing through in one piece anyway. There's some serious stuff on the way.'

Menéndez and Maria looked out beyond the small semi-circular portion of the stadium that had been the focus of their vision for almost an hour and saw what he meant. The sky was now turning dark black just a mile or so away from where they were. Only a brief ribbon of blue separated them from the darkness and that was disappearing fast. The air was beginning to buffet around them too in the lee of the storm cloud. Hot, turbulent air, charged with static, swirled around the stadium and from far off there was the low, ominous growl of thunder.

'Shit,' said Menéndez as a flash of electric blue trembled behind the cloud, like an erratic street light winking through a dark curtain. 'That is *all* we need.'

'Well that's what we've got. Maybe someone should tell our bullfighting friend down there. He seems to think he's got all day.'

53

On the floor of the stadium, Mateo was feeling fine. Just fine. He had played the bull for everything it was worth. Which was not a lot. Usually they gave him better material than this, good fighting stock from the plains near Jerez or Cadiz. This was more like a backyard beast, slow and plodding and stupid. They'd prodded and goaded it and still it refused to come to life, to show that sudden rush of anger, that sudden murderous surge, that gave the day its spark, its meaning. His doubts were forgotten now, and cocaine had little to do with it. He was in control, master of the ring, able to coax the stupid, brutish animal into doing whatever he wanted before he slaughtered it. But every matador was limited by the material he was given to work with, and this was dross. He could sense the mute, sullen mood of disappointment, near boredom, in the crowd, as could any matador worth his salt. This was the focal point of the week and they were not getting their money's worth. Maybe the next bull – and there were three more for him to fight this afternoon – maybe it would be better. But he could still despatch this one as best he could.

The animal now stood in front of him, exhausted. Its back was rent with wounds. Blood poured from its shoulders and hung in great snotty gobs from its mouth. It was using all its strength to stand, its legs trembled and shook with exhaustion and fear. Its eyes – he could not see the eyes. They were too small and too dark. He liked to see the eyes.

They could tell him things about the beast. He could read them. But this was an animal not worthy of the ring. It simply stood there, inanimate, shuddering dumbly, waiting to die.

He threw the muleta and the sword to one side and fell to his knees. From the crowd there was a faint ripple of applause, of recognition. Mateo raised his hands above his head, in the position of a dancer, elegant, balletic.

He closed his eyes tightly and began to shuffle slowly forward on his knees, experimenting, improvising with the creature in front of him. There was a moment, there was always a moment, when the play acting ended and the death dance became real. When he could no longer think about the crowd, the TV cameras and what the press would say. When he fought on instinct, without thinking. This was the purest, the most real time of his life. He sought it out hungrily, savoured every second that it lasted, from the first sudden dimming of *outside* to the act, the thrust of the blade, that brought it to an end. This was the simple, perfect heart of his being and everything else, everything *outside* stood as dross in comparison.

Mateo shuffled closer towards the animal. Now the sound of the crowd had almost faded, become transformed into a low, hushed whisper, an off-stage, admiring susurration from a single, communal throat. And he could feel it. It came just as he thought it would, at the exact moment; soft and hot and physical, the creature's breath blew gently on his face like the subtle panting of a lover after the act.

He moved even closer, felt the air hotter now, with an animal rankness that did not offend him, and he opened his eyes. The bull stood above him, gasping, dripping bloody saliva onto his knees. Its eyes – its eyes were still impenetrable, even so close, small, beady black pools that defied interpretation. Sightless, blind to everything but the physicality of the beast in front of him, he shook his head, heard the growing rumble of the crowd – *and something else?* It was looking not at him but *through* him. It had moved beyond the contest, beyond the ring. It was somewhere else, waiting to escape. Or waiting to die.

He shut his eyes tight, reached up and touched its jowls. The muscles twitched beneath his fingers, the skin, the velvet skin, was hot and wet with warm, slippery mucus. Slowly, he stroked the animal's muzzle, its head, its eyebrows. It bent down, only a little, but enough for him to reach the horns. He caressed them in short, loving strokes, feeling the shaft, feeling the tip, ecstatic in his dark and private little world. What lay beyond, what lay *outside*, was gone now. He could not feel the pulsing of their vicarious excitement, could not hear the low-pitched drone of their mutual, wordless approval. He was one with the creature he was about to destroy and his being, his existence began and ended with that knowledge.

He stroked the cheeks, hot and twitching, then looked at the creature again. The bull was now returning his gaze, its eyes no longer opaquely black and expressionless, but dark and deep and filled with light. In them he saw his reflection, the image, distorted by the curvature of the muscular lens, of a man in a suit of lights, kneeling on the sandy floor of a great arena enthralled by some vast and mystical ritual that united him and it, and the thousands around them, in a mystery of life and blood and death.

Joy, naked, painful and unrelenting, raced through Mateo's heart as he stared wildly into the creature's eyes. Then without knowing, without thinking, he reached forward, took its huge, majestic head in both hands and closed his lips upon the creature's mouth, tasting the blood and the phlegm, kissing it, mouth wide open, licking the gore from its cheeks, its nose, its flesh, gripping its skin so tightly it now bunched in his fists like rumpled fabric.

'We are one,' said Mateo, through the slime and the blood, the coke rush racing wildly through his brain. 'We are one.'

Across the ring, a man prepared to run.

A hundred feet above, Quemada put down the glasses and said, 'Shit. This fucking lunatic's really done it this time.'

The sky was rent by the roar of lightning, the world turned black as the storm cloud rolled overhead.

'He's gone crazy, I tell you,' yelled Quemada. 'For Christ's sake. Take a look. He's kissing the fucking thing!'

Menéndez and Maria moved their glasses off the crowd and into the ring. Mateo still kneeled there, the bull's head in his hands, his fingers entwined around the bottom of its horns. His mouth was locked onto the animal's, moving madly. From the crowd came the first angry shouts, the growing rattle of disapproval.

The sky shook again, and this time there was rain, first a few sporadic drops, then, in a matter of seconds, it turned into a downpour, hard sheets of water, coming down in silver rods. They hammered on the roof like cannon fire above them and turned the ring almost instantly into a swimming sea of sand. Still Mateo kneeled there, the animal now twitching slightly in his hands.

'They're getting him out of there. Look,' said Quemada.

From behind one of the fences came one of the *banderilleros*, a figure dressed in dull gold, moving swiftly, purposefully, across the ring towards the two figures locked together in the centre.

'He's crazy. They're gonna have to take him off.'

Maria watched the figure stride through the streaming rain and something inside her went cold. She pushed the binoculars back up to her face so hard they hurt, dashed them around the arena, trying to focus, trying to catch him. He still had a good ten yards to go and he was not hurrying. There was a smile on his face and he knew what he was going to do. She watched him bend over, pick up the muleta, pick up the sword, and said, without taking away the glasses, 'It's him. Menéndez. *It's him.*'

And she watched as the figure strode over to the man with the bull, stood erect behind him, pulled back his arm, then thrust hard, flat and then up, a single, planned movement that sent the blade straight through the bullfighter's chest, unobstructed by bone or muscle.

In the noise of the storm and the rain she could hear no screaming though she knew it had to be there. She watched Mateo fall back, mouth open, watched the bull recoil in shock, blood pouring from its muzzle where the blade had penetrated after it had gone through the man's body. And she watched as the man in gold let go of the blade, let the body fall to the ground, then turned and ran. Ran fast and deliberately, directly beneath them, out of sight, untouched by the small army of officials who did not know where to turn in the storm.

When she took down the glasses, Menéndez was already disappearing over the platform edge. Silently, without a thought, she followed them, down, step by step, into the dark, sodden bowels of the arena.

54

When he got to the bottom of the ladder Menéndez punched the keys on the radio, held it to his ear and swore. Nothing came out of the earpiece but static, crackling and fizzing senselessly. People were starting to climb over the barriers now, into the ring, towards the fallen body at the centre. Someone, one of the officials, was raising a pistol to the head of the bull. Events were starting to career, slowly, certainly, out of control. Menéndez pushed his way through the mill of people in the small arcade at the base of the ladder, found an official, a small man with a moustache, and pinned him to the wall.

'Police,' Menéndez said grimly, showing his badge. 'Did you see where he went? The man who came out of the ring.'

The official nodded, a wild, frightened look in his eyes.

'He ran in there.' The man pointed to one of three narrow doorways leading to the space under the east wing of the stadium, the oldest, most labyrinthine part of the ring.

'This is still the animal area, right?' asked Menéndez. 'Where they keep the bulls before they go into the ring.'

'Yes.'

'Is there anybody else in there at the moment?'

He shook his head violently from side to side. 'Not that I know of. The ring handlers stay at the front then go in when the next fight is about to start. It's not the sort of place you'd stay in out of choice.'

'Good,' said Menéndez. 'You have a house phone here?'

'There's one along the wall.'

'You ring for Captain Rodríguez. He's in the police office. You tell him you spoke to Lieutenant Menéndez and he says we've *got* to open the gates. You get that? We've *got* to open the gates. This crowd's starting to move. They won't stay where they are. They start shifting around this building with nowhere to go and we've got another crowd disaster on our hands.'

The official looked at the public end of the arcade, now a swirl of hot-tempered spectators looking for some way out, and said, 'I'll call him right now.'

Menéndez pointed to a small, cracked door in the wall and said, 'That way?'

'Yes,' the man nodded. 'You going in there?'

'Someone has to,' said Menéndez grimly.

'You know what it's like. You take the wrong turn in there, you could get lost for hours.'

'I'll take a ball of string,' muttered Menéndez.

'You could take this,' the man said. He unhooked a long rubber torch from his belt, tested the light for a second, then held it out in front of him. Menéndez took it, felt its heaviness, then passed it to Maria.

'Thanks,' he said, then shouldered his way through the growing mêlée, Quemada and Maria at his heels. When he got to the door he took out the automatic pistol from his shoulder holster, checked it, put it back in the grip, then ordered Quemada to do the same. From the crowd, the sound of unrest was growing. It cut through the atmosphere, an unnerving mix of fear, anger and physical discomfort.

'When we get in there, we stay together, you do as I say,' said Menéndez grim-faced. 'Exactly. Understand?'

'You're the boss,' replied Quemada, sheathing his gun.

'It will be dark and it will be hard to work out what's going on. There are only two ways in and out, at each end of the section. We have to assume he hasn't left through the other end, that the Captain is covering there too. We'll have to clear each part, area by area. Maria, you stay behind us, close in, use the torch when we can't see. I want you to watch out for us. We'll need all the sets of eyes we've got.'

'Hey!' said Quemada brightly. 'I did that when I was a kid in the army. I remember that game.'

'Good. But it's not a game.'

He opened the door, they walked through the narrow stone gateway and entered a world of near absolute blackness.

'Torch,' yelled Menéndez.

Behind him, she fumbled for the switch, found it, and saw a thin yellow beam penetrate weakly into the gloom.

'Wait,' whispered Menéndez. 'We wait here. Let our eyes adjust.'

They stood, breathless, backs to the cold, damp stone inner wall of the arcade. To their left, a bright narrow trapezoid of dull white stained the stone floor through the small open doorway. Above them they could hear the tramping of the crowd through the banked rows of benches. They sounded like animals on the move. Water, rain from the storm, dripped relentlessly from the ceiling, making small plashes on the stone floor, dropping, with sudden, tiny shocks, on their faces and hands.

Inside, the place seemed silent at first, then they began to pick out sounds in the dark. The shuffling of cloven feet in straw, low, panted breathing, animal grunts and groans. They could smell them too, the earthy, warm smell of bulls and their dung.

'Feel for the light switch,' said Menéndez in a low voice. 'It's got to be near the door.'

411

He stepped through the light of the doorway, stood in the dull whiteness and ran his hand across the wall. Nothing. Quemada and Maria did the same on the other side of the entrance. The stone was cold and dank. They could feel the oily slickness of layers of ancient paint under their fingers, the rippled outline of old brickwork.

'Got it,' said Maria. Beneath her fingers lay the round shape of an old-fashioned Bakelite switch. They heard it click, then click again.

'It doesn't work.'

Menéndez crossed back over the doorway, joined her, tried it for himself.

'There's got to be another one. This must be old.'

They searched again, everywhere around the door.

'There's no other switch, Lieutenant,' said Quemada. 'That's got to be it. Either it don't work or he's disabled it somehow.'

'*Shit!*' spat Menéndez, and there was some added bitterness to his voice that neither of them could understand. He was silent for a moment then muttered something to himself, turned away from them and yelled, as loudly as he could, into the empty blackness, '*Police!* We are armed. Make your presence known *now*!'

The noise reverberated around the cavernous space, shattered into a chorus of different voices. It died slowly, faintly, hovering on the rank air.

When the last traces of Menéndez's voice had gone, they listened, listened so hard that they thought they might be hearing their own breathing, the pumping of the blood in their veins. There was nothing that was not there before, nothing but the nervous shuffling of the animals, their low breathing, and the endless drip-dripping from the roof now rumbling to the sound of a crowd on the move.

Then it came, faintly at first, then a little louder. The

sound of laughter, low-pitched, deliberate, calculating. Maria felt her senses leave her for a moment, felt the world dissolve into craziness. It was not the sound of a trapped man, it was not the sound of defeat.

Menéndez reached into his jacket and took out his gun. Quemada heard the noise and did the same. The Lieutenant's voice boomed out again into the darkness.

'Antonio. We know your name. We know your address. We know what you've done. There is no way out of this enclosure we're not covering. It is *over*.'

The laugh came again, a little louder. It bounced around the walls, taunting them with its presence.

Then he spoke. 'Fucking cops.'

The words brought it all back to her. The phone calls. The night of the attack. When he spoke she could see his face clearly etched in her memory. 'Fucking cops, you know nothing. *Nothing*.'

Something moved. Something solid. The animals began to low, began to become restless.

'He's in with the bulls,' said Quemada. 'He's got to be in there with them. The Captain's right. This guy *is* crazy.'

'The torch. Maria. The torch. Try it in front of us, to the left.'

The thin yellow beam shot out wildly into the dark. She had difficulty controlling it at first. It dashed too high, illuminating the curved, bricked ceiling of the enclosure. Then she took hold of the heavy rubber body with both hands, pointed it down, moved it slowly from side to side.

About ten yards away dark shapes moved anxiously from side to side. When the light caught them, the beasts' eyes flashed back like dead mirrors, silvered in the beam. There were barriers, horizontal and vertical lines that cut across their shapes like black stencils. It looked as if there was a

413

small herd corralled for the market. Their shapes, the curves of their horns, the long, sleek lines of their backs, intermingled in the dark, silhouettes covering and re-covering each other constantly, tramping to and fro with a nervous, impatient frequency.

Briefly, for less than a second, something else flashed through the beam: a different shape, a different colour. It reflected the light, it was the shape of a man crouching.

'You see him?' asked Quemada.

'I see him,' said Menéndez. 'Maria. Keep the torch in that area. Keep it covering the animals. He's inside with them. He's using them for cover.'

'Some kind of cover,' mumbled Quemada. 'How the fuck we get him out of there?'

'We wait. He's not going anywhere.'

At the end of the hall there was a sound and then a sudden flash of daylight. The shadows of men darkened the door, their soft voices bounced around the velvet blackness, then they disappeared into the dark.

'Captain?' shouted Menéndez.

'Lieutenant. You've found him?' Rodríguez's voice sounded cracked and tense. 'You think he's here?'

'He's here. In the animal pen. We've seen him.'

There was a pause, then Rodríguez said, 'You are near the other door? He cannot get out?'

'He can't get out. All we have to do is wait. Get the lights back on – bring in some floods, fix the lights we've got, whatever – and he can't get out.'

'Good. I have plenty of men here, uniform men. We have him.'

Rodríguez's voice took on a kind of theatricality. 'You hear us in there? You hear all this?'

From the blackness, from nowhere in particular, came a subdued, sullen voice. 'Why don't you just fuck off? I killed

414

one of you guys already, I stuck him like a pig. You want to know what he sounded like?'

A thin animal screeching noise pierced the gloom, then subsided into ironic laughter.

Quemada sucked in between his teeth and whispered to Menéndez, 'I got to tell you, Lieutenant, this guy, when we finally do get him down the station, he's gonna have a hard time walking up and down the steps. Without falling over that is.'

Rodríguez's voice echoed down the hall. 'Lieutenant? You say he's in with the animals? In the enclosure?'

'Yeah. We're pretty sure of that. We've seen him a couple of times but he keeps dodging behind them. I guess he thinks we won't come in for him there.'

'I guess he's fucking right,' whispered Quemada.

'I see,' yelled Rodríguez. 'Then we will get him out.'

Menéndez heard the click, metallic and unmistakable, found himself saying, 'But he's not armed . . . he hasn't got a gun . . .'

And then the roar of the weapon drowned out everything, so loud it sounded as if their eardrums would burst. A yellow flame shot through the blackness, momentarily lighting up the entire cavernous hall. It stamped itself on her mind like a photograph: the animals shocked, scared in the enclosure, a figure, prone – *prone?* – in their midst, Quemada, Menéndez, covering their ears to keep out the sound, faces contorted in pain. And at the end of the chamber, outlined in the pale yellow light, frozen, three or four faceless men scattered around the Captain who had a hand raised, a pistol pointing into the air.

Then it disappeared. There was another shot. Something ricocheted, whistling around the stone walls.

'Ground!' yelled Menéndez, and they dived to the floor, listening as they did to the roar growing in front of them.

415

The wild, relentless roar of the bulls, in fury, in rage, in fear, and over them the screaming, loud, full-throated, agonised.

'He's killing him,' said Quemada, crouching on the ground. 'The Captain's gone crazy. He's gonna drive them so mad the bulls will kill him.'

They were close enough now to see the dim reflections of light in each other's eyes. There was something in Menéndez's blind, blank stare she did not recognise, did not like. The noise from the animal enclosure was now excruciating. The confidence, the arrogance, were now gone. He was screaming to be released, to be saved.

In a single, swift movement Menéndez stood up and walked into the arch of the doorway. His outline was silhouetted against the light. His voice boomed through the long, brick cavern. 'Antonio. Walk towards me. Walk towards the door. You will be safe, you will be . . .'

Nothing human moved in the enclosure. She had the torchlight there, she was trying to see, to comprehend everything that was to be seen there, but nothing human moved an inch.

'Menéndez, there's something . . .' she said.

And then the world roared again with the sound of a gun, louder than ever; the animals themselves began to scream; pitiful, primal sounds came out of the pen; they were trampling, goring, savaging each other in the beam of the flashlight. Behind the hulking shadows, dim white, was the form of a man, being trampled underfoot in the panic, dark stains growing large upon his torso.

'Oh, my God,' said Quemada and she felt something soft fall next to her, hit the ground with a sickening, physical thump.

She turned the torch away from the savagery and looked to her left. A foot away from her, Menéndez lay, curled in a foetal position, mouth, eyes, wide open, half his head

416

blown away, the shattered brain, the ridge of broken white skull given an unreal filmic quality in the thin battery light.

It was a short distance to the door, a short distance she covered in an instant, then Quemada held her as everything erupted from the pit of her stomach, and she choked and vomited an acid stream of bile onto the damp and sand-covered ground.

55

The storm was over now. It had moved on, taking with it the stifling heat and the pressure that made the blood feel as if it were about to boil. In its place was a fine, warm drizzle, and a flat overcast sky the colour of thin milk. She sat on the steps to the terraces, covered in cold sweat, the taste of vomit still burning in her throat. Quemada pulled a little silver flask out of his jacket pocket and offered it to her. She shook her head.

'Don't mind me,' he said, yanked off the top and knocked back a big draught. The smell of coñac came drifting across to her. She changed her mind, reached over, took the flask, and tipped it into her mouth. It felt like liquid fire and the pain, fierce and shocking, was good, cleared her mind, made her try to think straight, try to control the whirr of semi-formed ideas, memories buzzing around her head.

'I want to see him,' she said.

'The Lieutenant? They took him away. You don't want to see him again.'

'No,' she said. '*Him.*'

Quemada looked at her and shook his head. 'You're sure? The Lieutenant was no picture, but this guy . . . I tell you, it's not nice.'

'I want to see him.'

Her face looked like it was made from stone, pale, hard stone. No teaching the ice queen, Quemada thought to himself.

'Stick with me. Some point they're probably gonna bounce you out. They've got scene of crime guys going all over the place. There'll be an inquiry, you know. The Captain, going shooting around like that. I don't care what the guy was saying about Bear. You don't do that kind of thing. Just stick close to me.'

They got up and walked back to the little doorway. Inside, the place was well lit now, forests of bare light bulbs made it look like a Christmas grotto getting ready to be decorated.

'What was wrong with the lights?' she asked. 'Menéndez wondered that. What was wrong?'

'The guy had taken the fuse out. Boy, was he prepared. Got himself in there using someone else's ID. Somehow worked his way in as a *banderillero*. Guess he had the time to do pretty much as he liked.'

A group of men in plain suits and jackets hovered around the central enclosure, making notes, taking photographs. The bulls had been cleared away. The floor was covered in straw and piss and shit. It smelled like an abattoir. Quemada wandered over nonchalantly, she followed on behind.

'Excuse me,' Quemada said, then pushed to the front of the group and leaned on the metal bars of the enclosure. 'Lady here could identify him if you like, boys.'

A man with a cold, sour face and neatly trimmed goatee beard smirked and said, 'Really? Now that would be something.'

She joined Quemada at the railing.

In the centre of the stall lay the body. It wore the same golden suit of lights she had seen in the ring, now dirty and bloodied and contorted beyond belief. One leg was broken and turned around on itself, shattered at the knee, where bone and gristle showed through the flesh. There were big bloody stains which she presumed to be puncture marks in the groin, the stomach and the upper chest. The head was twisted grotesquely to the left, the neck clearly broken.

She stared at the face. Beneath the dark wavy hair, starting a little short of the forehead, it was torn in two. A large wad of flesh and gristle running from above the mouth, through the nose, to the left eye, had been honed off the front of the skull, exposing the bone and brain behind. It sat back on the head like a flap of meat, flesh side uppermost. Flies fed and buzzed happily around the blood and gore.

'You seen enough?' asked Quemada. 'Believe me. This man is *dead*.'

There was movement through the group. Rodríguez walked to the front and stood by the railing next to them. His face was immobile, passive, unreadable. He looked at the pile of meat on the floor and his chin sagged down onto his neck.

'You killed him,' she said and she could hear the strangeness, the odd pitch in her own voice. 'You killed them both and all you had to do was wait.'

Rodríguez closed his eyes briefly. She watched his hands grip tightly on the dirty metal railing, she tried to imagine what he might be thinking. Tried to find some sympathy for him.

'I made a mistake,' he said and his face seemed to be set in stone: impassive, incapable of expression.

'When he started to speak . . . about Torrillo, I made a mistake. I thought I could frighten him out of there. I was wrong. These men?'

He jerked a thumb back at the team working behind him.

'You see them? You know who they are? The investigations people. They were here already. I had called them in as extra support. There is an irony for you, Professor.

420

They will have my job for this if I don't resign first. You make a mistake. You pay. Menéndez . . . was a good man. How could I know? It is a tragedy. For him. For me. And all for . . . *this*.'

He pointed at the heap on the floor, distaste evident in his face.

She could feel the blood pounding in her head, could feel herself dancing at the very edge of her sanity.

'This,' she said, and hoisted herself onto the railings.

It took them a moment to realise, and then they were shouting, screaming at her to come back. She swung one leg, then the other, over the metal bar, dropped gently onto the bloody straw of the pen, then walked over to the body. Slowly, recording every image, she bent over, picked up the flap of bloody flesh on the corpse's face, pulled it back, and let it fall back into place.

Even then, the face was not a face any more. It was tissue, it was flesh, disfigured, ripped apart. A human being reduced to mere organic matter. She stared at it, stared harder and harder until something inside her head began to hum gently, insistently, like a little living creature, and then the arms gripped her, shook her, forced her away, out again, out into the milky light, the faint, warm rain, and the world.

Maria Gutierrez realised her eyes were streaming. She wiped them with her sleeve, then wiped her nose, and walked out of the open gateway of the ring, into the park, through the mud and the litter swirling gently in the wet, choppy wind, thinking to herself, over and over and over again . . .

No rain, Bear. We agreed. No rain . . .

56

The elation was not there. The streets should have been strewn with people, full of noise and colour and gaiety. Instead the city was indoors, driven there by the rain, the atmosphere, the curious, sinister mood that had hung in the air for days on end, then made its savage outburst in the ring. Rumours swept the streets, of murder and deceit and tragedy, they flourished in the little bars of the barrio, now full to the doors with ill-tempered, truculent men, young and old, feeling cheated, dispossessed. They drank cheap red wine, coffees thick with coñac, spoke little, watched the television, watched the rerun of Mateo's death, over and over again, first on one channel, then on another, replaying, reliving every second, looking for answers that never seemed to come. The week had ended in ugliness, an ugliness that infected them all, and what made it worse was that they recognised their infection, they could feel, could touch the virus within them, and knew that, in hating it, they hated themselves.

Through cobbled streets of muddy water, through piles of floating debris and litter, she walked, not stopping, not looking to see where she was. Her hair was now plastered to her skull, dank and greasy with the rain. Her clothes were soaked, they stuck to her skin, chafing it to redness. Her legs ached, her feet felt sore and blistered.

Finally, she stood inside an unlit doorway, wiped her face with her sleeve, stared blankly at the darkened window.

Distorted by the rain, the glass flashed back the reflection of a neon light from across the street: red, green, blue and yellow. She turned around and looked across the road. The optician's shop. To her right, the bar on the corner where, a lifetime ago, she had declined a drink with Torrillo.

Maria shuffled across the street, put the key in the door and walked upstairs.

57

In the city morgue, in the bowels of the police station, Quemada coughed phlegm into a grubby handkerchief and swore. This weather was getting to him. He could feel Velasco's cold coming on and his head hurt. He looked at the body on the bright shiny metal table and thought: what a lousy day, what a lousy fucking day.

It was naked now, the flesh, where it was unmarked, the pale, olive grey of death. The wounds caused in the goring looked like miniature dried-up oil wells. The blood, caked around the entry holes in the abdomen, the neck and the face, was being carefully wiped away with cotton swabs by the medical examiner. Quemada knew him vaguely: Castares. Creepy Castares, they called him, to his face too. He looked a little like a cadaver himself, thin, tall, with a whey-coloured face and a permanent smell of booze about him.

Quemada had once got drunk with him after a particularly nasty autopsy and, in his cups, asked, 'Why the fuck you do this job, Creepy? I mean, there's lots of nicer jobs you could do. Like being an asshole surgeon? Or a dentist? Or a gynaecologist? Spending your day with your hand up someone's ass, down their throat or messing around with ladies' doo-dahs sure beats spending it inside a dead person? Don't it?'

Creepy had taken a big swig of his drink, grinned and said, 'Yeah, but, Quemada, what you don't understand is, in this job I get to put my hands in all three. And anywhere else I like.'

Quemada looked him in the eye and tried to reassure himself the man was joking. 'But, Creepy, these people are *dead*. They're *dead*.'

'Yeah. I know.' He had a big, wide grin on his face now, the tobacco-stained teeth shone brown in the half-light of the bar. 'And you know what they say in my business: "Dead people don't complain."'

After that Quemada didn't make any jokes with Creepy Castares any more. After that he didn't go to any bars with him either.

Quemada watched him moving around the corpse on the plate, muttering asides to his girl assistant who wrote them down in a plain ringbound police notebook. He was taking his time. There was a lot to look at.

'Hey, Creepy,' Quemada said.

The pathologist shot him a venomous look. Off duty, in places he marked out as *sociable* places, he didn't mind the nickname. In the morgue, and in particular in front of his nice new girl assistant, he liked a little more respect. Quemada spotted his error.

'Sorry. *Doctor*.'

'What you want?'

'I'm curious about this guy. Something bugs me about him and I thought maybe you could help me on it.'

'What?' said Castares, and poked a metal probe into a hole in the corpse's abdomen.

'That wound on his face. The one that nearly took his face off. You think a bull could do that?'

'I haven't got that far yet. I'm working from the bottom up.'

'All a matter of taste, I guess,' said Quemada, automatically. 'See. We didn't actually see this guy buy it. We *heard*

425

something. But it was very dark. There was some shooting too. And I was curious. That wound on his face. I guess I never saw anything quite like it. And I just wondered . . .'

Castares grimaced, not a pretty sight, then muttered obscenely. 'I hate these kind of interruptions, you know. I have a way of doing these things. A *method*. You interrupt me, the method goes out the window.'

'I just wondered what you think. That's all. You're the expert.'

The pathologist looked at the flap of flesh, picked it up in his hand, looked underneath it, into the red morass of the skull.

'See,' said Quemada. 'What interests me is, we know this man was in the middle of a pen of bulls going crazy. We *know* that because we found him there afterwards. And you got these marks on his body. But say I brought him in, brought him to you and all he had was that wound on his head. Nothing else. What would you say caused it? A bull?'

Castares felt the weight of the pad of flesh, like a house-wife weighing up a piece of fish in the market.

'I'd say it was caused by a powerful blow from some kind of broad, blunt instrument. Maybe one of the tools you see in roadworking crews – you know, the other end of the pick.'

'Not being gored by a bull?'

'Definitely not. A wound that comes from something sharp is very easy to pick up. Even you could do that.'

'That's kind of you to say so,' Quemada said.

'No problem. On the other hand, you say this man was in a pen of stampeding bulls. You'd have to consider the possibility that he was kicked, maybe trampled underfoot.'

'And that could cause that kind of wound?'

Castares shrugged his shoulders. 'Maybe. I wouldn't like

to say until I've taken a closer look. *When* I take a closer look.'

He picked up the flap again, then bent over to peer inside the skull.

'On the other hand . . .'

Castares motioned for his assistant to pass him something from the surgical tray by the table. It was a pair of long-nosed tweezers. He poked them inside the head, round about where an eye socket would have been if the flesh had not been pulled to one side to flap along the opposite cheekbone. Then he pulled them out. There was something small and shiny in the tweezer head.

'On the other hand, *that* didn't come from any bull.'

Quemada walked over, tried to ignore the meat smell from the thing on the bench, and looked at the tweezers.

'You're the expert in this, detective. What would you say that was?'

'A small-calibre bullet.'

'Yeah,' said Castares. His face was buried back in the skull again. He adjusted the bright examination light over the table, bent to one side of it, and took a scalpel to the brain tissue inside the skull. Quemada saw something being sliced, then turned away. Castares cut and fiddled for a minute or so then made some clucking noises, left the corpse, and put the instruments back in the tray.

'I get the benefit of your wisdom on this?' asked Quemada eventually.

'I take the brain out for these things in any case, you know. I always look so I would have got this anyway. Without you.'

'Sure,' said Quemada. 'You're a whizz.'

'My guess – and it stays a guess until I do a formal examination – my guess is that the bullet killed him. The way the blood behaves around the entry wound in the brain. He was alive when he was shot.'

427

'So maybe there was some unlucky – *what am I saying "unlucky"?* – some *ricochet* in the dark and it hit him. That's what you're saying.'

'What I'm saying is that my guess is that the shot killed him. And that there was some interval between the shot and these wounds to the body. That would explain the way he bled. If the heart had been pumping when the wounds were made, there would have been more blood. The wound on the face. That's different. That was probably closer to the shot.'

'So he got shot. Someone took a pickaxe to his face. Then some time later, in the dark, he got bumped around a bit by some bulls. When he was dead.'

'That's about it,' said Castares. '*Provisionally.*'

'I see,' said Quemada. 'You done the prints yet?'

The pathologist grimaced. 'Of course I've done the prints. That's what I meant when I said I worked bottom up. It's part of the method.'

'I'd like to see them.'

The assistant walked over to the far side of the room and pulled two pages of paper from a brown folder. She came back and handed them to Quemada. He put them on the desk by the examination table, then opened up a file marked 'Antonio Mateo' and let the contents slide onto the table. A set of old charge sheets and station reports – minor thefts, drug pulls, a reported robbery that somehow never came to court – fell onto the desktop. He picked up a set of prints from the pile and placed them side by side with the fresh ones from the corpse.

'You got a magnifying glass?'

The assistant took one out of a medical cabinet drawer.

'Say. You're young. Your eyesight's better than mine. Take a look at these prints. One against the other. Tell me what you see.'

The girl came and stood beside him, then bent over the pages. He could smell cologne on her body, something expensive, something exotic underneath the plain white nylon jacket with the stains of blood and less savoury things on the sleeve. She wore thick-rimmed glasses and had her hair tied back in a bun but, when he came to think about it, he could understand why Castares didn't like being called Creepy in front of her.

'What do you see?'

'They're different.'

He took the glass off her and looked at the prints himself.

'Way different,' said Quemada.

Castares blinked and looked puzzled.

'You mean this isn't who you thought it was?'

Quemada put down the glass and scooped up the papers. 'It's not who *I* thought it was. Somebody else might feel different. Castares. You do me a favour?'

'If it's legal, ethical and decent and doesn't cost me money.'

'You just go back to the bottom and keep working your way up. And don't feel in a hurry. Tomorrow, tomorrow this thing will be sorted. One way or another. But I'd be grateful if you could keep this between us just for the time being.'

'You get through on three counts but is that ethical?'

Quemada sniffed and wondered whether it was really a cold or just all the medical junk they kept in the air in these places.

'You tell me that tomorrow. I'm not saying you hide anything. I'm just saying – just *asking* – that you go back to working your own sweet way, at your own sweet pace, and give me some window room. For tonight. No more.'

Castares' face looked long enough to touch the ground.

'I hate it when you detectives do this stuff on me. I *hate* it. It'll cost you a drink.'

Quemada's heart sank. 'Agreed. Provided all we talk about is football, food and sex. On second thoughts, skip the sex. I'm not sure my stomach could take it.'

When he'd gone, the girl turned to Castares and said, 'Creepy? I think that's sort of cute.'

'You do?' he replied brightly. The tombstone teeth glittered several shades of brown under the medical lights.

58

Thirty minutes later, back in the deserted squad room, Quemada took a crowbar to the locked cabinet by Menéndez's desk, thrust it into the crack between drawer and frame, then heaved hard on the end. The woodwork came away with a groan. He reached inside and fished out three files of papers, each marked 'Private' in the late Lieutenant's scrawly hand.

Quemada sat down and started reading.

He bundled up the pile of papers with some new notes he had made, put them in a folder, tied it round with a couple of elastic bands, wrote a covering note, then found a routing slip for the internal mailing system. He looked at the form, paused over the 'To:' portion. Then he screwed it up into a ball and threw it into the waste basket underneath the desk.

Quemada picked up the phone and dialled his brother's number. It rang out half a dozen times, then a gruff male voice answered.

'Miguel, it's me. Carlos,' said Quemada. 'Sure. Sure I'm fine. No. I don't want nothing. Huh? Well, yeah. I *do* want something. It's important. You can come now? I need to see you. Outside the station in the square. Fifteen minutes, OK? I said it was important, didn't I? Sure. Why else would I be asking?'

He was late. He was always late. Thirty minutes later a shiny new Mercedes estate drew up in the square and a young, serious face poked out of the driver's window.

Quemada looked at the car and whistled. 'They paying you well these insurance people these days? I save a year, maybe two years, I just might be able to afford the servicing on one of these things.'

'What do you want, Carlos? I'm busy.'

'I want you to look after this,' Quemada replied. He pushed the bundle through the car window and let it fall onto the passenger seat.

His brother looked horrified. 'Oh, Jesus Christ. I hate it when you play these things on me. What the fuck is it?'

'Just some papers I'd rather not keep at the station.'

'Carlos. Is this one of your things? Should I be doing this?'

'You just keep 'em a day. Two days at the most. If I have an accident, something like that, you give 'em to the TV station, the newspapers, whoever you like. You just photocopy them and just hand them out on the street if you want.'

'Jesus. I got a wife and kids, you know. I can't go around playing these games.'

'These aren't games, Miguel. You been reading the papers. You been following what's been happening here this past week?'

'You bet. And that's exactly why I want nothing to do with it.'

'Well, you got something to do with it. You got me to do with it. Now be a good little brother, huh? Do like I say, will ya? No one knows I gave you this stuff, no one *will* know. You just go back home, turn on your stereo and your satellite TV, go make lots more money and in a couple of days we can all go back to normal. You can forget you ever knew me.'

Miguel gunned the engine with his toe and let the noise

432

do the talking for him. It sounded loud and powerful and angry. 'You're a shithead, Carlos. A real shithead.'

'Yeah. Maybe that's right. And fraternal greetings to you too, brother. Now run along now and careful you don't scrape the paintwork. Oh. And thanks.'

The estate car pulled away from the kerb with a pained screech and Quemada watched it disappear out of the corner of the square.

'They drive the car like that because of the car or because of they *want* to drive like that?' Quemada wondered silently to himself.

He flashed his ID at the gate then went back into the station and climbed to the third floor. His desk was just as he had left it. He picked up the phone, dialled a three-figure extension and heard Rodríguez's voice, muted and a little hoarse, answer the phone.

'Captain? It's Detective Quemada here. I was wondering if I could come and see you. I got some problems on this case. Some major problems. I know you're not on it any more. I know they took you off after Menéndez got shot. But I was wondering, still, I was wondering if you could help. I mean, like, you're the old man, OK. If I can't come talk to you, who can I talk to? Right now, if it suits you.'

Quemada listened to the voice on the other end of the line. He could hardly recognise it. When Rodríguez had finished, he said, 'Fine. I'll be over in one minute.'

59

Maria turned on the hallway light, walked up the narrow flight of stairs, and went into the apartment. The light was on. The policewoman's gun lay on the table. She tried to think. Surely, they would have called the woman off by now? She tried to remember her name. It wouldn't come.

She went to the bathroom, took off her wet clothes, wiped her face and looked in the mirror. Her eyes seemed twice their normal size: round and white and frightened. Her skin was pale, bloodless. She took off her underclothes, towelled herself down, rubbed her face into the thick, rough fabric and felt something like life begin to return. Still pummelling at her head with the towel, she reached behind the shower curtain, felt for the tap, felt her hand grip, unmistakably, the outline of a human head, hair underneath her fingers, wet, thick hair. Her hand jerked back, automatically. She looked at it. The fingers were thick with blood, red and fresh. It dripped slowly onto the tiled floor.

Maria reached forward, drew back the curtain, half knowing what she would see. In the bath, on her back, unseeing eyes open, staring sightless at the ceiling, was the policewoman. A crimson wound, like a deathly red grin, ran obscenely from ear to ear, through the fleshy folds underneath her chin. Her mouth was set in a bizarre grimace, the teeth stained red, like lipstick that had run. She pulled the curtain back further. The woman was still in uniform. Her knees were bunched up to fit the length of her frame in the bath. On a strap at her waist, hung her radio. Somewhere out of nowhere it turned itself on, hissed and crackled stupidly at nothing.

From behind, soft and low, came a voice that said, 'He told me to kill her. He told me. So I did.'

She turned round, automatically clutching a towel to her from the rack. He stood in the doorway, dressed in a tattered T-shirt, faded jeans, mouth half open, eyes, *dead* eyes, staring at her. A long knife, its thin blade half covered in blood, hung almost lifeless in his left hand. There was something lethargic, something spent, about him. She stared and stared and then it came, the tiny, unforeseen revelation. She was not afraid.

'Did he tell you to kill me?' she asked.

He nodded, slowly, reluctantly.

'Yeah. He uses me. He says I am *his*. My father. You understand?'

'Antonio. Your father is dead. He cannot order you to do anything.'

The man shook his head and laughed.

'Don't say that. He doesn't like it if you say that. My father is alive. He talks to me. He *knows* what you do. He *knows*.'

His eyes looked dead. Maybe it was drugs. Maybe it was simply exhaustion.

'He knows everything. Like a spider. Like he knew when I started talking to that university guy, started getting him too close to the secrets. How'd he know that? I didn't tell him. My brother didn't tell him. Like he'll know, you see. He'll know if I don't kill you. Like he'd know if I didn't kill Jaime. And then he would kill me. But he loves me too. That is why we did the thing. At the corrida. Fooled you all. Million ways out of that place the cops didn't know about, specially if you got a little help, specially in the dark.

We was laughing at you. You know that? Just setting things up in there with the bulls, waiting for the time, and I was out of there so quick, so fast, you didn't even see me gone. Before the shooting started. Before you got those bulls moving. Real clever stuff. Not that you need clever stuff for dumb fucking cops. Real dumb.'

'Except for him, you mean.'

'Yeah,' he said, a little puzzled. 'Except for him. How you know that? Maybe that's why he wants you killed. Yeah. Fucking right.'

'He's not your father. He's *not*.'

'You don't know. You just don't fucking know. He can hear you, when you say that. He can see you. Everywhere. Sometimes I do things, things no one can see. And still he knows.'

'Like the brothers?'

He laughed and a little line of spittle flew from his mouth. 'Yeah. The brothers. Me and Jaime, we did them good. They fuck around too much, so I did them. Like Jaime showed me to when I filled him full of dope. The old man, he thinks you turn this thing on and off. He wants me to do it when *he* wants. Like with the university guy. And the old man in the office. Then he gets pissed when I have a little fun on my own.'

'Did he know about your mother? The woman you thought was your mother?'

He stood up and flashed the knife in front of her.

'What the fuck do you mean "*thought*"? I *knew* the bitch was mine when I spoke to that dumbfuck husband of hers. The old man told me so. That's why it was easy, real easy, when it came to kill that college fuck. You should've heard him yelling. That bitch. I meet her and she comes on like she's on heat. With *me*? And when I say, yeah, OK, she fucks off. Like you do. You *all* do.'

436

He held the knife tightly now, waved it in front of him. His free hand was feeling at his groin. A tic twitched above his right eye. She had to fight to take her eyes off it.

'Get in the bedroom,' he said. 'I watched you on TV. Next to him. When you were just watching, there, watching, and you looked right at me. I knew then I'd do it. One day. I knew it was going to happen. He told me to kill you. Didn't say anything about anything else.'

He stood back from the door, knife held high in front of him, between the bathroom and the table with the gun on it. She looked at the cold, dull metal a few feet away, looked at the knife.

'Get in the fucking bedroom!'

She walked through the bathroom door, kept her back close to the wall, edged along and walked into the bedroom. The big double bed was made: all white and neat and tidy. The policewoman, Maria thought. The policewoman must have got bored, decided to help. Fat reward.

'Get on the bed. Take that towel off.'

She lay naked on the cover, knees together, arms folded over her chest. Antonio leaned over, ran the blade against the front of her shin. She could feel the blood on it, sticky, clinging to her skin, and she shivered.

'Open your legs. Open it up. I want to see it.'

Maria let her legs fall back into a wide V, put her hand on the soft hair, felt for the opening, felt the dryness there. He followed her fingers with his eyes, his mouth gaping open.

'Like this,' she said, and thrust her finger into the moistness.

'You fucking dirty bitch,' he gasped. '*You fucking dirty bitch!*'

She held her vagina open wide and let two fingers roam inside. He stared at the pinkness and started to undo his belt. The jeans fell around his ankles. Still gripping the knife in his left hand, he pushed down his pants with his right. His penis hung limply in the nest of dark, tangled hair. He took it in his hand and started to jiggle it.

'Fuck you,' he spat, flecks of white flying out from his mouth, and this time he wasn't talking to her. 'Fucking, fuck you, come on, come on . . .'

Maria watched him, watched the limp organ refusing to move. He reached into his pocket, pulled out a small phial, sniffed at it. The smell of nail varnish drifted across to her.

'You don't need that. Take your clothes off,' she said. 'Take your clothes off. I'll do something.'

'You'll do something?'

He was yanking at it now, and still it stayed inert. 'You fucking stay there.'

She took her hand away from herself and waited. In the corner of the room he shook his clothes off. She could smell the sweat, rank and animal, streaming off his body.

He climbed on the bed, between her legs, pushed himself against her, pushed the knife to her throat. She felt the blade, thin and lethal, pushed sideways to her skin.

He kneeled in front of her, jerked his groin helplessly. The limp flesh pressed soft against her hair.

'Do something,' he said. He put his head on her chest. 'Do something or I'll fucking kill you now.'

She felt lips brush against her nipple, rough skin, bristle against her breast. Her left hand went to her breast, she held it, fed it further into his mouth. He was sucking. With her other hand she felt down his body, felt the prick slapping faintly against her.

'Do something,' he said again, and she felt something warm, like tears, on her chest.

She arched her body upwards, whispered in his ear, and took his stiffening flesh in her spare hand. 'Who do you

438

think of, Antonio? When you come? Who do you think of? Whose face do you see in the dark?'

His head came damply away from the nipple. Spittle dripped from his tongue, fell on her chest, slipped between their skin. His eyes stared into nothingness, the pupils dilating, growing larger, blacker, deeper. He felt himself becoming firmer in her hand, lunged with his back, jabbed faster, faster. She gasped.

'No. *No*. Slowly. *Slowly*. You'll lose it. Rush, and you'll lose it.'

Her hand moved away from his groin, moved up the front of his stomach, felt the hair. She stretched her hand, stroked the skin with the tips, the inside of her fingers.

'Slow, slow,' she said. 'Think, Antonio, think. Who do you think of? Whose face do you see?'

He obeyed her hands now, moved to their rhythm, and something was happening, something he had never experienced before, something was shining, coming into focus inside his head. He screwed his eyes shut, tight, tight, tight, stared into the darkness with his inner eye, saw the picture, *saw her face* . . . fringed with blonde hair, smiling, *tempting*. Just like in the park. Just like the day in the park. When he'd seen her, when he'd told her, offered himself, as son, as lover, as anything she wanted. He kept his eyes shut and saw her mouth move, open, the red, red lips open, grow giant, grow *huge* in the hot bloody darkness, grow vast to consume him.

And then he was rock hard. He felt strange, superhuman, complete.

She touched his penis now, touched the stiffness, moved herself underneath him, opened her legs wider, her face like a rock, set in grim, stony determination.

'Hold my hands,' she said. He rocked there, above her, agonisingly slowly, in space. She screamed, threw out both her arms, thrust herself against the stiffness. 'Now! Now! Hold my hands!'

Then she found him. The hardness rolled inside her. He gasped, as if in pain, his eyes, dark and deep pools, opened, focusing on nothing.

'Hold my hands!'

He felt the rush inside him. She moved her palms towards his. She felt the handle, smooth wood, felt it fall away as his fingers opened, felt them entwine. She ground herself into him, took him far, far inside her, watched him gasping, waited, waited, waited.

The world gyrated between their arching bodies, locked in a slow and loveless dance and then exploded into fury. He burst inside her crying, shaking with the fever, locked in sweat and flesh and semen. His eyes rolled up, up into his head, then he lurched forwards onto her, head on her chest. The bristles scraped her skin like raw sandpaper. Almost instantly, he was out of her, as if repelled by the act, and lay, panting, on her body, looking down its length, at the small, curving stomach, the hair below, the tiny, dark puddle on the bed. Without a thought, his mouth opened, then closed, gently, once more, on the nipple. She fed it back into his mouth and sensed the tender, nagging sucking.

Then her outstretched arm felt slowly, silently across the sheet, found what it was looking for, tightened its grip.

She let him suck, then moved her shoulder in, against his body, so that the movement, the rubbing, might pass as an embrace. Slowly, she shifted herself, further and further into his body, moving the arm, her upper arm, against him, lifting the blade behind him, higher and higher, until it shone like a silver jewel behind his head, radiant in the bedroom light.

She looked at it there and felt that the world had come to a standstill, that there was nothing left but this strange, loveless mating. It was too long. She was waiting too long, she knew this, but there was nothing she could do. She closed her eyes, squeezed them, opened them again, willed herself to act, told herself: *live.* And still it hung there, above them, her arm growing weak and tired and feeble.

His breathing changed, became shortened, more shallow. The sucking, the pressure, ceased on her breast. She did what she told herself not to do and looked down at him. A single black eye stared up at her, dark and fathomless, stark with the agony of being alive.

His arms suddenly gripped her body, hard and tight and painful.

'Too late,' he whispered. *'Too . . .'*

Maria looked down again and saw his face, saw the room.

The green mask and the red velvet walls

'Fuck you,' she said. And the silver blade flashed down like lightning.

60

In the late-night still of the office, Quemada tidied his papers. He felt old and tired and drained. Next week, which seemed like years away, would make him forty-four. Only fifteen years or so younger than the Captain. The 'old man'. To an extent, they had shared the same space. He could remember the old days, around when Franco died, before the reforms, the Socialists came, when police work had narrower, better defined lines. You knew who you were protecting, you knew who you had to lock up. The machine ran smoothly, and if that was because someone upstairs was greasing the wheels then that was the way it was. It was only these last twenty years or so, when you started having votes and committees and 'accountability' that the lines began to get blurred and fuzzy. There were maybe ten per cent of people on the force now who could remember the old days, the days when you fixed *some* things with a phone call, not a warrant, when a woman could walk down Calle Mayor without someone trying to snatch her bag or some crack addict asking for money. And every month another one retired, another one took the pension, bought a little *casita* out near the coast, relaxed into an early old age of watching the big blue Atlantic go in and out, sipping the saltiness of a morning manzanilla and thinking: fuck it. At least it's over.

And if they eased those years with a little extra top-up from some ancient gangster's slush fund, who cared? Now you gave the money to the government instead and a third went to the bureaucrats straight away, then the rest went on the social, the taxes, the public works.

The money, Quemada figured, the money didn't matter really. Killing people for it, particularly killing cops, now *that* was a different issue.

Quemada wondered how many times he'd greased those wheels this last quarter-century without even knowing it, wondered if one day the Captain would have called him in, explained a few things, then asked him to grease a few more. Then he dismissed the thought: who the fuck cared? You came in, you did your job, you went home. You didn't take it with you, the good *or* the bad. You switched on the TV, you opened a beer or maybe the coñac bottle and you sat in the low, peaceful light of a table lamp letting the world wash over you. Take it home, good *or* bad, and it just festered, then one day it came back to haunt you. And there were too many haunted people in this job already, too many ghosts flitting around the shadows.

Haunted. Just like the ice queen, he thought. All these people who couldn't face it, couldn't just sit back and let it roll. And let themselves get eaten instead.

The idea sparked something in the back of his head, made some nagging thought go walkabout, and he sat there trying to work out what it was. It hung around just out of reach and Quemada found himself wishing Velasco was there to help, there to bounce something off, even if it was just some gratuitous insult.

'What are friends for?' he said to the empty room.

And then it came to him. Two sets of initials, clear and unmistakable in a fine, female hand. At the bottom of the paper, the most damning paper, if Menéndez was right, right alongside the Lieutenant's own notes, just two letters: MG. *MG.* Maria Gutierrez.

'Oh shit,' Quemada muttered, and the words bounced lightly off the fading paint of the walls. 'Not that.'

He swivelled round in his ancient office chair. The sweat glistened on his head now and there was something that might have passed for panic in his eyes. He ran down the corridor again and looked in Rodríguez's office. It was empty. The sweat was cold on him now, the air chill.

Quemada walked back to Menéndez's desk, pulled out the dead man's mobile phone, picked up the small canvas sack of surveillance kit, then half ran out of the door, down the stairs and out through the main station yard, punching up numbers out of the phone's memory as he went.

61

She was hunched by the doorway of the bedroom, a pale, stone-coloured towel now stained with blood around her body, the knife clutched tightly in her right hand. She didn't make a sound. Quemada could taste the bile in the back of his throat. Things were bad enough when he first looked into the bedroom. Then, automatically, he had gone to the bathroom to find something to give her to wipe her face, her hands. What he saw there was just too much. He threw up hard and painfully on a dry stomach, retching and retching until he thought his heart would burst.

Quemada crouched down in front of her, held out his hands, thought it best not to touch her and started to beg.

'Lady.' He hunted for something, anything to say. 'Maria. *Please.* We've got to get out of here. We've got to move. The guy's dead. Mike's dead. There's nothing more we can do. We gotta go.'

He went back into the bathroom, trying not to look at the bloody mess in the tub, picked up a spare towel, dampened it under the tap, came back in and tried to wipe her face. She recoiled, savagely, and for a moment held the knife out towards him.

'Jesus.' Quemada sat down hard on one of the little cane dining chairs, hunched over and put his head in his hands.

'Maria. You've got to trust me. I don't know where the old man is and until I know I daren't call anyone in here, not while you're around. We're looking for him. We'll catch him. But I have to get you out of here. I *have* to.'

She stared at him and there was something – a hardness, a determination – in her eyes that made him want to run away, want to leave it all to the clean-up men, regardless of whether the Captain was out there a-hunting just around the corner. He'd had enough.

Quemada looked at her again, felt cold inside, and said, 'Maria. I can try to talk you round. I can try and act sympathetic. But I'm not *good* at this. I have to get you out of here. I don't know what the fuck's going on right now. We have to go. Before either or both of us ends up crazy or dead.'

She closed her eyes and he wondered, for a moment, whether she'd snapped already, whether he shouldn't just try to take the knife off her, then drag her out anyway. Then he hated himself for the thought.

She opened her eyes and there were tears, big, liquid tears, brimming in them.

'Thank Christ for that,' said Quemada, and for a moment he thought he was going to join her.

She spoke slowly, deliberately. 'Where will we go? Where *can* we go? Where's *safe?*'

'I thought of that. Don't worry, Maria. I've thought of it. You don't need anything. No clothes. Nothing. It's taken care of. We just need to go. Like *now.*'

He went to the back of the main apartment door and took down a long, fawn raincoat and held out the arms for her. She stood up and let him wrap it around her shoulders. He could feel her shivering underneath the fabric. He found the belt, knotted it loosely around her middle, then opened the door.

She wouldn't look into his eyes. It was more than he could expect and he knew it.

'Everything's going to be OK, Maria. Believe me. Trust me. Everything's going to be OK.'

She walked slowly down the stairs, opened the front door herself, then stood on the threshold and turned to watch him following her. Quemada waddled down the stairs like a penguin, slightly out of condition, took hold of the door from her and found himself staring out into the blackness of the night, the blackness of the city he knew so well, and wondering what the hell was out there.

62

'You're lucky you caught me.'

Maggi Bartolomé was flashing eyes that darted from amusement to suspicion in equal measure. She was made up to the nines and wore a sleek red satin tube dress.

'Another fifteen minutes and I'd have been gone for the night.'

Quemada looked at her and found himself wishing, against his own best judgement, he could keep her at home a little longer.

'Your little girl could have let us in.'

She shook her head.

'Walked out this morning. Found some stupid creep who says he'll keep her. I didn't ask in return for what.'

'I'm sorry.'

'Don't be. I'm not.'

She nodded towards the first floor and the sound of water rattling through old piping.

'She looks like she's dead.'

Quemada said, 'Yeah. She nearly was.'

'This all to do with that *thing* we were talking about? Our friend from the past?'

'You don't want to know what this is all about, Maggi.'

'Don't you believe it. I did you a big favour here. I deserve something.'

Quemada thought about it, thought about how, in one way, she was involved in it already, tried to figure out what would come out eventually and what would stay hidden, wondered if it mattered anyway.

'It was your fault.'

'*My fault?*' She stared at him amazed.

'In a manner of speaking. You told us about that fair-haired girl who meant something special to old Antonio. So we figured that maybe it was his daughter. Maybe that somehow that linked in the whole thing.'

'And it wasn't?'

'Nah. She was just . . . well, you know what she was.'

She watched him and waited, letting the pause stretch between them until it had to break.

'Truth is, we were looking for a daughter when we should have been looking for a son. A son he was real proud of. So proud, in fact, he put him in place, put him in charge of something that was real important to Antonio.'

'He was a cop?'

'Did I say "was"?'

'He *is* a cop!'

'Not for much longer. He tried to keep the lid on things but it didn't work real well. Sometimes you use the wrong people. And then they can't leave these things be.'

'Ah.'

'That's the trouble these days. You can't get good menials. And that's as much as you *need* to know. I paid my debt.'

'Not really.'

'Maggi. I didn't come here to tell tales. I came here 'cos of a woman who's had a real bad time from some shitbag and needs help. I figured you'd sympathise there.'

She smiled. 'You're smart. I don't understand how you happened into your particular line of work.'

'I hide it well sometimes.'

'Yeah.' She stubbed out the cigarette and reached for a

449

worn leather jacket hung on the back of an armchair. 'I gotta go earn a living.'

'I need something else. I need your car keys.'

'Jesus. Can I give you *money* too?'

'No. Just the car keys will do.'

'Here. The licence ran out in January and the tyres make you look like you got hair. Don't come back with any tickets.'

'Thanks.'

'You promise me something, Quemada?'

'What?'

'When she comes down, you go easy on her. I've seen women like that before. When they get a bad guy. Get beaten up. Worse. Women who never thought things like that happened. She's just opened the door on something she didn't even know existed and she needs some *gentle* treatment right now. You understand? Gentle.'

Quemada swallowed hard, tasted the bile still there at the back of his throat, and said, 'Gentle. Yeah. I'm trying. It's not what we do well.'

'Cops, you mean? Or men in general?'

'As a ha-ha comment I think that maybe merits one ha.'

'Yeah. You'll find some decent coñac underneath the sink. I keep it there for special occasions. She needs it. Ask me, you *both* need it. You look gruesome.'

'Thanks,' said Quemada, then went over to the little kitchen, found the bottle, picked up two glasses from the washboard, sat down and waited.

A few moments later he heard the sound of the front door opening and closing. Then he took out Menéndez's mobile phone, dialled up Velasco's number from the memory, and listened to the spacy whirrs and fizzes in the earpiece. Eventually, the call was answered.

'I should have stayed in bed,' said Velasco, sounding like

he was talking from Mars. 'I'm running a temperature, my nose is pouring like it's sprung a snot leak, and I feel like shit.'

'They found him yet?'

'Nothing. *Nada*. He's probably halfway to Brazil. You sure about this? You really think the Captain had something to do with the policewoman buying it? With Menéndez? Jesus. I just can't believe it. That woman – I worked with her way back and she was one decent person. You best be sure. We'll be driving the buses otherwise. Or worse.'

'Yeah,' Quemada grunted. It was the 'worse' he worried about most. 'I'm sure. And I don't think the Captain's gone. It just don't sound right. You just keep everything going like we said anyway. Just to keep me happy.'

Velasco sniffed then pushed the red button to cut the line.

When she finally came down the stairs she was wearing light-blue jeans and a red nylon shirt. Maggi Bartolomé's daytime outfit: cheap, but not without taste, and a little too big on her. Maria's eyes were red-rimmed and staring, her hair, long and damp and straggly, covered half her face. He poured half a glass of brandy, handed it to her and waited.

She downed most of the drink in one go, then said, 'I can't stay here. Take me somewhere else. Take me to see Bear. Anywhere.'

'Jesus, Maria.' Quemada couldn't believe it. 'They say Bear's getting better. They say he's probably going to be OK. He doesn't need us there.'

'I need . . .' She spoke in a slow, deliberate voice and he didn't like it at all. She wondered if he would understand. She wondered if she understood herself. She hated this place, with its foreignness, its plastic furniture. But more than that, she wanted to keep moving, keep running, until it was all behind her, a long way behind.

Quemada found he was wringing his hands and hated the discovery.

'Maria, you're *safe* here. No one knows about this place, no one even in the . . .'

He kicked himself for almost saying it.

'No one even in the police. That's what you were going to say, wasn't it?'

He picked up the glass and finished the coñac even though it tasted foul.

'Yeah,' he said and hated the undertone of anger in his voice. 'That's what I was going to say. I got Bear in hospital. I got Menéndez dead. I got that poor cow Mike dead for no good reason at all. You're alive. Think of it that way.'

Maria thought of the policewoman she had never come to know, her quiet strength, that sense of calmness, of resigned serenity that seemed to hang around her.

A small, firm interior voice said, 'If I could have chosen then, I would have taken her place. I would have died in her place.' And she wondered if this was true.

Quemada covered his shining head with his hands and looked like he could begin to weep. 'I'm sorry. I didn't mean that. I apologise. This is one *big* thing for me. For all of us. We're losing friends out there. Real friends. We got a cop we thought was a hero running around doing God knows what. *That's* why I say we stick around here until we *do* know what's going on.'

And it still wouldn't stop spinning. Inside her head. Around and around.

'The old man,' she said. 'He called him that. "The old man."'

She stared at him and he didn't like it at all. 'Just like you do. "The old man." Antonio thought his father was *alive.* That he talked to him through someone. Through "the old man".'

Quemada looked at her and thought: I do not know this person, I do not understand her.

'You don't have to talk, Maria. You don't have to say anything. What you been through, I can only begin to guess at. It takes a long time to get over that kind of stuff. You don't have to say anything at all. In the morning, in the daylight, I can get you help. People to talk to. Experts in this kind of stuff. Right now you're just lumbered with me and *I am not good at this.*'

'I want to talk. I want to.'

She looked at him and found she had nothing to say.

'Then you talk,' said Quemada. 'You just go ahead and do what you damn well want.'

'I . . .' A picture suddenly came into her head out of nowhere and hung there in her mind, bright and lustrous, full of the colours of death. It was the painting in the hospice, the Valdés Leal, and in her mind it *glowed* blazing and triumphant in the dark.

'When I came here, Quemada, you saw me, you *hated* me.'

'Gimme a break, Maria. I made some lines. That's all. I make lines all the time. That's me. That's who I am. *Hated* you? That's crap.'

'When I walked through the door into that office you looked at me and thought, here comes some tight-assed, frigid northern bitch out to tell us how to do our jobs. You *saw* that and you *hated* it.'

Quemada took a deep breath then asked, 'Does this have a point? Are we going somewhere with this?'

She had her arms folded in front of her now and he was alarmed to see her rocking, slowly, rhythmically, backwards and forwards.

'You saw *what*, Quemada, *what?*'

'I saw some kind of prissy little ice queen walking through that door. OK? That what you wanted to know? An ice queen who looked as if she was running, running from anything that might come even this close' – and he pinched his thumb and finger together – 'to touching her.'

'Running.' She closed her eyes and found her head flooded with images: of Luis, with a dark shadow over his head, of Bear and the bloody wound in his side, the policewoman, dead in the tub, a mess of flesh and blood and hair. And then the faces, young faces, the faces of children, flooding through her head in a swelling, tumbling, never-ending stream.

Her voice had a chill, cold clarity about it; she could hear herself speaking the words as if they came from another person. 'You saw in me that I had no capacity for love. No capacity for charity. Nothing but fear. Not even enough inside me to hate.'

She stopped rocking, uncurled her arms, and looked at her hands. The room was silent except for the slow ticking of an ancient wall clock that stumbled uncertainly over its cogs and wheels somewhere behind them.

'I almost . . .' she said, then hesitated. 'Tonight I almost let him kill me. Something inside wanted that to happen. Something inside of me just didn't *care*.'

Quemada sweated inside his suit and wished to God he was somewhere else.

'You been through a hell of a lot, Maria. Don't make it worse.'

'I tried . . .' She struggled to shape the words. It was hard. She shook her head and held out the glass for more brandy, took a deep swig, started over again. 'There was a picture, a painting, the one that they used as some kind of inspiration when they killed the Angels. I recognised that as soon

454

as we went there. I remember Menéndez's surprise. I saw that picture years ago and I always thought it was about death. Always. It seemed so obvious. And I was stupid. It's about life. All of this. The city, the rituals. It's a mirror. And all I could see was the other side. And I want it too, Quemada. *I want it.*'

She looked at him and there was a directness, a stability in her face that he realised he had never seen before. The moisture from her tears hung in a little pool beneath her eyes then ran in two long, narrow rivers down her cheeks.

'Does that make sense, Quemada? Does it?'

He thought about it and said, 'Jesus, Maria. That makes more sense than anything I ever heard you say in your life.'

There was a sound from her throat, a little choking noise, that showed some promise: one day one of its children might grow up into a laugh, he thought.

'I want to see Bear,' she said. 'I want to see him now. And I'm not taking no for an answer.'

The unseen clock ticked on behind her back, louder, louder, louder.

'You're stalling, Quemada.'

'Maybe. But there are a couple of calls I got to make first. And a couple of points we got to discuss. I need to know what *you* know, Maria. This thing isn't all in black and white yet.'

'All that stuff this afternoon. The fused lights. The body. Antonio, he couldn't *do* that on his own. He was half crazy. And Menéndez . . .'

'Yeah. Menéndez.'

She poured another brandy and set it on the table.

'Are you going to tell me?'

Quemada pummelled his mouth with one hand and sighed.

'You know it already, don't you? You saw the papers. Leastwise, the Captain *thought* you saw the papers.'

'I don't know what you mean?'

'Those financial inquiries. The ones where we were looking to see who Alvarez's beneficiaries were, whether anyone had entered any legal claims against his estate.'

She thought back to the mountain of files she had seen.

'You signed something, Maria. Two initials at the bottom of the page. I saw it tonight, when I broke into Menéndez's desk. The Captain saw that stuff too. Soon as he did, you were on the list. Along with Menéndez.'

She tried to remember and it was all a blur. The thing that had brought her into it, Menéndez into it, was just a faded piece of paper she couldn't recall.

'There was big money involved there,' said Quemada. 'God knows how much in the end. And Antonio didn't leave it to any individual. He just filtered it out into companies, trusts, charities, a big wide umbrella of things. Really hard to track. Really hard to get to.'

'Where did it go?'

'Who knows? The lady who owns this house told us something we should have thought about more, *I* should have thought about more. She said Antonio was a *real* gangster. Not just some failed politician who liked messing round with young girls. He was the real thing. Understand that and it all begins to fall in place. Politicians. Cops. And money for his bastards. Kids like Antonio, Jaime too, they must have been getting some regular income. Not too much, seeing as they were the kind who'd likely put it up their nose anyway. And not too little either.'

She could start to see it now. She could see the picture building inside her head.

'Tell me, Maria,' said Quemada, and he looked really interested. 'You finish it.'

'It went along well until Luis Romero came along and met Jaime. Then one thing leads to another and Jaime introduces him to Antonio who can't keep his mouth shut.'

'That's my guess. Maybe Romero got involved in this sex and drugs thing the brothers had going. I don't know. But pretty soon Antonio is blabbing out his past, *their* past, about the war, about secret little funds, and Luis is digging and digging and digging. And then, I guess, the old man just thought it was a matter of time before Romero found out and it was plastered all over the front page of *El Diá*.'

'Antonio *believed* that Romero's wife was his mother.'

'There's the Captain for you. He's a believable sort of guy, isn't he? He pulled the trigger and he wasn't even there. Smart. But Bear was right. Antonio started to like it. He and Jaime, what I guess, what I think Menéndez guessed, is they got used to going out together, get real doped up, do some sex things, that's how they met the Angels I guess. What a monument to brotherly love those two pairs must've made. Then once or twice it gets out of control, the dope gets so *big* that they don't really care what they're doing any more. The Angels, maybe things just got out of hand. That American runner, Famiani, the guy Bear smacked around a little. One of them, Antonio, I guess, was just playing. And once or twice, the old man still uses them to do his business. Keeping things quiet business. Keeping quiet people who know a little too much about this money thing. Like Romero. Like Castaneda. Like . . .'

'Like me,' she said. 'Like Menéndez.'

'Yeah. But it only works so long as we think the guy who's doing it is a crazy. Some nut in a red gown. So I don't know, maybe the old man even went along with some of those other killings, like the Angels, just to keep up the picture. You think about it. How'd all this begin? With someone waking up that old woman Lucena. She'd got those two bodies upstairs going mouldy on her and she didn't even know about it. Maybe someone jogged her memory a little so's we'd start on this tack. Maybe the calendar said it was time to get moving if they wanted to kill Castaneda the day after and blame it all on the guy in the red robe. Same goes for Famiani. It would have helped the story. I guess we'll never know unless the Captain gets religion.'

Maria looked around the little living room. It seemed too lived in, too normal. The clock showed close to midnight and she felt a sudden chill.

'You know what I think?' said Quemada. 'The old man is just a lone little operation these days. The rest of his guys, all those old fixers from the Franco days, they got the sharp end of some natural wastage. They just got ancient. They died. They took their pensions, and a little more from old Antonio's slush fund to keep them warm, and they turned into quiet, cosy old people who wanted to forget about all that stuff. And can you blame them? These are different days. You can't go around muscling and cheating like that any more. We're dealing with dinosaurs here and even the money, even *that* amount of money, won't keep them alive.'

Maria thought of Rodríguez's quiet, insidious charm, and the way she had warmed to it in the bawling rabble of the station. The way she had allowed him to engage her, even reluctantly, in some hidden little conspiracy as if it were a given thing, a thing that mattered nothing. She could imagine, she could *see*, him talking rapidly, insistently to the Mateo brothers, telling them what they had to do, telling them that this, *this*, was what their father wanted of them.

'How do you go about arresting a captain?' she asked. 'How do you do it?'

'Same way as we arrest someone else. We aren't there yet. But there are ways.'

458

Maria blinked. 'You aren't there yet. What do you mean? *What more . . .*'

Quemada waved his hands at her. '*Whoa, whoa, there.* What I mean is there are ways of doing things and ways of not doing them.'

'He's killed people, Quemada. He's *killed* people.'

'No. We think he's had people killed. That's different. It's harder to prove for one thing, particularly as the people we think he used to do the killings are both dead themselves now. The investigation into Menéndez is just a start. He's living on borrowed time. He knows that. But pitching all this at his door . . . that's not necessarily so easy. Unless he steps out of line again.'

'So maybe tomorrow he'll be out of the country. In Colombia. Wherever. With all that money and out of reach.'

Quemada tugged at his ear and tried to think how to phrase what he wanted to say. 'Don't get me wrong on this, Maria. What he did, that's bad, but to him it all made sense. These people work to their own kind of internal logic and you can't beat that. You just got to use it. And that logic, it's telling the old man now it's over, he's lost, and my guess is there's no one left to hand over to, no one to carry the baton. Why'd you think he took all those risks? Why'd he get the Mateo kids involved in the first place? Ten, fifteen years ago, stuff like this would be handled in-house. Get my drift?'

'You were here ten, fifteen, twenty years ago. You handled some of this stuff in-house?'

'Probably. Not that I knew about it. See, I did as I was told. Being a cop is like that. You don't ask, you do. Nowadays, we're always asking and look where that got us. As for the Captain, he knows we know something, he knows he's out of the force at the very least, and, if we're lucky, we'll pick up something concrete to link him into all this. Meantime, we sit tight.'

'I want to see Bear.'

'Aw, Jesus. I thought we'd forgotten that one.'

'You said he was getting better. I *want* to see him.'

Quemada pinched his nose and tried to think.

'I'm going to the bathroom now, Quemada. When I get back I'm finding a coat in this place and I'm walking out to go to that hospital. If you want to come, you're welcome. If not . . .'

He watched her disappear upstairs to the bathroom, thought about it, then reached again for the phone. Two calls was all it took.

63

In Maggi Bartolomé's battered Renault 5, limping through the night, she turned to him and asked, 'Quemada?'

'Yeah?'

'That call. From Melilla. That made us think Teresa Romero was his daughter. You took it?'

He looked at her closely, trying to see if she really still had doubts, then shook his head. 'You're one clever cookie, aren't you? Maybe you should be here full time. No, Maria. I never took the call. But tonight I called Melilla back to find out who did make it. They didn't know what the hell I was talking about. They never phoned here. Whoever did make the call was doing it on the Captain's orders.'

'And you're doing nothing with this. Nothing at all?'

Quemada made a face like he had toothache. 'Maria, this man is clever. We are doing what we can but he knows his business. He *taught* most of us. What we have on him now, we can get him for screwing up the show when Menéndez was killed. There's just not enough there for anything criminal. Not yet. Maybe never. You ought to get used to that possibility.'

She pulled away from his eyes, but Quemada didn't notice. The idea was buzzing crazily around his head looking for somewhere to settle.

'You know what I'd really like?' he said eventually.

She didn't answer.

'I'd like the old man to know for sure you're OK. To know for sure he's starting to lose.'

He took one hand off the wheel, dived into a jacket pocket and pulled out the phone, used his free hand to scroll through the stored numbers, found the one marked Rodríguez, clearly on the little LCD screen. He thumbed the green call button, put the handset to his ear, the phone rang three times, then a familiar voice said, '*Digame.*'

Quemada coughed, listened to find out if he could make out any particular background noise, then identified himself. The voice on the other end went silent.

'Captain?' said Quemada. 'You still there? We got something to talk about.'

He listened to the fizzing of the airwaves then, finally, Rodríguez barked back, 'I doubt it.'

'See, Captain, I'm here with Maria. She's a little shook up but she's fine. I thought you might like to know. Seems our man, you know the one we thought got killed at the bullring, he couldn't resist one last go. Seems it wasn't him in the bullring at all. Some poor guy running a food concession there is missing. Good family man. Looks like Antonio and his' – Quemada paused and gave the word some extra emphasis – 'his *accomplice* killed this guy, put the body in the bull pen while he got out some way – beats me where, but that's a real old maze down in that part of the ring, and we'd be fooling ourselves if we thought the only way out was through the doors. Then Antonio went after Maria. More fool him. I got a team down there now checking out the body. We lost the policewoman too. She was a good woman. Two good cops in one day. That's a real waste, a real shame. I guess you'd agree with that anyway.'

They listened to nothing except static, but the line still didn't go dead.

Maria snatched the phone from Quemada's hand, the hate, the resentment buzzing in an inchoate mass around her head. 'I am alive, you bastard,' she said. 'He killed your policewoman. *Your* policewoman. He's as good as killed Torrillo. Who the *fuck* do you think you are to visit this on people? To treat them like *things* you can dispense with when you feel like.'

She could hear him laugh somewhere out there in the night. The voice filtering into her ear through the phone sounded distant, ancient. And it mocked her.

'Ah. The clever little professor from the university, full of facts and theorems and certainties. You people, you grow up with such certainties. It must be nice. When I was young, this city was safe. The streets were safe. The crooks, the whores, the trash, they knew their place. Look at it now. Look at the *mess*. Do you have some cold little lifeless theory to explain all that away, Professor?'

The words stung her and she couldn't believe it, couldn't believe them. Was this all it came to?

'It's losing power that matters, isn't it?' she asked. 'It's not the money at all. It's the power, the respect, the control, and "the old man". Where the f—?'

There was static again then, as they approached the hospital gates, she had to take the phone away from her ear as an ambulance, its klaxon screaming into the night, flew past them.

'You talk nonsense,' Rodríguez spat down the line. 'I have had enough of this now.'

Quemada grabbed the phone roughly off her.

'One more thing, Captain. One more thing before you go.'

Nothing but the crackling, like cellophane catching fire.

'Captain?'

Quemada was talking ever more slowly, like a tape

463

running down. The words came crisp and clear and deliberate from his lips. 'I just wanted to say. *I. Was. Sorry. To. Hear. About. Your. Mother.*'

The voice at the other end was almost a whisper. 'The court jester tries to make his final joke.'

Then, with a click, the line went dead.

Quemada nodded and put the phone back into his pocket.

'I hate to say this but I enjoyed that. He say anything to you I ought to know about?'

'Nothing.'

She realised she was trembling. 'Quemada? You think it might make a difference? He was so ... there was no remorse. These people, people he worked with, people who respected him, dead, and he feels no remorse, no sadness?'

'You expect him to start throwing up his hands? He's not that sort of guy. He doesn't come from that kind of generation. My guess is he'll try to brazen it out with just some kind of dismissal from the force. Unless we get lucky, and then maybe he'll do the decent thing. Cops have a habit of killing themselves, you know. Happens all the time. Usually I get to feel sorry, even if the guy's a real shitbag, but in the case of the old man I think I could make an exception.'

The hospital entrance loomed up out of the dark.

'I spoke to the doctors while you were in the bathroom. They said there was a real change.'

'A change for the better?'

'We're not relatives. If it was a change for the worse, would they be telling us?'

Feeling a little incredulous, she asked, 'You're sure he's getting *better*?'

'You know Bear. The man's built like a mountain. Are you *surprised*?'

She thought about it and said, 'No.'

He bore right, past big white squares for the ambulances, towards the entrance, then parked in a spot marked 'Doctors Only'.

'Quemada?'

'Yeah?'

'Do you always get this hard? Do you just grow a shell and let it bounce off you? I killed someone this evening. I saw that poor woman dead. It was . . . it was a *nightmare*. And I don't feel anything. I just feel numb. And dead inside somewhere.'

The car drew to a halt outside the front steps. Quemada glanced around at the empty forecourt.

'You'll feel it. Believe me. It sneaks up, then hits you when you're not thinking. They got some programmes. In the force. People you can talk to, people who help. You should talk to them. Usually I don't like this mumbo-jumbo stuff, but these people, I think they got a point.'

She watched the lights flickering inside row upon row of hospital windows.

'No, you don't,' she said.

'Excuse me?'

'You think, she's a woman, she needs the shrink. If I'd been a man, you'd be slapping my back, congratulating me, taking me out for a beer.'

Quemada thought about it. 'Yeah. That's right. Sure. The ice queen knows best. Let's forget about Bear. You want a beer instead?'

'Not right now.'

'Ah.'

'And I don't want a fucking shrink either.'

'Ah.'

They climbed out of the car and felt the night air hit them.

'You know, Professor? You don't mind me saying this? Well, frankly, I don't give a fuck if you *do* mind. You kill me. You people from the north. Really. You kill me. You come down here, you say, whoa, it's so hot here, it's so tense here, it's so *real*. And that's nice for a visit, that's nice when it's a little local colour. But it's a little *too* scary for real life, it's a little too scary if something starts to touch you. This city. It's a little too close to the edge. So you scuttle back and you wrap yourselves in your closed little lives and go to your dinner parties and talk, talk, talk, and inside, you keep saying to yourself, well, it may be boring, no, let's be frank, it *is* boring, as boring as watching sheep screw, but be honest, it's safe. You can't see the edge. You can't feel that little nerve ticking away on the side of your face saying, it's running out, girl, day by day, it's running out. Yeah. Go back. Wrap yourself in your little cocoon. I just hope the blanket's thick. You're going to need it.'

She looked back towards the city centre and the halo of light there. The storm was over now. The night was clear, the sky a sparkling curtain of stars. In the gardens, palm trees swayed and whispered in the light breeze. The fragrance of oleander, heavy as the smell of a red-light-district bar, danced in the air. She could hear Quemada's pump running down like an overheated steam engine running out of fuel.

'That is the greatest number of words I ever heard you string together in one go, Quemada. Does it happen often?'

He looked exhausted. Exhausted and deeply, deeply miserable. She wished she had never started this. 'I believe it last occurred in 1987. Round October time. Shortly before my divorce. These two things may not be unconnected. It is also a pile of unmitigated shit. I'm sorry, Maria. I'm real sorry. I'm sorry you're messed up in this, I'm sorry for the

466

pain. And I wish I could do something about it. But I can't. You're not the only one who's still taking the human being lessons. It's a really popular course in this job. OK?'

She looked at the little fat man and wondered how many complexities you could hide so well in so small a frame.

'OK,' she said. 'Can we see Bear now?'

Quemada patted his jacket, felt the bumps underneath it. 'That's why we're here.'

Behind, in the dark, there was the sound of tyres on asphalt, and the headlights of another car lit up the broad, palladian steps to the hospital entrance. They walked up, checked at reception, then pushed their way through the revolving doors, and made their way to intensive care. The hospital was silent except for the tapping of shoes down polished linoleum corridors. Somewhere, she thought, somewhere lies the corpse of Caterina Lucena. Unvisited, unremarked. And across the city her son sits wondering what remains of his life.

Maria looked through the glass window and her heart stopped. The big man was surrounded by white coats. Doctors and nurses bent over the bed, completely obliterating the view. They could hear the beeping of the monitors through the partition, and see nothing but this wall of white backs, bent over the body.

'Oh shit,' said Quemada. 'Oh fucking shit. Don't do this to us, Bear. Don't do it.'

Then a white coat pulled back, followed by another. Clipboards moved, pens scribbled, a ragbag collection of medical implements went back into pockets and sanitised metal sleeves attached to the bed. Torrillo was propped upright in bed, his huge chest bare and covered in bandages. He looked at the doctors and nurses around him with polite, only faintly disguised boredom, stifled a yawn, then looked out through the window. A big, broad smile broke on his face and he made a massive round O with the thumb and forefinger of his right hand.

Maria blinked like crazy to keep the tears out of her eyes and saw that Quemada was trying to do the same.

'You big fat bastard,' muttered the detective. 'You big fat bastard.'

One of the doctors followed the line of Torrillo's gaze and saw them behind the glass. His face dropped to a sub-zero temperature and he walked briskly out of the room.

'Who the hell are you?' He had thick horn-rimmed glasses, a bald head and an excess of negative charm.

'Police,' said Quemada, flashing the badge. 'Colleagues. We just stopped by to see how he was.'

The doctor stared at the silver and leather badge, looked them up and down.

'He's getting better. He'll live. He doesn't deserve to. If he didn't have enough fatty muscle on him to float a whale he wouldn't have done.'

'But he's going to be OK?'

'No sign of any permanent damage that I can see. More's the wonder. I give him a month in here then he's back with you. Doing whatever he does.'

'He's a . . .'

'No. Please. I don't want to know.'

Maria smiled stupidly at him and felt she was pouring a small glass of tepid water on an iceberg. 'Can we see him?'

'See him? *Of course* you can see him. There. He's the other side of the glass.'

'I mean. Can we visit him?'

'Go down to reception. Look on the wall there. You'll see a list of visiting hours. *That's* when you can visit him.'

'No special favours, huh?' asked Quemada. 'Us being police and all that?'

The doctor gave a passable impersonation of a basilisk.

'You can get the hell out of here. That's what you can do.'

Quemada peered through the glass, got Torrillo's attention, jerked a thumb at the doctor and stifled a very deliberate yawn.

'You'll tell him,' she said. 'You'll tell him we'll be back. Tomorrow.'

'Yes,' the man said testily.

'And tell him this too,' added Quemada. 'This is very important. This will make him feel better. Tell him it's *over*. Got that? It's *over*.'

Something about the tone in Quemada's voice knocked the edge off the doctor's roughness. He wondered, for a moment, if he hadn't just stepped on the toes of something very nasty indeed.

'I'll tell him that.'

'Good,' said Quemada, then they waved a couple of times. 'Then we'll be going. You get good medical care here, doc? From what I see.'

'We think so.'

'Yeah. Guess that must be the case. Let's face it. You sure as hell didn't *charm* him better now, did you?'

There was a touch of colour on the face of the basilisk and Maria shot Quemada a glance that said: let's go. He stuck his hands in his jacket pockets, smiled, then walked out into the corridor. She followed him, watching the floor, and they went downstairs into the big airy marble reception.

He was shaking his head. 'We tell Bear it was the Captain it's gonna set him back weeks. You know that, don't you? He hero-worshipped the old guy. We all did. But not like Bear.'

'He'll cope,' she said.

'Yeah. Bear's a coper. Bear's an object lesson in coping for all of us.'

He stared her straight in the face. 'You sound better. You

sound like we can talk now. You can't stay here. You know that. It don't make any difference. He's going to be OK. And we can look after you better some place else.'

She didn't say anything at first. He knew he'd won on that one.

'Quemada?'

'Yeah?'

'Does your mouth get you into a lot of trouble?'

He stopped, looked at the visiting rotas, wrote down the times in his police notebook.

'Lots. *Lots.* Captain once said to me if only I could keep a lid on it I would've made sergeant one day.'

He turned to stare at her, genuinely bemused. 'This was an *incentive?* I asked him.'

Maria laughed, and it felt clean and good. 'You are an appalling human being.'

'This, I have to tell you, is not an original observation. But before this discussion goes any further, can I please make a request? I am hungry. I am thirsty. I am tired. I got to get you somewhere to stay before I find out what the rest of our merry men have been up to this night. Can I drive you to the hotel now?'

'I think that would be a very good idea.'

'Yeah,' he said, and they walked out into the fresh, fragrant night. She took a deep breath and felt the air rush into her lungs, clean and heady and soporific.

I will sleep tonight, she thought. There will be no dreams, no nightmare visits to La Soledad. Or anywhere else.

Quemada slipped around the far side of the car and got in the driver's seat. She opened her door and almost fell inside.

'I hope this is a comfortable hotel, Quemada. I want first class at the very least.'

He said nothing, so she turned to look. The gun shone

dully black at the window and poked Quemada's right temple. Beyond it, pale and tense in the darkness, Rodríguez stared at them, mouth half open, his breath painting condensation clouds on the air.

With his spare hand he felt inside Quemada's jacket, pulled the revolver out of its holster, then stuffed it into his coat pocket.

'I am going to get into the back of the car now,' he said, and his voice sounded different, sounded as if it belonged to someone else. 'When I get in, you're going to drive to the river front. The old port. Where the pleasure jetties were. When I tell you to get out, you get out. You do anything I don't like, I'm going to kill you. You understand?'

'I'm getting overtime for this, Captain?' spat Quemada. 'See, if I'm just the cab driver, that's OK. But I'd like to know, kind of, either way.'

The big service revolver flashed in the dark and hit him in the temple. She watched the line of blood come through the skin, run down his forehead, form a dark stain down his cheek.

'I've listened to you for twenty fucking years, Quemada. I'm tired of listening now. You drive.'

Quemada wiped the blood away with his sleeve and listened to the door opening and closing behind him.

'Now,' said Rodríguez. 'Drive slowly. Down the avenida. Down the ring road. You know the way?'

'I know the way.'

'Then do it.'

They pulled out into the broad avenue, now almost deserted. Only a few cabs cruised the streets looking for early-morning revellers on their way home.

'This is crazy,' said Quemada.

'Shut up.'

'Captain. This is crazy. There's records stacked up against

471

you by the million. What you gonna do? Tomorrow, the next day, they'll be coming for you. Sure as hell. You're just making it worse.'

'Records? You read those records, Quemada?'

'Yeah. Some of them.'

'They're just names. They're just companies. You can change those details. The rest is just circumstantial. You were a better cop, you'd know that. You were a better cop you'd know not to make phone calls from hospitals. Listen to those sirens in the background, everyone knows where you are. Stupid.'

'Sure. I'm just some dumb fucking detective. Menéndez was smart. He went back through the records. He found out who was signing off all those accusations against Alvarez all those years ago. For a long time it was people who are now dead. Then guess what? Somewhere around 1960, some new guy comes on the scene. By the name of Sergeant Rodríguez. And from then on he takes a real interest in signing off all the complaints against Alvarez. Surprise, surprise. Menéndez found out whose name was behind some of those companies he found in Castaneda's office. Same name. You been taking all those years.'

'Yeah. Menéndez *was* clever. And you try to work this out. They know someone in the force has been siphoning money out somehow. They know you're gone, no trace, and your name's on the records.'

'It *is?*' asked Quemada in a mock surprised voice.

'By the time *they* get to see them it will be.'

'And Maria here? She raking it too?'

'Try to think, Quemada. I know it's hard. But maybe you can make it one last time. A cop disappears with a close involvement in these murders and a heap of cash. A woman who'd been working with him disappears too. Even you can figure that one out.'

472

'You know me. I'm just a dumb fucking detective. I figure she's just not my type. What you think, Maria?'

She watched the street lights flash by, saw the long low silver ribbon of the river grow bigger up ahead of them.

'I think Maria agrees, Captain, but she's just too polite to say so. So why don't we just wrap this thing up? Fair's fair. I thought I was giving you a chance when we called back there, a chance you could get out of all this shit with some dignity, you know? Still get buried in sanctified ground, all that stuff? Your wife would still have got the pension – you blew yourself away, it didn't make any difference.'

'Jesus, you're stupid.'

Rodríguez waved with the gun, towards the right. 'Take the service road down there.'

The car ran down a narrow cobbled lane, beneath a line of trees, turned past a dark and deserted factory store. The silhouettes of idle cranes stood outlined against the horizon like jagged stumps of decaying teeth. The wharf looked neglected, abandoned, in the bright silver light of the moon.

Maria looked at the river and shivered. The car lurched forward onto the cobblestones of the dock. The overhanging warehouses, vast and tall and derelict, blocked out the light of the moon. The river stood black and sluggish and huge at this point, deep enough to have taken big freighters, when the business was there. The surface looked like thick oil, broken only by the odd piece of flotsam moving fast in the current.

Rodríguez barked at Quemada to stop the car. It pulled to a halt at the foot of a small, ramshackle jetty that protruded out a good thirty feet over the water. The planking was as full of holes and gaps as a tramp's smile.

'You go in there, with this tide,' said Rodríguez, 'thirty

minutes later you're floating in the Atlantic. Feeding the tuna.'

He jabbed the gun in Quemada's back.

'You first. Get out. Stand by the front of the car. You' – he poked the barrel into her back – 'you get out the driver's side. You come over. So I can see you. Stand by him.'

'Captain, Captain . . .' Quemada still had that joking edge in his voice, and she was sure it would get them killed. Right there. Right in the car.

'The meter on that fucking mouth is running out real fast, Quemada.'

The little detective turned round, ranged his arms over the back of the seat and stared at Rodríguez. 'You mind if I just say one thing? *One* thing?'

Rodríguez pointed the gun straight into his face and smiled, smiled with neat little white teeth that shone like tiny mirrors in the night.

'See. You're a clever guy, Captain. You're right about so many things. Like the tide, for instance. That's real interesting. I didn't know that. And the numbers, those accounts we got. Menéndez got real close to you on that, but he didn't get close enough. Not for a man of your *standing*. A captain and all that. You're a clever guy.'

Rodríguez stared over the seat and there was that dead look in his eyes again.

'Trouble is, you just got one thing wrong.'

'Yeah?'

'Me.'

She thought Rodríguez was about to laugh. Or kill them. Or both.

'See,' said Quemada, 'see, maybe I got a big mouth, maybe my clothes sense is a crock of shit, my hairline don't look so good, and all the rest of it. But' – and she couldn't believe, she couldn't believe his voice could rise like this,

could get so loud that he was shouting, bawling at Rodríguez
– '*one thing I'm not is fucking dumb!*'

The sound of his words died in a quiver of febrile rever-
berations inside the car.

'Not at all.'

He bent his head down, and patted his waist.

'That right, boys? Huh? That right? You hear that?'

Rodríguez blinked. And suddenly the blood began to
drain from his face.

'Just a little trick, Captain. Like you know, these radio
things, they just work the one way. Unlike me, they don't
talk back.'

There were figures around the car now, and lights. The
sound of feet on cobblestones rebounded around the wharf.
A hand fell on the car roof and faces appeared at the
windows. Velasco, a revolver in one hand, a tissue clutched
to his nose with the other, peered through the glass.

'They been with us all the way, Captain. Since we left
the house. I thought, I *hoped*, you might take the hint I
gave you and just kind of cooperate one way or another.
But I had to be prepared in case you didn't. It seemed like
a reasonable idea to stick in the wire too. Just in case. You
wouldn't believe the toys I found in Menéndez's desk when
I broke in there. Along with all the other stuff too.'

Rodríguez raised the gun and, for a moment, Quemada
found himself lost for words, found himself thinking that
this time he just might have gone too far. Then the barrel
went higher, the dull metal gleaming, turned round, and
Rodríguez pushed it gently into his mouth.

'Out of the car, Maria,' Quemada said. 'Nice and slowly.
Out of the car.'

She opened the door and stepped outside. The air made
the sweat cling coldly to her body. Around the vehicle,
slowly and deliberately, men waited, guns in their hands.

Quemada looked over the back of the seat, opened his mouth to say something, thought better of it, then climbed out the driver's side. He walked around the car, took her by the arm, and they walked to the river.

On the far side of the water, beneath a line of fairy lights, couples slow-danced to the music of a small latino band. The notes floated across to them, lazy and lilting, a sax playing catch with the keyboard, the mellow, whispered voice of a female singer drifting in and out of the melody.

She listened to the song, the words meaningless and banal, and suddenly, out of nowhere, she was crying. The tears slipped warm down her cheeks. She could taste them salty in her mouth and they felt good. Quemada's arm slipped gently, tentatively, around her shoulders. Briefly, there was a commotion behind them, the sound of a short, sudden report, and then Quemada walked her silently along the riverbank, to a squad car, put her in the back.

She looked at him through the window.

'It's over,' she said.

Quemada nodded, struggled for something to say, wondered at this new-found feeling of being lost for words, and walked off, back to the little crowd of quiet, serious men, now bunched around the car at the foot of the jetty.

In the back of the police car, on the torn and grubby bench seat, Maria Gutierrez lay down and let the darkness engulf her.

Six weeks later she sits in the little bathroom in this new place. She wears only a light cream shift. Her hair is cut short now, a tight bob that just touches the ear, the collar of her gown. The lines, at the corners of her mouth, around her eyes, are more marked. She looks older, different. It is eight in the morning and there is no noise, nothing to disturb her thoughts, the big, bright wheeling thoughts that whirl and circle her mind like great primeval birds. Maria sits and feels a mix of physical emotions, great strength, great weakness. In her hand she holds a small clear plastic phial, the liquid in it changing colour, yellow to blue. A bright, peacock blue, a blue full of life and beauty and hope. A blue she has seen before, only to let it slip away from her.

She gets up from the toilet, places the phial on the little ledge by the side of the sink, washes her hands, washes her face, then walks into the living room. It is large and airy, with a big, well-polished teak table at its centre, the sort of table where people gather and eat and drink and talk late into the night. She sits at the table and rubs her palm along the wood, enjoying its smoothness, its calm, unfussy solidity.

There is a diary on the table and she pulls it over to her, a big, office diary, with the name of a real-estate agent on the top, the kind they give to people who buy or sell when the money comes through, when the removal vans come and go. She looks at the little scribbled appointment for the following Tuesday, makes a note by the side of it to make it firm, no longer provisional. Then she starts to count, down the side of the calendar, week by week, slowly, exactly, since this is important. As she turns the pages, she can feel something inside her, something a little nauseous, and it grows, it gets bigger as her fingers walk up through the weeks, into the teens, into the early twenties. She looks at week twenty-five and the pen hovers over the line, the memories come back, of deadlines and decisions and necessities. Then she carries on counting, through thirty, through to forty. There is only one possible date of conception. It makes the counting easy, and when she has finished she draws a line, big and bold, around a three-week window some nine months hence and wonders what the rules are about sorting this out with the job.

These are things she must learn, in this new place, this new existence.

Maria walks to the window, the big panoramic window of this bright, new, shiny apartment, on the seventh floor, above the noise and the fumes and the dirt of the street. She looks out over the skyline, the now familiar skyline, with the cathedral, the Torre del Oro gold in the early sunlight, the old square, the barrio, and, beyond, the slow, lazy mass of the river curling away into the distance.

An image comes back, from the night before. In the hospital, watching Bear walk gingerly, a little unsteadily, around the room, watching the smile on his face grow bigger and bigger until it stretches from ear to ear. His hair is longer. It is pulled back from his face, the ponytail falls softly on his shoulder, a yellow elastic band around the end. Somehow he looks younger.

'Not tomorrow,' he says, eyes still wide at the wonder. 'Not this week. But soon. Soon. I'll be back.'

She looks at him, thinks before saying the words, then asks, 'Bear, do you mind if I ask you a question?'

He stands placidly by the bed, holding onto a white plastic cabinet weighed down with fading flowers, waiting.

'This sounds crazy,' she says. 'I know it does. And if it is crazy, then fine. I don't care.'

His eyes glint back at her, something amused skittering around their depths.

'You know *Woodstock*? The movie? The rock festival? I was wondering. Did you ever see it? I know it's a strange thing to ask a cop ... but ...'

The impossible happens. The grin gets wider and Torrillo leans forward, speaking quietly, speaking in confidence.

'That's a very strange thing, Maria,' he says. 'And I'll tell you the truth, so long as you promise to keep it to yourself 'cos if that loudmouth Quemada ever gets hold of it my life's a misery.'

There is a tiny, faint chill walking down her spine.

'I promise,' she says and there is nothing in the world now except the two of them, in the bright, airless room.

'Maria. I didn't need to see the movie. I was *there*. You believe that? Right there, the whole three days.'

He watches her expression. 'You OK?'

She nods. Her throat is dry and there is a rushing sound in her ears.

'OK. Go on.'

'I had a cousin from Miami who humped gear for Santana, enough money for the air ticket, the rest all came together. A different me. A different Bear. You see the movie, you see the part where Country Joe and the Fish come on. I'm in it. Right close to the front. More hair, less weight. But that's me.'

She stares at him and the air looks a little fuzzy around his head, the bright evening light plays tricks with her vision.

'No rain,' she says.

And he laughs, a slow, pleasant, physical sound.

'No rain, Maria. No rain.'

The morning nausea is receding now. She looks out of the window, places her hand on her stomach and feels the warmth of another life.

SOLSTICE

ONE

Blood

Central Siberia, 37,000 feet, 0417 UTC

British Pacific flight 172 had left Tokyo for London Heathrow right on schedule, every one of its 332 seats occupied, every ounce of weight, every moment of balance, accurately calculated. The route was standard these days: no more long, circuitous detours to avoid the Soviet Union, no more boring stopovers in Anchorage. Just a sharp hook to the west after take-off, on to Vladivostok and then a dead straight line along the great circle, coming down over Finland into Britain from the North Sea.

This was a two-man operation: one captain, one first officer, both watching the LCD screens of the new all-digital flight panel, pulling the big plane around the sky through the effortless servos of the fly-by-wire controls if, on occasion, they felt like unhooking the auto-pilot and injecting a little human activity into the process.

Ian Seabright looked at the schedule and tried to imagine what it was like back there in steerage with everyone fighting to stuff their hand luggage into the overhead racks, screaming for drink and food, trying, and failing, to sleep these next eleven hours or so. If there'd been a few spare seats he might have gone aft, smiled at the punters, tried to make them feel at home. Not today. A quick run through first and business, not passing for one minute through the curtains that separated them from the heaving quarters of economy, was all they were going to get. And that was for purely selfish reasons alone.

Seabright didn't like to admit it to anyone, particularly not the inquisitive little buggers in the company's human resources team at Heathrow, but these days flying just plain bored him. It had been different when he first got into the game, straight from the RAF, in the seventies. Then you used your brain, used your muscle too sometimes. There were routes to plot, courses to steer. You handled the machine. Today you just minded the computer, watching the dials flash and alter on some screen, making sure the silicon pilot didn't do anything wrong. And if it did, switching in its partner, the back-up system, instead. Reading the manual. Radioing ops for advice. Doing any damn thing except flying the plane.

He was fifty-three, in reasonable health, a little overweight from all those longhaul stops in hotels where the food was free and good and there was precious little else to do. The first officer on the run was Jimmy Mulligan, a bright, red-haired Irishman who'd worked his way onto the flight deck the hard way, through a private pilot's licence and then the low-paid graft of flight instruction in the States, building up the hours, building up the qualifications. He liked Mulligan. The man was smart, polite, hard-working. And yet, at just pushing thirty, he was already starting to look bored. Seabright didn't envy him. His own career had two years to run before compulsory retirement under the licensing regulations. Then it was a nice fat pension, a villa in the Algarve, the quiet life, golf and family and maybe a little sailing, not another damn plane to fly ever again. Mulligan was twenty-five years, a quarter of a century, away from that, with nothing to look forward to but this tedious round of routine, watching the dials flash, wondering how long it would take before you got that last two minutes of activity on the approach, when your brain still had to work, a little anyway, and it wouldn't be long before the ATC geeks took that away from you too. The idea of all those wasted hours in the cockpit appalled him.

Seabright looked at the moving map on the GPS. They were three hours out now, cruising in still air at 37,000 feet in the middle of nowhere with the weather looking fine and sunny all the way, every inch of the route in daylight, straight into Heathrow. Out of the window some god-forsaken part of Russia passed slowly by, even with a ground speed of 530 knots. A piece of nothingness in western Siberia, he guessed. What the hell. You reached a stage in flying these things where you no longer bothered to look at the map, where the world just became a web of beacons and waypoints, with impenetrable names that gave you no clue about where they might really be on the face of the earth.

'Are you going to marry that girl, Jimmy?'

The Irishman smiled, such a pleasant, charming, disingenuous smile Ian Seabright wanted to laugh, and would do, too, in a couple of years, when these stripes on his shoulders didn't weigh so heavily.

'You mean Ali?' Mulligan said, pointing backwards with his thumb through the cabin door.

'I believe that was the young lady you seemed to be proposing to last night.'

Mulligan thought about it. 'Now did I really do that? In so many words, sir?'

Seabright closed his eyes and thought: they can fill these bloody things with all the computers they want, but this little ritual just won't ever go away. You just coop up a crew in some foreign hotel, leave them there for three days, see what happens. This is the birth and death of marriages, he had seen both, experienced both himself. And was glad this too was all over for him, had subsided, with the years, into a delicate state of truce that passed for peace in his own personal life. A truce he enjoyed, looked forward to more each time he returned, wanted to turn into something else, something more positive in two years' time, in the Algarve, anywhere they bloody well felt like.

'She is a very sweet girl, mind,' Mulligan said. 'A man could do a lot worse.'

'A lot worse,' Seabright agreed.

'Which makes a man think, don't you see, that maybe, just maybe, he could also do a lot better.'

Seabright stared at this wiry, clever little fellow, arched his eyebrows and grunted, wondered why this short, meaningless exchange sparked a little flame of anger inside him. It all just comes round, he thought. There are things you can never tell another man, you just have to wait, let him discover it all for himself, and then look him in the eye and say: yes, me too. The casual drift from bed-hopping first officer to married (happily or otherwise) captain was one such journey in life.

'Looks like we've got company,' Mulligan said, staring out over the starboard wing. Seabright followed his gaze. A good ten miles off, on a parallel course tracking the same flight level, was a white 747. He dialled up the inflight frequency and put out a half-jokey call. There was no reply.

'Miserable buggers,' Mulligan muttered, reaching for a pair of pocket binoculars in the seat pocket. 'The least a chap can do is talk to his fellow aviators once in a while.'

Then he focused on the distant shape and let out a low, sweeping whistle.

'Jimmy?'

3

The first officer took away the glasses from his face.

'There was something in the paper about a summit in Tokyo or something, wasn't there?'

'Why do you think we're packing them into every square inch we've got right now? There was a world summit. Ended yesterday.'

'Well,' Mulligan replied, passing over the binoculars, 'it looks like we've got classy company on the way back. Can't expect them to talk to the likes of us now, can you?'

Seabright looked at the long white shape through the glasses. This was a new one for the book, an occurrence he rarely encountered lately.

'I think you're right there, Jimmy . . .'

He snatched the binoculars away from his face in a rapid involuntary physical jerk, and felt, for a moment, as if he was victim to some sudden muscle spasm.

'Jesus,' Mulligan moaned. In the right-hand seat the first officer had his hand to his forehead, eyes closed, and was visibly in pain.

'You OK, Jimmy?' This was unlike him. Mulligan rarely swore, never complained about anything. He rubbed his head for a moment or two, then unclenched his eyes, and looked at Seabright. His eyes were more than a little pink, unfocused, watery too. Maybe, the older man thought, it had been a long night with Ali, too long.

'Damned headache,' Mulligan complained. 'Came straight on me like that. You been sleeping OK back there? Last night I mean?'

'As good as ever. Which is to say not well at all. Damn hot in that hotel, I know that. I asked them to turn up the air conditioning more than once and all they said was it was running full tilt already.'

Narita airport in boiling hot weather. Three days in purgatory, Seabright thought.

'Yeah,' Mulligan said, and took away his hand from his head. There was sweat on the skin there. He really had been in pain, Seabright thought, then hated the way he told himself this might have to go down in the log, might have to go onto the report. 'Me too. And before you say anything, sir, that was nothing to do with anything else either.'

He juggled inside his trouser pocket, came out with a pack of soluble aspirin, threw a couple into his mouth, let them dissolve there.

'Been eating these flaming things like sweets ever since yesterday.'

And saw the look in Seabright's face.

'Just a headache, though. Everyone gets them, that right, sir?'

4

'Yes, Jimmy.'

Seabright thought: that was right. He had them too. He had the makings of one right now. And the tension of the sudden muscle spasm had not gone away entirely either.

'You feeling any better?'

'You bet. No problem.'

'Good. Because you've got an amber alert light on the main gear. Came on with your headache, isn't that sod's law for you? Nothing to worry about I'm sure but take a look. I can't see any counter indications anywhere but you know the drill.'

'Sir . . . ow!'

And the strange thing was, Ian Seabright felt the selfsame thing right then. A sharp, stabbing pain in the right temple, so hard it made him wince, just like Mulligan. Then it went away as quickly as it came, leaving a dull throb behind.

'What the hell was that?'

Seabright wiped his forehead, felt the sweat there, scanned the panel as he ran through the possibilities.

'You check the cabin pressure too, Jimmy. I felt that one too and I don't think we're both imagining it.'

They scrutinized the dials, went through the routines they knew by heart, confirmed the pressure, stable at the equivalent of 6,000 feet.

'You think it could have dropped, just momentarily, without us noticing it?'

Mulligan's face was close to the colour of his hair, and Ian Seabright felt, deep in his gut, something hard and cold and angry start to form, start to knot there and wait for him to recognize it.

'No,' he replied. 'That's just not possible.'

He looked at Mulligan again. This time it didn't seem so bad. Not quite. The man was flushed, for sure, but that much? Maybe it was just an illusion, or something temporary that his mind had exaggerated in the aftermath of the sudden stab of pain.

'I can pull out a record of the pressure if you like? See if it took a sudden drop?'

Seabright nodded, just for something to do, knowing this really wasn't the cause of it, knowing the pressurization system was behaving just like it should, feeling that with the gut certainty you got from thirty years in the air, even when you were up front, ostensibly in charge, at the helm of some tedious flying microchip.

5

Mulligan punched away at the control deck, watched the displays shift and change on the colour LCD screen. Then, when he was finished, looked at Seabright, saying nothing, visibly baffled by it all.

'Maybe it was one of those things,' Mulligan said, hating himself for it the moment the words came out of his mouth.

Seabright just looked at him and neither of them needed to say it, the phrases just passed unspoken between them, the old pilot's doggerel they drilled into you, year after year. All those half-smart, half-true little maxims ran through both men's heads at that moment ... that there really is no limit to how bad things can get, and how you shouldn't believe in miracles but you should rely on them. And, in particular, this one: when in doubt, predict that the trend will continue.

They sat in silence, in trepidation, and then they heard the security key turn in the cabin door, saw Ali Fitzgerald walk through, her face pale, taut with anxiety. The very appearance of her made the knot in Ian Seabright's stomach turn on itself once more until this tangle of pain in his gut was rock hard, icy and immobile.

'We've got a medical out there,' she said, and Seabright could see how close she was to real panic, how hard she was fighting to hold all this in. 'It's a bad one, sir, and I asked. There's not a doctor on the plane.'

Seabright stared hard at his first officer, checked the panel and made sure nothing else was blinking there except the one errant amber light on the main gear.

'You OK on your own, Jimmy? Don't just say yes. Think about this. I don't want more than one emergency on my ship.'

Mulligan thought before he answered; he knew the old man would demand that.

'I'll be fine. Best leave the door unlocked anyway.'

'Yes,' Seabright said, then unstrapped the shoulder harness, pulled himself out of the left-hand seat, and followed the stewardess to the door, held it half-closed, not letting her through.

'Sir?' She looked into his face, not understanding, not far from the edge, he thought.

'Ali,' Seabright said, as quietly, as gently as he could. 'Your shirt. You need to change it. You need to put a jacket on. Something. You can't go back through the cabin like that. I don't want those people thinking this is worse than it is.'

6

She looked at herself, at the broad red bloodstain that marked the entire front of her white blouse, down onto her skirt, marked her skin too, around her neck, where she'd held the man's head, trying to do something, anything.

'No, sir,' Ali Fitzgerald said, then waited for him to open the door, stepped behind the bulkhead that separated them from the first-class cabin and pulled out a clothes carrier. It happened so quickly he scarcely had time to tear his eyes away. She stripped off the blouse, then the skirt, washed her neck and forearms rapidly with a damp Kleenex and a bottle of Malvern water, and put on the dirty set of uniform she was carrying back from the outward journey.

'He's in business, sir. We've got the medical kit.'

'Good,' Seabright answered and watched her step in front of him, turn into the first-class cabin, smooth down her dress, start to do her job.

He followed her down the aisle, felt the eyes on him, the tension in the seats, and thought to himself that Jimmy Mulligan could do a lot worse. A hell of a lot worse if he wanted to.

Epiphany

David Hewson

'Mystery, menace and guilt . . . building tension to a seismic
explosion'
Daily Telegraph

Christmas 1975. A group of Californian students frequent
a remote old house to experiment with LSD. One of them,
Michael Quinn, is both highly intelligent and truly evil.
The search for pleasure turns to nightmare when a child is
killed. Quinn is responsible for this and other crimes, but
implicates the others, who include the gentle Paul
Dunsany and the pragmatic Hal Jamieson. As the police
net begins to close, it is Jamieson who leads the search for
an escape.

Now, twenty years later, just as Quinn is unexpectedly
released from jail, a mysterious young Englishwoman
named Joni Lascelles begins to ask questions that will
unravel the past. She seeks out Dunsany. Does he want to
get involved again in this dangerous business? In the end,
he will not have a choice. Because as the trail leads back
into the closed world of software mogul Hal Jamieson, it
becomes apparent that the horror of the past is poised to
engulf the present, leaving no one untouched by its power.

Turn by turn, shifting effortlessly between two eras twenty
years apart, the story is played out with relentless compul-
sion to an overwhelming climax. Evoking music and the
hidden world of quantum science, murder and the search
for redemption, *Epiphany* is a superb thriller of our times.

'John Fowles on acid'
Guardian

ISBN 0 00 649706 3

An Image to Die For

Mike Phillips

Independent TV producer Wyndham Davis unearths crucial evidence that could overthrow Leon Ross's conviction for the brutal murder of his wife and children on a tough London housing estate. Invited to attend an interview on the estate where a mystery witness is being questioned, black journalist Sam Dean is sickened by the vicious stabbing of one of the programme's researchers. So when Wyndham offers Sam the job of tracking down Amaryll Johnson, Helen Ross's lover, he isn't wild about taking it on... but emotional pressure is brought to bear by a figure from Sam's past.

As he embarks on his search for Johnson, Sam realizes there's more than one agenda here. There are secrets from Wyndham's life influencing events and Sam is getting sucked right into the dark heart of the mystery. Tough, vivid and shocking, *An Image to Die For* is a disturbing and compelling read from one of Britain's foremost crime writers.

'This is Mike Phillips's best novel, brutal and caring, totally authentic' *The Times*

ISBN 0 00 649671 7

A Grave Talent
Laurie R. King

Kate Martinelli, a newly promoted Homicide detective with a secret to conceal, and Alonzo Hawkin, a world-weary cop trying to make a new life in San Francisco, could not be more different, but are thrown together to solve a brutal crime – the murders of three young girls.

As Martinelli and Hawkin get nearer to a solution, they realize the crimes may not be the sexually motivated killings they had seemed, and that there is a coldly calculating and tortuous mind at work which they must outmanoeuvre if they are to prevent both further carnage and the destruction of a shining talent...

'If there is a new P.D. James...I would put my money on Laurie R. King'   *Boston Globe*

ISBN 0 00 649354 8

The Four Last Things

Andrew Taylor

Suffer the little children to come unto me . . .

Little Lucy Appleyard is snatched from her child minder's on a cold winter afternoon, and the nightmare begins. It is as if the child has disappeared into a black hole with no clues to her whereabouts . . . until the first grisly discovery in a London graveyard. More such finds are to follow, all at religious sites, and, in a city haunted by religion, what do these offerings signify?

All that stands now between Lucy and the final sacrifice are a CID sergeant on the verge of disgrace and a woman cleric – Lucy's parents – but how can they hope to halt the evil forces that are gathering around their innocent daughter?

The Four Last Things is the first novel in Andrew Taylor's Roth Trilogy, linked psychological thrillers set against the changing face of the Church of England.

'Andrew Taylor digs deep to explore the tangled roots of sex, violence and religion. This is a fine thriller, with clues complex enough to tax a Morse'   REGINALD HILL

'This author knows precisely how to wield suspense'
Independent on Sunday

ISBN: 0 00 649653 9